Includes Bonus Story of
*Desert Rose*

# *Wildflower Harvest*

# COLLEEN L.
# REECE

BARB
An Imprint of

Published by Barbour Books, an imprint of Barbour Publishing, Inc., P.O. Box 719, Uhrichsville, OH 44683, www.barbourbooks.com.

*Our mission is to publish and distribute inspirational products offering exceptional value and biblical encouragement to the masses.*

 Member of the
Evangelical Christian
Publishers Association

Printed in the United States of America.

*Chapter 1*

Red Cedars shimmered with light and laughter. Carefully hoarded candles flickered and danced. Lamps held high to guide guests through the early autumn darkness cast a welcoming glow. Flames leaped and whirled in fireplaces. Not since the firing on Fort Sumter in the spring of 1861 that resulted in the formation of West Virginia had such an affair been held.

During the Civil War Thomas and Sadie Brown's farm, tucked into a fold of the Allegheny Mountains near Shawnee and the Virginia border, had somehow escaped detection by destroying Yankee troops. Neither had Rebel forces discovered the farm. Grateful, Thomas and Sadie shared what had been spared with those who had little or nothing. When in 1865 the War Between the States, a war of brother against brother, was officially resolved, new trials emerged: despair, starvation, and the need to begin again. Yet the Browns and others like them refused to be beaten. They started over or went on from where they were. The same pioneering spirit that created a new state brought them through tragedy. New lines of sorrow etched themselves on sturdy faces but their souls remained unwrinkled.

Now the Browns' home, Red Cedars, was host to a well-deserved celebration. September 1, 1873, felt centuries away from past misery. Without apology families wore their mended, treasured best; bonnets turned and freshened by determined, nimble fingers nodded. No one noticed or cared that curtains and portieres, damask tablecloths and napkins bore as battle scares cobwebby patches of darning.

In a secluded corner of the front room, made larger by open, dividing doors, Mountain Laurel Brown quietly observed the excited crowd. Still as the cool evening air, she caught sight of her older, married sisters. Blue-eyed Gentian was proudly displaying her new baby; Black-eyed Susan was flirting with her brand-new husband. A smile twitched Laurel's curved lips. Neighbors never had understood why Sadie Brown chose such outlandish names for her girls! But Laurel knew that beneath Sadie's starched corset cover and petticoats lived a heart made glad by beauty. Sadie could no more resist choosing flower names—and how well they fit—than she could allow muddy boots in the house.

A pang went through her. Although her older sisters both lived nearby, new homes and responsibilities claimed them. Mama said it was right and natural but Laurel missed them deeply.

"Stop it," she whispered to herself. "One of these days it will be your turn." She could feel her color rise from the modest round neck of her blue gown, up her white throat, and into her face. For pity's sake, why did she lurk here in this corner? Wasn't this also her twentieth birthday party?

She raised herself to her full five-foot, six-inch height and stretched her slim body. She took one step toward the crowd and paused, gazing across the room at her uncanny mirror image.

Large, dark brown, glowing eyes met hers. Light brown curls caught up in back to cascade to her shoulders shone in the light. Laurel objectively examined her reflection. A wide mouth and an upturned nose might be considered charming but they weren't beautiful.

The thought brought a wry twist to her mouth but, surprisingly, her image's smile remained sparkling. Even more amazing was that her identical dress had miraculously changed from forget-me-not blue to rosy pink!

Pride mingled with envy. Would she ever catch up with Ivy Ann who had been born five minutes before her and, in spite of her clinging name, managed to lead in everything the two girls had ever done?

*Who cares,* Laurel demanded of herself, but the uneven beat of her heart said otherwise.

*I wish that for just one day, one week, one month, I could trade places with Ivy Ann,* Laurel confessed silently. *How can two girls—no, women—look so much alike even Daddy and Mama mix us up yet be so different?*

She examined her twin's face and figure. Nothing there to separate them. Her gaze traveled to Ivy's head, cocked to one side while she listened to the praise heaped on her. High color made her especially lovely and again Laurel felt the familiar surge of pleasure that such an enchanting creature was a special part of herself.

"Laurel, what are you doing standing over here by yourself?" Thomas Brown's hearty voice boomed into her hideout. "Everyone's asking for you. Come on." With a large, work-worn hand he caught Laurel's small but sturdy one and led his daughter across the room.

"Where have you been?" Ivy Ann reproached. Vain, selfish, and thriving on admiration, the love she had for her twin matched Laurel's.

"What a pair!" someone called.

"Only problem is, how do you ever know which twin is which?" a young man muttered. A shout of laughter followed. Eligible suitors knew only too well how one could never be sure that Laurel and Ivy Ann weren't playing tricks.

Suddenly Laurel felt tired of it all. The wish to be herself and not just half of Ivy Ann almost choked her. Only her strong training received from determined parents kept her from bolting.

Instead, she forced a smile and suffered herself to follow the wave of gaiety that lasted through supper and into the morning hours.

Even when she escaped she found no relief. The twins had shared a large room since babyhood. Laurel slowly removed her birthday present dress, brushed her hair, and climbed into bed. But Ivy Ann had been too tightly wound to run down yet.

"I am so glad Mama and Daddy encouraged us not to marry young," was her amazing remark once she emerged from the soft pink gown and slid into a ruffled nightdress.

Laurel couldn't help laughing. Trust Ivy Ann to come up with such a comment right on the heels of her splendid success at their party. "What made you think of that?"

"Oh, I don't know." She turned toward her twin. White teeth gleamed and the eyes that became provocative when a handsome neighbor appeared opened wide. "Gentian's baby is precious and Susan's husband is almost as wonderful as she thinks he is but I don't want to get married for ages and ages." Her smile melted some of Laurel's resistance. "I know we're considered old maids, but who cares?" She stretched white arms and yawned. "As long as there are men around to choose from, why marry? Are you willing to stay single until we're really old—twenty-five, maybe?"

"Mercy!" Laurel stared. "No man wants a wife that old."

A little frown marred Ivy Ann's forehead. "You're probably right, but my goodness, with all the nice young men coming to call, how can we ever make up our minds?"

Laurel refrained from reminding her twin how often those young men, even those who liked her, soon flitted from the quieter twin to the more daring, vivacious girl.

"Laurel, promise me that no matter who we marry or how far apart we may be, you won't ever let anything come between us."

Laurel sat up straight. Such serious conversation from Ivy Ann usually heralded some startling announcement. "Why would you want such a promise? What could come between us?"

"I don't know." Some of Ivy Ann's good mood had vanished. With troubled eyes, she stared at Laurel. "Sometimes I get the feeling we aren't as close as we used to be. Remember when we were small and always dressed exactly alike?" Nostalgia softened her face. "We don't now."

Laurel bit her lip. One of her small cries for freedom had brought about the change. "I like blue best and you like pink."

"I know, but somehow. . ." Ivy Ann's voice trailed and then died. "We don't like the same books or music either." Genuine sadness flickered in her eyes. "I just wish nothing had to change."

Understanding flooded Laurel. "You miss Gentian and Susan, don't you?"

"A lot more than I ever thought I would," she confessed with a quirk of her beautifully arched eyebrows. A deep dimple that had its counterpart in her sister's right cheek became obvious. "I thought I'd be glad when they left, they always bossed us around so. Especially Susan after Gentian married."

"Mama says she felt left out because we couldn't be separated."

Ivy Ann yawned and covered her mouth with her hand. "Perhaps. Anyway, now that we're women instead of girls we don't have younger sisters to boss! Too bad we don't have a brother." Her eyes gleamed. "They're mighty useful at bringing home young gentlemen."

"You are totally incorrigible," Laurel told her. "Goodnight."

"Goodnight."

Only after she heard her twin's soft breathing did Laurel remember she hadn't promised what Ivy Ann asked. Why should a strange feeling of relief fill her?

*✒*

A week after the Browns' celebration Laurel sat mending on the wide front porch. The never-ending basket of household linens and clothing rested next to her rocking chair and her quick fingers stitched and wove until a second pile formed. Accustomed to the work, she could keep sewing and still enjoy the stately red cedars from which her home took its name. September continued to be beautiful. Only a faint touch of frost had come and leaves that in some years had cascaded in golden showers from hardwoods remained green.

From her viewpoint, Laurel could look down the sloped hillsides to the river below or up steeper hills to distant mountains. Daddy said when God created West Virginia he forgot to put in any flat land. She secretly rejoiced. How could people live where the country lay straight as a table top? Distant figures scrambling up and down ladders into laden apple trees foretold canning and cider making. Her fingers stilled. As much as she loved Red Cedars, an undefined longing deep inside touched her in quiet moments. Perhaps Ivy's foolish chatter about not marrying until they were twenty-five had triggered her melancholy. Or the look on Susan's face when her tall husband snatched her up and lifted her over the stile. The feeling that went through her when she held Gentian's baby or intercepted the flash of love between her sisters and their husbands was still very real.

"Please, God, I want to belong to *someone*." Her barely audible prayer shocked her. Proper young women didn't talk to God about such things, did they?

*Why not?* a small voice whispered in her heart. Every girl and young woman's dreams are important to God; anything that touches His creation interests Him.

A rush of skirts interrupted her new and thrilling reverie. "Out here mending and talking to yourself?" a lively voice demanded.

Laurel whipped around toward Ivy Ann and felt herself redden. "I thought you were making beds."

Sadie Brown believed every girl must be head of her own household and know everything about housekeeping there was to know. "It's disgraceful how many Southern girls can't do anything but flirt," she indignantly maintained, and churned faster one day when Ivy Ann complained about the work. "I'd be disgraced to have my daughters so helpless." Her lightning glance at Ivy brought a flush of shame to her cheeks.

"The day is long past when southern women have nothing to do but be petted and admired. If the South is ever to rise and regain her strength, it will take every man, woman, and child working together."

"I thought you were for the Union," Laurel teased.

Sadie's sharp eyes softened. "I am and always will be but that doesn't mean I'm not also a Southern woman, just as my daughters will be if I have any say in the matter."

When Gentian and Susan went to their own homes, they possessed every housekeeping skill known to their mother. Their husbands rejoiced and gave thanks, especially after hearing stories from friends who had married helpless southern belles!

"I made the beds." Ivy Ann flounced into a chair. "And dusted. And prepared a dessert for supper. All while you're out here enjoying the sunshine."

"Want to trade jobs?"

Ivy barely restrained a shudder. "Never. You know I hate mending." She broke off a late bloom from the fragrant rosebush that climbed up and over the porch roof. "Mmmmm. Smells good. That reminds me. We must have enough rose petals saved to scent our clothes."

Laurel's needle flashed silver in the sun. In and out, in and out, weaving together frayed edges. "There will also be enough to put in the soap." When Ivy Ann didn't answer, she glanced up. Her gaze followed her twin's down the road and up the hill that led to Shawnee. "What are you looking at?

"Our fate."

Laurel dropped the needle. "Our *what?*" She looked at the empty lane then back at her sister, whose dreamy eyes were half-closed.

"Our fate. Can't you just see it? One of these days—" She dropped her voice to a mysterious tone. "Just when we least expect it, our fate will come riding down that hill and up the road. I wonder if we'll be ready for it."

"Are you stark, staring mad?" Laurel asked. "Whatever are you talking about?" Her pulse quickened in spite of her protest.

Ivy Ann dropped her indolent pose. Her eyes sparkled like dark molasses nuggets. She clapped her hands. "There is absolutely no romance in you, Mountain Laurel Brown! You should see as plainly as I that the most perfect young man God ever created is somewhere just waiting. When the time is right he will come riding, riding."

Laurel's heart filled with mischief. " 'Oh, young Lochinvar is come out of the west. Through all the wide Border, his steed was the best. . . .' " She rocked back and forth. "No Sir Walter Scott knight for me."

"Why not?" Laurel forgot her mending and concentrated on Ivy Ann. Not for a long time had the twins looked so alike with their teasing faces and hair loosened from good honest work. A vagrant breeze shook perfume from the roses and cooled the warm afternoon.

"Think I want to be carried off to who knows where, away from my family?" Ivy shook her head until her curls bounced. Some of the joy fled from her expressive face. "Could you stand having to live in some God-forsaken place, even with a husband?"

"You know what I mean." Ivy Ann impatiently brushed aside the remark. A brooding look replaced her fun. "I never did care much for Ruth in the Bible."

"Ivy Ann, are you criticizing the *Bible*?" Laurel gasped.

"Don't be a ninny. I just don't see how she could promise to leave everything and go off down the road. Especially when it wasn't even with a husband, just a mother-in-law. A former mother-in-law, at that!" She glared at Laurel. "Don't tell me you could or would leave this and—and me."

Laurel silently considered it, while the breeze increased, rustled leaves, and flirted with the rosebush. *Could she? Would she?* Yet the Bible said husband and wife were to cleave to each other and never be parted in this life. She slowly said, "That's what the Bible tells us. God created man and woman to be so closely entwined they could face whatever hardships might come."

"Pooh! It's all very well to quote from the Bible but when it came right down to it, you couldn't leave Red Cedars except to settle real close, now could you?" Ivy Ann's eyes darkened until they looked almost black.

Laurel hedged. "You mean if you really and truly met a man you felt God wanted you to marry, you'd say no—even if you loved him and he loved you—unless he agreed to live in West Virginia?"

"Yes!" But an impish look crept over her face. "I just bet any man would be glad to stay around here if it meant marrying me." She leaned back in her chair and daintily crossed her soft white shoes.

"But what if his work were somewhere else?" Laurel couldn't drop the subject that had somehow become strangely significant to her. "What if he *had* to live elsewhere?"

"He'd have to make other arrangements," said Ivy Ann nonchalantly, dismissing the imaginary situation with a wave of her hand. "You still haven't answered my question." For some reason she turned a little pale. "Would or would you not be a nineteenth-century Ruth?" Her clear voice hung in the ripening September air.

"I would." Laurel spoke from her innermost being. *Why did she feel the words committed her, like a solemn vow to something that would never happen?* "I would follow my husband wherever God called him to go." Her gaze never left Ivy's.

"Good for you!" Loud clapping followed the approving statement.

Laurel and Ivy Ann turned, torn from complete absorption in their discussion by the deep, masculine voice. A stranger stood on the bottom step, still applauding. Dark, interested eyes surveyed the twins. One fine hand held the reins of a spirited filly. Tall, straight, dark-haired and strong. . . .

*There never was knight like young Lochinvar.*

These words echoed in Laurel's brain. Laughter bubbled inside and to her horror escaped. Her dumbstruck twin just stared. But the stranger's dark eyes twinkled with merriment and Laurel couldn't help but wonder. The man had certainly come riding out of the west, down the hill and up their road. Could he possibly be the fate Ivy Ann predicted, stealing up while they talked, over-hearing their girlish conversation?

And if so, whose fate might he prove to be? Two young women, one handsome man.

Laurel gasped. And in the split second before her twin recovered her wits enough to hold out her hand in greeting, Laurel thought, *I'm glad I didn't promise Ivy Ann what she wanted.*

*Chapter 2*

D r. Birchfield?" The plain-faced, middle-aged woman who came in daily to clean his cottage and office tapped lightly at the open door.

Adam raised his head from the medical journal he had stolen time to read. "Yes?" Although his mind stayed on the report of new advances in treating contagious disease, his alert eyes caught the telltale twisting of Mrs. Cutler's hands.

Her firm mouth trembled. "Is it true what they say? That you'll be leaving Concord soon?" Before he could stifle his amazement and answer, the good woman added, "Why, Birchfields have lived in Massachusetts as far back as anyone can remember. None ever wanted to live anywhere else, until—" She broke off and dull red suffused her face.

"Until my older brother Nathaniel refused to fight in a war he hated and left home," Adam grimly finished. He set his lean jaw and his dark eyes flashed. "Where did you hear that I might be leaving?"

"I couldn't help overhearing you argue, er, your discussion with your father this morning." She stared at the floor then looked straight into Adam's furious face. "Begging your pardon, Doctor, but Jeremiah and Patience have already lost one son. Surely you won't desert them, too."

Only strong regard for Mrs. Cutler's long, well-meaning friendship kept back the hot words that sprang to Adam's lips. "I'd appreciate it if you keep what you heard to yourself," he told her. "I don't know what I'm going to do—yet."

Mrs. Cutler sighed. "You'll have to do what you think is right. Every tub has to stand on its own bottom. But isn't there a way for you and your father to part without anger if you feel you must go?"

Adam didn't reply and Mrs. Cutler vanished from the doorway, leaving him more disturbed than he cared to be. He stood, walked to the window open to an early August afternoon, and stared unseeingly into the perfect day that at another time would have enticed him outside.

Without anger—if only it could happen! He could not deny the restlessness that had filled him ever since he finished medical training and returned to Concord. Had it started when his father exploded at his idea of setting up a separate office when Jeremiah had long planned that Adam would join him in practice?

*First Nat, then me.* Adam drummed his fingers on the white-painted windowsill. The admission opened Pandora's box. Memories Adam wished he could forget crowded into the sunny room.

From the time he could toddle Adam worshipped his brother Nathaniel. He followed after him, never realizing until he grew up how unusual it was for a boy six years older to suffer the presence of a small child and make him feel welcome. Jeremiah and Patience looked with approval on the boys' relationship. Dr. Birchfield's dream of having Nathaniel march in his own steps inspired Adam. Someday he, too, would study medicine. How wonderful if all three of them could work together!

Like a thunderbolt came news of war with the South. No man in New England carried the fire of patriotism higher than Jeremiah Birchfield. He could not volunteer because of a heart problem, but his face flamed when he summoned twenty-year-old Nathaniel home from his medical training in early 1862.

"I can't go, but I proudly send my best, my oldest son."

Patience, whose name matched her God-fearing personality,

wrung a fine handkerchief mercilessly but made no protest. She seldom took a stand against her rock-ribbed husband. His streak of granite resembled those found in the stern New England hills.

Adam, whose fourteenth birthday had just passed, started to speak. A single glance from Nathaniel quelled his words. The next instant Nat spoke.

"I am sorry to disappoint you, Father, but I cannot go."

Patience's nervous fingers stilled.

Adam could only stare at the white radiance in his adored brother's face.

Jeremiah rose to full height, towering in his shock and disbelief. "What is this foolishness? You *must* go."

"I cannot."

"To think I would see the day my own son turned coward and refused to fight for his country!"

Jeremiah's rage brought misery to Nathaniel's dark eyes but his steady gaze didn't even flicker. "I am no coward. I cannot fight in a war I don't believe should happen." He warmed to his subject, given opportunity by his father's stunned silence. "Don't you see? The North condemns the South for slavery. Yet how many families living here keep colored servants?"

Speechless, Jeremiah raised a warning hand but Nat rushed on.

"If I thought this conflict was about preserving the Union or bringing equality to all people, it would be different." The fight went from him. A beseeching look replaced his determination. "Father, please, if you can't understand, at least respect my decision."

Adam held his breath, silently praying to God to do something, anything.

Jeremiah got his second wind. Anger overrode reason. "As long as I furnish you with meat and drink and shelter you will obey me. I say you will put aside these blasphemous ideas and serve the country your forefathers sought to be free and worship God." Every word beat into the room with the force of a physical blow.

Patience roused from her submissiveness. "*Don't do this!*" She ran to her husband and caught his arm. The strings of the morning cap she wore loosened.

"Woman, be still."

"I will not be still!" she cried. "He's our son, yours and mine. Nothing can ever change that."

"He has changed it of his own free will," Jeremiah stormed. "Nathaniel Birchfield, if you refuse to do a man's duty, you are hereafter no son of mine."

"Jeremiah, *no!*" Patience burst into mournful weeping.

"It's all right, Mother. Father may not claim me as a son but he can't stop me from loving him. I am truly sorry."

When Nat marched from the room Adam choked. His brother's shoulders squared in such an erect position Adam had the feeling Nat stepped to the sound of martial music only he could hear.

That same afternoon Nathaniel left Concord. "Don't blame Father too much," he told his brokenhearted brother. "Someday, when the war is over, perhaps he will change." He tousled Adam's raven hair, so like his own. "Try and make up for me if you can. Godspeed."

While the war raged and Patience and Adam grieved, Jeremiah Birchfield permitted no mention of Nathaniel's name. He could not control his younger son's thoughts though. Adam held tight to a dream that one day, when he had the resources, he would find Nat. Years and miles meant nothing compared with the brother enshrined in Adam's heart. A few scattered letters came. Twice Jeremiah saw them first and tore them into bits without reading them. The others told little except that Nat was well and had worked at everything from being a farmer to a blacksmith. He also wrote he missed his family.

Adam took a deep breath and held it. When it rushed out he turned back to the desk, his mind still turbulent. "I've been faithful, Nat," he said half under his breath. "I became a doctor as Father wished. But I'm twenty-five years old now. You're thirty-one. Lately I feel you need me." The same prickle that had caused the earlier argument with Jeremiah returned. A trivial comment had slipped out in spite of Adam's guarded tongue.

"I'll wager that if Nat had become a doctor he'd be a far better one than I." He instantly clamped his mouth shut but it was too late.

"I know no Nathaniel and if you are as wise as you ought to be you'll do the same."

Adam had learned patience and pity for the father who had aged so in the past eleven years. Yet he had also inherited Jeremiah's quick temper and his own sense of justice. "Father, why can't you forget the past? I've heard you read stories from the Bible about the need to forgive—"

"Are you daring to tell me what to do?" Slumbering fires fed by guilt and stubbornness flared.

Adam shook his head. "No, I just know how much Mother misses Nathaniel. If you can't forgive him for yourself and for him, can't you do it for Mother's sake?"

Jeremiah's features turned to chiseled marble. "I believe you had something you wished to consult me about?"

Adam's despair at his family's estrangement caused him to lose control. He clenched his hands and said slowly. "I want to leave Concord."

Suspicion reddened the old doctor's face. "You're not considering going after—him?"

Adam had never lied in his life. Nat had taught him from babyhood that lies and deceit lead to dishonor. Of all the sins, Adam learned to despise dishonesty most.

"Someday." Before Jeremiah could answer he added, "Besides, I'd like to take my medical skills where they'd do more good than here in Concord."

"Perhaps to the Wyoming Territory?" His father's loaded question confirmed Adam's belief that Jeremiah had kept far more careful track of Nat than anyone realized.

"Perhaps."

"You'd give up all you have here, a secure practice, the respect of the town, the chance to prosper..." Jeremiah's face grayed.

"Father, didn't you and Mother come to Concord not knowing what it held, not sure if you could establish a practice here? Adam spread his hands out, palms up. "Look at these hands. They are skilled in surgery and caring for the sick but they aren't needed here. You and Dr. Partridge can handle things while I'm gone."

"And how long is that to be?" Jeremiah folded his arms in a gesture that warned Adam the discussion was not settled.

"I don't know."

Jeremiah grunted. "I thought so. Adam, if you walk away from everything I've given you—" He hesitated. Did he remember another gauntlet thrown down to a son who had no choice but to pick it up? "We'll discuss this later." He strode away, his shoulders slumped but still determined.

*No wonder Mrs. Cutler's plea haunted him,* Adam thought. The arrival of afternoon patients and several calls on horseback swerved his mind from the problem. *How old and tired and ill Jeremiah looked. Could his one remaining son leave him, even for the best of reasons?*

"Dear God, what shall I do?" Adam reverted to his usual

way of solving problems. "Go? Stay? Or merely wait?" When no answer flashed into his brain and heart he decided God's signal must be to wait.

It didn't take long. A few days later Jeremiah Birchfield commanded Adam to come for supper and startled both wife and son with an announcement.

"You've been wanting to see what medical practice out in the wilds is like. Can you be ready to leave tomorrow morning?"

"Leave? For where?" Adam put down his fork and swallowed his last bite of molasses-sweetened apple pie.

"West Virginia." Satisfaction oozed from the older man's entire being. "I have it all arranged. You'll visit mountain areas where everything you've learned will war with the conditions you find there. You will see poverty and squalor, superstition and apathy until you'll be ready to come back and appreciate Concord."

Adam ran the full gamut of emotions: anger at his father's high-handed disposal of himself; unwilling interest and a sense of adventure; compassion for his wide-eyed mother; even amusement at Jeremiah in foiling his plan to head West.

"I can be ready." Adventure had won, but the war between father and son had not ended. This trip to West Virginia was simply the first skirmish between them.

Adam's departure had to be postponed a day. Such a furor over his going ensued that Jeremiah gruffly said, "Wait until tomorrow. The neighbors are determined to bid you Godspeed." A dazed Adam was only half aware of the impromptu covered dish supper, an expression of the townspeople's regard. Not surprisingly, his leaving rekindled village gossip of years before about where "that ungrateful Nathaniel Birchfield" had ended up. Adam stumbled onto one such conversation and effectively stopped it with one steady look at the offenders.

He secretly rejoiced when everyone left and he could go

back to the cottage for his last night there. When would he see it again? Despite what Jeremiah thought, Adam instinctively knew all the miseries he faced in West Virginia wouldn't send him running for home like a whipped dog.

"Dear God," he wondered aloud, "Is this the first step toward Nat?" The soft night wind blew in from the west and brought cooling relief and an invitation. He wished he could have gone that morning instead of having to wait. Yet the next day he gave thanks to God it had not been so. Just before he locked his cottage door for the last time, Patience Birchfield's hired girl rushed up to him. From the folds of her voluminous apron she pulled a letter that showed stains of travel. "Miz Patience says take it." She scurried away just before Jeremiah arrived.

Adam quickly pocketed the worn letter. His heart pounded from the glimpse of bold writing and it took all his concentration not to betray himself to his father.

"I'll be expecting reports of your work." Eyes undulled by age and heartache bored into Adam.

"I'll write. I promise." The younger doctor held out a slim hand and grasped the other's lined one.

"Godspeed." After a moment Jeremiah added, "Son."

"Godspeed, Father." Other words trembled on his lips but refused to form. Adam watched his father turn away heavily and walk down the road toward the red-brick traditional house that had been built a few years after the Birchfields came. Jeremiah didn't look back. If agony and the same uncertainty of father and son meeting again in this life touched him as it did Adam, no one knew.

The trip by rail to West Virginia always remained a blur in Adam's mind. Enthralled by the long letter Nathaniel had sent, irretrievably caught by the older man's plea for him to consider coming West, Adam's eyes saw the changing country but his heart and mind could not take them in. Snatches of the letter haunted him.

*Medical help is practically nonexistent.*
*It will come as a great surprise, I am sure, but I made the greatest decision of my life a little over a year ago.*
*I feel God has called me to be His servant. After much prayer and study, I have accepted a tough assignment and am building a church in the small but wiled hamlet of Antelope in the rugged Wind River Range of the Rocky Mountains.*
*Here will I live, serve—and one day lie.*
*How much you could do, if you came. . . .*

The next days and weeks tore at Adam. Father had been right: Many of the West Virginians struggled and overcame, but some did not. Bound by tradition and mountain superstition, bereaved and desolated by heavy losses of both family members and crops, Adam found he had more to do than three doctors could handle. The old doctor who should have retired years before demanded and got a fine horse for Adam. Beyond that and his food and shelter, Adam received little. Yet mountain-proud patients gave what they had, simply and quietly—a haunch of venison, turnips, apples, and once, a worn but still usable quilt.

At first Adam protested but his host soon stopped that. "Everything's been taken from them but their pride. Tuck yours away in your pocket and let them keep theirs," he advised when Adam insisted the families needed things more than he.

August ended and September slipped in. One beautiful afternoon Adam found himself free for the first time since he came to the hills.

"I don't know quite how to act," he confessed to his good mentor.

"Now if I were forty or so years younger and had a free day, I'd ride out and say thanks to the folks who donated the filly." The mountain doctor's eyes twinkled. "Being it's such a nice day and all."

Adam distrusted the twinkle but eagerly snatched the idea. He'd sent thanks but wanted to let the generous family know how much he appreciated the loan. The filly's easy stride gobbled up miles and Adam had found to his amazement that he was a natural horseman.

Adam whipped his face from the burning September sun and recognized from Doc's directions the land he sought. A flash of blue from the wide porch showed someone was home. A little hesitantly, he rode closer to the house, dismounted, and paused with one foot on the bottom step. Cool vines and a climbing rose offered no obstruction to the clear voices.

"Would you or would you not be a nineteenth-century Ruth?" a light voice demanded.

"I would. I would follow my husband wherever God called him to go."

Why should the rich voice send joy through Dr. Adam Birchfield? "Good for you!" he called and applauded.

Not one but two bewitching young women whirled to face him. Then the one in blue laughed, and Adam thought of bubbling water.

# Chapter 3

Dedicated to medicine and determined to learn everything he could, Adam Birchfield had wasted no time on romance. When he saw a particularly attractive woman, a vague realization that one day he'd have to find a wife pierced his studies. He laughed then reassured himself that when that time came God would provide. His fellow medical students jeered at the idea.

"God? Why, He's busy enough keeping this old world from going to ruin. How can you expect Him to be a matchmaker?"

"I don't." But Adam grinned and laughter lurked in his dark eyes. "You have to admit, though, getting married is one of the biggest events in a man's life. I talked with God about becoming a doctor. Why not about marriage?"

"You sound like a parson," his chief rival for top honors accused. "Maybe you should have gone into preaching."

"I thought of it." Adam raised one eyebrow. "But I believe no one should take that honor unless called of God and I feel no such call." He yawned. "Enough talking. I have one tough examination first thing in the morning."

Even when he completed his training and became established in Concord, Adam shied away from the droves of young women who hounded him. Something fine inside refused to succumb to those who set traps for him and generally were nuisances. Once he exploded to his father, "Why can't they see real men can't abide their silliness?" His face softened. "Mother isn't like that and I bet she never was."

A poignant look of remembrance touched Jeremiah's craggy features. "Patience lived and continues to live up to the Proverbs description of what a godly woman and wife should be. My boy, no man has ever had a better companion." As if regretting the moment, he snapped, "Now, let's get back to business. Have you convinced old man Trescott to let you treat him or is he still insisting on seeing me?"

They launched into a medical discussion but Adam's heart warmed to his father in a way it had seldom done since Nat left.

Now a pair of dark eyes—no, two pairs of dark eyes—haunted him. Sadie Brown issued an invitation for the visiting doctor to have supper with them and Ivy Ann prettily concurred. Laurel's quiet look convinced him. Before Adam remounted to ride back to Doc's, he had accepted further invitations to drop by any time he could.

The second time he came ended with a discussion of the opportunities out West.

"Is it true that women are really allowed to vote and to hold office in the Wyoming Territory?" Thomas might be a farmer but he loved to keep up on events outside his own domain. His eyes glistened.

So did Laurel's. When Ivy Ann whispered, "Who cares?" her sister whispered back fiercely, "I do! Be still and listen, will you?" Ivy's eyes opened wide like a spanked kitten's but she acquiesced.

"My brother Nathaniel writes that it's all true." Adam glowed with pride. He had sketched in why Nathaniel went West, surprised and pleased that the Browns bore no resentment toward a Northerner who wouldn't fight. He had also shared how Nat wandered until he came to a point where he truly believed God wanted him to serve as a minister. Nat chose Antelope in the opening territory because, Adam quoted his brother, " 'The fields are white already to harvest.' "

"He sounds terribly good to me," Ivy Ann put in.

Adam glanced at her sharply but her innocent face gave no

sign of criticism, only admiration.

"Tell us more." Sadie echoed Laurel's unspoken plea. "What about Indian trouble? And women's voting rights?" Her eyes snapped. "About time wives and mothers were allowed to have a say."

"Mama's all for women being given the vote." Ivy Ann couldn't keep out of the conversation long. "So's Laurel." She shot a look of mischief toward her twin.

"How about you?"

Ivy Ann covered a dainty yawn with slender fingers. "Dear me, I'm not sure I could choose." A shout of laughter followed but Adam took her seriously.

"Just surviving in a new and untamed land is hard. The women work alongside their men and bear children as well." He saw the shocked look that passed between the girls. "I ask forgiveness if I'm indelicate, but as a doctor I see the bearing of children as natural." He quickly changed the subject. "About women voting, Congress created the Territory of Wyoming in 1868 and in 1869 the Wyoming Territorial Legislature gave women the right to vote and hold elected office. In 1870, Esther H. Morris became the nation's first woman justice of the peace."

Inspired by all but Ivy Ann's rapt attention, Adam went on, quoting from Nathaniel and from everything he had read, in fact all he could find about the new western frontier.

"Lieutenant John Fremont explored the Wind River Mountains way back in 1842 and 1843 but fur trade began just after 1800. Over the years it resulted in the Indian wars we've heard about. But the discovery of gold in the 1860s in Montana triggered off trouble."

"Then you'll be going into danger?" Wide-eyed Ivy Ann leaned forward, making a pretty picture in the firelight and softly shaded lamplight.

Adam shook his head, "No, Red Cloud and other Indian leaders signed a treaty about five years ago. They agreed not to interfere with the building of the Union Pacific Railroad in southern Wyoming in exchanged for the army's abandonment of Fort Phil Kearney and two other forts. This gave northeastern Wyoming back to the Indians who hated this fort." Doubt filled Adam's eyes. "Nat says it's an uneasy truce and peace."

Laurel spilled over. "I don't blame the Indians at all! If reports are true, they've been lied to again and again."

"All the more reason for Nat to establish a church in Antelope. He hopes not only to reach the cowboys and miners and ranchers in that area, but perhaps take the Gospel to the Indians."

"You are really going, aren't you?" Ivy Ann asked. "But what about your wife? Will she leave Massachusetts and live in the place called Antelope?"

"Wife!" Adam's hearty laugh filled the room and brought answering smiles to the others' faces. "I have no wife. Anyway, what decently brought up girl would give up everything and trail along with me to such an untried country? Would you?" He looked deep into Ivy Ann's dark eyes.

Ivy wrinkled her nose in disgust. "Go out where there's nothing but cowboys and miners and ranchers?"

"Oh, there are other things," Adam said solemnly. "Jackrabbits and mule deer, elk and black bears. There are grizzly bears and mountain lions, lynxes and coyotes, foxes, skunks, and wildcats."

"Please, no more!" Ivy covered her ears.

"I haven't even begun." Adam's excitement knew no bounds and lighted fires of interest in the others. "We mustn't forget the fur animals such as beavers, raccoons, martens, and otters. Or the pronghorns—"

"What's a pronghorn?" Ivy Ann took down her hands and

pouted. "Another dangerous animal?"

"They're like a deer and like an antelope and roam the Rocky Mountain plains area by the thousands. Nat says they're so beautiful they make his throat hurt. Tan with dark markings and short black horns, their varied coloration protects them by blending into their surroundings.

"You know, the Wyoming Territory has flat land *and* towering peaks and rugged canyons, racing rivers *and* waterfalls."

"I've heard that it's dreadfully cold." Ivy Ann shivered.

"In winter, yes, but a dry cold that men can stand." Adam breathed deeply.

"Men, but not women." Ivy Ann tossed her curly head. "Why don't you just settle around here? There's plenty of need for a new doctor." She smiled provocatively. "Lots of pretty girls, too, and, as you said, no decently brought up girl would go out there with you—"

"I would." Laurel said. Then red blood flooded her smooth skin. "I mean, that is, not with Dr. Birchfield, but if I were in love with someone. . . ."

For the second time in their acquaintance something passed between Adam and the quiet twin who had so bravely spoken out. For a single instant a feeling of kinship existed before being suddenly shattered by Ivy Ann's laughing accusation:

"You know you'll marry someone right around here, Laurel, so don't sound all noble! You couldn't bear to be away from Shawnee more than a few miles, any more than I could." She gracefully rose, linked her arm in Laurel's, and pulled her to her feet. The twins' wide, soft skirts rustled and swayed with the movement.

"See, Dr. Birchfield? You don't really think young women like us should go to the Wyoming Territory, do you?"

Adam's heart plummeted and he silently called himself a

fool. After twenty-five years of walking alone, why should the impossibility of such a thing affect him? He stood, better able to think while on his feet. He paused in the way he had of thinking before ever committing himself. When he spoke it came from a belief that had crystallized while reading and rereading Nathaniel's letters.

"Miss Brown," Adam's gaze turned from Ivy Ann to Laurel. "Whether Christian young women such as you *would* go to the Wyoming Territory I have no way of knowing. But yes, I believe such women *should*. Without decent women to establish and maintain homes and schools and churches, wild and lawless men can only live rough lives, shorn of the beauty only women can provide. Nathaniel says the few wives who have accompanied their mates are already making a difference. They are almost worshipped by those very men who shoot and gamble!"

Undaunted, Ivy Ann tossed her head again. "I've heard the women in the West are—are—" She struggled to find an acceptable but significantly telling word. "Are bad," she finished triumphantly.

Adam folded his arms and looked stern. "There will always be bad women and men as long as strong Christian followers balk at inconvenience, danger, and hardship." He clamped his lips into a straight line then deliberately smiled, hoping to erase the impression of criticism. "I must go. I am grateful for your warm Southern hospitality. We who live in the North should be so gracious."

"Goodnight, Dr. Birchfield." Ivy Ann extended one hand and clung to her twin with the other. "Perhaps your mission *is* to convince certain Christian followers. Do come again."

Adam hid a grin. He had nettled this young woman more than she cared to admit. He bowed over her hand, then Laurel's. "If time permits, I will." He turned toward Thomas and Sadie.

"Forgive me for monopolizing the conversation. I never could resist Nat's enthusiasm. As soon as I finish my promised stay here I plan to go West." He smiled. "I frankly admit I'm glad I can ride the Union Pacific across country. I'm not yet skilled enough at horseback riding to relish the thought of traveling that way."

In true Southern custom, the Browns accompanied Adam outside. Thomas insisted on helping him saddle the filly and all four stood in the cool night air until the sound of hoofbeats dwindled and faded into distant silence.

"He's a bit of a crusader, isn't he?" Ivy Ann flounced inside and away from her family's protest. "Can you imagine?" She folded her arms and said in a passable imitation of Adam's pronouncement, "*Whether Christian young women such as you would go to Wyoming I have no way of knowing. But yes, I believe such women should. . . .*" She broke off and mirthfully grasped her sides. "For pity's sake, deliver me from earnest young men!" Still laughing, she lightly ran upstairs.

Laurel felt reluctant to follow. The entire evening had quickened her senses as nothing had done before. Before Adam Birchfield's arrival the vague sense of wanting something more than her present way of life had smoldered. The intense young doctor had fueled her discontent. She also remembered his challenging words. Not lightly, as did Ivy Ann, but in a way that she couldn't fully comprehend.

Her own faltering explanation flashed into her mind like a sunrise over mountains. "I mean, that is, not with Dr. Birchfield, but if I were in love with someone. . . ."

Laurel slowly climbed the stairs, treasuring the surprised and admiring glance Adam had given her, the feeling of kinship. Even Ivy Ann had been excluded from that moment. If only he were staying longer, perhaps the fragile thread could strengthen.

She sighed and reached the top of the stairs then walked down the hall to her room and to Ivy Ann.

Laurel's heartfelt wish changed in the short time before Adam Birchfield went West and out of her life forever. Obviously piqued by the way the doctor had at first equally divided his attention between the twins, Ivy pulled out every trick from her enormous store of enticements. A soft hand laid on Adam's arm when it wasn't necessary. The cocked head and intense concentration on what he said. Downcast eyes followed by a quick upward sweep of long lashes over melting brown eyes.

Laurel secretly raged, angry with Ivy Ann and even more furious with herself. None of the tricks were new. She just hated seeing them used on Adam. "He's too fine for cheapness," she whispered to herself, then wondered why she cared.

Yet she quietly rejoiced the day Ivy Ann overstepped herself. Clad in one of Laurel's favorite blue gowns, the scheming young woman met Adam at the door, made up an excuse about her sister not feeling well, and prepared to keep Adam to herself. She didn't identify herself as Laurel but neither did she act like Ivy Ann. A half-hour later when a perfectly healthy and unsuspecting Laurel came into the big living room calling, "Ivy Ann, Mama wants us," she met Adam's shocked gaze.

"How do you like my little trick?" Ivy Ann asked Adam, but Laurel saw her twin's fingers tremble in the folds of the blue gown.

"I find deceit in any form totally abominable. It is nice that your sister has recovered—so rapidly."

Ivy Ann turned crimson and cast a resentful glance at Laurel who just stood there.

"Miss Brown, may I have the pleasure of your company while getting my horse?" Adam asked Laurel.

"Oh, we'll both go with you." Ivy Ann tucked her hand under his arm in the way that never failed to obtain forgiveness.

Adam didn't unbend. "Miss Brown?" He offered his other arm to Laurel, who felt torn between wanting to laugh and ignoring Ivy's glare. Flanked by the young women, so alike and yet so opposite, Adam reached his horse, bowed, and rode off "stiffer than Mama's starched petticoats," Ivy Ann complained. Unholy glee filled Laurel. If they never met another man Ivy couldn't twine around her finger, at least Adam Birchfield hadn't succumbed to Ivy's tricks.

Adam only had time to visit once more. Several times Laurel caught his glance resting on her but, as usual, Ivy Ann kept herself on center stage. Never had she been more vivacious and lovely, bewildering and changeable as in a rosy gown that modestly left visible only a little round of white neck and dimpled hands below her ruffled sleeves. If she felt embarrassment or contrition over Adam's last visit, even Laurel couldn't see it. By mutual agreement, neither twin had told their parents what had happened. Thomas and Sadie well knew their daughter's ways but Laurel never carried tales and Ivy seldom confessed anything that would mar her image.

Adam appeared restless and Laurel knew how eager he must be to get going. When Ivy vanished for a few minutes he shared his heart's concern. "It's close to twelve years. I wonder if Nathaniel and I will have to get acquainted all over. There's a lot of difference between twenty and almost thirty-two."

"No more than between fourteen and more than twenty-five," Sadie reminded. She patted the young doctor's hand. "The same love you and your brother shared while he lived at home is there." She pointed to the fireplace, well banked for the night. "See?" Sadie tossed a twig and flames shot out to snatch it greedily. "That's all it will take."

Laurel watched Adam's bowed head and saw his throat work. God grant that he would find his brother well. Envy swept through her. If she were a man she would do as Adam Birchfield had chosen to do—go where decent, law-abiding people could make a difference. But Daddy and Mama would never agree to her going West. *Unless you married someone who lived there,* a little voice said inside.

Glad for once of Ivy's renewed chatter Laurel silently enjoyed the final minutes of Adam's company. *Why did she have to be so tongue-tied? Why couldn't she be more like her twin?* Yet even her special love for Ivy Ann couldn't blind her to the fact Adam simply hadn't fallen at her sister's small feet. His voice remained the same when he bid each of them goodbye.

"May God go with you," Thomas said when he gripped Adam's hand. "I almost wish I were going, too."

Laurel saw the blaze in Adam's face and the way his hand tightened. "Perhaps, sir, one day you will."

"Leave Red Cedars?" Thomas acted surprised yet something in his face when he turned toward his wife and daughters sent a strange spurt of hope through Laurel. What if they did go West, all of them, in spite of Ivy Ann's fretting? Her traitorous heart skipped a beat then rushed on. The prospect of seeing Adam Birchfield again sent flags flying in her cheeks and in her heart.

# Chapter 4

Every mile of the long journey between Shawnee, West Virginia, and Antelope, Wyoming Territory, strengthened Adam Birchfield's belief in the rightness of his decision. Every mile proved a revelation to the once provincial young man who had been born, raised, and schooled in Massachusetts. Not until his West Virginia odyssey had Adam seen anything other than his own state or been on his own. At home and school Jeremiah had dominated. In West Virginia the good old mountain doctor took a father's place. The intoxicating allure of freedom flowed in Adam's veins and consumed his every thought.

With every mile he thanked God for this opportunity and asked for Jeremiah's eventual forgiveness. At times he felt remorseful over the way he had sent news of his departure too late for his father to respond. Yet what good would more arguments have done except to worsen things between father and son? Better to follow Mrs. Cutler's advice and go without more anger. Mother must never again be forced to stand by helplessly and see a son cast out.

Adam thrilled to the ever-changing scenes that fled past his window seat. Rolling hills gave way to gentle farmlands; cities that had meant little more than a test of memory in geography sprang into solid, unforgettable places. Time after time he marveled. How could even the sturdiest pioneer have traveled the weary miles, walking behind covered wagons that stirred up dust? A little pang went through him. How many of those same men, women, and children lay beneath the prairie sod, mute witnesses to the settling of the West? A little prayer of gratitude filled his heart.

He resented the darkness, boyishly afraid he would miss something. As long as twilight showed even the most open, empty land, Adam strained his eyes to see. "I may never be here again," he whispered then straightened, shocked at himself. Had he so fallen in love with Nathaniel's West he was ready to disown the East forever? Impossible! Mother, Father, everything he knew lay waiting in Massachusetts.

Yet across the grassy plains, beyond the distant mountains, the unseen hamlet of Antelope in all its wildness had already staked a claim in his heart.

*I will probably be the only doctor for hundreds of miles,* he admitted. *How can I care for patients in such circumstances?* He had prayed that his skills might be used. If all he expected came to pass, God's answer to his prayer could be overwhelming!

Even while Adam glued his gaze to outside the window, his mind and heart remembered Red Cedars. There was Ivy Ann, shallow but charming. Did a sound, true heart beat underneath all the frills? He closed his eyes and a rosy vision danced before him. A man could find excitement enough for a lifetime if he could get beyond the Southern belle pose and reach Ivy's heart.

An involuntary smile crossed his face at the thought of Laurel. At first he had found her a quieter version of Ivy Ann. Adam shook his head. Laurel's passionate outbursts about leaving all to cleave unto her mate had turned her glowing dark eyes to almost black. A lot of banked fire burned within the sometimes-overlooked twin. What if Thomas and Sadie answered the call of the West? Thomas's excitement when they discussed it betrayed an untamed, pioneer spirit. What an asset that family would be to Antelope!

Adam awoke to a gradual slowing of the train as it climbed. Rubbing the sleep from his eyes, he looked straight out at snowcapped peaks he wouldn't have believed existed outside of an artist's rendering. Amazingly, even though the train steadily chugged on for hours, the peaks came no closer!

A grizzled man with well-worn boots and an over-sized hat laughed at Adam's astonishment. "Son, out here the air is so clear things look a powerful lot closer. Are you aimin' to stay?"

"Yes, at least for a while." Adam threw a sop to his conscience.

Shrewd eyes measured the young doctor. "Let me give you a word of advice. Never hop on a cayuse and head out toward the mountains—or anywhere—without findin' out from someone who knows how far you have to go."

"Thanks." Adam felt humbled before this man's direct concern and friendliness.

"How come an easterner like you is in the Wyomin' Territory?"

"Why, my brother is here. I'm a doctor and he asked me to come."

"A *doctor?*" The rancher clapped Adam on the shoulder so hard the younger man nearly fell out of his seat. "That's a whole bushel of good news. Where you aimin' to settle?"

"In Antelope." Adam regained some of his composure. "My brother's building a church there and—"

"Jumpin' grasshoppers, if you ain't Nat Birchfield's brother!" The welcoming grin accompanied another backslap but this time Adam braced himself. He could feel his blood pound in his head.

"You know Nat?" he asked eagerly.

"Half of Wyomin' Territory knows him and admires what he's doin' to help make Antelope a place for decent folks to live and raise their families." His unqualified approval warmed Adam to the tips of his travel-stained shoes.

"My name's Hardwick." He thrust out a weather-beaten hand in the kind of grip Adam expected from such a man. "I own the Lazy H spread a few miles out of Antelope. Run quite a few cattle and horses."

*What luck!* Adam leaned forward and his dark eyes flashed. "I don't mean to pry but how many is 'quite a few?'"

Hardwick grinned again. "Consider'ble more than last year, maybe less than next year." He laughed outright at Adam's raised eyebrow and relented. "We drove a bunch of cattle rustlers out of the country about a year ago, so the Lazy H and other ranches are prosperin'." His eyebrows pulled together and the corners of his mouth turned down. "Who knows what kinda varmints will come creepin' back? Or if the good Lord will choose this year for a ripsnorter of a winter that freezes critters where they stand? Then there's the little matter of hail and drought, flood, and fire from lightnin'." He jerked his big hat down over his eyes and mumbled, "Man's a fool to try and beat this crazy country."

"But you wouldn't live anywhere else." Adam's newly gained wisdom prompted the comment.

Hardwick shoved his hat to the back of his grizzled head. Adam caught the same approval in his eyes that had been there when they discussed Nat. "Reckon you're goin' to be all right out here." For the second time he pulled his hat forward. A few minutes later snores rumbled in time with the train wheels.

There was no sleep for Adam. Hardwick had given him—a tenderfoot—the highest possible compliment. Too bad Ivy Ann Brown couldn't hear Hardwick. What had he said about Nat? Oh yes, that half the Territory knew and admired him for helping to make Antelope a place for decent folks.

"Dear God, what if I hadn't come?" Adam barely whispered. Hardwick might be sound asleep but a rancher who lived on guard against two- and four-legged varmints would certainly be a light sleeper.

"Good thing I run onto you, like I did." Hardwick drawled the next day. "It's a lot of rugged miles between Rock Springs and Antelope." He eyed Adam's strong body. "Can you ride?"

"If you'd asked me that six months ago, I'd have said no." The young doctor laughed. "I can now, though. I've been in West Virginia where they have some great horses."

"No better than our cowponies, I'll wager." Hardwick jealously defended his own. "They might be faster but, by jingo, a man needs a horse that's half human and can get him out of trouble when the shootin' begins."

"Is there a lot of shooting?" Adam tensed.

"Tolerable amount. Not so much since your brother came."

The last miles of the long journey raced as Adam continued to learn from the rancher. "I won't be totally ignorant when I get to Antelope," he confided in his new friend, "thanks to you. By the way, why do you call your ranch the Lazy H? I can figure out it's *H* for Hardwick but I wouldn't think you'd have time for laziness."

His companion's shout of laughter drew the interested attention of everyone in the car. "You're right about that, son." Hardwick's eyes twinkled. "It's just a name. See this?" He drew in the dust that had collected on the windowsill. "We have to brand our cattle and the lazy part just means the H is layin' down on its side. See?" He pointed at his lazy "H".

Adam solemnly regarded the little figure. He sighed. "I have a lot more to learn, I guess."

Hardwick sobered. "Adam, any man who's willin' to admit he don't know it all is a jump ahead of the game. Just do your doctorin', keep your ears and eyes open and your mouth closed, and you'll do fine."

"Say, do you have a gal back East?"

Adam couldn't keep from squirming. "Well, not really. I mean, I met a girl, that is, two girls this summer."

"They ain't keen on the West?"

Adam felt Hardwick could see right through him. "One sure isn't." He shifted position again.

"And the other?"

Adam felt his lips curve up into a smile. "If she weren't a well brought up young woman, I think she'd—" He broke off and stared out the window across the aisle over Hardwick's shoulder. "*Look!*"

Hardwick whipped around and unconsciously grabbed for the Colt sixshooters he had earlier showed Adam. With a motion so fast the fascinated doctor could scarcely follow it, the guns were out of their holsters and into his hands. Hardwick's gaze never left the band of Indians on horseback that stood statue-like watching the train.

"Are—are they friendly?"

Hardwick muttered something under his breath and slowly sheathed the six-shooters as the color came back to his face. "Friendly? No. Peacable? Maybe."

"Do they bother your ranch?"

Hardwick shrugged. "Now and then a steer's missin' and all we find is the hooves. Can't say if it's hungry braves or someone else." His lips tightened into a grim line.

"Do you—I mean, it's hard back East to get any kind of picture of what the situation out here really is." Adam waited, sensing more beneath Hardwick's actions than stolen steers.

For a long time the rancher didn't answer. "There's right and wrong on both sides. I saw what was left of a wagon train after the Indians hit it. Then I saw an Indian camp after a cavalry raid." He turned toward Adam, his eyes molten steel. "I don't ever want to see either again and neither do you." He cleared his throat. "You'll ride along with me from Rock Springs to Antelope."

Adam knew the subject had been closed, permanently.

Nothing Adam had seen so far compared with the ride from Rock Springs where they got off the train up through western Wyoming Territory to Antelope. Those hundred miles offered Adam a hundred new experiences and every emotion known to humankind. Humbled, Adam numbly followed in his guide's tracks.

The sheer beauty of autumn in the Wind River Range made Adam speechless: cliffs with narrow trails that clung to their rock sides and broke off sheer into gorges far below that thundered warning in white water; peaks he could only see by craning his neck, especially Wind River Peak, over thirteen thousand feet high, that dwarfed all else, yet Hardwick said Wyoming Territory had other peaks even higher! How magnificent was God's creation, Adam realized fully for the first time.

Adam lost count of the times they had to ford creeks, streams, and young rivers that roared their way downward. He learned to hold on stonily and let his horse do the work. Now he knew what Hardwick meant when he had observed that this country called for half-human horses to keep riders out of trouble. The beautiful filly the Browns had graciously let him use might do well in her own environment but out here she'd prove useless.

Yet the danger, fear, and restless anticipation of what might come next couldn't dampen Adam's spirits. Never had he appreciated food as he did now. Even his mother's cooking paled before the hearty fare served on tin plates after being cooked over the open campfires. The rancher never praised Adam for starting campfires but Adam saw growing friendship and respect to match his own and treasured this rare opportunity.

Sleeping on pine needles with nothing between him and

a million blazing stars brought rest beyond belief. Not even in medical school where he had cherished sleep had Adam slept so well as on the ground with smoky blankets to keep off the frost that formed every morning.

They heard Antelope before they saw it. Tinny piano music and the yells of cowhands and miners in town for Saturday night reached Hardwick and Adam when they dropped down the last fairly steep incline from the forest to a fairly level area below. "Antelope at its noisiest and worst," Hardwick warned. Only the thought that Nat had a long way to go to provide a better place for families dampened Adam's raging enthusiasm.

They swung around a bend. Antelope lay ahead a few hundred yards. Etched into Adam's brain were a few neat, peeling log cabins flanked by hastily thrown together buildings. Dirty tents were on one side and saloons bordered each end of town, the Pronghorn and the Silver. Adam shuddered, yet he only had to lift his eyes to the hills: Like wasted tea leaves that lay in the bottom of an exquisite teacup, such was the contrast between Satan's meddling and God's handiwork. *No wonder Nat pleaded for help*, Adam thought.

Adam squared his shoulders and silently rode forward. On closer inspection he saw a blacksmith shop, a dressmaker's business, and a sprawling building that Hardwick explained held everything from food and clothes to trapping equipment. The main street, if such a dusty thoroughfare could so be called, looked three times wider than any street in Massachusetts and held horses and riders, a lone buckboard, and half a hundred shouting men.

"What's happening?" Adam raised in his stirrups to see better.

The yelling stopped and the roughly dressed men spilled to each side of the street.

"We'd better go back and head for your brother's," Hardwick suggested, as he neck-reined his horse to the right.

The sound of a shot—and a cry from the crowd—stopped Adam from following. What impulse led him to spur his horse on down the street he could not explain. A man loomed in the dust, his feet apart and steady. He still held a Colt in his right hand. Another man lay face down in the road, his fingers still clutching his six-shooter. Although Adam saw a ray of sun glint from the silver star on the erect man's chest, he ignored it and flung himself down beside the fallen cowboy. "Bring a light," he ordered in the same way that kept his assistants in surgery hopping.

"Here, who are you?" the sheriff bellowed. He strode to Adam, gripped his shoulder, and rocked him back on his heels.

With a mighty effort, Adam threw off the restraining hand. "Get me a light," he repeated, his voice razor-sharp, as he slipped his hand under the wounded man's body. "Good. Bullet went clean through. He's alive but needs surgery. Where's that light?"

"Right here." Hardwick shouldered the sheriff aside and held out a lighted lantern he'd evidently snatched from someone.

"I want to know who you are and what business this is of yours," the sheriff demanded at the top of his lungs.

Adam glanced up only long enough to see a slow smile spread across Hardwick's face. In the dusk outside the circle of lantern light, Hardwick cleared his throat.

"Folks, meet Adam Birchfield, brother of Nat and our new doctor."

Adam ignored the silence followed by a cheer. "I want three strong men—Hardwick, Sheriff, and you." He pointed to a burly man standing nearby. "Where can I take this man to treat him?"

No one answered or moved.

"Confound you all, if I don't get him sutured he's going to

die." Adam faced the crowd. "Take him to Nat's."

"The range is better off without Mark Justice," the sheriff grumbled, but he subsided when Adam threw him a fiery glance of scorn.

Each holding a leg or arm, the quartet carried the young cowboy who didn't look over twenty away from the main street to a new-looking peeled log cabin. Too concerned over his first patient in this violent land to pay attention to anyone else, Adam vaguely heard Hardwick say, "Preacher must not be home. No light."

"Then make one," Adam ordered when they got inside and had laid the cowboy on a bright, blanket-covered bed. "This boy's lost a lot of blood." A half-hour later, Adam turned from his task. Not a word had been spoken while he cleansed, stitched, and bandaged the gaping hole.

"I oughta take him to jail," the sheriff blustered, but a reluctant smile erased some of his truculence. "Guess it ain't necessary. You'll be responsible for him, Doc?"

"Of course. What did he do, anyway?" Adam's voice struggled to sound matter of fact.

"Got drunk, lost at cards, shot up the Pronghorn, and pulled his gun on me when I tried to arrest him. I had no choice but to shoot—"

"What are you doing in my cabin?" An icy voice asked.

Adam pushed through the others toward the door. "Nat, I'm here!"

"*Adam?*" Strong arms caught him and that single moment of reunion with his beloved brother more than made up for everything that had gone before.

# Chapter 5

D r. Adam Birchfield's first month in Antelope brought more and different kinds of cases than he had seen during his entire Concord practice. "Did they all save things up until I got here?" he demanded of Nat one evening after wearily finishing up with his last patient.

Nat lifted black eyebrows so like Adam's. His younger brother noted with satisfaction that Nat looked years younger than the fateful night he burst into his cabin to discover it had been turned into a temporary surgery. "Now how could Mrs. Fenner have saved up falling out of a tree until you came?" he teased.

"With no doctor in town, she probably was scared to climb the tree until I got here." Adam stretched his muscles and rejoiced in his newfound strength, the result of riding out to folks who couldn't come in for his help. "And Mrs. Trevor obviously wasn't due to have Junior earlier." He yawned. "Seriously, Nat, what did people do here with no medical help? I know you did what you could. . . ."

"But patching up heads after fights isn't operating on Mrs. Hardwick and having her appendix burst just after you removed it."

Adam shuddered. That particular situation had been a nightmare. Bound by friendship to the first person in Antelope who had welcomed him, it had taken intense prayer, a steady hand, and all his concentration and skill to save Mrs. Hardwick. "A few minutes more and it would have burst inside her and shot poison through her system. Little chance of saving her if that happened. Thank God it didn't."

Nat rose, ruffled his brother's hair the way he did when they were small, and gruffly said, "Your being here means everything on earth to me." He cleared his throat and Adam saw the convulsive motion when he swallowed. "I know it's way too early for you to make any kind of permanent decision, but I'd be the happiest person alive if you decided to stay."

Before Adam could answer he swung out the door of the extra room that willing hands had built for "the new Doc." Long and low, partitions divided it into a small waiting area, a work area, and a tiny bedroom with a bunk for Adam. The smell of freshly peeled logs bore witness to the friendship and appreciation of the rugged families served by both Adam and Nat. Although the saloonkeepers and gamblers never came to the small church, they had been generous with money and labor in adding on to the preacher's cabin.

"I wonder what Miss Ivy Ann Brown would think of my new home," Adam said to himself as he headed for his bedroom to wash up before supper. "Or Laurel. They couldn't fault the town's friendliness. It matches what I received from them."

The thought recurred an hour later. Nat sat preparing his next sermon, deep in thought and Scripture. Adam idly flipped through an old medical journal. Suddenly he said, "I'll do it."

"Do what?" Nat raised his dark head. A few silver threads glistened in the lamplight.

"Write to the Browns." Adam searched out the necessary materials. Yet Nat had gone back to his sermon long before Adam collected his thoughts. He hesitated then plunged right into his adventures since leaving Shawnee. He neither overstated nor downplayed the lawless element and crudity but he also included the good done by such solid citizens as Nat, the Hardwicks, and others.

*At first encounter I thought the sheriff worse than the so-called outlaws. However, after experiencing a few more Saturday nights in Antelope I understand a lot better. It takes strong persons to build this country. In the past month I have dealt with men who were thrown by horses, clawed by mountain lions, and gored by mean steers. One boy not yet in his teens suffered a broken leg from trying to tame a mustang, a wild horse.*

He paused then mischievously added the next paragraph.

*I attended a basket social in the brand-new schoolhouse a few nights ago. Imagine buying a basket and finding it stuffed with venison steak instead of fried chicken and containing dried apple tarts in place of apple pie or chocolate cake. The women out here make do with what they have and rely heavily on the country. They have cellars filled with hundreds of jars of home-canned fruit and vegetables. Bushel baskets of potatoes, squash, and other keeping vegetables line cellars dug into the earth. It reminds me of Mother and her pickling and preserving.*

Once more he stopped before concluding his thoughts.

*It is wild, raw, and uncivilized. Yet a spark of decency has been lit, a small flame ignited and the determination to make Antelope a good place to live burns high. I can't even begin to describe the beauty of this changeable land that smiles with sunshine one day and blusters the next. Snow crowns the nearby mountains already and Nat tells me the old-timers say we are due for a hard winter. I suspect my skills will be tested to the utmost. Oh, the rebellious young cowboy is healed and back on the range a wiser person. It amazed me to discover that he holds no bitterness toward the sheriff but feels he got just what he deserved for getting drunk and going crazy, as he describes it. He's so grateful to me that he even came to church the one weekend he could get in from his duties. Nat nearly forgot his sermon when he saw the boy come in.*

*I believe even more firmly than ever that if, no, when, Antelope gets enough godly people such incidents will dwindle and fade away. God grant that more pioneers and less of the lower element will choose to come West.*

*Respectfully yours,*
*Adam Birchfield, M.D.*

Let Miss Ivy Ann and her family shiver and exclaim over this. Would his letter be a seed, planted and waiting for the right climate to make it grow? The Bible story of the sower came to mind as Nat had told it the week before. Adam adapted it to the Brown family, using what knowledge he had gained while there.

The seed that fell by the wayside to be eaten by fowl could represent Ivy Ann. He suspected she'd be easily distracted from serious things and let the most precious ones be taken away without ever realizing it.

Perhaps the seed would sprout with Laurel or Thomas, maybe even Sadie. But could it withstand stony places such as the Wyoming Territory must appear to them? Or scorching heat and thorns that represented leaving all they knew for the unknown?

Adam sighed. Not many places could offer the rich soil from which pioneers and explorers sprang a hundredfold as the seed in the thirteenth chapter of Matthew did. He stretched and stared at Nat's bent head. A rush of love that had been planted in childhood and carefully nurtured through all the years now bloomed stronger than ever. Good old Nat, preaching and visiting, never too busy to lend a hand raising a cabin for a new family or too weary to answer a call in the middle of the night along with Adam when a crisis came! Heroes in history and storybooks dimmed alongside Nat, and Adam felt that every day in his company wound more invisible chains to keep the brothers together in Antelope for a lifetime. *What would Father say? And Mother, whose aching heart longed for her sons?* Yet in the past days a great tumult in his heart warned Adam such might well be his fate, his call, his service.

He bade Nat goodnight and sought sleep in his own room. The next day his letter began the journey east.

✒

Never could Adam Birchfield have imagined the furor that accompanied the arrival of his letter in West Virginia. Life at Red Cedars had gone on undisturbed, like a quiet pool that stills once the waves from a rock thrown into it subside. Ivy Ann continued charming every male who chanced on her home. Laurel became quieter than ever, often wondering at herself and even more at Ivy Ann. She couldn't believe how quickly even her fickle twin forgot Adam after going to so much effort to enslave him. "Ivy by name, Ivy by nature," Laurel muttered to herself when the laughing girl clung to the arm of the handsomest man at different gatherings.

The family worked hard harvesting and storing up for winter. Yet Laurel knew restlessness as never before. More often than she cared to admit, she found that her gaze turned west. Once Ivy Ann petulantly demanded, "What's out there?"

Laurel felt streaks of red stain her smooth skin. "A sunset worth watching," she quietly answered, glad for the truth that covered a deeper yearning.

Then The Letter came, forever capitalized in Laurel's mind.

As usual, Ivy Ann snatched it with a cry of joy. Her dark brown eyes sparkled. "Everyone, come! A letter from Adam Birchfield." Her long pink skirts swayed as she childishly clutched the letter with both hands.

"Well, for land's sake, open it," Sadie commanded. A pleased look settled over her face. "How nice of the young man to write when he must be so busy out there in the West."

Laurel ached to take the letter and read it privately. Above all she resented the way Ivy Ann acted as if it had been written just to her, especially when Laurel saw it had been addressed to Mr. and Mrs. Thomas Brown and family.

"He says things are going well and—" Ivy Ann maddeningly started to put the news in her own words.

"Just read what Dr. Birchfield wrote, daughter." Thomas didn't often issue commands but when he did he expected immediate obedience.

Ivy Ann looked injured but complied, except when she got to the most exciting parts. She then interjected little shivers of mock fright until Laurel wanted to shake her.

"The basket social sounds like fun," Ivy dreamily said when she finished and let the pages drift to the floor.

"Is that all you got out of his letter?" Incredulous, Laurel stared at her sister.

"Why, you don't really believe all that about people being clawed by wild animals, do you?" Ivy's eyes opened wide in consternation. "Surely Adam just put that in to entertain us."

Laurel glanced at her father. He looked skyward then back before sharing a secret grin with her. "Remember what he said before he ever went out there? I don't doubt that every word is true."

"Besides—" Laurel couldn't keep a little malice from her voice. "Adam said he hated and despised deceitfulness above anything else. You must remember that, Ivy Ann."

Her twin turned scarlet. "Oh, that's right." She bent to pick up the pages and looked innocent enough when she straightened. "Imagine him hinting for us to move West. Can you think of anything sillier?"

"I can," Laurel told her, but Ivy Ann just sniffed. Laurel saw the unreadable look that passed between her parents and her heart skipped a beat. Of course they wouldn't think of leaving Red Cedars but the flicker of longing in her father's eyes matched what lay in Laurel's heart. "I wish I were a man. I'd go out there and be part of creating a new land," she burst out.

"You must have stayed out in the sun too long today," Ivy Ann said sweetly and felt Laurel's forehead. "Dear me, what a tempest Adam's letter caused! But then, perhaps he intended it should." She yawned and patted her mouth with her well-cared-for-hand. "Oh, I'll answer his letter tomorrow. Poor dear, he's probably starved for companionship with his own kind." She clutched the letter and swept out.

"It would be nice if you also wrote to the young man," Sadie told Laurel.

"Why? Ivy will tell him the news." She tried to keep the bitterness from her voice and deliberately yawned as her twin had done. "Goodnight."

"Goodnight, dear." Their voices followed her up the stairs.

Why should Ivy Ann expect and take all the happiness out of everything, draining it to the last drop and leaving nothing for anyone else? Laurel's love for her twin warred with the deepest indignation she had ever felt. *Why do I care so much? I never did before,* Laurel thought. *Those few looks I shared with Dr. Birchfield are meaningless.* She fell asleep troubled by strange dreams of a greatly changed Adam whose dark eyes glowed with welcome and whose lips whispered words of love Laurel had never heard before.

When she awakened, new resolve filled her. This time she would not allow Ivy Ann to take over. After her sister patted her light brown curls into place and hurried down to breakfast, Laurel made a hasty toilette and read Adam's letter. That afternoon she stole time from other duties to dash off a quick message of thanks and an invitation for Adam to write "to the family" when he could. Her heart beating rapidly at her unaccustomed daring, Laurel held her tongue when Ivy Ann sat down to write her own letter. When she nonchalantly said she'd put it in an envelope if Ivy liked, she surreptitiously slipped in her own note. The heavens might fall when an answer came but until then Laurel clung to her first show of independence and rejoiced.

Several weeks later a second letter came. Again Adam had addressed it to the family; again Ivy Ann appropriated it as her own and doled out its contents. When she came to the statement, "Thank you so very much for your messages," she frowned. *"Messages?* Why should he say that?"

"You shared more than one piece of news, didn't you?" Laurel stayed cool outside and felt reprieved when the frown faded and Ivy read on. Adam closed with a challenge, evidently in response to something Ivy Ann had written.

*Folks like you are still needed. The hunting here is wonder-ful. Fifty males to every female.*

"Whatever is that s'posed to mean?" Ivy Ann peered at the cryptic message. "That there are more female deer?"

"Don't you get it?" Laurel threw back her head and laughed.

"With only a few married women and even fewer single young women, the odds are in the females' favor."

"Don't be vulgar." Ivy Ann's face tightened and her eyes flashed. "As if decent young women like us would ever look at anyone in the Wyoming Territory!"

"You did enough looking at Dr. Birchfield when he visited here," Laurel reminded. "And he's in the Wyoming Territory."

Ivy gasped but Thomas backed up Laurel.

"That's right. From what I gather that brother of his is a cultured man as well." His eyes twinkled. "If you run out of beaux here you can always go West, girls."

"I doubt the westerners would have us," Laurel teased, and she felt rewarded when Ivy sat bolt upright.

"I guess I could do anything any old girl in the West could do, if I made up my mind to do it."

"But you never would," Sadie put in, smiling at the flustered girl. "Admit it, Ivy. You like comfort too well."

"You're all picking on me!" Storm clouds gathered in the fair face. "If I didn't love Red Cedars so much, I'd up and go West just to show you how wrong you are."

Laurel buried her face in a small pillow and laughed herself sick. How clever of Adam to needle Ivy Ann so subtly. Now if she could again smuggle a message in her sister's letter. . . .

Christmas came in a round of festivities. Spicy evergreen branches turned Red Cedars into a bower. Fruitcake ripened in the pantry. A multitude of gifts arrived from Ivy Ann's followers who vied to win her favor. Fewer came for Laurel but she honestly didn't mind. What gift could compare with the beautiful Indian moccasins Adam had sent the twins? Handmade of soft deerskin, Laurel cherished both the gift and the thoughtfulness behind it.

Ivy Ann scoffed at such a present but her twin noticed how

she made a point of displaying the moccasins when her beaux came. "Wasn't it just sweet of Dr. Birchfield to send *me* such an unusual Christmas gift?"

A curiously carved necklace for Sadie accompanied the moccasins as well as a hand-tooled leather belt for Thomas, along with a crude but surprisingly attractive small painting of the area near Antelope. Adam explained in a note that Mrs. Hardwick had done a similar one for him while recuperating from her appendectomy. He'd begged her to paint another and insisted on paying for it so he could send it to the Browns.

Laurel gazed at the rolling, tree-dotted hills that swept upward to solid timber then white peaks and the bluest sky she'd ever seen. The longing within her that had gone dormant from all the hustle and bustle of Christmas came to glowing life. *Someday,* she vowed, *I am going to see it for myself. How or when I don't know. But I will go West—someday.*

On Christmas Eve afternoon Laurel rode into Shawnee for a few last-minute items needed in the cooking of tomorrow's big dinner that would be shared with many friends and neighbors. She got what she needed, kept a sharp lookout toward the cloud-clotted sky, and stumbled when she stepped down from the porch of the store.

"Careful, Miss Brown." One of Ivy Ann's suitors neatly caught Laurel's arm and kept her from falling.

Laurel felt herself redden. "Thanks, James. You saved me from a nasty spill."

"May I present my cousin, Beauregard Worthington?" James stepped aside to let a tall, fair man dressed in the latest fashion come forward. "Beau, this is Miss Laurel Brown. Beau's here from Charleston for the holidays."

"My pleasure, Miss Brown." The strikingly handsome man bent over her hand as if she were the Queen of England.

"Beau will be coming to dinner with us tomorrow," James rushed on. "When your mother heard he'd be here she graciously included him in the invitation."

Laurel smiled up into the tall stranger's deep blue eyes. She could see her reflection in them, rosy-cheeked from the late afternoon chill, with a few curls escaping from under her bonnet. "You will be more than welcome, Mr. Worthington." She quickly mounted before either of the men could offer assistance. "I must hurry or darkness will overtake me." She smiled again and felt her heart flutter at the unmistakable admiration in the visitor's eyes.

"Until tomorrow, Miss Brown."

"Until tomorrow, Mr. Worthington, James." Her pony swung toward home. *What a handsome man,* Laurel thought. Ivy Ann will—no! she determined. Not this time. *I met him first.*

# Chapter 6

The twins wore the same gowns for Christmas dinner they had worn for their twentieth birthday party. Ivy Ann complained and begged for a new dress but soon ceased pouting for fear it would leave a wrinkle in her smooth face.

Laurel serenely donned the lovely blue gown and secretly smiled. She had stolen a march on her twin for once by offering to decorate the long table and do the placecards they no longer bothered with except for very special occasions.

"Who is Beauregard Worthington?" Ivy Ann demanded at her sister's elbow. "And why are you putting him next to you?"

"He's a visiting cousin of James." Laurel forced herself not to betray any kind of interest.

"What a name!" Ivy Ann threw her hands into the air. "What is he, a country bumpkin whose parents gave him a pretentious name he can never live up to?"

"No-o. I met him briefly yesterday at the store. He seemed so appreciative of being included at dinner it seemed right to seat him by one of the family."

"Oh, the shy and humble type." Ivy Ann tossed her head until the curls loosened and surrounded her laughing face. "Leave it to you to be kind to the misfits."

Laurel smothered a laugh and quickly diverted her twin. "I put James on one side of you. Do you want Stephen or Phillip on the other side?"

Ivy cocked her head to one side and a calculating look crept into her eyes. "Well, I like Stephen better, but Phillip sent me the nicest present so I guess I owe it to him." Beauregard

Worthington passed out of her consciousness, at least for the moment.

Laurel made sure she got downstairs before Ivy and instead of making a grand entrance she met James, his family, and their guest at the door. The same admiration that had shone in Beauregard's eyes the day before had deepened significantly. "Miss Brown, how charming you look!" He bowed over her hand, his immaculate clothing winning her approval. A little stir behind them made Laurel and her guest turn. She noticed he kept her hand in his.

"Why—who's that?" The blond man looked from blue-clad Laurel to the pink-gowned Ivy Ann.

"James, didn't you tell your cousin there are two of us?" Ivy tapped his shoulder with her furled fan. But the look she sent Laurel promised all kinds of dire things in retaliation. "You *are* Beauregard Worthington, aren't you?"

Under cover of the flowing conversation a bit later Ivy Ann managed to furiously whisper, "Why didn't you tell me the best-looking man that's been in this part of West Virginia for ages would be having dinner with us?"

Laurel opened her eyes wide in false innocence. "That shy, humble bumpkin with the pretentious name? Why ever would you want to hear about him?"

"You'll be sorry."

Laurel just laughed at the childish threat and smugly led Beauregard in to dinner. From where they sat, they could barely glimpse Ivy Ann between her devoted swains. At least until the feast ended she'd have no opportunity to carry out any scheme.

Laurel felt her heart pitty-pat the way she associated with heroines in the few romance novels she had read. *Why not use the time to make an impression on this well-mannered, interesting man?*

Before the end of dinner, she learned that Beauregard not

only was her senior by ten years but was deeply involved in politics, loved riding, and intended to someday run for governor of the state. Unfortunately, his deep voice attracted attention and the rest of the family and guests also gleaned the same information. Ivy Ann's avid listening warned Laurel that her twin considered Beauregard Worthington not only the best-looking man around, but the best catch as well. Yet even when the more vivacious twin, Stephen, Phillip, and a few other young men and women joined Laurel and Beau, Beau continued his discussion with Laurel, whose intelligent questions spurred him to share his ideas and aspirations.

At a disadvantage, Ivy Ann finally broke up the conversation by almost forcing the merry crowd to join in singing Christmas carols. Laurel grinned at the ploy. Ivy Ann knew how white and dainty her hands looked when she played the spinet. Flushed from the warm room and attention, Ivy had never been more beautiful.

To Laurel's delight and Ivy Ann's obvious chagrin, Beau merely thanked the musician for her playing when he left but lingered with Laurel. "Miss Brown, may I call tomorrow? I'd like to finish our discussion."

"Of course," said Laurel triumphantly as she closed the door.

Her triumph faded, however, before the blaze in Ivy Ann's eyes and the tight line of her mouth. Ivy didn't dare say anything in front of their parents but once upstairs she turned on Laurel.

"Just what do you think you're doing, hogging Beauregard Worthington all evening?"

Laurel could have laughed it off; she knew in her heart she should. God did not want families to quarrel. Yet the sore spot formed in childhood when everyone petted and praised her twin had been intensified over Adam Birchfield and irritated further by her own growing dissatisfaction of living in her sister's shadow.

The taste of victory lay sweet in her mouth. "Isn't it about time?"

Ivy Ann's eyelids half-closed in the danger signal Laurel well knew and usually heeded. "What do you mean?"

Laurel walked to the dressing table, seated herself, and deliberately let down her curls. Ivy's flushed, angry image stared at her over her shoulder. Suddenly Laurel had borne enough. She turned and faced her sister. "Ever since we were big enough to toddle you've had to be first. Pretty, popular Ivy Ann. Quiet Laurel, following a few steps behind. It has never mattered which of us found a new friend or beau. Always they've eventually turned from me to you, Ivy Ann. How many boys that I could have cared for did you deliberately take away, even when they meant nothing to you?"

Ivy's face turned to pearl but she didn't answer.

Laurel felt exhausted. "I love you more than anything or anyone except God. But it isn't right and it isn't good for *either* of us to continue the way we have. You need to learn that you can't have everything you demand in life."

"Meaning Beauregard Worthington?" A small smile crept over Ivy's face until she looked like a sleepy kitten. Yet Laurel knew how sharp her claws could be.

She sighed and didn't back down. "If he chooses to call on me, I am going to welcome him and enjoy his company." She carefully removed her blue dress and hung it away, noting her twin's unusual silence. But when Laurel pulled her nightgown over her head she caught Ivy Ann's whispered response.

"We'll just see about that."

*Was it worth it?* Had staging a tiny revolution done anything except challenge Ivy to do her best—or worst—and capture Beau's interest? *Dear God,* Laurel silently prayed, *maybe You created me to be the giver. But how can Ivy Ann ever become a woman if she takes and takes and takes? Or am I just excusing my own selfishness?* Troubled, she fell asleep without an answer.

If Thomas and Sadie Brown hadn't been so involved with the never-ending duties of Red Cedars, they would have noticed the latest romantic triangle. A hundred times before, Ivy Ann had charmed the young men who called on Laurel as well as on herself. But this time Laurel didn't meekly step aside. Deep in her innermost being she knew she cared little for Beauregard Worthington in spite of his eligible qualities. But the same flame of independence that had brought about the most serious argument the twins ever had steadied into resolve. What she had said in a moment of truth bore heavily on her mind. Going on as she had, giving in to her twin, set a silent approval to Ivy's idea she could and would be first in everything and with everyone.

*No more*, Laurel promised herself. And yet the new coldness Ivy bestowed on her almost shattered Laurel's stance. Childhood arguments and quarrels, conducted without their parents' knowledge, had always ended with the girls making up before bedtime in compliance with their Bible teachings. This latest rift did not and, for the first time in her life, Laurel refused to apologize for the disagreement and take the blame as she had done before.

"Dear God," she prayed one night when Ivy Ann had fallen asleep without even a goodnight, "your Son taught that blessed are the meek. Does meek mean being a doormat all my life? I don't think so." She remembered what their minister said in his last sermon concerning the Beatitudes.

"Moses is identified as a meek man. Can we picture him groveling or effacing himself to the point of losing his personality? No. When we study different languages from Bible times we learn that meek means *teachable*, not docile and spiritless as people now call it."

Ivy Ann's frosty treatment of Laurel in private matched the January winds that blew across Red Cedars and Shawnee. When others were present, Ivy clung prettily to her sister as usual. Beau extended his visits and often rode out in spite of the snow. Cutters called for the twins and sleighing parties that ended at neighbors' homes or back at Red Cedars for spiced cider or foamy chocolate brightened the twins' winter. Beau automatically took his place by Laurel and her natural vanity and pride swelled. Yet devious Ivy managed to sit on Beau's other side an amazing number of times. Laurel smiled to herself. Her pretty twin seized every opportunity, and prepared for them. A half-dozen times Laurel found her reading and discussing events of the day with their father. Before Beau appeared, such talk had left her bored and restless.

Wise Ivy Ann! Her knowledge of subjects that interested Beau never went deep, but a few well-chosen comments could keep the intelligent and dedicated young man talking for hours.

"I didn't think at first that your sister cared about anything but parties and dresses and flirting," he candidly told Laurel one evening while they waited for Ivy to come downstairs. "A person shouldn't go by first impressions, should they?"

" 'Man looketh on the outward appearance, but the Lord looketh on the heart.'" Laurel couldn't help quoting, thinking of Ivy's deceitful mind.

"Shakespeare certainly had a way of getting to the core of things, didn't he?" Beau said enthusiastically.

Laurel didn't have the heart to tell him the quote came from the Bible. Neither did she have time. Ivy Ann ran lightly downstairs in spite of her heavy cloak and shoes and warm gloves.

"Ready?" Her cheeks shone against the dark cloak.

Laurel sighed inwardly. The look in Beau's eyes betrayed the beginning of the end. At least he had made a good fight, far better than any young man before him. Laurel felt like tearing off her own heavy clothing and refusing to join the party calling from the sleighs gathered outside. An hour later she wished she had instead of silently submitting to Beau's hand under her elbow. Ivy's adoring gaze shone clear even in the starlight. Her upturned face and expression of deep interest sickened her twin. The chances of Ivy caring about anything political equaled those that the world would end before they reached home.

*Yet,* Laurel considered, *perhaps Ivy Ann did care.* If she captured Beau, she might one day live in the governor's mansion! Laurel let her lips curl into a reluctant smile. No woman of her acquaintance could better carry such a position. Ivy's charm would dazzle even opponents and prove a real asset to a young man on the rise to fame.

*So could you,* a reminding voice whispered.

She shook her head. The last thing she wanted would be the endless round of gaiety, soirées, and excitement that delighted her twin. An unbidden vision of a tall, dark man etched against a scene similar to the painting by Mrs. Hardwick shot into her mind. She longed to hear his impassioned voice sharing the conviction that God wanted him to go West.

She compared the two young men who had most touched her life. Beau—equally dedicated, but toward a profession that would bring glory as well as service. Adam—who turned his back on a lucrative practice and future, crossed swords with his father, and followed the dream in his heart to a rough but needy town thousands of miles from home.

Laurel felt herself tottering on the edge of an important and enlarged understanding. Not until the evening ended with Ivy twitting about her, letting her mind wander, did Laurel realize a startling truth: Every trace of annoyance with her sister's flirting had vanished. How trite, how unworthy to care when men and a few courageous women and children struggled to create a home in the wilderness!

Like a stranger in an unfamiliar land, Laurel observed the pretty young women vying for attention with Ivy Ann in the center. Even a few pitying glances aimed at Laurel when Beau hovered near her twin failed to penetrate the new armor she wore.

*I feel as if tonight I have put away childish things and become a woman while they are still playing with dolls.* Laurel smiled at the thought and continued watching her friends. Had Sally-Ellen always simpered so? Strange that she hadn't noticed how James brayed when he laughed, usually at the wrong times. One by one she considered those she had known for years and those who had entered her life later. She mentally measured them against Adam Birchfield and found them lacking. Only the older men, those who had fought and come home with too-wise eyes to razed homes and the need to start again, could meet Laurel's high standards.

Because of her experience, Laurel only smiled tolerantly when Ivy Ann triumphantly confronted her the next morning. "Beau is coming to see *me* today."

"That's nice," Laurel said absently. She poked up the fire until it roared into the time-blackened chimney.

"Don't you care?" Ivy Ann looked totally astounded. Her mouth dropped open in an unbecoming pose.

"Should I?" Laurel raised her eyebrows.

"But he's been coming to see you!" Ivy Ann petulantly flounced onto a chair across from her sister.

Laurel instantly caught her twin's mood. Half the joy Ivy Ann received from Beau's asking to call on her had been drowned by the fact her twin simply didn't care! Laurel threw her head back and laughed, a clear, ringing laugh that dispelled any idea Beauregard Worthington's transfer of affections would give her a moment's thought.

Ivy sullenly stared and, when Laurel settled down and put her feet toward the warm fire, she never let her gaze wander.

"Ivy Ann, do you really care for Beau or is all the excitement just to take him away from another woman?"

Ivy's eyes glittered. "He's nice. He's going to be someone. The woman he marries will have beautiful clothes, live in a home with servants, and be adored and cared for."

"Petted."

An angry flush marred the other's face. "Why don't you admit it's sour grapes, Laurel? I've got him if I want him and you're jealous." She held to her crumbling position with clenched fists.

"You don't believe that." Laurel knew she'd hit home by the way Ivy flinched and the way her color deepened. "Do you really think all the things you mentioned will make you happy? What about when children come and you're at home while Beau has to attend the parties for the sake of his office? What then, Ivy Ann? Or suppose he's terribly ill. Will you care for him gladly?"

Her sister's lips quivered like a butterfly poised for flight. "You're perfectly horrid to bring up all those things, Mountain Laurel Brown!"

Laurel felt a hundred years older than Ivy Ann. She rose and put her arm around Ivy's shoulder. "Mama and Daddy have taught us marriage is from God and unless we love our husbands with all our hearts—next to God Himself—we must never enter into it."

Ivy's slim shoulders stiffened and Laurel squeezed them. "I won't say more but never forget that once we say 'I do' only death can cancel that promise before God. " She left Ivy staring into the fire, silenced for once.

For a few weeks Beau shamefacedly sought out Laurel at times and talked with her as before. Yet all Ivy had to do was enter the room to claim his attention. Laurel discovered how sorry she felt for the young man. No boy to be teased, but a man to be reckoned with. Couldn't Ivy Ann realize her flirtatious ways wouldn't be tolerated forever?

Thomas Brown spoke out at dinner one evening when only the four gathered for the meal. He rested his forearms on the table after the blessing. "Is young Worthington courting you, Laurel, or Ivy Ann?" He scowled. "I don't like the tittle-tattle in Shawnee about one man and twin girls."

"Daddy!" Ivy Ann sounded horrified but Laurel caught a satisfied gleam in her dark brown eyes that went so well with a favorite pink dress. "Do you really think Beau would come courting us both at once?"

"Beau and I are good friends and always have been," Laurel quietly said. "As far as courting—" Her eloquent shrug said how little it mattered.

Yet all her lack of caring and common sense couldn't prevent shock spreading through her a few nights later when she discovered Beau and Ivy Ann kissing in a way no girl should allow unless she were betrothed.

When Ivy Ann pulled away with a trill of laughter and caroled, "To think I thought you liked Laurel best," righteous indignation rose to new heights in Laurel. She would break free from her twin, no matter how far she must go.

# Chapter 7

Now that Laurel Brown had the bit in her teeth, she prepared herself to run with the speed of a fine West Virginia racehorse. Item by item she smuggled into a large trunk: dresses; bonnets; plain things for the most part. She could work slowly, for not until spring would she dare attempt the long journey West. In the dark night hours while Ivy Ann slept and murmured in pleasant dreams, Laurel collected things that wouldn't be missed and spread her other clothing wide to hide the gaps. She hated the secrecy. With all her heart she longed to go to her parents and say, "This is something I have to do."

But she could not. They would forbid her to embark on such a mad escapade worthy of Ivy Ann and not her dependable self. She knew she would never go against their expressed command.

Now that she no longer paid attention to Beau, some of Ivy's interest flagged but she hid it well. Laurel suspected pride kept her from discarding him too soon. Besides, his promising future continued to intrigue Ivy. Until she met another and brighter star she found it desirable to stay high in Beau's esteem.

Laurel avoided any confrontations with her twin but, inevitably, Ivy Ann provoked her beyond endurance. The pretty blue dress remained Laurel's best and she saved it for special occasions only. Once or twice Ivy had asked permission to wear it and was refused. Laurel knew how careless Ivy was with clothing. The pink birthday dress already had a tiny tear in the hem, invisibly mended by Laurel but a reminder of Ivy's irresponsible attitude.

That same forget-me-not dress laid claim to Laurel's affections for another reason as well. She had seen Adam Birchfield's admiring glance when she wore it. When she got to Antelope, Laurel intended to wear that gown the first time she saw Adam.

Spring came early and Laurel rejoiced. Ivy Ann flitted between Beau and others. Then one afternoon Laurel returned from an invigorating ride that tossed her light brown hair and left her cheeks rosy. She burst into the parlor calling, "Ivy Ann! You should have come, it's just grand out."

A girl in a forget-me-not blue dress guiltily leaped to her feet. The china cup she held tilted and a stream of raspberry cordial cascaded down the soft folds of the dress.

"*Ivy, how could you?*" Laurel grabbed her twin's shoulders and marched her toward the stairs, ignoring the startled protest from her cowed but defiant twin. This time Ivy Ann would not escape justice. Sadie had stepped into the hall, back early from an errand in town. She followed the twins upstairs, scolding all the way.

"Did you have permission to wear Laurel's dress?" she snapped. None of her usual amiability softened her features.

"N-no." Ivy Ann looked six instead of twenty. Mama's wrath knew few bounds once provoked.

"The dress is ruined," Laurel cried, her anger turned to numbness while Mama helped get the blue dress off Ivy.

Mama's mouth buttoned itself shut. "This isn't the last of this, girls. There's company downstairs and you're to go back and apologize to Mr. Worthington for this scene," she finally ordered Ivy Ann. "Laurel, I need help in the kitchen."

"I can't go down." Ivy Ann shivered. "Beau will—won't—"

"I expect you dressed and downstairs in five minutes." Mama snatched a simply gray dress from the wardrobe. "Wear this."

Obviously frightened, Ivy Ann got into the dress, smoothed her hair, and followed Mama. Laurel held out the wide skirt panels and wondered if the front breadth could be removed.

"Why bother?" She wadded up the gown and threw it into a heap in the corner. "I'll never wear the spoiled thing again, anyway. Not after it's been ruined and made over." The numbness passed and an exultant wave of gladness filled her. In a short time she'd be gone. Never again could Ivy Ann selfishly take and ruin what rightfully belonged to her.

Beau didn't stay long and the girls avoided each other's company until supper. Afterward Thomas gathered Sadie and the twins into the parlor. "Ivy Ann, you have acted abominably and I'm ashamed of you."

Laurel couldn't help but feel a little sorry for the drooping figure huddled in a chair that heightened her deceptively frail figure. *If Daddy ever boomed at her like that!*

"Go get the blue dress," Thomas commanded Ivy Ann. "Laurel, bring down the pink birthday dress."

She started to protest but saw the stony look in her father's face and did what she'd been told, following thoroughly subdued Ivy Ann. Back in the parlor Thomas spread the stained gown out over his knees.

"Sadie, will the stain come out?"

"I don't know." She looked at the ruined gown. "It spread so far. We'll probably have to take out a panel and make it straighter but it won't be as pretty." She sent a sympathizing glance toward Laurel.

Thomas took the frothy pink gown in his big hands, careful not to let their roughness mar the delicate material. "Laurel, this dress is yours from now on. Ivy Ann will wear the blue until it is worn out, once it's been fixed."

Mutiny sprang to Ivy's face and protest caught in Laurel's throat. Before either could speak, Thomas spoke in the voice he reserved for only the most portentous times. "The matter is settled and *no one* is to say another word about it. Laurel, put the pink dress away. Ivy, put the blue gown to soak or whatever it needs."

Ivy Ann stumbled out, her eyes glazed with tears. Laurel took her new pink gown upstairs and reluctantly stowed it in the big trunk destined for Antelope. *Could she ever wear it without remembering this awful day?* She must. She had no other beautiful gown, just simple clothing and outgrown dresses.

The power of Thomas Brown's ultimatum had an effect on both twins. Neither mentioned the dress but it hung between them like a gauzy curtain of misunderstanding and resentment. Laurel wearily counted the days until she could slip away. She watched and waited until one afternoon both parents and Ivy Ann were absent from Red Cedars. Then she hurriedly arranged for her trunk to be taken to the railway station and shipped west. If her calculations proved right, it should reach Antelope just before she arrived.

Now every day became bittersweet. Saying goodbye to the horses and rolling hills and mountains brought pain. So did the gnawing knowledge of her deception. She had sworn to secrecy the old friend who picked up her trunk and shipped it. Nothing remained except a few days that stretched like an eternity in her heart.

In the closing chapter of her life at Red Cedars, Laurel often wondered if she should forget the whole thing, confess her sins to her parents, and have her father retrieve the trunk.

The sight of Ivy Ann as blithe and selfish as ever hardened Laurel's plans. "It isn't like it's forever," she mumbled to a swaying laurel clump already showing signs of swelling buds. "Someday I'll come back." She firmly refused to examine Adam's possible reaction to a madcap young woman who ran away from home and traveled West unchaperoned. Time enough to consider that on the train journey that loomed like forbidden fruit.

Before sunup that fateful spring morning Laurel's tears fell on the carefully written notes she placed on the tall chest of drawers. After tying the strings of her plainest dark bonnet, Laurel walked the miles to Shawnee and began her journey. She kept her head down so the few curious passengers wouldn't ask where she was going so early on a midweek workday. Once on her way, no one would know or heed her, she thought, never realizing that her lovely eyes and well-bred manner would attract attention all the way from home to the Wyoming Territory.

Laurel hadn't known what a mess of contradictions she was until she left Red Cedars and headed West. At times her heart quailed and she fought the desire to get off at every stop. Yet part of her exulted at her new freedom, and a fierce pride in breaking away from Ivy Ann sustained her. Months earlier Adam Birchfield had opened wide his dark eyes at the changing country. Now Laurel Brown gasped and frankly stared. How ignorant she had been of anything outside her own county, her own state, her own little world!

How many rivers did they cross? How many miles of free swaying grass? How many spring freshets and sunny days gave way to the relentless *clack-clack* of the wheels? How many small children did she wave to, barefooted, gap-toothed urchins whose longing for adventure clearly showed on freckled faces that watched the train out of sight? Each time Laurel hugged close to her heart that she actually was on this adventure. Once she secretly pinched herself to make sure it wasn't all a dream. Then she laughed until those around her gazed at the fresh face set off by the plain dark bonnet and traveling gown.

Cramped at times and wishing for a bath, nothing daunted Laurel for long. When she grew irritated at the lack of all the comforts she had taken for granted at home, she privately reminded herself how lucky she was, as Adam had said, to be riding a snorting iron horse all those miles instead of following in the dust of a creaking wagon.

Her first sight of the distant Rockies left her speechless. Never had she felt as insignificant as the moment her gaze beheld the jutting peaks that looked determined to pierce the bottom of heaven. Mountain after snowy mountain loomed until at last she heard the charmed call: "Rock Springs!"

*She had done it.*

Stiff from the long and tiring journey, Laurel stepped into a world she wouldn't have believed existed. A world of bellowing cattle being driven in for shipping, of dusty men in boots with impossibly tall heels, of curses and the jangle of spurs.

Suddenly her joy faded. Why hadn't she thought things through better? *How on earth could she get from Rock Springs to Antelope?* She grabbed her dwindling courage in both hands as she timidly queried a fellow passenger. "Where is the stage to Antelope?"

His open face showed astonishment. "Stage? There ain't no such thing, miss."

"Well, people go there. How?"

He scratched his head. "Blamed if I know. I never lost anything in Antelope so I never wondered."

Laurel wanted to scream with laughter. If Ivy Ann could see this friendly but simple fellow she'd absolutely die.

She wasn't Ivy Ann, so she'd best start wondering even if this man never had. Yet no one seemed to be able to help until a slender young man whose spotless linen and grooming made him stand out like sunflowers in a violet patch strode toward her. His high heels gave him the appearance of height but Laurel guessed him to be only a few inches taller than her own five foot six inches. Blond, cleanshaven, and thoroughly dapper, he could have stepped into any West Virginia home.

"Miss, did I hear you say you needed to go to Antelope?" Curiosity lit his glowing amber eyes.

For a second Laurel recoiled. Those eyes reminded her of the eyes of a tiger she once saw in a book—wild and dangerous. She hesitated.

"The reason I ask is that a crude wagon road has been built to haul in supplies. I'm taking a wagonload in tomorrow morning. A couple of men are going with me and one woman."

Laurel's joy knew no bounds. "A woman?"

The man smiled. "She's not exactly your type, but she's good-hearted. Storekeeper's wife. She came out for a burying."

Relief washed through the tired girl. "Where can I find her?"

"Boardinghouse." The man jerked a tanned finger with its scrupulously clean nail down the street. "You can stay there overnight. One thing—"

Her heart pounded. *What now?*

"It's a real bumpy ride." White teeth gleamed in his sun-warmed face. "Where's your baggage?" He glanced at the reticule she carried.

"I sent a trunk ahead."

"Must be the one the agent said was bound for Antelope. I'll see to it. It's been here a few days but we don't rightly have a schedule into Antelope. By the way, I'm Dan Sharpe."

She didn't offer her hand but she smiled. "I'm Miss Brown." Five minutes later she followed her self-appointed protector into the parlor of the boardinghouse.

"Mrs. Greer, meet Miss Brown. She's going to Antelope with us tomorrow."

The double-chinned face dropped open in surprise but Mrs. Greer snapped it shut and quickly smiled. "Why, nice to meet you!" Her eyes almost closed when she smiled. Laurel appreciated the way she obviously refrained from asking why a young woman from the East would be headed toward Antelope. Instead she merely chatted after Laurel paid for her supper, breakfast, and night's lodging. She told the girl they had about a hundred miles of the wildest Wyoming country ever to travel. They would put up at ranches that welcomed the chance to buy fresh supplies and get outside news. *Mama would approve of Mrs. Greer*, Laurel thought.

At last the good woman ran down. Laurel felt she must explain at least a little. "Dr. Birchfield visited our family in West Virginia," she said. Her heart pounded in her ears. "He said Antelope needed Christian women and families and that his brother was making it a place for decent people to live."

"Land sakes!" The moon face opposite her positively glowed. "Are you Dr. Birchfield's young lady? Why, Miss Brown, he and that brother of his are doing more to bring common decency to Antelope than you can ever imagine." She rushed on and mercifully spared Laurel from having to answer her question.

Dan Sharpe's promise proved true. Much of the misnamed road to Antelope jolted Laurel until her bones ached. Mrs. Greer laughed her cushiony laugh and told the weary girl, "You need more padding, like me."

All Laurel could do was grin feebly and hang on. When they came to places laboriously widened to accommodate the supply wagon, she gritted her teeth, closed her eyes against the canyons that plunged on both sides of them, and prayed. Only once did her sense of humor break through her misery. When Mrs. Greer cheerfully boasted how fine it was to have a road instead of having to ride horseback the whole way or be born in Antelope to get there, Laurel secretly wondered if she'd have the courage to leave it once she got there.

"We're going to make this into a real road one of these days," Dan Sharpe promised and lifted a tawny eyebrow. Again Laurel thought of that tiger. She sensed that like his feline counterpart, Dan Sharpe had the potential to spring.

The other two men said little but fixed their gaze on Laurel until she wished they'd fall asleep or off the wagon or something. Yet she found nothing sinister in their stares, just a frank-eyed admiration. When she smiled they turned rosy and hastily averted their gaze.

A warm welcome, hot water for washing, and a clean bed after a bounteous supper that left her ashamed of her unusual appetite did much to restore Laurel's optimism. Besides, if Mrs. Greer could placidly knit in spite of the narrow ledges and rushing streams they crossed, the danger couldn't be as great as Laurel feared.

An eternity later, but actually a few days, the wagon swung around the same bend that had hidden Antelope from Adam's view months earlier. Little had changed except more people now thronged the dusty street and a few new cabins had been built. To Laurel's fascinated, horrified gaze any expectations or romantic beliefs about the hamlet died an instant death. Antelope itself showed what a mirage her ideas had been. Here lay naked substance, a small but sprawling town at her very feet.

Mrs. Greer, sensing Laurel's dismay, calmed the troubled girl's whirling brain. "Look up, child."

Laurel automatically obeyed. Jagged mountains guarded the town and offered security, something to cling to in this strange place. They felt like old friends, friendly in spite of their scarred, snow-clad surfaces. *Small wonder the Psalmist had looked to the hills for the strength that cometh from God*, Laurel thought.

She inhaled and felt a rush of exhilaration renew her inner self. No matter what lay ahead, or behind, no matter where she went or if she stayed, those mountains had been etched permanently into her heart, mind, and soul.

"You'll want to see the young doctor right away," Mrs. Greer whispered when Dan Sharpe reined in his team.

Sheer panic destroyed her serenity. "Not yet," she said breathlessly. "I-I want to bathe and—and—"

"Of course." Mrs. Greer chuckled then frowned. "Hmmm. The hotel, such as it is, won't do for you. Let's see." Her face brightened and her double chins quivered. "The Widow Terry has a spare room since her daughter married. She's particular about who she takes in but she'll be glad for company."

Laurel had little chance to protest. Mrs. Greer swept her along in the falling dusk. They rounded a corner.

'Well, look who we're running into." Pleasure dripped from every word.

Laurel stared at the roughclad but unmistakable figure just ahead. Her intentions to dress up before letting Adam see her became futile. She gathered her travel-stained skirts in one hand, raced down the narrow lane off the main street, and clasped the dark-haired man's arm. Her heart pounded more from anticipation than exertion. "Hello!"

The man turned and looked into her face. "Excuse me, miss. You must have mistaken me for someone else."

Laurel nearly collapsed. Adam's steady voice was denying her. She turned to stone.

"What's all this?" Mrs. Greer hurried up, her pleasant face distorted by shadows dancing in the dusk.

"This young lady seems to feel she knows me. I've never seen her before in my life." Swiftly and surely he removed Laurel's clutching, desperate fingers.

# Chapter 8

This couldn't be happening. Laurel had expected shock, disapproval, and even a reprimand from Adam but not a refusal to acknowledge their acquaintance and friendship! Her knees felt lifeless. Would they give way any minute?

"Now, Reverend Birchfield, how could you not know her? This is Miss Brown, come all the way from West Virginia. She knows the doctor, and—"

The man Laurel belatedly realized was not Adam but an older version of him threw back his head and laughed. "And in this half-dark she thought she'd found him!" He laughed again and even in the dimness she could see Adam as he would be a few years from now. Relief and surprise left her stunned. At least Adam hadn't rejected her presence.

"I'm taking her to the Widow Terry's," Mrs. Greer said as she firmly grasped Laurel's arm. "Tell Dr. Birchfield Miss Brown will see him in an hour or whenever he's free."

"Gladly and a delayed welcome, Miss Brown." The minister whose voice and appearance so reminded Laurel of Adam left the two bewildered women.

"It will take a good hour for you to get freshened," Mrs. Greer said in her practical way. "Soon as I introduce you to Mrs. Terry I'll trot back and have Dan drop off your trunk. No girl wants to have her beau see her looking bedraggled from a long journey."

Again, Laurel didn't have the wits or heart to deny that Dr. Birchfield was her beau. All she wanted was time to settle down before he came.

✍

Mrs. Terry turned out to be as welcoming as Mrs. Greer had foretold. She not only heated water and helped Mrs. Greer unpack Laurel's trunk—with many an *ohh* and *ahh*—she quickly heated irons and pressed the fluffy pink gown. She also announced that she'd just walk a piece with Mrs. Greer since the doctor would be there to keep her new boarder company. "If you want to work, my dear, I can tell by your gowns you are a good needlewoman and I need help in my business."

"I'd like that." Laurel thought of her dwindling resources, the birthday and Christmas money now depleted by her journey.

The two chattering women, one billowy, one thin almost to the point of gauntness, but both unmeasurably kind, vanished through the door.

Ten minutes later a rapid knock on the peeled pine log door announced Dr. Birchfield's arrival and set Laurel shivering.

✍

Every day Dr. Adam Birchfield lived and worked in Antelope he more clearly saw the need for his skills and rejoiced. How much more opportunity to give real service here than back home in Concord, especially since it had grown and attracted other doctors. The long rides out to ranches and the ever-changing Wyoming mountains, hills, and valleys continued to thrill him to the soul. He rode in at dusk one snowy afternoon, content and at peace.

A blast of music from the Pronghorn saloon, defiantly mocked by another from the Silver, upset him as usual, but much of his business stemmed from saloon patronage. He rode down the street, turned his mount, and trotted toward home, feeling more peaceful with each mile. Being here with Nat had turned out to be everything he had hoped for and more. Adam led his horse into shelter, quickly rubbed him down, and strode into the sweet-smelling log cabin.

"Hmmm," he sniffed, "something smells good."

Nat's wide white smile flashed. His dark eyes twinkled. "Venison stew, hot biscuits and—" He triumphantly waved a glass jar. "Wild berry preserves."

"Donated by a grateful parishioner?" Adam shrugged out of his snowy coat and boots before making for the welcome warmth of the fireplace with its roaring flames.

"Not exactly." Nat turned the tables on his brother and his sparkling dark eyes showed how much he enjoyed doing so. "Sally Mae Justice made them with her own little hands and wants our good doctor to have them. It's the only way poor little her can show her appreciation and respect for the man who saved her brother Mark." Instant contrition replaced Nat's faithful imitation of Sally Mae's simpering. "I shouldn't mock her. Sally Mae really loves that cowboy brother and I'm sure she'd be grateful to whatever doctor saved his life. Even if he weren't 'the best catch Antelope's seen in many a year,'" he couldn't help adding.

"Forget that stuff!" Adam growled, but a reluctant grin found its way over his storm-wet face the same way the kitten Inkblot, yet another gift, always found herself close to the hearth. "Besides, I'm only the *second* best catch, you know." He clasped his hands in a ridiculous pose, gazed skyward, and said in a high falsetto, "Isn't it just too, too wonderful that with all Mr. Birchfield has to do he's getting up a choir for Christmas?"

Nat's face turned red and he muttered something that clearly told Adam his brother knew what it was to have to minister to silly young women who trailed and set traps for him.

"With all the cowboys and ranchers around, why do the few nice young women concentrate on us?" Adam asked later. Filled with good food and the prospect of a free evening together—a rare occurrence—the brothers lounged in front of the fire, safe from the pelting storm.

"We represent the East many of them knew and they haven't yet started to realize some of the cowboys and ranchers out here are among the finest men on earth." Nat's eyes glowed and he leaned forward. "I don't mean the hard-riding, hard-shooting, loud-mouthed showoffs. I mean those who will find a place in the pages of western history books. Not for deeds of daring but for their relentless refusal to let a new and untamed country beat them."

Adam's eyes opened wide at Nat's fervor. He shifted into a more comfortable position and stretched. A mighty yawn followed and he stumbled to his feet. "Guess our discussion will have to wait." He yawned again, so wide he wondered if he'd dislocate his jaw. "Nothing like a blizzard, hot food, and a warm fire to make a man sleep."

"Goodnight, Adam. I'm glad you came."

Adam gripped Nat's hand, strong as his own, yet never failing in kindness and blessing. "So am I."

An hour later he wondered at himself. *Why should he lie awake, reliving that poignant moment?* Wind shrieked around the corners of the cabin and through the treetops. The thud of snow too heavy for branches to bear sounded like intermittent explosions. God grant he would not be needed this night. No man or horse could get in or out of town until the storm abated. Gradually the warmth of wool blankets and the well-banked fire did its work and Dr. Birchfield slept.

He awakened refreshed and to winter beauty beyond words. Massachusetts had storms and snow, but Wyoming had outdone any Adam remembered. The first thing he noticed was stillness. Antelope had not yet dug itself out of the worst storm of the winter. His teeth chattering, Adam dressed in the warmest clothing Nat had provided, poked a single coal into the fire, and eagerly clutched the mug of hot coffee his brother thrust into his hands. "Whew! This is welcome." Adam, who seldom drank the bitter brew, was overcome by the rich fragrance and warm comfort and drank heartily. "How cold is it?"

"Ten below. A real winter heat wave." Nat laughed out loud at Adam's astonishment. "It cleared off after the storm. Look." He pointed out the cabin window, whose bottom half lay packed with snow.

For one crushing, unexpected moment homesickness attacked Adam like a living, breathing thing. How many times had he eagerly peered from the window at Concord into such a snowy scene? Sleighing parties with jingling bells and laughing young men and women, clam chowder suppers and pumpkin pie with whipped cream no fluffier than the snowdrifts made Adam's insides twist.

A heavy but compassionate hand fell to his shoulder. "I feel the same way. There hasn't been a winter since I left home that I haven't remembered Mother and Father, and you." The grip tightened and Adam had to strain to hear the next words.

"I wonder if I'll ever see them again."

A snowball-sized lump formed in Adam's throat and he blinked hard at the husky voice of his exiled brother. "We just have to keep praying that Father will realize. . . ." He couldn't continue and secretly welcomed the interruption when it came.

"Hey, Doc, Preacher! You fellers all right?" The stentorian yell effectively shattered the fragile moment.

Nat's hand fell and he strode to the door, pulled it open, and stepped back when a shower of accumulated snow fell.

"Well, I'll be!" Adam stared at the solidly packed wall of snow outside the door.

"We'll have you cleared soon," the same voice boomed.

"Snow stopped before daybreak. Folks've been digging out ever since. Some of us figgered as how we better get you clear in case anyone needs marryin' or buryin' soon." Ribald laughter followed the remark.

"I doubt anyone will want either but thanks, boys. We'll have hot coffee for you when you break through," Nat promised at the top of his lungs before closing the door.

Faster than Adam expected the door burst open and a dozen lusty giants surged in out of the cold. They looked like the snow and ice statues Concord citizens built each winter.

"Don't mind the dripping," Adam told them. "We'll mop up when you're gone." He pushed the rescuers closer to the fire. "Is everyone all right?"

"Why shouldn't they be?" One big man raised his frosted eyebrows. "With this much snow not even the Pronghorn or Silver's open. Unless someone fell out of bed or something, you'll get no customers today, Doc." He took a long swig of coffee.

The prophecy proved false. Just after noon a half-frozen cowboy leading a lamed horse staggered to Adam's door and collapsed after pounding on it. It took time to get his story but Adam finally learned that Mark Justice was in trouble again.

"We g-got c-caught," the messenger gasped, trembling in spite of the hot drink Nat had helped Adam get down him. Shivers made his teeth chatter until his words blurred. "I th-thought he w-was right b-behind m-me." Unashamed tears fell. "M-my horse w-went d-down and wh-when I got him u-up, I c-couldn't find M-mark."

"Drink some more of this," Adam ordered, and he helped steady the mug.

Finally the cowboy could continue. "I hollered and heard an answer but it sounded far away." He gulped and stared at Adam. "When I found Mark he had a broken leg. We got to the line shack, God knows how. Probably because Mark keeled over from pain and I tied him in the saddle. Anyway, I did what I could after buildin' a fire and we slept some. But this mornin' Mark was out of his head with fever." His eyes still held shock. "I was scared to leave him and scared not to." He leaped up and almost fell, too exhausted to do more than plead. "He needs you Doc. If you don't go, Mark's gonna die."

"I'll go. Adam set his mouth in a straight line. "Which line shack?"

"Follow my trail. It's a good five miles. Out toward the Lazy H but in the trees, not down by the river."

"I'll go with you." Nat reached for boots and coat.

"What about him?" Adam pointed at the patient who had sunk back once he had delivered the critical message.

"Be right back." Nat shouldered past him out into the brilliant day. Fifteen minutes later he appeared with a red-cheeked, well-bundled woman who took charge and shooed the brothers off on their difficult journey. "Land sakes, nothing wrong with this lad but worry and being tired. Go on."

"I knew I could count on Mrs. Greer," Nat said once they had decided snowshoes would be better than horses although it would take longer. "Best thing that ever happened to Antelope was when Greer set up his store and his wife stood right behind him." His tone turned somber. "It's going to take everything we have to save Mark."

"I know. I've been praying ever since the boy came."

Nat's radiant smile echoed Adam's statement but he said nothing. A long, tough trek lay before them. Wasting breath on talking could only make the ordeal worse.

The time of testing had come. Every ounce of muscle and strength gained in facing hard climbs and adverse conditions pitted itself against the worst odds known to humankind. A dozen times the young cowboy's words came back to Adam, tossed from the rising wind and spitting snow that heralded another storm.

*We got to the line shack, God knows how.*

Each time the words brought comfort, warming Adam's cold body that even the heaviest clothes and most strenuous exertion couldn't keep from chilling. Once he stumbled and noticed how quickly Nat came to lift him up, just as he lifts those who fall and stumble in life itself, Adam's dazed brain thought. He ploughed on, now leading and peering into the early gloom that had settled with the new storm at the rapidly filling tracks made by Mark Justice's partner. At other times, Adam simply followed in the footsteps of his big brother, as he had done so many times before. The journey became a parallel of life and tangled in it were the faces of two lovely young women from West Virginia.

"Think of something other than storm and whiteness," Adam ordered himself. He concentrated on Red Cedars. Would the Browns like the unusual gifts he had managed to find and have shipped? Ivy Ann's pert face, wide-open eyes, and smile when she saw the deerskin moccasins tantalized him. Laurel would like hers, too. She probably wouldn't exclaim in Ivy's manner but Adam felt sure of Laurel's pleasure. Would the precious painting of Antelope Mrs. Hardwick had done at his insistence tempt the family to leave everything comfortable and come West? Adam's laughter at the way Ivy Ann and Laurel would set Antelope upside down drifted off with the wind. What would poor, silly Sally Mae think of the twins?

"Adam, stop!" A strong hand grabbed him. Nat looked like a snowman. He put his mouth close to Adam's ear. "You've passed the end of the footprints."

Adam looked down. A pang went through him. Dreaming

of two gently bred young women had caused a lapse of concentration. He silently followed Nat back, chiding himself for his inattention. The treachery of this changeable land allowed no time to dream.

"Here!" Nat abruptly turned left. The footprints and hoofprints showed more clearly under the gigantic evergreens that had helped protect the ground from such heavy drifts. A little later Adam shouted with joy.

Through the fury of snow that proclaimed its defeat against the two travelers, a rude structure loomed, the line shack.

A lighted lantern, and a stirred fire later, Adam threw off his snowy outer clothing in one fluid motion. He bent over Mark Justice who tossed and muttered and whose hair lay in damp strands over a hot forehead.

"We have a fight ahead," he warned Nat.

"I know." Nat had already filled a large kettle with packed snow to melt and heat. "What are his chances?"

"Better than when he had the bullet in him but not much."

Adam kicked off his boots and pulled on the heavy dry socks they'd brought in their packs. Then he opened his medical bag and went to work.

For three days the storm raged outside the lonely line shack, a monster ready to devour anyone caught in it. For three days a war raged inside the shack, the fight for a man's life. Adam didn't close his eyes for the first thirty-six hours and only consented to snatch a little sleep with Nat's firm promise to rouse him should there be the slightest change. Twelve hours later he awakened to find Nat bending over him and smiling broadly. "The fever's broken. The snow packs you used worked, thank God!"

Every trace of weariness and sleep fled before the good news. Adam bounded from the bed. Never had Nat looked more beautiful than standing there unshaven and wrinkled, red-eyed but rejoicing. Careful nursing would bring Mark Justice back to the range again.

Limited by what supplies they had been able to carry, Nat made broth and tenderly fed it to the cowboy who was too weak to do it himself. Adam continued his almost twenty-four-hour care, whistling to himself when Mark's gaze followed him.

"I don't know who really saved me," were the first words that came when Adam finally permitted Mark to speak. "If my pard hadn't gone for help or if you hadn't come—" His fingers nervously twitched the edge of the rough woolen blanket that covered him. He licked dry lips. "I-I reckon it was God."

Adam glanced sideways at Nat. Did he want to burst out with what lay in Adam's own heart? Would he, could he resist taking advantage of everything that had happened to bring Mark to God?

Before either brother could answer, Mark went on. "This is the second time." The dawning of understanding showed in his eyes and brightened them against the dark circles of illness.

Adam held his breath. Saying too much or too little might destroy the opportunity.

Nat smiled a singularly sweet smile at the cowboy. "Mark, you're very wise."

Red color stole through the white face to the roots of Mark's hair. "God must care a whole lot about me to send help and save my life twice." He straightened as if jabbed with a spear. "Why, it's three times, isn't it?" His eyes lighted and a weak smile crossed his face. "That time I came to church, you said God sent Jesus to save us, didn't you?" His gaze bored into Nat. He laughed, a kind of wild but happy laugh. "I read in a book that some folks in the world believe if you save someone's life that person belongs to you. I guess that means I belong to you—no, to God—and that I'll have to be riding with Him from now on?"

Nat's steady gaze never wavered. "That is up to you, Mark. The same way it's up to you whom you choose to bunk with and make your pard."

Tired out by the extra effort, Mark dropped back but before he closed his eyes he mumbled, "Gotta tell my pard we're gonna have a new trailmate from now on."

Adam's eyes stung. *What would Father and Mother and the Browns think if they could see into this line shack?* Would they realize how all the heartache and struggle fell away when measured against the soul of one wild cowboy?

# Chapter 9

The conversion of Mark Justice rocked Antelope. Nothing had set tongues wagging and heads nodding as much as the dramatic change in the cowboy once shot by the sheriff in self-defense. When the second storm abated and an unnatural warm spell followed, Nat went for help. Mark bit his lip to hold back the pain when his comrades lifted him onto a steady horse. The curses they expected to split the air never came. Blood ran down Mark's chin from where he had driven his teeth into his lower lip but he said nothing and stuck on the horse.

At his request, the men took him to the Lazy H bunkhouse instead of into town. "What's a little old broken leg?" he demanded once Adam pronounced the break clean and healing well. "You poor fish will have to be out checking on how many cattle got caught in the storm. I get to lie in bed or hobble around a nice warm bunkhouse, shoot the breeze with Cooky, and take me a va-cation." He didn't add what he told Nat later. "I'll have a chance to read the Bible you gave me. Now that I'm riding with God, I want Sally Mae to know about Him. She always did listen to what I have to say and she'll be coming around soon. I better get ready." He clutched the Bible and jauntily waved goodbye to the Birchfields.

More of the story came from other Lazy H hands.

"Crazy kid," one rangewise cowboy told Adam. "Never preaches. Just lays there readin' that Bible." He squirmed a bit then looked square into the doctor's eyes. "He told us everything that happened there in the line shack. Blamed if I didn't go and get a cinder in my eye just then and have to rub it out." He cackled. "A lot of the other men sat there rubbin' their eyes, too. Guess it kinda got to us." He took a deep breath. "Makes a feller sort of wonder. I mean, Mark's never been out and out bad but you don't find them much wilder. He's shore changed."

"How come you never see Mark Justice around here no more?" became a standard question in Antelope.

"Aw, he's got religion," someone always answered, but a dozen times Nat or Adam saw the look in some of the other cowhands' eyes, the look that "made a feller sort of wonder."

"You know, Mark can be one of the best witnesses for Christ around here simply because he's one of the cowboys," Nat said one evening. "Any time a man or woman or child whose life isn't so spotless accepts the Lord, that person can be a powerful influence."

"I wonder how Mark can keep from preaching," Adam mused.

"I told him just to live it and baffle his friends!" Nat confessed.

Winter passed with a spate of spontaneous get-togethers with various Antelope families, the church program, and snow, snow, and more snow. The infrequent letters from Ivy Ann, always with a brief message Adam suspected Laurel tucked in secretly, brightened days made long and weary by the fight against cold, sickness, and accidents. Adam gloried in knowing if he hadn't been where God wanted him to be many of those who came down with pneumonia would surely be dead. If at times he longed for a companion, a wife, he quickly drowned the wish in the joy of being with his brother.

Suddenly, spring came, not stealing into Antelope like a thief in the night, but with a rush of warm days that release rivers from their captivity and sent them gleefully chuckling, free from winter hibernation under sheets of ice. Tiny flowers sprang up. New life abounded and Adam lifted up his head and gave thanks. Only one sore spot remained: It had been a long time since he heard anything from his friends, the Browns, or from Mother, who faithfully smuggled letters to him. How had they kept through the winter? What news Antelope had came slowly and only after a long time. If it weren't for Dan Sharpe, who had already made one round trip out for a top-heavy load of supplies, the world since the snowfall might as well not exist!

One early evening Adam felt more tired than ever. If only his patients would follow his advice. At times he despaired of ever convincing these people that when he ordered rest it didn't mean after all the usual work chores ended. Yet he couldn't blame them. Every family busy with spring work toiled from sunup to past sundown. How could they do anything else when duty called?

Adam sighed, wishing Nat would return from whatever errand had called him out. The cabin felt empty without patients, or Nat. Too tired to eat the warm supper he found saved for him by his thoughtful brother, Adam restlessly paced the floor longing for he knew not what.

Suddenly the door flung open and Nat came in, his mouth stretched wide in an expression of glee. He tossed his hat into a corner.

"You look like the Cheshire cat in *Alice in Wonderland*," Adam told him, unreasonably resenting Nat's obviously high spirits when his own were mysteriously low.

"I've just seen a vision."

"You've *what*?" Adam was jolted out of his doldrums.

"Not a religious vision," Nat quickly amended, "but a vision of fair young maidenhood."

"Sally Mae's in town again?" Adam taunted while a quiver of anticipate went through him. "Since when is she a vision?"

"My good man." Nat drew himself up as if offended, but his

twinkling black eyes ruined the attempt. "I am not referring to Sally Mae Justice. I am referring to a young and lovely woman who pursued me down the street, clutched my arm, and looked into my face then said, 'Hello.' Furthermore, a young lady I have never seen before."

"Are you making this up?" Adam demanded, while that same odd lurch of his heart pumped blood against all reason.

Nat's keen look replaced his teasing. "No, Mrs. Greer explained it all. In the dim light the young woman mistook me for you."

*"What young woman?"*

"You haven't heard from Ivy Ann Brown for a long while, have you?" Nat grinned tormentingly with the expression that contrasted so to his serious demeanor when ministering.

"Impossible!" It burst from the depths of Adam's heart. He must be mad to think of it. *Yet wouldn't a stunt like this be just like Miss Ivy Ann Brown?*

"I am to tell you that Miss Brown will see you at the Widow Terry's where she has taken up residence in one hour, or whenever you're free."

It was all Adam could do to keep from rushing to Mrs. Terry's cabin. He bathed, shaved, and dressed in fresh clothing from the skin out. He ignored the gleam in Nat's eye and his innocent comment.

"Wish I had a pretty girl from the East to visit." A few minutes before the appointed time, he presented himself at the front door of Ivy Ann's new abode, willing his usually steady heart to stop pounding.

⚘

The pink gown swirled around Laurel's unsteady feet as she slowly walked to the door. She hesitated, one soft hand on the latch. Then she took a deep breath, lifted her chin with all her heritage of southern pride, and opened the door.

A tall, deerskin-clad figure stood before her.

Laurel's quick survey took in the new man. Dr. Adam Birchfield in the western garb he had adopted for comfort and practicality outstripped the young man in fine broadcloth and immaculate linen she remembered.

"Hello, Adam." Why did she stand frozen before the familiar stranger? She anxiously scanned his face, lean from hard work and outdoor calls, and felt relieved to discover the beginnings of a smile. Yet what shadow lurked in the watching dark eyes? It couldn't be disappointment, could it? Her spirits that had been shored up by the warm bath and the pink gown fell. The next instant the look vanished and laugh crinkles half closed his eyes.

"Well, Miss Ivy Ann, you've done it this time! I thought you were the young lady who refused to give up the comforts of home for the good of our expanding country." He threw back his head and laughed, just as his brother had done in the street earlier.

An icicle pierced Laurel to her very soul. So Ivy Ann *had* won again, in spite of everything. She opened her mouth to cry out the truth, but was stopped by Adam's hearty voice.

"Don't look so stricken." He took her hand and shook it. Genuine welcome lightened his face. "It's wonderful for you to be here no matter what the reason." He led her to a settee and sat down beside her. "When I didn't hear from you for a time I thought you had probably forgotten all about your Wild West doctor friend."

"I could never do that." Laurel's lips moved of their own accord. Her mind ran in a dozen directions.

"How's Laurel? And your father and mother?"

With a tremendous effort the distraught girl managed to mumble, "All my family is well, or at least they were when I left." Inside she wanted to shriek. Any hope that the doctor had escaped Ivy's charms without regret faded when Adam continued.

"Nat told me how you mistook him for me in the dusk." Another laugh escaped. "Would you like to know what else he said about you?"

"Why, of course." She nervously pleated her frothy pink skirt, hating it with all her heart and wishing she'd worn calico. Yet, would it have changed anything? Although Adam had heard her feelings about the West, never in a million years would he believe the quiet twin capable of the escapade she had just completed.

"It's still hard for me to believe you're here." Admiration shone in Adam's face. "Say, but we'll have a good time. I have places to show you that will make you turn traitor to even your beautiful Red Cedars." He went on making plans while Laurel numbly prayed for Mrs. Terry to return before she betrayed her identity. She must think and decide what to do. Laurel had been prepared for disapproval, even shock. She hadn't even considered that Adam would take her for Ivy Ann.

By pasting a smile over lips that wanted to tremble, she oohed and ahed in all the right places and knew how a prisoner given a reprieve must feel when the Widow Terry swept in, greeted Dr. Birchfield, pointedly looked at the clock, and ushered Adam out.

"She's going to be here for a spell. Now you get home and get your rest... The good Lord knows there are few enough uninterrupted nights for you."

At last Laurel escaped from her landlady, if she could be called that when she obviously intended for Laurel to replace the daughter who had married and gone. In a tiny, piney-smelling room Mrs. Terry hastily cleared of cloth bolts and trims, Laurel stared out the single window at stars that looked near enough to pick. *What would she do now? Seek Adam out at the first opportunity and confess?*

She tossed and turned, remembering how above all else Adam hated deceit. Her courage failed. At least until she made new friends Dr. Birchfield must remain a staunch ally to whom she could turn in this faraway land. "If I can do all the wonderful things he has planned we'll be together," she comforted herself. "Dear God, it isn't that I won't tell him. I will, but just not now. Besides, I never said I was Ivy Ann. He said I was. I just didn't correct him." She moved again and kept her gaze on the majestic stars. "I know you hate deceit even worse than Adam does, but I just can't—"

Misery took over and the longing to be safely back at Red Cedars. She had thought nothing could be worse than living forever in her twin's shadow. Now the shadow of her own making lay long and dark over any chance for happiness in this forbidding land. A wail in the distance didn't help. A wolf? Coyote? She shivered under the warm, beautifully made quilts Mrs. Terry had brought out from her "saving for comp'ny" closet. Did everyone who broke free from home, especially those who slipped away without the family knowing, feel this way?

Before she finally slept, Laurel had wrestled with her knotty problem and decided she had no choice. Until she got close enough to Adam Birchfield to feel that he cared enough to forgive her, she must be Ivy Ann—not in what she said but in what she did. Perhaps he would attribute the differences she knew she could not hide to her being in a new place. Or maybe he had forgotten some of Ivy's little ways.

She sighed. All the times she had played parts in young people's entertainments hadn't prepared her for the monstrous role she faced in playing her own sister! Perhaps she should have corrected Adam immediately. The one other option lay in going home.

"*No!*" She sat upright in bed. A surge of protest drowned out the sensibility of that move. "I'm here and I'm staying." She slid back down under the covers and a hard core of stubbornness formed within her. *So what if Adam built on his gladness to see Ivy Ann and fell in love? It would really be with her, Laurel, wouldn't it?* She fell asleep hugging the thought to her heart. If that happened, surely he would forgive her. . . .

Laurel hadn't counted on a new complication entering her already topsy-turvy plans. Blond-haired, amber-eyed Dan Sharpe had ideas of his own. Before Mrs. Terry and Laurel had finished breakfast the next morning, Dan rapped on the door.

Mrs. Terry's cup hit the table with a little crash. Her thin face turned toward the door. "My, my, isn't your beau impatient?" She marched to fling open the door and welcome Dr. Birchfield, then scowled in surprise.

"Morning, Mrs. Terry." Early sun turned Dan's hair to molten gold.

"Land sakes, Dan Sharpe, what're you doing coming around here at the crack of dawn when a body's getting ready for work?"

"Just paying my respects. Is Miss Brown here?"

"Bees to the honeypot," Laurel heard her hostess mutter before she grudgingly allowed Dan to enter.

"I just wondered if you'd care to go riding a little later," Dan drawled. "Every unmarried man around's going to come calling." He sent a significant glace at her bare ring finger. "According to Mrs. Greer, Doc has a prior claim but I don't see any sign of it being staked out."

In the middle of Mrs. Terry's indignant gasp Laurel coolly replied, "I don't quite understand your meaning, Mr. Sharpe, but it doesn't really matter. I am to help Mrs. Terry and my work begins immediately. I'll have little time to go riding, at least until I get settled," she amended when she saw his reaction. "I do appreciate your calling, however. It's nice to have the local people welcome me to my new home." The next instant she wished she had bitten her tongue.

"You plan to stay permanently?" Dan's gaze sharpened and drilled into her.

Again she thought of that tiger, under control but still dangerous. Laurel smiled in the way she had seen Ivy Ann do a hundred times, a smile guaranteed to disarm her inquisitive suitors. "Who knows?" She shrugged her shoulders in a dainty gesture. "I suppose much will depend on how I like Antelope. Now, if you'll excuse us, I'm sure it's time for Mrs. Terry and her new apprentice to go to work." She held out her hand.

Danger signals in Dan's eyes warned her the battle had neither ended nor been won but he merely bowed over her hand. "Remember, I asked first," he said, then bowed toward Mrs. Terry and swung out, whistling the first few bars of "Dixie."

"Well, of all the—I knew Dan Sharpe was presumptuous but this really beats it all!" Mrs. Terry's astonished reaction sent Laurel into a fit of giggles.

"'Remember, I asked first,'" she mimicked. "Who does he think he is? I get the feeling he's convinced that any girl would just be waiting for him to confer attention on her."

"That's Dan Sharpe." Mrs. Terry's thin lips closed tightly. Then she added, "I'm not one to spread gossip but according to the whispers there's a whole lot about Dan Sharpe no one knows. Or at least if they do, they aren't telling."

Laurel stopped, her hands filled with the breakfast dishes she had gathered up. She impulsively said, "Mrs. Terry, I'm a stranger in a strange land who's going to need a lot of help in understanding the people and the place. I really need you to guide me."

A pleased expression lighted the older woman's face. "I think we're going to get along real well, child. Real well." She folded the breakfast cloth, shook it outside the cabin door, and smiled in a way that did more to settle Laurel down than anything since she left West Virginia.

# Chapter 10

I like your Ivy Ann," Nat told Adam one late spring afternoon. The brothers had reined in on top of a grassy knoll above Antelope to let their horses rest after a climb. "I wouldn't have thought such a girl as you described could so quickly adjust and become part of the community." His fine eyes looked into the blue heavens. "But something seems to be troubling her. Have you noticed the way she bubbles at times and still carries an almost brooding look at others?"

Adam relaxed in his saddle. "Yes, it's strange. The Ivy Ann I knew at Red Cedars cared for little except getting her own way." His lips curved in remembrance. Aspen leaves decked in new-leaf green whispered secrets not to be shared with the riders. A confession Adam wanted to make halted on his lips and a worry line formed between his dark brows. Even though the Bible said to share burdens, right now Nat didn't need a heavier load. Nat's efforts to get more law and order than Antelope wanted had resulted in bitterness, especially from the owners of the Pronghorn and Silver saloons.

Suddenly Adam's horse shied and Nat's whinnied. Like a stab of lightning, a dark form appeared in front of the startled brothers. Adam's mouth fell open. A magnificent Indian warrior, powerful and naked to the waist, calmly grabbed the reins of both horses.

"Who—what—?" Adam sputtered as fear gnawed at him. "What do you want?" Nat took charge.

"Grey Eagle." The Indian pointed to himself. "You come." He pointed to Adam, then Nat. "Son sick, maybe die. Running Deer no die! You medicine man. Make well."

In bits and pieces they learned Grey Eagle's story. When the tribes had been rounded up and forced to go on reservations, a small band refused and hid in the vast wildness of the Wind River area. The government could spare neither the time nor troops to find and capture the wily group. They moved from time to time and lived as their ancestors had lived for hundreds of years, free and drifting.

Grey Eagle, who seemed to know more about the area's happenings than the Birchfields, had discovered the presence of a white medicine man in Antelope. He had tucked the information away, perhaps never intending to use it. In desperation, he refused to accept the death sentence his tribe's medicine man prescribed and now stood before Adam on behalf of his son.

"You go with me. Both go."

Adam didn't hesitate a moment. "Of course we'll go with you, Grey Eagle. When I became a doctor I promised to go anywhere and to anyone who needed me." He held out his hand to show his good faith.

The dull black eyes glowed with dark fire and Grey Eagle took Adam's hand. "No tell where you go?"

Adam looked at Nat who quietly explained, "Grey Eagle is putting the safety of his tribe in our hands." With slow movements he loosened the catch of his saddlebag and took out his worn black Bible. "Grey Eagle, do you know what this is?"

"Great Spirit book."

Nat nodded. "My brother and I pledge by the Great Spirit we call God not to tell." He placed his and Adam's hands on the Bible.

Grey Eagle grunted and the semblance of a smile creased his aged, angular face. Without a word he slid into a cluster of trees and reappeared riding a shaggy horse, his only saddle a worn blanket. "Come."

Hours later they reached their destination, a cragbound valley only the tribe who called it home or an eagle on the wing could find. Ice-cold water bubbled from a spring, so cold Adam's teeth ached when he flung himself to the banks and drank. Spring flowers sent thrusts of color through the rich, green grass. A dozen tepees made up the village and horses grazed nearby. Grey Eagle led the brothers to the largest tepee. Wailing sounds sent chills through Adam. *Had they come too late?* He followed Grey Eagle and Nat into the smoky interior. A stripling Indian lay on a bed of rich skins. Sweat glistened on his copper skin. The look in his eyes when he turned toward his father pierced Adam's heart. Terror, pain, and hope combined in the age-old expression that binds father and son.

"White medicine man." A sinewy arm drew Adam nearer.

A cry of rage from the howling Indian medicine man was cut short with a single wave of Grey Eagle's mighty arm.

"Clear everyone out," Adam ordered Nat with such authority in his voice the huddle of Indians silently obeyed without question.

Adam quickly examined Running Deer. "You'll have to help, Nat." His lips felt stiff. "We've got a red-hot appendix."

"Not again!"

Adam nodded. "Just like Mrs. Hardwick." He pressed the lower right area of Running Deer's abdomen. A moan of pain escaped the tightly clenched teeth.

"Make you well." Grey Eagle stood to one side, his arms folded across his chest. A muscle in his drawn face showed his love for his only son, now lying defenseless against the white medicine man's probing.

Adam straightened and fearlessly looked into the dark wells of Grey Eagle's eyes that had seen bloodshed and peace, sunrise and sunset. "I will do all I can and my brother will ask the Great Spirit to help me."

"Bad spirit in son."

"We must let it out." Adam compressed his lips. What a setting for his second emergency appendectomy since reaching the Wyoming Territory! He quickly made what preparations he could, calling for boiling water and the tepee flap left open for extra light. Then with the most fervent prayer he had ever offered, he began.

Grey Eagle unflinchingly watched the thin red line that followed Adam's initial incision. He gave not a sign of inner turmoil yet both Adam and Nat knew how torn he must be. To go against his medicine man's advice, to let a white man cut his son, had been a terrible decision.

Again the years of training and prayers met to triumph. Again, the diseased appendix burst, but outside of the patient. Humility and thankfulness filled Adam and he quickly sutured and bandaged. "Nat, I want you to go back and leave me here for a few days. I have to be sure Running Deer gets the proper care." Adam stretched to full height. "Grey Eagle, I believe your son will live but I want to stay with him."

Grey Eagle solemnly nodded and turned toward the open tepee flap. "Tell tribe." A string of unfamiliar phrases followed his exit from the makeshift operating room.

"Why don't I stay, too?" Nat frowned.

"And miss your Sunday services? Antelope would have a search party out!" exclaimed Adam as he washed his stained hands in the clean water Nat brought. "Give me a week, will you? If anything's going to develop, it will by then." He watched Nat ride off with Grey Eagle, who would make sure he could find his way back, then called a warning. "Don't tell everything. Just say I'm staying with an out of town patient, will you?"

Nat signaled and disappeared after Grey Eagle.

Of all the experiences so far, the week in the small and hidden Indian camp affected Adam most deeply. Running Deer's young body healed incredibly fast. Adam spoke through him and his father to the old medicine man and pleased the ancient by carefully listening to what he had to say. Certain herbs and primitive knowledge made good medical sense and he gratefully expressed his appreciation. By the time Nat returned, Adam felt a certain reluctance to leave, although eager to get back to their own place. When they did go, they carried the pledge of the tribe's eternal friendship and gratitude.

Adam had also found time to think while in the hidden village. The problem he'd concealed from Nat came out into the open of Adam's mind and had to be dealt with. Ivy Ann's face danced in the firelit shadows, but so did another. After prayer and much consideration, Adam set his jaw firmly. The showdown with Ivy Ann had to come soon, for both their sakes.

Laurel had, as Nat said, settled into Antelope the way a broody hen settles into her nest. Her moments of homesickness had little chance against the enticement of spring in the Wyoming Territory. Although sensible enough to know part of the masculine attention could be credited to lack of competition, she couldn't help rejoicing over the unqualified approval of most single Antelope males. She treated them all alike, to Dan Sharpe's chagrin and Mrs. Terry's secret delight, and she never acted like Ivy Ann to anyone except Adam—and only when she remembered.

Sally Mae and the few other girls loved Laurel in spite of their jealousy. As Sally Mae told her brother Mark, who was one of Laurel's most faithful admirers, "It'd be different if she was flirty or stuckup. She's just nice to everyone."

The only real flaw in Laurel's world except for running

away from her beloved Red Cedars was the weight of deceiving Adam. It pricked at her like an imbedded splinter. *Soon*, she often promised herself, but days and then weeks passed and she still had not confessed to Adam and asked his forgiveness.

During that time the respect and attraction that had lighted a tiny fire in her heart grew into the steady flame of love. Although Adam could not suspect it, he had no rivals for Laurel, alias Ivy Ann. She also saw in his eyes when she caught his gaze in unguarded moments a growing feeling and she thanked God for it.

Widow Terry's business took a surprising jump after Laurel signed on as her apprentice. "You're my best advertisement," Mrs. Terry told the young woman. She eyed the tiny frills around the high neck and long sleeves of Laurel's work gown.

Laurel laughed. "Back home we—I learned to make the best of what we had and make sure I took care of it! New gowns can't compete with the need for new tools, seed, and all the things that wear out on a big farm." She industriously leaned closer to the window to catch a final gleam of daylight. The soft glow of lamplight didn't offer adequate light for the tiny stitches necessary to finish Mrs. Hardwick's new Sunday dress, a dark blue gown with fine tucks and a wisp of braid on the collar.

"Ivy Ann?"

Something in Mrs. Terry's voice stilled the flying fingers. "Yes?" She felt guilty answering to the name she'd never claimed.

Dull red suffused the gaunt face. "I don't want to pry but hasn't Dan Sharpe been around an awful lot lately?" She rushed on, obviously eager not to offend. "Some of the other boys come too, but. . . ."

Laurel sighed. "I can't very well ask Dan not to drop by. I avoid him when I can and turn down twice as many of his invitations as I accept." She impatiently shook her head until a light brown curl escaped its mooring and hung over her forehead, making her look like a troubled little girl.

"I know, child." Mrs. Terry took up the child's dress she had cut out earlier then folded it and put it away. "Tomorrow's time enough for this." Her sigh matched Laurel's and her kind face seemed strange without her quick smile. "I guess as long as you aren't spoken for the boys won't leave you alone."

Laurel felt warmth steal into her cheeks. She bent her head, wishing she could confide in her new friend but rejecting the idea immediately. Not until she settled things with Adam could she tell anyone else. She pretended far more interest in setting the final stitches in the gown than she felt. "There! Dear Mrs. Hardwick will get a lot of service out of this dress and I know she'll look nice in it."

The keen-eyed dressmaker took the garment from Laurel and examined every seam and the set of the sleeves. "If I'd known what a good apprentice I'd get, why, I reckon I'd have sent back to West Virginia for you long ago!" She smiled roguishly. "But I s'pose a handsome young doctor is a better reason to come West than an old lady like me."

"You aren't old and I love you." Laurel hugged Mrs. Terry. Her words and actions so flustered the widow the subject changed, as Laurel intended it would.

Only to Laurel did Nat confide his and Adam's adventure with Chief Grey Eagle and his people. She had learned to appreciate Antelope's minister and gloried in the fact that as Adam grew older, the same sterling qualities would deepen in his own life. Her first letter home actually spoke more about Nat than Adam. She praised his dedication to duty and devotion to his Lord and merely said Adam stayed extremely busy supporting his brother's spiritual ministry with physical healing. So when Nat called one evening while Adam was still in the hidden village, she gladly walked with him and thrilled to his tale.

"What's it like, the Indian village, I mean?" Laurel's sincerity loosened Nat's tongue.

"It's located in probably the most beautiful spot in Wyoming, inaccessible except to those who know the way. Even after going and coming back, guided by Grey Eagle, I'll have to look sharp when I go back for Adam. He could have simply had Grey Eagle guide him but he wants me to pack in a few luxuries for the tribe—candy, bright cloth, that kind of thing."

She stopped short, her heart pounding at her own daring. "Take me with you when you go. I'd love to see the camp and meet Grey Eagle and Running Deer and their people." She clasped his arm with both hands.

For a moment she thought he'd agree but then he shook his head. Regret clouded his eyes. "I can't, Ivy Ann. I'm sorry."

"Why?" she persisted. "Don't you think I can ride or hike that far?"

He threw his head back and laughed in the way the Birchfield men did when highly amused. "Gracious, it isn't that. Antelope's rampant with stories of your horsemanship." His eyes twinkled with mischief. "Did you really beat Dan Sharpe in a race a few days ago?"

"Who told you?" She clapped her hand to her mouth then joined in his laughter. Pride lent a tilt to her chin, a sparkle to her mobile face. "He was so sure he could beat me he offered me a headstart. I told him I needed no favors." She blushed, remembering how Dan suggested a wager, a silver dollar against a kiss. She had coldly told him she didn't wager, then beat him in the race by a full three feet.

Now she returned to her teasing. "Please take me."

Nat shook his head again, more decidedly this time. "Adam and I gave our word we would not reveal where the camp lies. I couldn't break that promise, although I'm sure you would enjoy the hard climb and scenery." A new thought brightened his face. "Tell you what. When I see Grey Eagle again I'll ask him for permission to have you visit the camp sometime. There's no guarantee he will agree but I can ask."

"Tell him he has nothing to fear from me," she said earnestly.

"I don't know about that." Nat's laughing mouth reminded her of Adam's. "According to Mark Justice and some of the other boys you are mighty dangerous. Seems a rash of heart trouble has broken out since you came."

His meaning brought floods of color to Laurel's neck and face. She controlled the desire to retort and meekly suggested, "Perhaps they should consult Dr. Birchfield."

"Perhaps they should," he blandly agreed, and Laurel wondered if the innocent words held a subtle, hidden warning.

◈

On a soft spring evening a week after Adam came back to Antelope he called on Laurel. For the first time he seemed restless and uneasy. After a short while Mrs. Terry took up her bonnet and decided to "visit Mrs. Greer for a spell."

Disturbed by the change in Adam, Laurel couldn't help dreading the inevitable conversation that must follow. Somehow he must have discovered her deception. Perhaps Ivy Ann had written, not knowing her twin's masquerade. Yet through the dread came relief. At least things would be clear between them.

"I have something I must tell you," Adam began. Embarrassment colored his tanned face. "It's hard to say without sounding pompous."

"Ivy Ann, I've really enjoyed spending time with you. You are so different from the girl I met in West Virginia. But I have to be honest with you, even though you may despise me for it. I hope we can continue to be *friends*." His voice underscored the word.

"You seemed so bound to your home that I never dreamed you'd come to the Wyoming Territory. Since you arrived I've tried to convince myself—Ivy Ann, when you used to write to me your sister always included a message. At first I had the two of you all mixed up together." He drew in a long breath and stood to full height.

"What I'm trying to say is that I do admire you, especially since you've become part of Antelope. But I've had time to think. I know now I fell in love with Laurel the first time I saw her. I don't know if she would ever consider me or leave West Virginia, but maybe someday." He looked at her bent head. "Forgive me if in any way I've hurt you, Ivy Ann."

*He loves me. He wants to marry me.*

Laurel wanted to shout it to the peaks and let them echo back to the valley. Exquisite delight she hadn't known existed burst into a beautiful flower.

But it died on its stalk, frozen by reality. Ivy Ann still stood between them. Not a flesh and blood Ivy Ann, but the shadowy twin whose name Laurel wore like a crown of thorns.

# Chapter 11

From the moment Ivy Ann Brown discovered Laurel had fled, everything about Red Cedars changed. Sometimes she wondered how she could have been so blind. "Shallow, foolish, vain!" she accused herself. "Why didn't I see it sooner, before my flirting and hatefulness drove Laurel away?"

Days and nights of soul-searching agony thinned Ivy to string bean proportions and left dark smudges beneath her deep brown eyes. Gradually the beaux who had once delighted her and fallen in droves for her charms deserted, lured away by jollier and more interesting girls. She cared little. Even when Beauregard Worthington's calls became fewer and fewer "due to the press of business" she only shrugged.

"Why didn't I know how much I loved Laurel and how good she was until she left?" Ivey wailed to her parents.

For perhaps the first time, they offered no excuses, no solace. "Most of the time we let the real treasures we have slip away and don't realize their worth," Thomas Brown sternly told his repentant daughter. He softened at the acute misery in her face. "We can't undo the past but we can use it to shape the future."

Sadie also suffered. Shocked by the defiance and secretiveness of her tractable Laurel, she haunted the front porch whenever anyone rode in from Shawnee. Laurel's first letter brought a certain uneasy peace.

"Thank God she's all right!" Thomas swept Sadie into a rare public embrace.

"She's happy, too," Sadie decided out loud once the letter had been read and reread. "This Mrs. Greer and Mrs. Terry sound like wonderful Christian women. Besides, Dr. Birchfield will look after her."

Thomas drew shaggy eyebrows together. "It doesn't excuse her going as she did."

"Would you have allowed her to go if she had asked?" Ivy Ann posed, not in her usual pert manner but seriously.

"Of course not!" Thomas faced west and a slow smile lightened his craggy features. "I didn't think she had it in her."

Every letter brought glowing reports of the beauties of the Wyoming Territory. Each message invited, not in words, but with the challenges Laurel had found, coupled with her experiences, the memory of Adam Birchfield's strong views on the need for godly men and women to help settle the West.

Ivy Ann could see the effect of the long family discussions, first on her father, then on her mother, and last of all on herself. Inspired by her complete confession to God asking for His forgiveness, she found herself tantalized and drawn by the vastness of the unknown frontier that had swallowed Laurel. She also missed her twin with every fiber of her being. *Strange, she had always believed Laurel relied on her.*

Not one of the three Browns could remember when the tone of the conversation changed from, "If we should ever" to "When we get to Wyoming. . . ."

"Shall we write and tell Laurel?" became the hotly debated question. Thomas favored a blunt admission that through business connections he'd arranged to buy a ranch near Antelope and that Red Cedars had been eagerly snatched up by some of Beauregard Worthington's contacts.

Ivy Ann definitely wanted to surprise her twin. She had begun and discarded a dozen letters to tell Laurel how much she had changed. None came close to what lay in her heart. "I need to look into her eyes so she will know it is true," she told her parents.

Sadie remained undecided about telling Laurel but sang louder than ever while she did the hundreds of things necessary to turn over the property to its new owners. Many a tear dampened her work apron at the thought of leaving Black-eyed Susan, Gentian, and their families. Yet her sturdy pioneer spirit rose up and sustained her. Soon she would be a part of the new flood of expansion sweeping America, and soon she would see Laurel.

At last Ivy Ann persuaded her mother to side with her and Thomas reluctantly gave in. Laurel would not be told.

"Just think of her face when we knock on Mrs. Terry's door and ask for Miss Brown." Ivy Ann gleefully clapped her hands. Sincere and repentant she might be, but her unquenchable spirit of fun had bounced back like an India rubber ball.

A flurry of farewell parties with a dozen suitors wondering how they could temporarily have thought Ivy Ann dull swept by until the perfect June morning when the Browns turned their backs on Red Cedars and faced west.

The long train journey offered time to hear all the details of the new life that lay ahead. Thomas looked ten years younger, so fired was he with enthusiasm and vigor. "The ranch we're getting is actually part of one of the largest spreads near Antelope."

Ivy hid a smile at the word *spread*. Ever since they started talking of going West, western colloquialisms, courtesy of Mr. Hardwick, sprinkled her father's conversation.

"Mr. Hardwick, who owns the Lazy H, had such terrible losses due to the unusually cold winter he's been forced to sell or go under," said Thomas as he took writing materials from his bag and drew squiggly letters. "This is the Lazy H cattle and horse brand. See? The *H* is lying down on the job."

"What will our brand be?" Ivy Ann peered at the paper with interest.

"Hardwick suggested we use the Double B." Thomas drew another figure ℞ ℞. "It will be easy to brand over the Lazy H because it only needs a few curves to change."

Sadie looked worried. "I'm not sure I like a purchase where we don't know the seller. What if he cheats us or doesn't furnish as many cattle as the contract calls for? We put most of what we got from Red Cedars into this."

"My dear, this Hardwick is so well thought of and trusted on the range that every person our agent talked with flared up at the idea he'd ever cheat anyone. Most of them just do business with a handshake and Hardwick's never been known to go back on his word." When Sadie didn't look totally convinced, Thomas continued. "Besides, it isn't like we're going into partnership. The sections of range we just bought are separated from the Lazy H by a parcel of land owned by someone else. That's one reason Hardwick let some of his holdings go." A frown flickered. "I kind of wish we were snuggled up to the Lazy H but, according to my man, whoever owns the in-between strip of land has never done anything with it except collect fees for grazing of Lazy H cattle."

Any time interest in the changing scenery lagged, the fascinating subject of the new Double B rose to be explored.

State after state surrendered to the steady *clack-clack* of the train's churning wheels until as Adam and then Laurel had done the Browns gazed in awe at the Rocky Mountains and knew their destination could not be far off. Like the two travelers before them, the clear distance deceived Thomas, Sadie, and Ivy Ann.

Once Ivy cried out, "Look! Those must be the pronghorns Adam told us about." Spellbound, the easterners watched a small band standing with raised heads and staring intently at the train. A heartbeat later they moved into single file and fled faster than anything the Browns had ever seen.

"They can reach speeds of up to sixty miles an hour," a fellow passenger told the enthralled travelers.

Ivy Ann pressed her nose to the train window until the last of the graceful animals disappeared from sight. *Would the rest of the Wyoming Territory prove as new and intriguing?* The answer would come soon enough.

✍

Adam's declaration of love for a girl he believed to be safely back home in West Virginia changed Laurel's troubles to disaster. All the sweetness of being loved by the finest man she had ever known turned sour because of her deception. The sword of Damocles that legend said once hung by a single hair paled next to the weight pressing down on Laurel.

*Tell him*, her conscience ordered night and day.

*I can't*, her weaker side protested. *What if he despises me and I lose his love?* Yet even the weak side had no answer to conscience's retort.

*How is waiting going to help? You have to confess sometime.*

So she stitched seams and hemmed gowns, smocked and tucked, and tried to ease her conscience and aching heart that leaped each time she saw Adam. How hard was the way of a deceiver! Basically honest, Laurel hated the role she played yet feared what Adam would say. His integrity that first won her respect then love worked against her now.

*Just a few more days*, she promised herself, then the days stretched into weeks. Early summer came in all its Wyoming glory and Laurel still had not confessed.

While she struggled, so did Adam to his own amazement. He had been so sure of himself about Laurel and his feelings he confidently expected every worry would slide away regarding the future. Nothing prepared him for the tumult that continued to rage inside him, stilled only by Antelope's demands on him for skill and comfort.

"I never dreamed Ivy Ann could change so," he told his horse a dozen times. "All the wonderful qualities I saw in Laurel are magnified in Ivy since she came!" As he raised his face toward the blue heavens where fleecy clouds played tag, he prayed, "Dear God, can a man be in love with two women at the same time?"

His question remained unanswered and a startling happening drove it and other things from Adam's mind. News came that the Rock Springs bank had been robbed. Antelope perked up its ears, especially when the amazing truth came out: No masked men had appeared. No dynamite or the usual paraphernalia of such robberies had been used. Someone, evidently in broad daylight, had simply marched in without being observed and helped himself. Or some wily, unauthorized person had a key and had come at night.

Rumors flew like cawing crows. Good citizens shook their heads and wondered. If anyone had information, it stayed locked behind securely fastened lips.

Following the robbery ranchers reported missing cattle and horses. Not in large numbers but enough that at first the range riders simply felt they'd drifted into draws. Horses known for their speed and endurance mysteriously escaped from corrals.

Hardwick reached the point of near explosion. "Here I've sold a piece of land and a stated number of animals in good faith," he said as he scratched his grizzled head. "Doc, it beats me how these dirty skunks can sneak in, cut out the best, and get away without someone seein' them." He held his muscular arm steady while Adam cleansed a nasty cut and dressed it.

"You say you've sold part of the Lazy H?"

"Had to." The terse reply said everything. "A few more hard

winters like this one and I'd be out of ranching." He fumbled with the button on his sleeve.

"Who bought it?"

"Some feller from back—"

"Hey, Doc!" The door opened and a freckle-faced gap-toothed boy burst in. "You're needed at the Pronghorn. Right now. There's been a fight an' a bunch of guys are about dead!" He slammed back out.

Adam grabbed his medical bag and overtook the excited youngster halfway to the saloon. Sometimes he felt like refusing to patch up men who fought for entertainment or because they wouldn't take anything off anyone else. He shook his head and lengthened his stride. Never in his life had he turned his back on need and he couldn't start now, no matter how disgusted he might be.

When he stepped inside the saloon, a strangely silent crowd parted like the Red Sea and fell back to make a path for him.

"Who's hurt worst?" He rolled up his sleeves and started to work, relieved that no one was "about dead" after all. When he had set a broken arm, staunched the blood from a head wound, and tended to various cuts and bruises he faced the motley group. "How many more of you are going to wind up like these men? Or like those? He pointed out the open window toward the little cemetery at the end of town. "Don't any of you have brains enough to know that brawling settles absolutely nothing?"

"Sounds like we've got two preachers in this town instead of just one," a lazy voice drawled.

Adam whipped around, furious at the contemptuous comment. Dan Sharpe lounged in a chair tipped back against the wall with the two front legs in the air. Voices nervously tittered but the laughter Adam might have expected never came.

"I'm no preacher but I'm fed up with this kind of thing." His deadly quiet voice stilled the shuffle of feet that had greeted his outburst.

The chair came down in a hurry. Dan bounded up like a tiger, and his mirthless grin made the resemblance even more striking. Every curve of his tensed body showed all he needed to spring was a single word from Adam. "Trying to make Antelope a better place for—the ladies?"

His meaning was absolutely clear. Everyone in Antelope knew Dan Sharpe had fallen for Ivy Ann Brown like a second-rate rider. Even those who admired Dan muttered an inaudible protest that spurred Adam into action. Black rage erased his hatred of violence. In two quick steps he reached Dan, snatched a handful of deerskin shirt, and threw the shorter man back in his chair.

Faster than hail Dan reached for the gun hanging low on his right hip. Before it cleared the holster a mighty kick crumpled him into stomach-clutching misery and disabled him. In silence Adam Birchfield turned his back and strode out of the Pronghorn. A moment later he came back in. "He may have a broke rib or two. If he does, haul him down to my office."

For a time Antelope held its breath and waited. How would Dan respond? No one knew, not even his most trusted henchmen. His ribs had not been broken. Neither had he suffered permanent damage except to his ego. Three days later he stepped from the saloon just as Adam and Nat came out of the Greers' general store.

"Hold on there!" he called, and rapidly walked down the dusty street.

Adam and Nat froze. Unarmed, they could only watch Dan advance. Faces popped into windows. Men, women, and children on the street scurried for shelter from the inevitable fight. Nat involuntarily started to step forward and shield his brother but an iron hand restrained him as Adam's hoarse voice ordered, "No, this is my fight."

To the town's astonishment, Dan stopped a few feet from the brothers, took off his hat with his left hand and held out his right. His clear voice reached everyone around. "Sorry, Birchfield. I was way out of line. No hard feelings?"

A little warning bell inside Adam told him not to trust Dan Sharpe any farther than he could see. Yet he had no choice but to accept the proffered hand. Someone coughed and a few cheered. Others looked disappointed at being cheated of a fight. But Dan clapped his hat back on his head, grinned a snowy grin, and marched into the Silver saloon.

Adam overheard one old-timer mutter, "That devil! Knows even the worst of us won't stand for some things. Now he walks off like a hero." A stream of dark brown tobacco juice pinged against a rock in the road. "Hope Doc's smart enough not to be fooled by that coyote in the chicken coop." He came over to Adam, walking with the uneven, bowlegged gait of a man more used to straddling a horse than hoofing it. "Sonny, don't you never turn your back on Dan Sharpe." He went on down the street before Adam could answer.

"I'm afraid you've made an enemy," Nat told him soberly.

Adam shrugged. "It won't be the last, I'm sure." He unseeingly gazed off down the street then looked up at the mountains. "Like you told me before I came, it's a rough land out here."

"You haven't changed your mind about staying?" Nat asked.

"No, but I've sure changed my mind about myself." Adam's clear laugh rang out. "I always felt I could be in control of any situation. Now I know that underneath the surface lies more anger than I ever dreamed possible!"

Before long the incident had slipped into the graveyard of stale news. Nat and Adam continued with their busy lives. Dan took advantage of the summer months to widen and better the rough wagon track into Antelope. Laurel gathered her courage to speak a dozen times and finally promised herself that the next time Adam came to see her she would trust in his love and tell him the truth. She secretly rejoiced when that time of reckoning was postponed due to a rash of illnesses and minor accidents.

One golden afternoon loud shouts brought her and Mrs. Terry to their cabin door. "Dan Sharpe's back," rang in the streets.

Widow Terry's face lightened. "Ivy Ann, go see if he brought back our bolts of cloth, will you?"

Glad to escape her own thoughts, Laurel lightly ran over to the main street. She saw Adam hastening toward the general store and she waved. He raised his hand, smiled, and froze when a familiar figure in a blue dress alit from Dan Sharpe's wagon.

She straightened her hat, and looked inquiringly around her. Suddenly she caught sight of the blue-clad statue whose hand remained upraised. "Laurel!" Ivy Ann gathered her skirts around her and sped down the street. "Surprise! We're here for good!"

Laurel watched her twin come as if in a dream. Surely it couldn't be happening, just when she had promised God to make things right with Adam, no matter what the cost.

Yet it *had* happened. She had waited too long.

# Chapter 12

The arrival of the real Ivy Ann Brown and her parents—and the untangling of why Laurel had chosen to masquerade as her twin—offered an even more interesting topic of discussion than the Rock Springs bank robbery. After the first initial shock, when Adam's heart had cried out in gladness at the sight of that blue gown, he fell prey to more emotions than he had known existed: disillusionment that the young woman he had put on a pedestal could have deceived him; joy that the real Laurel was not Ivy Ann; and wariness in his dealings with either twin. When Nat began squiring Laurel, all he felt was jealousy, pure and simple.

Dan Sharpe soon transferred his affections. Ivy Ann's welcome of him as part of her new life soothed the blow to his vanity that Laurel had dealt with her indifference. He even accompanied Ivy to church at her insistence. Caught up in gladness over being with Laurel again, Ivy took to the range like a rabbit to its burrow. Never a Sunday afternoon passed but what the wide porch of the old ranchhouse on the Double B was crowded with riders in their best.

During the week, Ivy Ann rode with whatever hand she could pry loose from her father's iron supervision. To the family's amazement, Laurel preferred to stay in town with Mrs. Terry and keep her job until winter when the married daughter and son-in-law planned to come back, build onto the cabin, and live with the kindly woman.

"I started a job and I'd like to finish it," she wistfully told her parents. She didn't add that even glimpses of Adam rewarded her diligent search for him every time she went out. Or that

Nat offered strong support. He had come the same evening her family arrived and asked to see her alone.

"It's been a terrible shock but I believe that in time he will forgive you," Nat comforted. "In the meantime, may I accompany you now and then?" He added irrelevantly, "That sister of yours could be quite a woman if she were more like you."

At last they arranged things so Laurel would go home weekends but stay in town during the week. Before long and in spite of her own preoccupation, Laurel saw small signs that convinced her Nat had fallen in love with Ivy Ann. Poor Nat! Although she could see some changes in Ivy, the chances she would ever consider marrying a minister were a thousand to one. Nat never expressed his feelings but Laurel felt sure she saw them in his dark, expressive eyes.

"Ivy Ann," Laurel said one Sunday evening just before she left to ride back to Antelope, "I don't want to interfere but you do know Dan Sharpe is in love with you?"

"As if any decent girl could care for him," Ivy scoffed and shook her light brown curls until they danced. "He is so stuck on himself I wouldn't be surprised if he tries to tell God when to make the sun come up and go down!" A shrewd look made her appear far older than almost twenty-one. "Besides, Sally Mae said Dan was crazy about you. The only reason he likes me is to get back at you for turning him down."

"Don't be foolish." Laurel blushed.

Ivy Ann stretched her round white arms, bare to the elbow. "You know who I think is the nicest man out here?"

*Adam*, Laurel's aching heart cried. She sat up straight on her sister's bed.

"Nathaniel Birchfield." Warm color added beauty to the lightly tanned face and her dark eyes shone. "I know he'd never look at me and I could never be good enough for him, but I do admire him. He's so much like Adam, and then some."

Laurel felt relief pour through her. Just having Ivy not interested in Adam meant a lot. She considered dropping a hint to her twin and changed her mind immediately. *Once before she had fallen into a mess because of Ivy Ann. Never again.*

The following Saturday dawned as one of the most beautiful days of summer. Laurel and Ivy Ann scorned the hopeful offers of a dozen escorts and set out for a long ride. Delicious and filling sandwiches, cookies, and two blushing peaches from some Dan Sharpe had brought rested in their saddle bags. Their canteens were full in case they chose to go up rather than down to the river or if they didn't find a stream to quench their summer thirst.

"Do you realize this will be the longest time we've had together since I got here?" Ivy Ann reined in her mount atop a low rise that afforded a view of the rolling Double B with its surrounding mountains.

"I know, it's wonderful." Laurel meant it. The new twin her sister had become didn't jangle on Laurel's nerves but offered the same companionship they'd known before Ivy Ann discovered beaux.

"We have to stay on main trails," she warned and nudged her horse's sides with her heels.

"You won't catch me getting lost in this place," Ivy Ann said emphatically and she lifted one eyebrow. "Of course, if the right person or persons came along to rescue us—"

"You're impossible!" Laurel couldn't help laughing and thinking it wouldn't be so bad after all, provided that rescue party included Adam.

Three hours later she paid for her daydreaming. With Laurel's hands slack on the reins as her horse stepped into a gopher hole,

Laurel pitched over the horse's head and landed in a heap.

"*Laurel*!" Ivy Ann screamed then slid from her horse and ran to her sister. "Are you hurt?"

Laurel shook her head and spit out a mouthful of pine needles. "Ugh! I don't think so, oh, oh." She tried to stand but went down when her ankle refused to support her. "I—I guess I sprained it." She felt her ankle gingerly. "I don't think anything's broken."

"Good." Ivy Ann pushed Laurel's hand away and gently pulled off her boot. "It's starting to swell."

Laurel's horrified gaze riveted on the ankle.

"Can you ride with it like that?"

Laurel shook her head. "You'll have to go for help."

"And leave you?" Tears streamed down her cheeks, and Ivy glanced around the country that had seemed so beautiful but now appeared threatening.

"We have no choice." Laurel knew she had to be strong. "Leave me some of the sandwiches and. . . ." She broke off and stared behind Ivy Ann.

"What's wrong?" Ivy turned.

"I thought I saw something move behind that big pine but I guess there's nothing there."

Ivy Ann cast a fearful glance then bravely marched to it. "I don't see anything." She looked at the sky and noted the sun's position. "Why can't I just stay with you? Daddy will send someone."

"But not for hours," Laurel pointed out, as she bit her lip against the pain and fear falling over her like a blanket. "We told them we'd be gone all day. Hurry home and get help."

Five minutes later she watched her twin bolting down the grassy hillside and out of sight as if the devil himself pursued her.

Another few minutes passed before a familiar drawling

voice cut the eerie silence. "Well, Miss Ivy Ann. I've been biding my time just waiting to cut you out of the herd. Looks like it's paid off."

Laurel twisted her body and stared straight into Dan Sharpe's tiger eyes, more amber than ever in contrast to his bay horse.

"I'm not—" *Ivy Ann*, she started to say.

He didn't let her finish. "What happened?" He stepped nearer and genuine concern showed when he saw her exposed ankle. "You really messed yourself up, didn't you?" He dropped to his knees and pressed here and there.

"That hurts!" Laurel tried to pull her foot free but Dan held it fast.

"I'm on my knees to you. Isn't that what every girl wants?" Again he gave her no time to answer but sauntered to her horse. He grunted when he found the sandwiches carefully wrapped in an old napkin and transferred them to a clean rock nearby. "I'm not skilled like the Doc but wrapping it will help enough so you can ride." He deftly made a bandage and tied the ends.

"My sister has gone for help, thank you." Laurel's icy tones didn't faze him.

"Oh, we won't be going exactly the same way." He shoved his hat back on his head, more predatory than ever. "I know this nice little place not far from here where we can stay, that is, until you promise to marry me."

*"Marry you?" Was he totally mad?* Laurel's brain seemed to explode.

"Look, Ivy Ann." He hunkered back on his boot heels. "If you're going to live out here you need a husband. The sooner the better. I've never asked a woman to marry me and I never thought I would but you aren't just any woman. First off, I fell for your sister but since getting to know you, I decided I like your spunk better." He smiled and she wanted to hit him.

"Now I'm going to get you onto your horse. Don't get any wild ideas about running away because I can catch you."

"You will be hanged for this," Laurel predicted, her tone cold and clear in spite of the hot day. "Even Antelope, wild as it is, won't allow a kidnapping."

"My dear, ignorant girl." He raised his tawny eyebrows in mock surprise. "An elopement isn't considered kidnapping even in the East, is it? I'll get you settled comfortably and go find a preacher. Sorry you can't have a church wedding and all that with the Reverend Birchfield presiding, but I know a justice of the peace who will come for certain considerations and keep his mouth shut about any story a timid bride might concoct."

*Dear God, are You here?* Laurel looked up with a silent cry in her heart. The same snow-topped mountains she loved reared against the same sky. Uneasy peace nudged aside some of her fears as she clung to her faith and trust in God with all her heart and soul.

Even when her lips whitened with pain as Dan lifted her into the saddle she held back tears.

"This is no good," he said as he lifted her off and laid her back on the needle-covered ground. The he smartly slapped her horse's rump. "He will head for home," Dan said. "They'll think he broke free." He picked her up and in spite of his small stature easily carried her to the bay and mounted, cradling her so her injured foot could be supported across the saddle.

"They will track us," Laurel warned through waves of pain when he started.

"Not where we're going." He chuckled and a few minutes later when he left the soft ground and his horse's hooves clattered on rocks it took everything Laurel had to keep her from despair.

Too engrossed with carrying the injured girl to heed his

surroundings, Dan's usually keen hearing missed small, cautious sounds that warned someone pursued them. Ivy Ann had no more than ridden out of sight when she realized she still carried the water canteen. Wheeling her horse back the way she had come, uneasiness filled her as she glanced around. *Why did she feel another presence? Had Laurel really seen something move?*

The thud of hooves roused Ivy and she swung her horse out of the way of the approaching steed headed straight toward her. Her eyes widened. Laurel had ridden that very horse this morning! She watched the frightened beast rush by, obviously headed for the Double B. *What had happened to terrify him like that?* she wondered.

Ivy Ann set her mouth in a straight, unyielding line. Something peculiar must be happening where she'd left Laurel and she had to know what it was. She slid from the saddle while still a short distance from the site of Laurel's accident and tied her horse to a tree, making sure the knots would hold. "Stay here and be quiet," she ordered.

Dodging behind trees Ivy sneaked back, her heart pounding from exertion, fear, and caution. Low voices reached her. A spurt of gladness vanished when she peeped out from her sheltered position. She shoved her hand over her mouth to keep back a cry.

In the clearing before her Dan Sharpe was mounting a strong bay, and he had Laurel in his arms.

"They will track us." Laurel's faint words reached her twin's straining ears.

"Not where we're going." Ivy hated Dan's laugh. Rebellion rose in a wave of protest but she sensibly stayed out of sight. *That's what you think*, she thought to herself. Her busy fingers jerked off the scarf she wore under her chin and methodically tore it into narrow strips. "Just like in the storybooks." She grinned in spite of her worry and slipped back for her horse.

Step by careful step Ivy Ann followed the doubly burdened bay. When they reached the rocks and the horse ahead clattered on them, Ivy's hope failed. "Dear God, now what?" A few minutes later the pampered girl who must now become resourceful managed to fashion pads for her own mount's hooves of Sadie Brown's worn tablecloth.

Ivy Ann listened hard to make sure she was still on the right trail. The distant crack of sturdily shod hooves on rock rewarded her and she swung back into the saddle, hot and tired but filled with the most satisfaction she had ever experienced. The next instant she bowed her head. "Thank you, God. I know You helped me think what to do."

All afternoon she trailed her quarry from afar. She only caught glimpses now and then. To allow her horse to get too close to the bay could result in disaster if either whinnied.

Just when the drooping girl felt she couldn't stay in the saddle one more minute, she heard Dan Sharpe's "Whoa." She straightened and stopped her horse. Again she tied him. Again she sneaked forward and peered out from cover like a ground squirrel from under a bush. Dan had dismounted and the open door of a rude shack bore witness he had reached his destination.

Ivy Ann crept closer. *If only the shack had a window!* She wormed her way around back and confronted a blank, weather-beaten solid wall. A little sob reached her throat and she backed toward the side of the cabin. Concern for Laurel overcame prudence. She stepped on a large dry pine cone and its disintegration came with a riflelike crack.

Strong hands fastened on her shoulders and whirled her around. "Who—what—?" Dan Sharpe's mouth fell open but his grip didn't diminish.

"Hello, Dan." She jerked free in spite of the searing pain it cost her.

"Laurel? No, Ivy Ann. But—" He turned his head toward the shack. The next instant he had forced her ahead of him around the corner, onto the rotting porch and through the door of the shack.

Laurel sat on a blanketed cot, her injured ankle straight out before her. Her eyes darkened when Ivy Ann burst in with Dan just behind.

"Why didn't you tell me you weren't Ivy Ann?" Dan raged. "Some more of your smart tricks?" When neither girl replied he flung his hat onto a dirty table and wiped the sweat from his forehead. His smile slowly replaced the anger in his face but its chill roused more fear in Laurel than his accusations. She glanced at Ivy who had closed her eyes, swallowed convulsively, and then opened them with a disarming expression.

"Looks like you won the jackpot, doesn't it, Dan?" Her rueful smile and the way she rubbed her aching shoulders made Laurel gasp as well as Dan. "Here we are. Now what?"

In the split second Dan's gaze left her and traveled to Laurel, Ivy glanced around the cabin for a weapon. If this were a novel an old knife should be sticking in the wall. Even if she could find one, could she bring herself to stab Dan? She shuddered at the thought then steeled herself at the gloating in Dan's eyes when he turned back to her. Laurel couldn't help; anything done to free them must come from Ivy.

"Just what *are* your plans?" tore from her throat.

"I had planned to tie up my bride-to-be and go get a justice of the peace," Dan responded.

Horror showed in Laurel's face and in the heartbeat before Ivy Ann spoke a hundred thoughts thundered into her brain. For the first time in her life she had the chance to do something worthy. If it meant sacrificing herself to save Laurel, then she had no choice. *Dear God, give me strength.* Ivy clasped her hands in front of her in a demure pose. She glanced down then up through her lashes in the coquettish way she had done so often.

"You went to all this trouble just to marry me? Why, Dan, I'm flattered beyond belief." She forced herself to smile and look around the cabin as if considering every spider web and speck of dust. "It isn't the exact surroundings I'd have picked, but if people are in love, it doesn't matter, does it?" *All true*, she soothed her protesting conscience. Her keen gaze hesitated on the untidy stack of cut branches near the rough fireplace then turned back to Dan. He must not know her plans. She proudly lifted her chin in the best Brown manner.

"Laurel, you will be my bridesmaid, won't you?" She laughed into the two faces staring at her like white blobs and triumphed over her fear.

"No, oh no!" Laurel leaped to her feet without regard to her ankle then crumpled to the floor.

With an oath Dan sprang to lift her back on to the cot but not as quickly as Ivy Ann. With a silent cry to God for help she bounded the few steps toward the wood pile, snatched the strongest looking length of pine branch, raised it, and sent it crashing against the back of Dan Sharpe's head.

He collapsed without a single cry as Laurel fell to the cot.

# Chapter 13

Ivy Ann stood frozen to the dirty cabin floor, still clutching her weapon. A slight moan and movement showed she had not knocked Dan completely out, only stunned him. With wisdom born of prayer and desperation she ordered, "Quick, Laurel, we have to tie him."

Laurel pushed back the nausea that had risen when she jumped to her feet and ignored her throbbing ankle. "Help me tear the blanket," she cried. Four hands working as two rent the old blanket and Ivy Ann put the strips round and around Dan, tying strong knots where the pieces joined. By the time Ivy rolled him onto another cot and wound more blanket strips to pinion him exhaustion threatened her.

"You'd better look at the damage you did to his head." Laurel's faint reminder sent her twin into hysterical giggles that ended with healing tears.

"A big bump but it didn't break the skin," Ivy said after examining Dan. She shrank back when he blinked and opened his eyes. Even in anger there had been a certain respect. Now hatred made him more dangerous than ever.

"I'll get even," he threatened. With mighty efforts he fought against his bonds. They didn't give as the twins had feared they might. But his struggles and twistings accomplished a lot more than he expected. Stubbornly refusing to admit defeat at the hands of two young women, Dan tipped over the cot and landed on the floor. The force of his fall broke the cot free from the moldy wall where it had been attached.

"*Look!*" Laurel pointed at the gaping hole exposed just under where the cot had come free. "A hiding place."

"*Don't touch that!*" Dan lost control and for the first time fear mingled with his anger.

It was too late. Ivy Ann had already grabbed the contents of the niche and carried it to the tottery table. She threw open the mouth of one of the sacks. Money spilled out. Bills, gold coins, and eventually the incrimination papers lettered *Rock Springs Bank* were all there.

"Well, Mr. Bank Robber. It looks like you'll have more to face than abducting Laurel." Ivy Ann's contempt was thick enough to cut.

Game to the very end, Dan merely smirked. "You can't prove anything."

"You had a reason for coming to this cabin, Dan," Ivy reminded.

Dan managed a shrug in spite of his position on the floor. He shifted his weight and growled. "Help me up, will you?"

It took all Ivy Ann's remaining gumption to right the cot then she faced him squarely. "Dan, if Laurel and I tell the ranchers what you tried to do today they'll hang you." She shuddered and some of her fearlessness left. "If you confess to the bank robbery it will mean prison but not death. Which do you choose?"

Dan's jaw dropped in amazement. A flicker of something neither twin had ever seen in him surfaced into his eyes. "You mean you'll say nothing if I admit to the robbery?"

Ivy Ann turned to Laurel who nodded. "You have our word."

"But why?" Dull red marred the tan skin, the red of shame before such generosity. "I'd think you—"

Ivy took a long, deep breath. "If this had happened a few months ago in West Virginia only Laurel would have spared you. After she left, and especially since I came out here, I've learned that a child of God cannot harbor hatred, no matter what." She spread her hands wide. "Dan, letting you off even when I boil inside to think how you might have actually forced Laurel into marriage—" She choked then determinedly went on. "It's for my sake as well as yours." Understanding lit up her face. "No, it isn't! It's for Jesus' sake."

An indiscernible murmur came from Dan. He ceased fighting and sagged against the blanket ropes. "You sound just like Preacher Birchfield." Astonishment still filled his face. "You and he would make a real pair."

Ivy Ann couldn't keep the hot color from her cheeks. If she had been honest, she'd have retorted, "I think so, too," but pride sealed her lips.

Laurel's anxious reminder switched her thoughts back to the present and away from some vague future possibility. "What are we going to do now?"

Ivy Ann looked at her then at Dan. With a lithe movement she stepped closer to the old cot and looked down on him. "If I untie you will you give me your word of honor you won't try to run or hold us here in any way? That you will confess you robbed the Rock Springs bank?"

"*Ivy!*"

Laurel's shocked cry didn't change her twin. "Will you?" she repeated.

The tawny eyes blinked. "You'd take my word for it?"

"If you swear to do what I say." She staked her claim on the good Thomas Brown had taught her was in every man, often hidden but there.

"I swear." The husky words brought relief to Ivy's tense body. "Do you have a knife?"

"In my belt." Dan acted dazed by the turn of events.

"We made them pretty tight," Ivy matter-of-factly stated as she began hacking away at the confining strips. When she finished, she felt relief at having come through the ordeal without real harm and a fervent prayer left Ivy's heart. One day, with God's help, Dan Sharpe might accept Jesus and leave the life he had embraced in this wild country.

Ivy dropped into an old chair. "Now all we have to do is wait until help comes." She stared out the open door, dreading the night that must pass before a rescue party arrived.

Some of Dan's sardonic humor remained. "No rescue party can find this place. Remember all the rocks we came over?" He looked down at his hands, still showing faint red streaks where Ivy had imprisoned him tightly.

"Oh, they'll come. I dropped pieces of my scarf all along the way," she told him confidently.

"Well, I'll be!" Dan threw back his head in the same way as Nat and Adam Birchfield. His laughter rang through the little cabin and the twins couldn't help joining in. Bank robber, would-be bridegroom, and rascal he might be, but that clean laugh brought back pleasant memories of when he had squired first Laurel and then Ivy Ann.

Long after Ivy Ann had served a sandwich supper supplemented by the few stores in the shack, a naughty wind wakened, came to life, and howled its protest for miles around. It left only after greedily claiming the torn scarf markers Ivy Ann had so carefully left on the trail.

All day Adam had been restless. For some unexplainable reason few patients claimed his time and by late afternoon he restlessly paced the floor of his small office.

"What's troubling you?"

Nat's voice from the open doorway stopped Adam. "Just thinking. Probably too much." He took another turn.

"About Laurel Brown." Nat's dark eyes offered sympathy.

Adam stared unseeingly out the window then glanced back

at Nat. "Why didn't she tell me? You've been with her lately." He hoped Nat hadn't caught the bitterness in his tone.

"I've thought about it even though she hasn't told me any more than you know," Nat confided.

Adam's heart beat faster. Relief nudged aside his still smoldering resentment at being made to look like a fool. Nat didn't sound as if he had fallen in love with Laurel.

Nat's fine features clouded. "Perhaps much of it goes back to always being in her sister's shadow." His gaze met his brother's frowning look. "Remember, she never—according to you—claimed to be Ivy Ann. You just assumed it."

"But she should have told me when I told her I—I—when we discussed certain things," Adam protested. Fresh disappointment pressed heavily into his soul. "She didn't lie but her silence consented to the deception."

"The one thing she ever said that gave me a clue was simply to relate what you once told her about hating deception more than anything on earth." Nat stepped inside, closed the door, and spoke boldly. "I believe Laurel cared so much for you that she followed you out here, felt cut to the heart when you mistook her for Ivy Ann, and grew terrified that you'd despise her when you learned the truth. I also think she hoped you would grow so close that you could forgive her once she found the courage to confess."

Adam listened silently, wanting to believe.

"I don't want to preach, but how many times has our Heavenly Father forgiven us when we've stumbled and been afraid or when we've made bad decisions?" For a moment his mouth twisted. "Adam, don't ever be like Father, miserable in Concord with his two sons thousands of miles away because of his unforgiving spirit." He laid one hand on his brother's shoulder and Adam felt he'd been given a blessing.

"Thanks, old man." His hand clasped Nat's. To break the quivering moment he added, "I've been coming to that conclusion. Just one thing." He paused and tightened his hold on Nat's hand. "Do you care about Laurel?"

"Very much." Mischief sparkled in Nat's dark eyes. "But I'm not in love with her. Someday, God and Ivy Ann willing, we may be brothers-in-law as well as brothers!"

A knock on the outside office door came simultaneously and Dr. Adam Birchfield found himself extremely busy for the next few hours.

Dark had encroached when a loud knocking sent Adam and Nat both to the door. Thomas Brown strode in without waiting for an invitation. His agitation showed with every jerky sentence.

"The twins didn't come home. We didn't think anything at first. They'd planned to spend the day and they know the country as far as they were going. Then Laurel's horse came in just a little bit ago. The boys rode out but it's too dark to find out anything. They're still out and we thought it would be good to have you at the ranch—both of you—just in case. . . ." His voice trailed off.

Nat and Adam sprang to attention and a few minutes later pounded down the pale moonlit road behind Thomas. Adam longed to leave the others and plunge off to the rescue but he restrained himself. He didn't know the country as well as those already searching, and if, no, *when*, the twins came in he must be at the Double B.

One by one the groups returned. Lanterns bobbed from horses' backs in a weird yellow glow that competed with the feeble moonlight. Rising wind and dancing shadows made searching impossible until morning. Somehow they lived through it, the Browns, who had faced and conquered similar fears all during the War Between the States, and the Birchfields, bonded closer than ever by their love for Laurel and Ivy Ann. Now and then one attempted to reassure the others by commenting on how trailwise the twins had become. For the most part, each kept a silent and prayerful vigil and thanked God the night stayed warm despite the screeching wind.

"At least there's two of them," said Hardwick, who had come immediately when summoned by one of the Double B hands. "We'll find them in the morning all curled up together and just waiting for us to bring breakfast."

But his prophecy was doomed from the start. Before morning the wind changed to rain and washed out the tracks needed to follow the twins.

Adam impatiently waited for dawn's gray light with a prayer for his own stubbornness following his petitions to God to be with them. First to be ready and mounted, he looked down in disbelief when pale but calm Nat stopped him from heading out in the direction the twins had first taken the morning before.

"Adam, you can't do a thing the hands can't."

Protest and denial rose in his throat but Nat never let him speak.

"Listen, the only one I know who might still find some sign after the rain is Chief Grey Eagle or Running Deer. Ride as fast as you can and ask for their help. They will never forget their debt to you for saving Running Deer." He gripped Adam's hand. "Ride as if life depended on it but still use care in the high and treacherous places."

Adam never remembered much of his ride to the Indian village. Filled with fear and worry, he scarcely saw the trail except as a hurdle that must be leaped so Laurel and Ivy Ann could be saved.

Cries of gladness greeted his arrival. He sprang from the back of his sweaty horse to greet his friends. All looked well and he rejoiced at the way Chief Grey Eagle's dead black eyes lighted. He quickly sketched the crisis: the lost young women, the wind and rain, the loss of all tracks.

"Running Deer will go." Grey Eagle gestured and in moments fresh horses stood ready. "Grey Eagle's eyes grow old but his son's are new like the morning."

"Thank you." Adam blinked hard. Not a question, not a second of hesitation, just the sending of his son. How like another Father who sent His Son to help save the lost!

He silently shook hands with Chief Grey Eagle, nodded to his old friend the medicine man and the others, then sprang to the back of the now-saddled Indian pony and rode away, humbled by the depths of gratitude in the hidden tribe.

✺

Ivy Ann awakened from her uncomfortable bed on the floor beside the fireplace to the steady drum of rain. She rubbed sleep from her eyes and stole glances at Dan and Laurel, still asleep on the rickety cots. Dan had been furious when she insisted on making a nest of old blankets and a saddle blanket for herself. "You think I'm going to sleep on the cot and let you huddle there?" He staggered a little but fiercely glared at her.

"Dan, I don't like the way your face is flushed," she told him. "I'll be fine. You have to rest." She observed again the dull color in his cheeks and his listless eyes that showed even an inexperienced nurse such as herself the presence of a low-grade fever. Only when he tried to get up and fell back from sheer weakness did Dan stop arguing.

He looked cooler this morning and Laurel's tousled light brown curls spilled over the coarse blanket in utter relaxation. At least Ivy Ann wouldn't have two patients here in this forsaken shack.

She thought of Dan's full confession the night before. His freighting in of supplies had won the confidence of those he bought from and sold to. One day he'd noticed how the Rock Springs banker carelessly left his keys on the desk while talking with Dan. A niggling idea grew. The next time Dan went to see the banker he carried a lump of soft clay in his pocket. This time the keys didn't appear but several visits later they did and when his banker acquaintance was called away for a few minutes, Dan made an impression. Later he constructed a crude key and polished it. Then one night he stole down a dark street, used his key, and helped himself. At first he secreted the money in the bottom of his wagon. When he heard of the deserted trapper's cabin he painstakingly gouged out a cache in the wall, covered by the cot.

"Why, Dan?" Ivy Ann had burst out.

He shrugged. "I always wanted a cattle ranch but never could afford one."

"And now?" Laurel's soft voice accused him as her sister's had done.

Dan's brittle laugh little resembled his earlier honest mirth. "Prison. A long stretch." He yawned and Ivy Ann saw his hand tremble. Then Dan closed his eyes and the twins sat silently. A little later, all three slept.

All that day they waited for someone to come. Dan never fell unconscious or grew delirious but Ivy Ann wouldn't let him ride out for help.

"Are you afraid I won't keep my word?" he challenged.

Surprise underlined every word. "Of course not. You just aren't in any condition to ride." One dimple showed as she couldn't resist saying, "Look, Mr. Sharpe. We're keeping still about something that could end with you dead. I'm not going to let you ride out of here, fall off your horse, and lie somewhere hurt. It wouldn't do any of us the last bit of good."

He subsided, too tired to care. "You sure pack a mean wallop." He gingerly rubbed the goose egg on the back of his head.

"I'm sorry you had to do it," he mumbled.

"So am I," Ivy Ann quietly told him. Then she gathered up the rag ropes and burned them.

Ivy Ann managed to clean up the shack a bit and, by using a few more of the old stores, get a creditable meal. "Good thing we always pack a lot more food than we need," she said. They ate and she scrubbed the battered tin dishes she'd had to wash in boiling water before using.

Evening melted into dusk. Now nothing remained except to wait.

# Chapter 14

*W*ait. The most difficult word in the English language, Adam thought. He stared into the curtain of rain just outside the rude shelter of boughs that Running Deer had constructed when a downpour caught the two on their way back to the Double B. *What went on in his companion's mind behind the dark eyes that betrayed nothing?* Running Deer seldom spoke, and when he did, only in response to Adam's direct questions. Yet in the space of an hour the Indian, with Adam's less skilled help, had found dry roots in spite of the cloudburst, built a roaring fire, and provided shelter.

*Could he have done as well?* Adam wondered. Probably not. He still had a lot to learn about survival in the Wyoming Territory. *You still have a lot to learn about forgiveness, too,* a voice inside prodded. The memory of Laurel's expression haunted him. He had originally considered it triumphant that her little joke had gone on so long. Now he knew it for pleading. If she cared as Nat felt sure, the hurt must have gone deep.

By the time the rain let up enough for Adam and Running Deer to reach the ranchhouse then follow to the spot where Nat led them to the rest of the rescue party, despair filled Adam. No one could find a sign after the rain, not even Running Deer. "How do you know they were ever here?" he asked Hardwick, who slouched low in his saddle, his hat brim down and collar turned up against the weather.

"Found tracks we recognized under a tree where the rain hadn't soaked through." Hardwick's terse reply warmed Adam but he chilled again when Hardwick continued. "Found somethin' else, too." His keen eyes bored into Adam. "You said the twins rode out alone?"

"That's right," Thomas broke in. The hours since his daughters failed to ride in had aged him.

"Well, they weren't alone all the time."

With a southerner's quickness to take offense, Thomas drew himself up and his voice turned icy. "What are you implying, sir? That my daughters planned to meet someone here?"

"Simmer down," Hardwick told the irate father. "I'm just sayin' we found tracks of three different horses." His voice softened. "Look, Tom, no one in this country would believe anythin' bad about your girls. It appears some galoot came along and—"

A call from Running Deer a little to one side of the clearing interrupted Hardwick's speculations. Adam, Nat, and the others hurried to him. The Indian silently held out a sodden bit of color-dulled cloth.

"Why, that looks like the scarf Ivy Ann wears so much." Thomas Brown reached for it.

A rare, slow smile crossed Running Deer's unreadable face.

"Where did you find it?" Hope flared in Adam's chest.

Running Deer pointed to a nearby clump of trees and Adam reached them in one leap, closely followed by Nat. Yet a thorough search disclosed no more clues.

"Spread out and search every inch of ground," Hardwick ordered. Adam stuck with Running Deer. Nat joined Thomas. The hands paired up and agreed to meet again in an hour, or to fire three shots if they discovered anything more.

For the second time that day Adam realized how far short his newly acquired woodcraft fell compared to Running Deer's skills. If the situation hadn't been so terrifying in its unknown possibilities, Adam would have rejoiced in the education he received in noticing seemingly trivial things. Running Deer left no area until he had examined the smallest patches of ground. Even when their steps clattered on rock, the tracker's intent scrutiny checked out each broken branch or overturned stone. Fifteen minutes later he dug a second bit of torn cloth from under the edge of a dislodged rock.

"Running Deer, you are a wonder!" Adam burst out in admiration. He fired into the air three times to summon the others, excitement sending relief through his tense body. But when the rescue party reassembled, to their dismay two other pairs had also found bits of scarf!

"Wind blow hard." Running Deer's sweeping gesture told the sad story. Then he turned back to his search, closely followed by a discouraged Adam.

It felt like a month later when the tracker's pleased grunt brought Adam out of his misery to stare at a track in the softer earth alongside the rocky path. Deep, partly filled with rainwater, it offered a spurt of hope.

Hardwick pushed his hat back from his grimy forehead and his eyes glistened. "Isn't there some kind of old tumbledown shack back a ways from here?"

The Indian straightened from measuring the track with his open palm. "Pony carry two. Make heavy track."

Again Adam's spirits dragged in the muddy earth. He saw Nat's concern, heard Thomas gasp, and noticed the way the searchers shifted uneasily from one foot to the other. If the horse that made the track carried two persons, one must be hurt. Hardwick's observation about three horses plus the return of Laurel's horse could mean just one thing and Adam didn't want to consider it. *Maybe not*, he told himself. Perhaps someone came along and offered assistance because the twins only had one horse between them. On the other hand, why would a Good Samaritan of the mountains head toward some

COLLEEN L. REECE

obscure hut miles away from Antelope instead of going back to the Double B?

A frantic prayer for their safety sprang from Adam's trembling heart and he silently followed Running Deer, who methodically continued his tracking.

Darkness descended before they reached the long-forsaken and overgrown trail Hardwick vaguely remembered might lead to the shack. A few more tracks and his statement that "one pony go, one follow" dished up speculation while the men drank hot coffee and ate the steaming supper Hardwick handily prepared.

Hardwick's persuasive voice and bright eyes in the firelit circle of rescuers splashed into a little pool of silence. "The way I figure it is, whoever's ridin' that second horse is the one who kept droppin' those little bitty pieces of scarf. Maybe they were tied and came off in the wind. Or maybe the person leavin' the trail didn't count on a storm."

"But what's it supposed to mean if that *is* what happened?" Thomas wanted to know. His hands gripped his tin cup until they resembled claws.

"I'd say someone—" Hardwick paused and Adam's nerves silently screamed for him to continue.

"Someone for some reason and none of us knows why must have put one of the twins on his horse and the other moseyed along behind leavin' signs for whoever came when Laurel's horse got home." Hardwick raised his coffee cup in tribute and silently drank to the resourcefulness of a tenderfoot woman smart enough not to panic but to leave evidence of her pursuit.

Hours later Nat stirred beside a wide-awake Adam. "Are you asleep?"

"No."

The strong hand that used to comfort a small boy now

gripped Adam's. "We may not know where they are but God does."

"I know." Yet dread never left Adam's heart and mind. He shifted on his pine-needle bed. "Nat, sometimes God lets things happen. Even to those who love and serve Him."

"And sometimes He doesn't." The big hand squeezed harder. "Remember what Jesus said? 'Where two or three are gathered together in my name, there am I in the midst of them.'* I'll bet there isn't a man here tonight—including Running Deer who prays to the Great Spirit—who isn't thinking of and praying for them."

Strangely calmed, his faith bolstered by the unshakable tone in his older brother's voice, Adam clasped Nat's hand until his own ached, and a little later he fell into an uneasy sleep. He awoke to a fiery, red-streaked sky that made Hardwick mutter. The search party gulped hot coffee and ate meat slapped into cold biscuits as they traveled behind Running Deer into a world where faces, rocks, and even trees reflected the awe-inspiring heavens. Deeper into the mountains they went, buoyed by Running Deer's steady progress and infrequent pointing to tracks. The red in the sky died. Gray-black clouds roiled and gathered. Running Deer stopped dead still and sniffed the air.

"By the powers, *smoke!*" Hardwick gave an exultant yell. Running Deer's rare smile came once more and he bounded down a little corridor made where branches along the little-used trail had been broken by the passage of animals. Minutes later the little group rounded a bend. Before them stood a rotting shack. Moss splotched the roof but from a crooked tin pipe came a white wisp of smoke.

"Laurel? Ivy Ann?" Thomas pushed aside the others and ran to the weathered door of the dirty cabin with his rescue party close behind. Without stopping to knock or use the caution

Hardwick would have advised, Thomas Brown crashed open the door.

"*Daddy!*" A woman with a soot-stained face from trying to heat water in the decrepit fireplace rose and flung herself into her father's arms.

Adam looked past the twin he knew was Ivy Ann, but a changed Ivy Ann with a look of maturity he'd never seen in her face. Laurel sat propped on a blanketed cot, her bandaged ankle straight out in front of her. Her pinched face had never been more beautiful to Adam. He crossed the small room with giant strides and loomed over her. "Laurel, my darling, are you all right?"

Bright tears gathered. So did color more glowing than that morning's sky. "I hurt my ankle. Mr. Sharpe, Ivy Ann, we came here and—" she faltered.

Dan Sharpe shrugged his shoulders, the flush of fever dulling his eyes but not his audacity. "I might as well 'fess up. The girls just captured themselves a bank robber." He pointed to the sacks on the rickety table, still gaping open and spilling out incriminating evidence. A ripple of shock filled the cabin.

The doctor in Adam took over. He marched to the second cot and examined Dan's head. "How did you do this?"

Dan's mouth twitched. "Took a bad fall." His eyes laughed.

"Is that right, Laurel? Ivy Ann?" Adam looked from one to the other. Something about the whole thing didn't feel right.

"He took a terrible fall," Ivy confirmed from the depths of her father's embrace. "I wouldn't let him ride for help."

"That's right." Laurel told the stunned group. "We made him swear he'd confess the robbery. He gave his word."

Hardwick said heavily, "He may be a robber but I never knew Dan Sharpe to go back on his word." He sent a piercing glance at Ivy Ann. "I reckon 'twas you who rode the horse that followed the first one. Why'd you leave pieces of your scarf?"

"I wasn't sure I could find my way back out of here," she admitted. "You see, I'd started back for help after Laurel got hurt. Then I went back to leave the canteen with her and saw Laurel's horse heading for home." She paused. "Anyway, Dan had come along and found Laurel hurt so I came after them." She rushed on. "We got here and Dan fell and I've been taking care of them and praying for someone to come." She looked up into Nathaniel Birchfield's face and something passed between them, something to be taken out and examined when the present crisis became nothing but an adventuresome memory.

"If it hadn't been for Running Deer you'd have been here a lot longer," Nat said soberly. With one accord they turned toward the open doorway.

"Why, where is he?" Adam left Laurel and raced back out the shabby door. Only the grumble of thunder in the distance and a few large rain drops spattering on the ground greeted him. "Running Deer?" Adam cupped his hands around his mouth. *"Running Deer!"*

A rough hand that still held kindness fell on Adam's shoulder. "It's no use, son. He's gone." Hardwick lowered his voice. "He did what Chief Grey Eagle sent him to do."

"I didn't even thank him."

"The way I hear tell you did that a long time ago when you and that brother of yours went to a certain hidden village and you saved Running Deer's life just like you saved my wife's."

"How did you know?" Adam whirled. "We promised not to betray the location of the tribe."

"Son, this is my country and I pretty much know what's happenin'." Hardwick grinned but his steady look never wavered. "I'm also known for keepin' my mouth shut, so don't worry none. Now come back inside. We've got to decide whether to make a run for it or stay here tonight." He glanced at the storm-laden sky. "I person'ly vote for stayin'. The horses are tired and it will give the girls and Dan a little extra time." He sighed and his good humor faded. "Sure hate to find out Dan Sharpe's a thief. He's gotta be punished and they'll give him a lot of time for this. Maybe since he surrendered nice and gentlemanlike, and since everyone will get their money back, the judge won't go too hard on him."

Later that night when the newcomers disposed of themselves as well as they could on the floor and were joined by Dan who refused to let Ivy Ann sleep on the floor again, Adam heard Hardwick whispering. He strained his ears to hear.

"Sharpe, if I thought there was more to all this than the girls are tellin' I'd horsewhip you 'til there wasn't enough left for trial."

Adam's heart skipped a beat when Dan retorted half under his breath, "Go to the devil, Hardwick. Are you questioning the word of the two finest girls that ever hit the Wyoming Territory, or anywhere else?"

Hardwick grunted and subsided. Adam lay awake to marvel. Rogue, rascal, and bank robber, Dan Sharpe still recognized and bowed before the simple goodness of Christian women. How right Nat had been about the need for such women in this wild place! How many would-be Dans remained for the Brown twins and others to influence, to catch before they turned to crime and wickedness?

He thought of Mark Justice who continued to baffle his pards by accepting Jesus Christ. One or two even came to church with Mark occasionally. God grant that the tiny seeds being dropped along the way, as Ivy Ann had dropped pieces of her scarf, would take root and not be blown away with the first wind that came.

For another day and night the new fall storm imprisoned the group. The cowboys made no attempt to hide their admiration for the plucky twins or their disgust for Dan, the fallen. Thomas beamed and lamented, "If only Sadie could know everything's all right!"

Hardwick offered the opinion that Running Deer would stop at the Double B before heading home. Adam couldn't keep himself from staring at Laurel and checking her ankle often merely to be close to her. Nat and Ivy Ann exchanged furtive glances that brought color to both faces and warmth to Adam's soul.

Pale sun greeted the new day. A weary band of riders swept into the Double B in late afternoon. Laurel and Ivy Ann waved goodbye to Nat, Adam, and Hardwick who officially escorted Dan Sharpe back to Antelope and to jail. Limping inside, they bathed and fell into their beds.

Laurel woke first. Ivy Ann lay in the abandonment of deep sleep, her arms spread wide like a broken doll's. Laurel studied her twin's face. A new set to Ivy's red lips showed the results of taking responsibility and facing fear.

Laurel stretched and slid deeper into her quilts. Her ankle barely twinged. Now she had time to take out of hiding the look Adam bestowed on her when he followed Thomas into the shack and the timbre of his voice when he called her darling. Instead of the censure she had learned to expect, forgiveness and something more made her heart pound and her pulse race even harder than that awful moment when Ivy Ann struck Dan and he tumbled to the floor.

"Laurel?" Ivy Ann sat bolt upright in bed. Her cambric nightgown rose and fell with her breathing. Hair tousled and face flushed, the new love and concern in her face touched Laurel deeply. "Are you really, truly all right?"

Sheer happiness spilled into laughter and Laurel stretched.

"Thanks to God and Adam and Running Deer and the rest,

I'm really, truly all right."

"You left out Nat!" Ivy Ann protested.

"I wouldn't want to do that," Laurel teased and caught the telltale color in Ivy's face. She propped herself up on one elbow and rested her chin in her hand. "You'd better not, either. I have a strong feeling Nathaniel Birchfield isn't about to let himself be left out, especially when it comes to one Ivy Ann Brown.

"You really think so?" Could this be the remote, heartless twin who had delighted in collecting and discharging beaux the way children do dandelions?

Ivy Ann interlaced her fingers and stared at her sister with a new humility. "If he doesn't love me I'll—I'll—"

"Not die. Only heroines in novels languish away, not pioneer young women in the Wyoming Territory."

"Of all the callous individuals! Never in all my born days did I expect that my own twin sister would be so unsympathetic." Ivy Ann snatched her lacy pillow and fired it at Laurel with some of her old imperiousness. But the next moment she sank back into a little heap and stared at Laurel from tragic dark eyes. "If you had any feeling in you at all you'd know the very idea Nat may still think I could never make a good minister's wife leaves me sick and so scared I don't know what to do." She sighed and stared. "I wonder how long it will take me to show him I've changed?" She didn't seem to notice how Laurel flinched.

*Chapter 15*

Dan Sharpe received a sentence of twenty years of hard labor in prison for robbing the Rock Springs bank. The town of Antelope buzzed with the men upholding the sentence and many of the girls and women were secretly regretful that "such a pleasant, courteous young man" could be so wicked. Sally Mae Justice and others Dan had never deigned to notice sighed at the loss of an eligible man they had considered a little above the cowboys who called on them.

Laurel and Ivy Ann, no worse for their escapade but far more careful, soon rode out again and marveled at the coming of autumn. Nights grew crisp. Skies took on blue tones that provided a perfect backdrop for golden aspen and cottonwood leaves by day and giant, white stars by night. Along with their new neighbors, the Browns canned and dried and pickled for the coming winter. Distant peaks, then those nearer, accepted their white winter coats while bears stuffed themselves to prepare for hibernation and squirrels and chipmunks gathered nuts and seeds and acorns against the inevitable cold.

Adam and Nat had long since visited the Indian village with packhorse loads of supplies to help Chief Grey Eagle and his people through the winter should they be snowed in and without adequate food. Their thanks to Running Deer had been brushed aside but his rare smile showed his pleasure at their visit. On that trip Nat broached the subject of bringing the twins to see the village.

"Are women your wives?" Chief Grey Eagle demanded.

Adam and Nat looked at each other and grinned. "Not yet but we hope soon," Nat confessed and dug his toe in the ground

145

like a small boy caught in mischief. Adam wanted to laugh.

"Will betray Chief Eagle's nest?"

"No, Chief. Laurel and Ivy Ann know how to keep secrets." Adam's heart added, *and how!*

"You bring them. Soon, before snow comes."

The following Saturday Nat and Ivy Ann and Adam and Laurel rode out from the Double B the way they had done many times. No one paid any particular attention except one of the cowboys perched on the rail of the corral. "I wish I had a purty gal to ride with instead of bein' a pore, lonesome cowpoke." His grin flashed white. "Maybe I shoulda been a doc or a preacher." He scratched his head when everyone laughed.

"I don't see nothin' funny but then I'm just a—"

"Pore, lonesome cowboy," Ivy and Laurel finished for him.

They rode away from his good-natured complaining into the happiness only the young and in love can know on a western Wyoming autumn day.

Adam suddenly realized something that had been nibbling at him for several weeks. "You don't dress alike anymore, do you?" He glanced from Laurel to Ivy Ann and back.

Laurel's long lashes hid her eyes as she sounded demure. "We're afraid someone might take us for each other and we can't chance that." She looked up and smiled.

Adam causally added, "Good idea. It can save a heap of trouble, as Hardwick says." The minute the words left his mouth he regretted them. Laurel's face turned scarlet and her smile faded. *How sensitive she was,* he thought. A protective wave of love flowed through Adam and he reined in his horse. "Laurel, there's something I must say to you."

"I know." It came out as barely a whisper but she courageously raised her head and looked directly into his eyes. "Before you do, I want you to know I really meant to tell you I wasn't

Ivy Ann." The words rushed out like the gurgling brook back home. "I had promised myself that the very next time you called I would confess but then Ivy Ann came. I had waited too long." Her lips trembled. "My only excuse is that I couldn't bear for you to think badly of me." She seemed to droop in the saddle.

The last trace of lingering resentment fled forever. Adam dismounted more rapidly than ever before, reached up both hands, and helped Laurel to the ground. But instead of releasing her, he put his hands on her shoulders and drew her close. "I've been mule-stubborn and unforgiving and for the rest of my life I'll regret it," he told her. "Laurel, a long time ago I told you how love came without my realizing it when I first saw you on the porch of Red Cedars in your blue dress." He saw hope spring to her dark eyes and tenderly pulled her unresisting form so close her head rested against his chest just under his chin.

"If you think you can forgive me, Miss Mountain Laurel Brown, I'd like to ask your father for your hand in marriage." The formal proposal in all its foolishness covered his rapidly beating heart but he knew she would understand.

Laurel started to reply but Adam gently laid his fingers across her mouth. "Before you answer, you need to know I'll never live anywhere except Antelope, unless of course God calls me to another place. Once you said you would be like Ruth and follow your man where God led. Do you still feel the same way?"

Adam, the mountains, and the sky waited for her response. Even the slight breeze that lifted the light brown curls from her temples hesitated for a moment.

" 'Whither thou goest. . . .' " Laurel's whisper came only to Adam's waiting heart and ears, so low he strained to hear her, yet shouting the wondrous news of her love. He tipped her head back and kissed her. Her arms went up and around his neck and tightened. Like a frightened baby bird that has been returned to its nest, she clung to his strength. Whatever life in this still-primitive land held could not defeat her with Adam as her husband, lover, and shield.

A long time later they remounted, their faces glowing with love and reflecting the holy moments when they had knelt together and dedicated their coming oneness to the service of their Lord. Nat and Ivy Ann had no need to ask why the other couple had lingered far behind. When Adam and Laurel finally caught up with them before they entered the hidden Indian village, their entwined hands gave them away.

"You're *engaged*!" Ivy Ann blurted out the instant she saw them.

"Yes, and we're going to be married just as soon as we can." Adam flung his head back. "I've waited too long already. Late October or at least the very first of November we'll be giving you some business, parson."

Nat's dark eyes twinkled. "I'll be ready." He turned to Ivy Ann and a tiny pulse beat in his throat. "Seeing as how you're twins and all, how about making it a double wedding, Ivy Ann?"

Her laughter died. Her face paled until her eyes looked enormous and she cast a frantic glance toward Laurel. *Surely Nathaniel wouldn't joke about such a sacred thing as marriage,* she thought. Yet when she glanced back she could read little in his lean face. To cover the hot tears crowding behind her eye, she flared, "How—how could you, Nat Birchfield? I hate you!" She touched her heels to her horse and pelted down the trail.

"For mercy's sake, stop her," Laurel cried. Adam headed after Ivy but Nat sat on his horse, shocked and bewildered.

"What did I do? I thought taking her by surprise might give me an advantage." His troubled gaze turned from the two racing figures back to Laurel.

"Have you ever once told her that you love her?" Laurel

demanded, torn between fear for her twin's physical safety and annoyance with Nat, whom she adored.

Misery crept into his face and settled it into lines that made him look far older than his years. "I thought at the cabin that perhaps she cared but I couldn't be sure and—"

Compassion blotted out irritation. "Nat, Ivy Ann loves you more than life, just as I love Adam." The words sent a thrill through Laurel's heart. "She has changed so much and for weeks has feared you would only see in her the shallow person she used to be." This was no time for more misunderstanding but a time to fight for her sister's happiness. "Mama told me the minute I left she saw a change in Ivy Ann. She will make a wonderful minister's wife. We've talked how there will be times you cannot share with her those private confessions from your people's lives. She knows and accepts this." Laure slapped her mount's neck with the reins to get him moving.

"I guess I don't know much about women." He soberly clucked to his horse and followed Laurel. "I've even wondered if the age difference is too much."

"It would have been in West Virginia, but not out here." Laurel relented and gave Nat a dazzling smile. "Get things made up with Ivy Ann as soon as you can, brother."

His old audacity that added charm but never detracted from his vocation brought a sparkle back to Nat. "I will."

By the time they reached the next cluster of trees Adam had overtaken and slowed Ivy Ann. She sat proudly, chin high, and stared straight ahead.

Nat slid from his horse in one fluid motion that reminded Laurel of Adam and marched over to the now-flushed girl. "Ivy Ann, I—"

"Do you want us to go ahead?" Adam interrupted.

A violent shake of Nat's head preceded his simple declaration of love. "Ivy Ann, you're all I ever dreamed of in a woman during my long, lonely years of wandering. I love you and always will. Do you think an old bachelor like me can make you happy?"

Laurel felt she had glimpsed heaven when she saw the look in Ivy's face, a look that matched her own soul at the moment Adam had asked her to be his wife. "Come." Laurel held out one hand to Adam and they quietly rode on, confident that Nat and Ivy Ann never knew when they left.

A poignant moment came when the Birchfield men introduced Laurel and Ivy Ann to Chief Grey Eagle and his people. The erect old man looked at one then the other. "It is good. Always there will be friendship between Grey Eagle and you." The two couples left the Indian village bathed in afternoon sunlight, feeling they had been given a blessing of peace.

That night after the excitement and rejoicing over the two engagements, Ivy Ann and Laurel huddled close whispering secrets. Once Laurel hesitated then nodded. Once Ivy Ann raised her voice then quickly lowered it. The next day a cryptic message left Antelope and sped on its way.

The twins didn't care about a big wedding but soon realized they couldn't avoid one. When Thomas and Sadie, Widow Terry and Mrs. Greer, and the Hardwicks pointed out how the town and range felt a certain ownership in their doctor and minister and would feel slighted if left out, the twins gracefully gave in. On the first of November the sweet-smelling pine log church would be smothered with the outdoors. Dozens of willing hands would bring in scarlet leaves, still-green vines, and whatever else they could find for decoration. Ivy Ann blinked wet eyes when Nat proudly led her to the cabin Antelope had raised for their new home so Adam and Laurel could have Nat's former cabin that now included Adam's office.

"They keep bringing us things I know they can't really afford to give," Ivy protested, as she laid her hand on a gorgeous patch-work quilt. "Why, Mrs. Terry could have made several dresses in the time she took to make ours and it was all Mama could do to convince her the bride's parents must at least pay for the heavy silk!"

"I know, but Adam says they feel they can't afford *not* to give." Laurel stroked the frame of a fresh painting Mr. Hardwick had dropped off just that morning. It pictured a valley at sunrise. Molten silver edged the clouds and with the skill of a true artist, Mrs. Hardwick had painted a feeling of peace in the rolling hills and mighty, watching mountains the twins had come to love. "Real giving comes from the heart."

"I hope *our* present comes in time." Ivy Ann broached the thought Laurel carried constantly.

"So do I but there isn't much time left."

The double wedding day outdid itself. " 'Happy is the bride the sun shines on,' " Ivy Ann caroled while she and Laurel hurriedly dressed. "Come on, Laurel. We have to give our present to Nat and Adam before the wedding." She giggled. "Doesn't Antelope frown that those eastern girls are taking such a chance on bad luck by actually letting their husbands-to-be see them on their wedding day before the wedding?"

"Who cares?" Laurel's exhilaration matched Ivy Ann's at her wildest. "God is in charge of these weddings, not superstition." She exchanged a secret glance with her twin. "I can't wait to see Adam and Nat's faces when—"

"Ivy, Laurel, your young men are here! Come down for breakfast right now!"

Too happy even to laugh over their mother's orders, the twins bounced downstairs and demurely took their places at the table.

"Can you believe they are sitting there stuffing themselves?"

COLLEEN L. REECE

Adam demanded of Nat. "I thought brides got so nervous they didn't eat and sometimes passed out during the ceremony."

Nat lifted arched eyebrows. "Let them eat. It will save us embarrassment at the town covered-dish dinner. They'll be too full to disgrace their new husbands by displaying such wholesome appetites."

"I notice neither of you is turning down extra biscuits," said Ivy Ann as she calmly reached for another. So did Laurel.

"Hey, that's different!" The whole family broke into laughter at Adam's involuntary protest.

"Run along, children." Sadie admonished them, but she gave the twins a stern stare. "Mind that you be back here by eleven o'clock. It takes time for brides to dress and I won't have it said my girls were late to their own wedding." She turned to Nat. "Did your minister friend from Rock Springs get here?"

He nodded. "Yesterday afternoon. Right after I pronounce Adam and Laurel husband and wife I'll step down and stand next to Ivy Ann for our turn." He beamed and she blushed becomingly.

An hour later the two happy couples reined in at the top of the rise that overlooked Antelope. Laurel looked at Ivy Ann who then nodded as she took a deep breath. "We have a very special present for you. It's from both of us to both of you."

"I thought getting you was present enough," Adam teased.

She felt delicate color rise from her high collar but chose to ignore his comment. Instead she reached into the pocket of her riding skirt and drew out an envelope.

Adam and Nat looked apprehensive. Nat protested, "You aren't giving us money, are you? We agreed not to accept what your parents called your dowry. They need it to build up the Double B."

"It's better than all the money on earth," Ivy Ann cried, her eyes shining. "Laurel, read it out loud."

*Dear Misses Brown,*

*Your letter made me very happy, more than you can ever know. After much prayer I felt led simply to leave it on my husband's desk. In fear and trembling I waited, hoping and pleading with God that your gentility and beauty of expression and deep love for Adam and Nathaniel would speak for themselves.*

*The next day when he left to make a call in the country, I entered his office. My heart sank when I saw how crumpled your letter was, as if a heavy hand had crushed it. In despair I felt all was lost. Then dark, black writing I recognized as my husband's caught my attention. The wrinkled envelope bore the inscription, Numbers 6:24–26.*

*I hurried to find my Bible, torn between hope and fear. Oh, dear children, the joy that came to me as I read the beautiful words: "The Lord bless thee, and keep thee: The Lord make his face shine upon thee, and be gracious unto thee; The Lord lift up his countenance upon thee, and give thee peace."*

*Jeremiah has not mentioned your letter nor his response. Yet my prayer of years has been answered and I praise my God and King and offer you this greatest of gifts.*

*Deepest love from your mother,*
*Patience Birchfield*

Laurel's voice broke on the last words. Diamond drops sparkled in her lashes and in Ivy Ann's. Nat and Adam's strong shoulders bowed before the message that made their wedding day complete.

"The harvest of Mother's faithfulness has come," said Adam,

choking on the words.

Laurel's heart lurched at the exalted look in the brothers' faces. *How right it had been to brave a stern father's wrath on behalf of his sons*, she reflected. All the way back to the ranch, through the donning of her bridal white, and even in the midst of the lovely service that gave her into Adam's keeping Laurel treasured that memory. The part of her that was Ivy Ann knew her twin had also tucked it away into her soul, the harvest of faithfulness. How fitting for this November wedding day!

Yet when the last congratulations faded, the final bit of food had been packed away, and Reverend and Mrs. Nathaniel Birchfield slipped away by themselves, Laurel told Adam, "Let's take a walk out of town." She lifted her white skirts, carefully avoiding the ruts made by wagon wheels. After they reached a little rise that gave a splendid view of the darkening sky, the jutting white mountains, and the village she'd come to love, Laurel leaned against Adam's strength. The harvest of love she had so long sought and often despaired of winning lay before her. God grant her wisdom and courage to keep it green and growing in all the seasons of their lives.

# Desert Rose

Enjoy Your
Bonus Story

# Chapter 1

Her auburn braid flying and brown eyes sparkling with determination, Desert Rose Birchfield reached her roan horse Mesquite and swung astride while her best friend and cousin Nate lagged a few steps behind. Five feet seven inches tall and one hundred and twenty-five pounds, in the half-worn jeans she looked like a slim boy.

"Race you to the point!" Rose took advantage of her lead and touched Mesquite lightly with her boot heels.

"No fair!" Nate bellowed. He stepped into the stirrup and slid into Piebald's saddle. "You could give a fellow warning." He thundered behind the laughing girl. His dark hair tossed and his dark eyes, so like his father Nathaniel's and his Uncle Adam's, glared at the lithe figure already a hundred yards ahead of him. With that kind of lead even faithful Piebald had little hope of catching Mesquite before they reached the bald knob overlooking the Double B ranch. The aerial vantage point provided a panoramic view of Wyoming's breathtaking Wind River Range.

By the time Nate dismounted, Rose had already flung Mesquite's reins over his head so he would stand and thrown herself face down on a soft bed of pine needles. She rolled over and patted a fake yawn. "What took you so long?"

"One of these days..." Nate could never bring himself to list the dire consequences, and Rose just laughed at him.

"Pooh, you know you can't get the best of me."

Her cousin dropped to the ground beside her, fingered a single pine needle, and tickled her bare arm with it. "I've been ahead of you ever since we were born, if you'll remember."

She indignantly sat up and her thick braid with the curl at

the end flopped over her shoulder. A little candle of irritation lit her dark brown eyes. "Just because you were born exactly one month ahead of me doesn't mean a thing."

"Dear child," he said pompously, pulling his mouth down. "Don't you know the Bible tells you to respect your elders?"

"As if that meant you," she scoffed and moved out of his reach. "Why don't you go back to Concord, Massachew-sets, so we can have some peace again?" But Rose held her breath waiting for his reply. The past year that he had spent living out East with his paternal grandparents and attending school had been miserable, although she wouldn't tell him so.

"I'm not going back. Ever." Nate forgot his teasing and straightened to a crosslegged position. "Grandpa and Grandma Birchfield want me to live with them and study medicine, but I can't."

"Why not? You—you don't want to be a minister like your father, do you?"

"And if I do?" He shot a searching glance at the cousin who was more like the sister he never had.

"Why—" She faltered as she felt her tanned cheeks redden. "You don't act like a minister. I mean, you'd have to be a lot different from what you are." She stopped, embarrassed and sorry when a hurt look crept into the dark eyes observing her so carefully. "Nate, are you *serious*?"

He didn't answer.

In desperation she babbled, "You don't have to decide now, do you? What does your father say? And Aunt Ivy?"

"They don't know anything about it. No one does." Nate clenched his teeth and moodily stared out over the beautiful valley sheltered by saw-toothed mountains. "You aren't to say anything, either, Miss Smarty."

"As if I would. Have you ever known me to tell anything,

especially anything you shared?"

"No." His short reply hung in the clear air. After a long silence Nate glanced at her. "As far as making up my mind, don't forget that we'll both be eighteen before 1893 is over." In a fluid movement, he stood and walked to the edge of the promontory. A magnificent eagle soared by above them. They could even distinguish the cattle that dotted the valley floor: Lazy H cattle owned by their friends, the Hardwicks; Double B cattle with the mingled BB brand that showed the twinship of Laurel and Ivy Brown who had married the Birchfield brothers. One section of land between the Lazy H and Double B ranches remained unsettled.

Rose came to Nate and slipped her arm through his. "I'm sorry I teased you," she whispered. "If God asks you to preach for Him, I know He will help you do it." When he didn't respond she added, "Do you—is—has God called you?" Funny how hard it was to discuss this new possibility. Never before had there been such constraint between them.

"That's the problem. I don't really know yet." The word *yet* rang a little bell inside Rose.

Nate's stumbling confession opened the floodgates and all his hesitancy vanished. "Sometimes I think it's just that I see the good Dad does, the way people say that he and your father have changed Antelope for the better in spite of all the trouble the past few years. Other times I know it's because of what Dad *is*. If I can be half the man he is, I'll be a success. Then once in a while when I'm riding alone at night the moonlight and mountains and foothills and trees shout that their Creator is present and that I must serve Him. I'm just not sure how. That's why I haven't said anything. This summer I have to make up my mind."

Rose felt as if her childhood companion had suddenly gone far away from her. She clutched Nate's arm. "Then why not enjoy this summer all you can and wait for God to help you know? Eighteen isn't so old."

Nate grinned the crooked grin that melted Rose every time. "That's what I thought until I went to Concord last year. Then I found out eighteen's a whole lot older out here than back there."

"Really? How?" Rose eagerly snatched at the subject, eager to rid that lost, little-boy look from Nate's face and the need to look at the future from her mind.

"Maybe it's because of all that's happened since we were born in 1875, or even before. How many times have we heard our folks and Grandpa and Grandma Brown tell how thousands of white people violated the Indian treaties and rushed into the Black Hills after gold was discovered in 1874?" Nate's face flushed with resentment and a sympathetic throb filled Rose's heart. Only too well did they know how the Indians held the Black Hills sacred and that the Sioux and Cheyenne tribes had retaliated. Peace in the summer of 1876 had been won at a terrible cost: at the Battle of the Little Bighorn, Sitting Bull, Crazy Horse, Gall, and others, along with two thousand Sioux warriors, the largest gathering in Western history, wiped out General George Armstrong Custer and his entire unit of over two hundred soldiers.

"I don't blame the Indians," Rose declared. She clenched her shapely hands into fists. "If anyone tried to take our homes away from us or desecrate what we held sacred, I'd fight, too."

"So would I," Nate agreed. "I feel sorry for the Indians, and I'm glad we haven't had trouble here."

"Have you seen Chief Running Deer since you came home?" Rose asked.

Nate shook his head. "No, but I will. Dad says he and his father Chief Grey Eagle proved themselves to be staunch friends years ago."

"My father always goes to take them medicine and never lets anyone know where their little tribe still lives," Rose put in. "They swore friendship before we were even born when Dad took Running Deer's appendix out and saved his life." She sighed. "I wish I could do something big and courageous like that. Not much chance here, though. Nate, I love Antelope, but at times I feel I'll smother. Nothing ever happens."

"You ungrateful wretch!" Nate swung toward her, only half jesting. "What about oil being found in Wyoming in the early 80s? And you're certainly old enough to remember the winter of 1887!"

"Who could forget it?" she returned, feeling hot blood seep into her face. Rose tossed her braid and her exasperated grimace showed the tiny overlap of front teeth that lent pixie charm to her heart-shaped face.

"I'll never forget it as long as I live," Nate muttered.

Neither would Rose. Bitter temperatures and savage blizzards had killed thousands of cattle. Frozen carcasses littered the valley, and Thomas and Sadie Brown had been among the few to survive the ruin and hang on to their ranch. As the only doctor in the area, Rose's father, Adam, had been literally run off his feet; Uncle Nat had officiated at burials and comforted the sick, an equally demanding job.

Rose stirred restlessly. "I didn't mean *that* kind of thing."

"What did you mean?"

She stared at the tranquil scene below and focused on a tumbleweed idly moving but getting nowhere. "I don't know. I just feel that if I don't do something soon I'll explode like a bad jar of canning."

"Too bad you aren't more like Columbine," Nate teased.

"Columbine?" A vision of her brown-haired, brown-eyed coquettish sister shimmered in the heat waves before Rose's eyes. "That flirt? I heard Mother say she thanked God I took after her since Columbine's the spitting image of Ivy when she was fifteen."

Nate cocked his head to one side and smirked. "Granted Columbine's the flirtiest fifteen-year-old girl I've ever known, but just keep in mind how Aunt Laurel kicked over the family traces and rushed out here after Uncle Adam to get ahead of my mother!"

Before Rose could catch her breath he continued. "I just bet you wouldn't have the spunk to do something like that."

"Who says so?" Rose planted her hands on her hips and glared at him. Would she? *Perhaps,* she thought, *if I followed someone like Dad.*

"I do." Nate's natural lightheartedness and tendency to pester never stayed down long. A glint in his eyes struck fire to his volatile cousin. "Look, Rose Red—"

"Don't call me that. My hair is *not* red, it auburn." She twitched the single heavy braid around for inspection.

"I could call you Roan Red. It's almost the same color as Mesquite." The quietly grazing horse lifted his head and nickered. Nate rolled on the ground with laughter. "Wonder if he's flattered?"

"You are so—so—I'm leaving." In a flash she had vaulted to the saddle with the barest touch of her toe to stirrup. "Come on, Mesquite."

"Hey, I'll come, too." Nate sobered quickly and headed toward Piebald who showed signs of restiveness.

"Don't bother!" The words floated back over the girl's shoulder.

"I didn't mean to make you mad, Rosy."

"*Rose*, Nathaniel Birchfield the Second." There, that would get him. Nate hated being called his full name. If he insisted on being the bane of her life, he should get used to the thorns she could show.

Mesquite settled into the comfortable, rocking-chair gait that permitted his rider to dream while he did the work. Over the grassy slopes, still green from the unusual summer rains, the roan horse and auburn-haired girl seemed to move as one. From the back of Piebald, Nate observed how much taller she had grown in the year he spent back East. At five feet ten inches and still growing he could look down on her, but deep inside he knew he also looked up to the beautiful girl. *Would he ever find a girl to match her?*

"God willing," he muttered. "And that she finds someone who will be worthy of her." He frowned until his black brows met above the dark eyes that could change from laughter to deep thought so quickly. "There's not a man on the range who is good enough for her," he told Piebald in a voice too low to carry to the girl ahead. "In fact, I've only known one man outside of Dad and Uncle Adam who could handle her with love and the firm hand she's going to need." His mouth twitched. "Herein is a matchmaker born, but how?"

*~*

For several days Nate put aside his own weighty considerations and plotted. Over two thousand miles lay between Wyoming and Massachusetts. Besides, if Rose were allowed to go to school back East, what guarantee had anyone that she wouldn't follow her headstrong ways and fall in love with some rotter? Living in a so-called civilized part of the country didn't ensure ideals and morality. Nate had found as many scoundrels in his year in Concord as in Antelope. They wore finer clothes and looked down their haughty noses at westerners, but Nate's keen vision penetrated to their core. He couldn't take a chance on a bedazzled Rose getting tangled up with a skunk in Harvard clothing!

COLLEEN L. REECE

Perhaps he should go back with her. Yet not even for Rosy would he endure another year in a strange land. He had studied hard and proved himself, but he had counted the months, weeks, and days until he could come home. The same restless, seeking spirit that had lured his father and uncle to the frontier more than twenty years earlier ran strong in Nate's veins.

*Did he dare to pray about his scheme?* If he prayed and God said no, that would be it. Better to simply set the stage and let God take over at that point, he assured his conscience. He did relent enough to say, "Dear God, You know how much I think of Rose and I do have her best interests at heart. All I want her to do is have the chance to meet him. Then it will be up to You." No lightning flash or thunderclap came, so Nate quickly added, "Amen," and rode off to find Rose, determined to wait and watch for the perfect opportunity.

He almost missed it when it presented itself the next day. He came down the stairs of the Double B to find Columbine and Rose giggling over a magazine they hastily stuffed under a pillow when he entered.

"What's this?" Nate pounced and withdrew a copy of *Hand and Heart*. He disgustedly tossed it aside. "What are you two doing reading this, anyway?"

"There's nothing wrong with it," Columbine defended in her haughtiest Southern belle fashion. "Why shouldn't people advertise for wives and husbands?" She dissolved in laughter again.

"Some of them are hilarious." Rose wiped her eyes and snatched the magazine back. "Listen to this. 'Wanted: Wife to cook, bake, and sew. No ridin', ropin', or brandin'.'"

"That's not in there!" Nate peered over her shoulder.

"It sure is. This one's even better. 'You kin have yore own stove, you kin have yore own pony. Wyomin' winters git mighty lonely.' Here's another. 'Young, healthy female wants to keep

164

company with strong, healthy rancher. Object: matrimony.' Oh dear, do you think anyone ever answers these?"

"You bet they do." Columbine suddenly dropped her affected air. "Mrs. Hardwick said her own sister answered an ad in a magazine like this only it was called *Heart and Ring*, and she married the advertiser and they've been happy for over twenty years!" She shivered and the mischief faded from her pretty face. "A girl would be taking an awful chance, though."

"She sure would. She might get someone like Nate," Rose tormented.

Nate didn't say a word. An idea had popped full-blown into his fertile brain. "How about a ride, Rose?"

"I'll be ready by the time you saddle Mesquite for me," she told him and ran to change her clothes.

"May I go, too? Columbine asked.

"Not this time." Nate barely saw the disconsolate droop of her lips. "Sam will be out later." He knew his sixteen-year-old brother adored Columbine and never had been able to understand why they didn't get along the way he and Rose did.

"Oh, Sam." Columbine drifted away, leaving Nate feeling uncomfortable. Someday he would include her but not today, not when he held the means to carry out his plan concerning Rose.

No matter which direction they rode, Nate and Rose almost always ended up on the point. They never tired of the changing sky, the slight breeze there on most days, and the feeling of solitude.

Today they mutually turned Mesquite and Piebald toward the flower-strewn slopes and came out on the bluff that ended in the bald knob viewpoint. As usual, Mesquite and Piebald grazed with reins hanging loose.

"Red Rose, Roan Rose, Rosy, what kind of man do you want to marry?"

Nate's question burst a moment of absolute silence. Rose turned her astonished gaze toward Nate. "Whatever makes you ask that?"

"Most people get married when they're younger than we are," he reminded her. "We haven't talked about it for ages, but you used to say you wanted someone to ride straight out of a storybook. Come on. Who's your hero now?"

She hesitated so long he looked at her closely and followed the line of her watching eyes to the distant mountain peaks. "Someone strong and gentle like Dad and Uncle Nat."

Nate's heart leaped. He thought of his candidate for Rose's hand. *So far, so good.*

"And?"

"He has to love God above anything, even me."

Nate leaned closer to catch the final two words. "Is that all?"

Rose abandoned her seriousness. "Of course not. He has to be rich and exciting and handsome and. . .why are you looking at me like that?" she demanded.

"I'm just wondering if you have the courage to do something really exciting and new, something you've never done before and will never do again." He laughed until his white teeth gleamed in the sunlight against his tanned, handsome face.

"I have the courage to do anything you can think up," she said rashly.

"Promise? You're a scaredy cat if you don't," he taunted. He saw her hesitate and he pushed his advantage. "I knew you wouldn't do it."

"I will," she flashed, all imperiousness and determination.

Nate pulled the crumpled issue of *Hand and Heart* out from under his shirt where he'd stashed it. "I dare you to send an advertisement to them."

Rose's hand flew to her mouth. Her eyes looked enormous.

"Dad would kill me. So would Mother."

"How will they know? How many *Hand and Heart* copies have you ever seen?"

"None," she admitted. "Columbine brought it home from visiting in Rock Springs."

"Well?" Nate held his breath, counting on her well-known unwillingness to let him get the best of her and pushing back the thought this wasn't fair.

"All right." But she sighed. "I don't know why I let you get me into pickles all the time, and this will probably be another one, but I said I would and I'll do it. Why don't *you* send one?"

Nate had already prepared himself for that question. "Too much competition. Anyway, there are hardly any from girls. You're sure to get answers." *At least one,* he promised himself.

An hour later an announcement more exaggerated than any in *Hand and Heart* had been composed. "I'll write it out and send it," Nate promised. "That way there's less chance of your getting caught." That night he kept part of his bargain. He copied and mailed the advertisement and sent a picture, but *not* to *Hand and Heart.*

# Chapter 2

Carmichael Blake-Jones stared at the ivy-covered walls that had held him ever since he graduated from college and began teaching. The late afternoon sunlight that turned the stone walls rosy flickered in his curly golden hair and reduced his twenty-three years until he looked more like one of the boys who came to the private school than an instructor. A pang of regret slipped through him. *Had he been insane to give up this privileged teaching post? Had the whim of a moment resulted in folly?*

He could go back into the dean's office and retract his resignation. Yet Carmichael hesitated and the moment passed. He turned on his heel and walked away, only pausing at the stone-arched gates to look back.

An imaginary parade of teenage boys marched between him and the school. Tall, short, overweight, underweight, timid, bold, good, and mischievous, he had loved many, despised a few for their cowardice or cheating, but served all. His fun-loving personality sympathized with their dilemmas, and he had often been hard put to keep from laughing instead of meting out the necessary discipline. Even the boys who thought him a pushover on first acquaintance soon learned that B.J., as they called him, offered friendship as well as education but never allowed himself to be maneuvered.

Now his new freedom sat heavily on his broad shoulders. *What next?*

The unspoken challenge echoed in every footstep between the school and his ancestral home. Born and raised in Concord, "one of those dyed-in-the-wool New Englanders," a fellow teacher had labeled him, Carmichael loved his home. And yet. . . . He tossed his head back and laughed aloud. If that teacher and the others only knew! How often in dreams had the dedicated teacher longed to step from the rut he could feel growing deeper and more comfortable daily—to strike out and travel, to search for more adventure than he could find here.

Carmichael automatically returned greetings from those who hailed him, left the business district, and walked on, glad for the considerable distance between home and the school. In bad weather the walk had proved inconvenient, but on an early summer day with a beckoning sun spilling its joy Carmichael was unaware of the distance. His steps dragged, however, when he came to the corner of the Blake-Jones property. Not large enough to be called an estate, the spacious grounds and solid brick home showed the permanence of long standing. Sparkling white columns gave the mellowed brick a clean and welcoming look. Carmichael sighed. In the weeks since his parents had been killed in a railway accident he hated coming home. The youngest of the children and able to live at home long after the others married and gone, a special bond had strengthened between him and his parents.

The mouth that stayed etched in a smile twisted bitterly. Since the accident Carmichael had been bereft of even his heavenly Father's comfort. A dozen times he had cried out, "Why, God? They loved and served You. You could have protected them. Why didn't You?" Only the high ceilings replied, with silence. At last his prayers dwindled to formal recognition and he suffered alone.

"Michael, is that you?" a girlish voice called from the top of the curving staircase that led to the second floor.

His heart lifted. "Here. What are you up to?"

Sixteen-year-old Mercy Curtis pelted downstairs, her skirts

clutched with one hand to keep her from tripping. Plump and just a little over five feet tall, she wore her gold curls, so like her mother Caroline's and Uncle Carmichael's, in a topknot that threatened to topple at any moment. Her blueberry-blue eyes twinkled. "I've come to take care of you, of course."

"You have *what*?" Long familiar with her impetuous actions, her blunt announcement still surprised him while her warm hug took away some of his emptiness.

"You know I'm as good a cook as Mandy and can keep house a whole lot better. I just told Mama and Daddy that it didn't make sense for you to be rattling around all alone in this ark, excuse me, house—" She paused to grin and her teeth flashed against the healthy red lips. "Anyway, now that school is out, I don't have anything to do except help Mama, so here I am."

For the second time this afternoon Carmichael laughed spontaneously. Mercy had dressed for the part by adding one of Mandy's voluminous aprons over her gingham dress and wrapping it around herself twice. She wore a cap whose origins looked suspiciously like a dish towel. Now she bobbed a little curtsy and assumed a meek expression that her twin dimples somehow defeated. "Will Master Michael be ready for his tea in five minutes?" In her own voice, she added, "He'd better. I helped Mandy make popovers, and they'll fall if you don't hurry."

Still laughing, Carmichael sped upstairs, hastily washed, and arrived at the tea table where the popovers sat puffed and waiting. For the first time in weeks he actually enjoyed a meal. "You aren't serious, are you?"

Her blue eyes opened wide. "Of course I am. Once I convinced Mama it would be good training for me to have charge of a house because I'll be getting married one of these days—"

"Married!" He set down his teacup with a little crash that brought a cry of dismay from Mercy until she saw it hadn't cracked. "Why, you're still a baby!"

"Oh?" Red flags of color flared in her face but her voice stayed sweet. "Let me run this house for one month and you'll see how much of a baby I am." She fixed him with a stern stare. "In case you've forgotten, I am almost seventeen years old."

Delighted at her reaction, he added, "Your birthday isn't until December."

She hurriedly changed the subject. "Can I stay?"

He wasn't to be sidetracked. "Just who do you have in mind to marry, that you need this practice?"

"How should I know?" She shrugged her plump shoulders and grinned again. "Your school's filled with boys, isn't it? I thought maybe you could pick out a few of the extra nice ones. Oh!" She jumped up so quickly the little tea table rocked. "You got a letter." She ran to the mantel and brought back a fat envelope, then perched on the arm of his chair and peered over his shoulder. "Nathaniel Birchfield. Isn't he that boy who went to your school last year?" An undercurrent of excitement pinkened her smooth face.

Carmichael eyed her suspiciously. "How do you happen to remember him? I don't think I ever introduced you."

"You didn't have to. He came to church with his grandparents. He was—different. Sort of nice different."

Totally amused but intrigued, he let the letter lie unopened on the table. "What do you mean by that, Mercy?"

She traced the damask pattern on the tablecloth with her forefinger. "He just smiled and didn't act smart or try to flirt."

"Well, I would certainly hope not," Carmichael retorted. "Nice young gentlemen don't flirt with little girls." Storm warnings in his niece's eyes made him add, "After all, last year you were only fifteen and didn't even have your hair up."

She relaxed and smiled. "Aren't you going to open your letter?

171

Carmichael scowled. "If you take over as housekeeper, you are going to have to learn your place and not show such vulgar curiosity about the Master's mail." But he hugged her and smiled, then slit open the letter. A flat, tissue-wrapped card fell out and to the floor.

"I'll get it." Mercy swooped off the arm of the chair and scooped it up. The wrapping fell back. "Why, it's a photograph!" She stared. "Uncle Michael, have you been keeping secrets?"

Carmichael grabbed the photograph and gasped. A girl mounted on a fine-looking horse smiled back at him. A long, thick braid with a curl on the end hung over her shoulder. The likeness had caught sparkling eyes and a wide, white smile. Dressed for riding, she was clad in boys' jeans and a long-sleeved shirt.

"Who is she?" Mercy demanded.

"I have no idea." Carmichael couldn't take his gaze from the picture.

"She's beautiful. No, not exactly, but better than pretty." Mercy judged. "She looks like she'd be fun, and see the way she sits her horse? Oh, if Mama would let me ride in pants! I hate riding in skirts, they bundle so."

Carmichael's keen eyes caught the rearing mountains in the background and he turned toward the letter. "I wonder why Nate Birchfield sent this picture. Perhaps he put it in by mistake."

"Read it and find out," Mercy said practically and resumed her seat on his chair arm, avidly following Nate's letter.

*Antelope, Wyoming*
*June 1893*

*Dear Mr. Blake-Jones,*
*You probably didn't think you'd ever hear from me once*

*I got back home. I'm not coming back to Concord, as I told
you when I left. I learned so much from you, but now it's
time to move on and out here in the West is where I belong.*

*I want to thank you for everything you did for me and I
will write again after I decide what to do with my life. I'm
taking this summer to consider and I just may have surprising news for you a little later. In the meantime, I wonder if
you'd do a favor for me. It's this way:*

*My cousin Desert Rose Birchfield is always trying to
get ahead of me and she usually does! Now I have a chance
to have some harmless fun if you'll help. I talked her into
writing an advertisement for Hand and Heart magazine,
the one where people advertise for wives and sometimes
husbands. . . ."*

Mercy interrupted with a little scream. "My stars, how did
she have the nerve?"

"If you *have* to read my mail, kindly refrain from commenting on it," Carmichael told her, tipping the page so she couldn't
see it. As usual with Mercy, he relented and read aloud.

*Now, fun is one thing but having someone answer who
will get angry when she turns him down—as she will—or
even worse, someone who will hang around her wouldn't be
funny at all. Besides, her parents and mine would lambaste
us for doing this.*

*Anyway, I just thought that you might write her a
letter. She probably won't ever answer or, if she does, you
can stop corresponding at any time and she'll think you lost
interest. I am enclosing a picture of Rose and her letter to
Hand and Heart and will be much obliged if you will at
least write one time.*

*Respectfully yours,*
*Nathaniel "Nate" Birchfield II*

*P.S. If you write, please don't tell her how you got her advertisement.*

"Of all the ridiculous requests!" Carmichael dropped the letter to the table.

"*I* think it's perfectly splendid," Mercy cried. She caught the single sheet of paper that had drifted out and laid it to one side. "Will you read Desert Rose Birchfield's advertisement or shall I? Oh, what a pretty name!" All eagerness, her greedy fingers unfolded the page but she waited for Carmichael's permission.

"Go ahead." He leaned back in his chair and feigned indifference even while he glanced again at the laughing girl in the photograph. Desert Rose. Her name suited her.

"Just listen!" Mercy giggled until he couldn't understand her. In exasperation, Carmichael took the advertisement from her.

*Wanted: Young man to correspond with almost-eighteen-year-old girl.*

"I wonder when *her* birthday is," Carmichael broke off to say. "Go on!" Mercy ordered.

*Must be at least five foot ten, have sense of humor, faith in God, be willing to relocate in Wyoming should correspondence lead to a closer companionship. No drinkers, smokers, or dandies. Must have good education but not be stuffy, no younger than twenty or older than twenty-five. Financial stability required. No ranching experience necessary, but must love horses and be willing to learn range lore. The*

*ability to adapt to scorching and freezing temperatures,
blizzards and droughts, hailstorms and gully-washers
mandatory. Must be good-natured and not easily provoked.
No divorced men or widowers need write. Will exchange
photographs only after advertiser determines it worthwhile.*

"Is that all?" Mercy tried to see the page.

"What more do you want?" her uncle demanded. "You can see that this Rose deliberately made up an impossible person in order to best Nate." He tossed the advertisement to the table.

Mercy immediately took possession of it. A golden curl fell over her forehead as she perused it. "Hmmm. You're exactly five foot ten, have a sense of humor, faith in God—"

"For goodness sake, Mercy! Stop your foolishness." But Carmichael had all he could do not to show curiosity as she ignored him and rattled on.

"You don't drink or smoke and you're the right age. Now that you've inherited a tidy sum from Grandpa and Grandma you are financially stable. You aren't a dandy and haven't been married and I'd hate to see you go to Wyoming but you could adapt if you had to and you love horses and already ride well. You're good natured, at least when you get your own way, and, why Uncle Michael! You're everything Desert Rose made up!" She stared at him admiringly. "May I read your letter to her?" Mercy's eyes shone with plans and dreams. "What if you write and she answers and you fall in love? You could use your inheritance to buy a ranch in Wyoming and I'll come out and keep house for you until I find a cowboy who'll carry me off on his horse and marry me and we'll all live happily ever after!"

Why should a wild leap of excitement shoot through him at his niece's nonsense? For a single moment her eloquence had swayed him. Common sense came to Carmichael's rescue. "I thought you said you were grown up enough to run a home? This kind of talk certainly proves how wrong you are," he said sarcastically. "I have no intention of getting involved in a childish prank."

Mercy's dismay seemed out of proportion to his decision. Her blue eyes darkened. "You mean you won't answer? But you have to! What if you don't? Desert Rose will think no one likes her well enough to correspond. She will feel absolutely terrible." Mercy dramatically pointed to the photograph. "You can't be so mean you won't write just one little letter to her! I know how I would feel if I never got a reply." She managed a woebegone expression that sent Carmichael into fits of laughter.

Mercy seized her advantage. "Just one letter, Michael?" she pleaded.

"I'll consider it." He shut his lips tight in the way that warned the subject had been closed.

Mercy said no more—then. But in the days following after Carmichael and the girl's parents agreed the responsibility of housekeeping might do Mercy good, she quietly began a campaign that made the most illustrious army general look like an enlistee. Innocent little phrases such as, "Desert Rose will start looking for a letter soon" crept into her conversation. Now and then she sighed, "I wonder if Desert Rose would like to have me write to her? No, that would spoil Nate's plan."

Finally Carmichael capitulated, aware of how the simple photograph propped on the mantel (where Mercy placed it) drew his attention each time he entered the well-kept, comfortable room. "All right, I'll write tonight."

"Good!" His tormentor became his ally and clapped her hands in victory. Never had her eyes glowed more like sapphires, and Carmichael recognized a startling truth. His not-yet-seventeen-year-old niece indeed trembled on the brink of womanhood. In spite of her small stature, Mercy no longer could be considered a child. Even Mandy admitted it.

On one point he held firm against her half-pouting pleas. "No, you may *not* read my letter. In the first place, all I'm going to do is tell her the truth—that I've been a teacher at a private boys' school and am in the process of making some changes in my life."

"Are you going to tell her you know Nate?"

He drew his brows into a straight line and a rueful smile played on his lips. "I think I'll have to. She's bound to discover it or ask Nathaniel."

Long after Mercy slept in the guest room she had appropriated, the one with the canopy bed she had always adored, Carmichael struggled with his letter. He wrote and discarded a dozen letters and finally settled on a simple message based on the outline he had sketched for Mercy's benefit. His golden curls grew damp with effort. His blue eyes brightened and dulled in turn. At last his sense of humor won over the feeling he wasn't being quite square with the girl who wore the odd name Desert Rose so well.

He sealed the envelope, exhilarated yet half-disgusted with himself. An hour later he lay wide-eyed and sleepless. Tales Nate had shared with the teacher who had seen through his bravado to find a homesick but determined young man crept into Carmichael's thoughts. Never once had he felt Nate exaggerated.

"He didn't have to!" Carmichael whispered and chuckled. The Old West and its fight against the elements certainly hadn't faded into history. Just living and winning in Wyoming could challenge a man or a woman to the utmost.

What was she like, the young woman in the picture? Obviously as filled with a love of fun as her cousin Nathaniel. She must also possess a tremendous faith or she wouldn't have included that in her ridiculous advertisement. Something in her eyes showed innocence wedded to mischief, the same traits Caroline once said her younger brother Carmichael possessed.

Surely suitors flocked around Desert Rose. For some strange reason Carmichael resented the thought then wondered why. Yet, knowing one Birchfield as he did, and judging from Desert Rose's advertisement, he'd bet not a man in a hundred would so much as carelessly attempt a caress.

Carmichael jerked upright in bed, appalled at his train of thought. Good heavens, if just writing a letter to Nate's cousin affected him like this he'd best tear up the letter and write to Nate in no uncertain terms that he disapproved of the whole scheme and would have no part of it.

He tossed and turned and awakened more determined than ever to retrieve the letter from his desk in the writing room and replace it with a scorching missive to Nate. Tired, out of sorts, and thoroughly ashamed of his weakening before Mercy's assault, Carmichael dressed and strode down to the writing room.

The desk lay empty.

"Mercy?" he called, his heart thumping.

"Here," came the answer from the hall. "I just ran out and got your letter posted."

# Chapter 3

To Carmichael's amazement, Mercy turned out to be capable and thrifty in running his household. Mandy, who had felt without direction since the elder master and mistress died, gave thanks and sang Mercy's praises. "I can cook most anything that's fried, baked, boiled, or stewed," she stated, "but I needs someone to tell me what they want cooked." She added a little forlornly, "Master Michael, you just ain't so good at that."

He sighed, thinking of his lack of interest in food the past months, but his eyes brightened and he patted faithful Mandy's arm. "You won't let Mercy boss you, will you?"

"Land sakes, why would she do that?" Mandy settled into her favorite pose, her arms akimbo. "We works together. Like two hands on one person."

Carmichael's keen observance confirmed Mandy's claim. The girl-woman and the old cook complemented each other and the household machinery never creaked under their joint efforts.

To Carmichael, Mercy's abnormal curiosity and romantic views were the only thorns in his life. Long before the letter to Wyoming could have reached its destination Mercy haunted the post for an answer. Her uncle laughed at her until his blue eyes crinkled at the corners. "You don't honestly think she'll reply, do you? Writing to such a magazine on a dare is a far cry from actually responding to an unknown man over two thousand miles away."

Mercy's round chin set stubbornly. "She'll answer. Any girl with Desert Rose's spunk is bound to. *I* would," she belligerently added.

"I don't doubt that!" her long-suffering uncle agreed. He clasped his hands behind his head and looked at his pretty companion. How nice to have someone across the table at meals! To hear singing while Mercy cleaned and dusted and proved how well trained she had been by her conscientious mother. Carmichael knew he had always avoided girls, especially those who showed eagerness for his company. Having sisters so much older than himself had been a disadvantage. He didn't feel comfortable around giggling girls. Teaching at the boy's school had only compounded the problem. He never had difficulty dealing with mothers, but his situation offered little opportunity to meet the opposite sex. Besides, his studies and work had absorbed him. Someday he'd marry, but with the comfortable home his mother provided he had been lazy about pursuing such a relationship. Only since living in the big and empty house alone had Carmichael realized how much he missed the presence of others. Once he suggested that Mandy eat with him but she had thrown her apron over her head.

"It ain't proper," she announced.

He hadn't pursued the idea. Now Mercy filled a gap he hadn't even known existed until recently. It made all the difference in the world to come downstairs and see his plump niece tucked into a chair, her pretty hands busy with needlework or mending.

One evening he told her, "You really are going to make a good wife someday."

Her silver knitting needles slowed and her dimples appeared. "I know."

He laughed the joyous laugh that had returned with her arrival. "Of all the smug and complacent girls, you're the worst."

"Why?" she dropped her half-knitted sweater and squared off. "Don't you know that you're a good teacher?"

"Of course I do." He had the grace to turn red and grin

weakly, thinking what an attractive picture she made in her simple pink dress with something white and frothy at the neckline.

"Uncle Michael, what are you going to do at the end of summer? I still have a year of school at least. Mother and Daddy want me to go to college—can you beat that? Me, in college!"

He couldn't help teasing. "From the sound of your grammar, college wouldn't hurt you."

Her laughing blue eyes darkened. "Don't change the subject." Concern showed in every line of her body.

Carmichael respected that concern and answered accordingly after staring out the window into the summer dusk. The heavy scent of night-blooming flowers drifted in to color the conversation. Night birds crying sent a pang of loneliness through the young man at a crossroads. "I don't know, Mercy," he told her quietly, speaking as if to a contemporary rather than a girl. "Now that I'm alone I don't relish the thought of staying here. That's why I resigned." He felt her stir but she remained silent, perhaps from shock. He hadn't even told Mandy about his resignation.

"You laughingly said a few days ago I could sell this place and go buy a ranch out West. At first I laughed at the idea. . . ." His voice trailed into the twilight.

"And now?" Mercy leaned forward and kept her voice low.

"It isn't such a bad idea." In a wave of companionship he opened up hopes and dreams he had never shared with anyone but God. "I love Concord and all it stands for, but something inside me cries out for adventure. What am I doing here spending my time teaching mostly sons of rich parents who will send them to all the places I long to see? I have the money to travel, to see and do and go. Once I marry, what chance will there be for me to experience foreign places or the West or a hundred other things?" His well-shod feet paced the costly Oriental rug.

"I also wonder if I could succeed in a place where I am not known and accepted because of our long line of worthy ancestors. You know what I'd really like to do? Go somewhere and work with my hands. Sweat and become exhausted and know hunger and cold. If I could find a place that requires manhood and hard work, I'd leave Concord tomorrow!" His eyes glowed and he could feel excitement surge through his entire body.

Mercy stared at him. He saw how her face gleamed in the deepening dusk. "Then go, Michael. Don't let anyone stop you." The glitter of tears in her tangled lashes confirmed how much she meant every word. "If I were a little older or a young man, I'd go with you." A small smile hovered on her lips. "Remember Desert Rose's description of Wyoming? It sounds an awful lot like the place you described."

Blood rushed to Carmichael's head. The feelings he had denied ever since looking at the jutting mountain background against which Desert Rose Birchfield so easily sat her mount returned in full force. "Who would hire anyone like me in a country like that?"

Some of Mercy's usual dreaming joined with her New England practicality. She impatiently brushed away her tears. "If you owned a ranch you'd have a job just as you said you wanted." She jumped up and hugged him. "Will you let me come out as soon as I finish school next spring?"

"Whoa!" His arms tightened around the niece he had really only discovered in the last few weeks. "You're going too fast for me." Yet he thrilled at the pictures that frolicked in his mind. Away from everything he knew, among new people, facing a new land, might he lose the anger he held toward his heavenly Father for not intervening and saving his parents? If mountain peaks, rolling hills, and green valleys could offer healing to his spirit and a return to his childhood faith, any amount of money would be well spent.

For hours they sat up talking until even Mercy couldn't keep her eyes open. The next day they continued their conversation, weighing and considering. Finally they decided Carmichael should write, not to Desert Rose, but to Nathaniel Birchfield II, casually inquiring about the availability of small ranches in the area near Antelope. The letter would contain a strict warning for Nate to say nothing to anyone concerning Carmichael's questions.

A reply arrived in record time. Nate obviously had hopped on his horse and thoroughly researched every ranch within miles. Carmichael could picture the eager young man who stood as tall as his former teacher interviewing various cowmen, his hat shoved back on his forehead, his dark eyes giving nothing away. Nate's enthusiasm was evident.

*There isn't a lot for sale but what there is will knock your eyes out. I had no idea Old Man Turpin wanted to sell out and go live with his daughter in Rock Springs. The Circle 5 is a pretty little spread that could be made into a paying proposition if a man had the money to do it. The house and out-buildings are a little rundown. I guess since Mrs. Turpin died, the old man hasn't cared enough to keep them up. Besides, he doesn't look too well.*

*There are only a couple hundred cattle but the range will hold many more. The spread is quite a ways from Antelope but not so far from Gandpa and Grandma Brown's Double B ranch.*

*Are you serious or just asking? So far nobody but I knows the ranch is for sale but news like that leaks out fast. You won't have any trouble getting good hands and the view's grand. A dandy trout stream runs through the upper part of the property and there's enough timber to build a dozen ranchhouses. Besides, you'll have great neighbors! Let me know pronto if you're interested and send along a few bucks to hold the deal until you can get here.*

Nate had scrawled his name below and sketched in a crude drawing of what must be the Circle 5. On one ferocious-looking critter that must be a bull he had drawn the Circle 5 brand. The miniature 5 that held Carmichael's attention seemed to draw the disapproving looks of all his New England ancestors pictured in gold frames around the living room.

"Are you going to buy it?" Mercy hung over her uncle's shoulder in her favorite position for inspecting his mail. She took a long breath. "If you do, I want Indian rugs on the walls of my room and a soft bed and two windows overlooking that." She pointed to the rough portrayal of rolling hills that rose to serrated peaks.

"Your room? My dear young woman, how you run on."

She smiled her bewitching smile that so often won whatever she wanted. "You'll be busy at first, but you have almost a year to get your log house built and you may as well know before you start how I want my room to be."

He threw up his hands at her daring. "The idea. Why, you're ready to move into an imaginary bedroom in a house that isn't and may never be built on a ranch I don't own!"

Unfazed, she merely reached for the sketch and began making outlandish suggestions for a house of lodge proportions that any Astor or Vanderbuilt would be proud to occupy.

Mercy received more fuel to add to her growing fire of reasons why her favorite uncle should go West. The morning post brought a squeal from the excitable girl and put her more practical uncle in shock.

Desert Rose had answered Carmichael's letter.

He could hardly believe his own eyes when he saw his name and address in a clear, firm handwriting that had no "feminine" swirls. He could see that Mercy itched to tear open the letter, but a newborn loyalty to the girl in the picture made him say, "It wouldn't be fair for me to let you read it."

She looked so downcast he quickly added, "I'll tell you what she says, though."

"Good." Mercy settled herself in a nearby chair and Carmichael could feel her eyes boring into him as he read. Unwilling to keep her in a suspense too long, he skimmed each paragraph and condensed its contents.

"She's quite surprised that anyone so far away would run across her advertisement. She says she hadn't realized that *Hand and Heart* would ever penetrate the august walls of a private boys' school."

Mercy giggled and her eyes flashed. "What else?"

"Oh, she says she asked Nate about me and he assured her that it's safe to correspond, that I'm not the kind of man who would take advantage of her letters or would bother her." Carmichael exploded. "Confound the rascal! I'll bet he's laughing behind both of our backs."

"Don't stop there," his niece begged, sitting on the edge of her chair.

"She says it's kind of me to write and that she appreciates the opportunity to learn more about the East than her parents and Nate have told her and that—" He stopped reading but his gaze traveled on.

Mercy couldn't restrain herself. "What does she say? What does she *say*?" She bounced up and down despite the danger of falling off her chair.

COLLEEN L. REECE

Carmichael couldn't keep back his grin. He folded the letter and put it back into the envelope. "Just that if I ever decide to visit Nate, all the Birchfields will welcome me." He didn't repeat the final part of the last sentence: *Nate speaks highly of you and I am thankful that you are the one to answer my advertisement.*

Mercy crossed her arms and looked at him suspiciously. Carmichael maintained an expression of bland innocence to match her own and diverted further questions. "I think I'll write to Nate and send those 'bucks' he talked about. Even if I don't decide to become a cattle rancher this Circle 5 sounds like a good investment."

"I agree. As your friend Nate said, you'll have such nice neighbors." With this parting shot Mercy ran toward the kitchen. "It must be time for lunch and I'm starved." She paused in the doorway and mischief surrounded her like a halo. "Better eat civilized food while you can, Uncle dear. If things get tough in Wyoming you may end up dining on rattlesnake and prairie dogs." A smothered laugh later, she disappeared.

"Good little scout," Carmichael said out loud. Mercy had kept quiet about his affairs and even Mandy didn't know all the possibilities floating around the Blake-Jones home.

Carmichael's half-formed determination to buy the Circle 5 wavered when he suddenly thought of Mandy. Could Caroline and her husband take her? Never, ever would she be turned out after the decades of service to "her family." Widowed and child-less, she had come to them while still a young woman and had grown old caring for the different children. "Dear God," he whispered, "is this all some ridiculous plan to escape everything here, even me? Or is it something You want for me?"

For the first time since the double funeral Carmichael Blake-Jones felt a little warmth stir in his frozen heart. He quickly added, "Please, help me know. . . ."

186

Letters raced between Massachusetts and Wyoming. The price Old Man Turpin was asking for the Circle 5 was both fair and sensible, Nate wrote. His investigation and knowledge of Wyoming land values confirmed it. More and more Carmichael picked up Mercy's trick of saying, "When I get to Wyoming" rather than "if I go." At last he finally faced the final hurdle.

Mercy's usual quick understanding caught the frustration in his voice one day while he raised various objections. Suddenly she burst out, "By the way, if you're worrying about Mandy, don't. I asked Mother and Daddy a week ago if we could have her in case you ever decided to teach somewhere else. Mother clasped her hands and looked like I'd offered her a good-sized chunk of heaven."

Mercy mimicked Caroline perfectly. " 'Having Mandy here would mean free time for me to read and maybe even gad a bit, especially now that Mercy has been working with her. I could turn the housework and cooking over to them and be a lady of leisure.' "

"I wonder how Mandy would feel." Carmichael dreaded even bringing it up with their faithful friend.

"Want me to find out?" Mercy offered. Her eyes narrowed and she tapped her lips with one finger.

"Would you? Can you, without giving anything away?"

"Just watch me." She raised her voice and called, "Mandy, could you come in here for a moment, please?"

Carmichael held his breath while Mandy entered and perched on the chair Mercy indicated.

"Mandy, I can't bear the thought of having to go home when Uncle Michael doesn't need me any longer. We've had such fun and you've taught me so much."

Her wistful voice and eyes told Carmichael how sincere Mercy really was and brought a wide smile to Mandy's face.

Mercy continued, twisting her handkerchief but keeping her blue gaze on Mandy. "Would you ever consider coming to live with us? I mean, if Uncle Michael didn't need you anymore?"

Mandy solemnly stared at her then at Carmichael. "It'd be pure joy being with Miss Car'line and you, child." She turned a longing look at the teasing girl. "I reckon if ever Master Michael takes him a wife he could spare me."

A great load fell from Carmichael. He impulsively crossed the room, knelt at the old woman's side, and took her worn hands in his. "Mandy, I'm not taking a wife, but I am seriously considering going away from Concord."

"It's a mighty good thing, Master Michael." Mandy smiled when his mouth dropped open. "This place ain't really home now that Master and Missus are gone to heaven. I been expecting this. Don't you worry none over old Mandy." She beamed at Mercy. "That child will warm my heart just as you did."

A thought made Carmichael ask, "Suppose I got a home somewhere else, a long way off, maybe. Would you come, as far as Wyoming, maybe?"

Mandy considered for a long while. Then her lined face brightened. "I reckon it would depend on who needed me the most, you or Miss Car'line and this here child."

"You know you'll always be part of our family no matter what," Mercy put in. She bounded over to hug Mandy. "We'll have the best time. I can just hear mother singing praises when we take over her work so she can rest."

With the final problem overcome, Carmichael succumbed to the lure of the West. He and Mercy decided that he should not tell Desert Rose who he was when he reached Antelope. "She'd think you raced out there posthaste and it might spoil everything," Mercy wisely pointed out. She frowned then her face cleared. "I know. Tell her you'll be traveling and to send her letters in care of me. No, that's not so good. She might think Mercy Curtis is a rival."

"How about just having them come in care of M. Curtis?" Carmichael inquired, wondering how deeply he was going to get involved and what might result.

"Perfect." Mercy glanced around to make sure Mandy wasn't in hearing distance. "Michael, why don't you do something really daring? I read this book where an easterner bought a ranch but didn't know much about running it so he used a different name and then went out and got a job on his own ranch so he could find out all about it."

"Spies and counterspies?" Carmichael grinned. Yet the boldness of the plan appealed to his new, adventuresome nature. Why not? He could meet Desert Rose Birchfield without her knowing his identity, for a while.

# Chapter 4

Dr. Adam Birchfield believed range lore and survival skills as important to his daughters' health as good food and plenty of sleep and exercise. His wife Laurel agreed, as did her twin sister, Ivy, and her husband, Nathaniel Birchfield, Antelope's beloved minister. These beliefs worked in favor of Desert Rose and Columbine and Nate and Sam who spent all the time they could on their grandparents' ranch, the Double B.

Rose's interest in keeping up with the daring Nate dismayed a score of would-be suitors who often found themselves left to young Columbine's mercies. Even the most devoted and love-stricken cowboy had not touched her heart, although many had won her admiration with his riding, roping, and marksmanship skills.

Yet when a triumphant Nate sought her out waving a letter and whispering, in case Columbine or Sam lurked about, "It's come!" Rose's heart lurched.

"So soon? How did they get it published already?" She snatched the envelope and her eyes opened wide. "Why, this isn't from *Hand and Heart*. It's from Concord, Massachusetts."

"Of course it is." Nate's dark eyes flashed with mirth. "Some eager swain evidently wrote the moment he saw your advertisement. Open it, will you?" The letter from his former teacher had been carefully removed from the larger envelope that came so the one Rose now held could be delivered intact.

Fun filled Rose's expressive face. She ripped open the letter and silently began to read. "Why, he knows you!" she gasped. "Listen to this, Nate. He says there must only be one Nate

Birchfield in Antelope. What an odd coincidence."

Nate bent over to twitch a piece of sage off his pant leg and mumbled, "That's probably why he felt it would be safe to write, seeing as we used my address."

"Oh." Rose returned to the letter. "He sounds nice. Is he?"

Nate didn't need to pretend. "He's just plain grand and the only reason I even considered going back for another year." His enthusiasm showed in every word and Rose listened hard, holding one finger to mark the place in her letter where she stopped reading.

"Carmichael Blake-Jones. What a name!" She threw back her head and laughed until the hills echoed with her joy. "What does he look like?"

"About my height but heavier, fair instead of dark. Better than that, he's willing to see the other man's side of things."

"Is he a Christian?"

Nate cocked his head to one side. "Well," he drawled. "He attended chapel and church. I don't know how deep his faith goes. I know even the most critical of those at school never knew him to do an unkind or unfair thing. Several times for someone in trouble he—"

"Were you one of them?" she demanded, her dark brown eyes glowing.

"Let's just say that even someone as angelic as I slips now and then," he teased then made a halolike motion above his rumpled dark hair.

"Do you think I should answer?" Rose quickly finished the rest of the short letter. "Oh, I know he isn't interested in moving out here or doing any of the things I put in that silly advertisement. He just sounds nice and maybe a bit lonely."

All Nate's mischief fled. "Both his parents were killed in a railway accident a few months ago and he lives in the family home alone except for a housekeeper, Mandy."

"Doesn't he have brothers and sisters?"

"All older and married, busy with their own families. He has a young niece Mercy. I vaguely remember seeing her a time or two."

"Aha!" Rose seized on his statement. "Pretty?"

Nate shrugged. "I guess so. Plumpish, fair. Pretty skin." He surveyed Rose's tanned complexion. "Pink and white, not tanned like yours."

She bristled and he quickly added, "On you it looks good. On her it wouldn't. What else did he say?"

Rose's firm chin shot skyward. "It's my letter, not yours."

"Don't forget I'm your go-between," he warned.

"Not for long." She tucked the letter back into its envelope and shoved it in her shirt pocket. "When I write I'll ask Mr. Blake-Jones to write directly to me from now on."

"How will you explain to your parents the sudden influx of letters in a masculine hand from two thousand miles away?" Nate fired his best shot.

"There won't be a sudden influx," she reminded him. "Besides, I'll tell the truth, well, part of it. I'll tell Mother Mr. Blake-Jones is lonely and you fixed it up for us to correspond."

"Thanks a heap!" He glared at her. "She'll tell my folks and there won't be a doghouse in Wyoming big enough for me."

"Don't be silly," Rose told her irate cousin. "Mother knows what it's like to want to do out-of-the-ordinary things." Her white teeth flashed. "Writing to a perfectly respectable teacher at a private boys' school is a lot different from leaving home and traveling alone to the Wyoming Territory a generation ago!"

Out maneuvered, Nate couldn't help prodding, "When are you going to answer?"

Rose just smiled. "Shame on you, trying to get at the secrets of a maiden's heart."

Nate parried her thrust with a quick retreat, only stopping to call around the corner, "I see you've been reading romances again. Ohhhh, love is soooo grand." He crossed eyes, stumbled in a mock swoon, then recovered himself and vanished with a mocking laugh.

She couldn't help joining in the laugh. Good old Nate! Suddenly a pang went through her. What if *he* had met a girl back East he cared enough about to move there himself? *If that ever happened, well, life would hold no surprises for her. He didn't, she told herself. So stop building mountains.*

Her fingers stole to the letter and a warm feeling for the lonely young man who had so courteously answered her advertisement took root in the rich, sympathetic soil of her heart. Perhaps it wasn't proper to reply at once, but who cared? Rose tossed her head and went to find writing materials....

Summer opened in a new and different way from any other. Almost before Rose caught her breath and confessed to her mother that she had actually answered a letter from one of Nate's former teachers, a second letter came. In a way, it offered relief. Rose openly showed it to her parents.

"I wouldn't have chosen this way for you to begin writing to the young man," Dr. Birchfield said. "On the other hand, having a friend from back East can benefit you both, and Nate assures me this Mr. Blake-Jones is above reproach." His dark eyes so like Rose's twinkled. "Although Nate isn't always the most reliable judge of character, when it comes down to what really counts I value his comments. Write away, Rose. Just don't encourage your friend to pull up stakes and move to Antelope, at least not until you're eighteen."

"Adam!" Laurel sounded shocked then laughed until her

pretty face crinkled and she looked almost as young as her daughters. "I distinctly remember some other easterners pulling up their stakes and look what happened."

"That's what I'm afraid of," he told her solemnly, but Rose saw the twinkle deepen when he kissed her mother.

*ℒ*

One evening before sunset Rose saddled Mesquite and rode up to her favorite overlook. She carried with her the latest letter from Massachusetts. New feelings stirred in her heart that thrilled yet frightened her. *Was this what falling in love was like?* To wait impatiently from the time she wrote to Michael, as he had begged her to call him, until a letter came? To seek solitude rather than open the letters in front of curious Columbine and taunting Nate?

With her new awareness, Rose mulled over the changes in herself. "I spend more time dreaming," she admitted to the fiery edge of the sun still visible over the peaks. Color brighter than the blushing sky crept into Rose's cheeks and a wistful sigh escaped. Just this evening after supper she had come upon her father and mother in a rare moment of freedom from their duties. Adam and Laurel had ridden out from town to eat with the Browns and the Birchfield offspring, then had slipped away for a quiet walk. Screened by a drooping cottonwood, Rose stopped short at the picture before her. As Dad faced Mother with their hands joined, their profiles showed clear against the big rock where they stood.

Not wanting to intrude on their precious privacy, Rose took a silent step back then halted, transfixed by Dad's words that fell like beads from a broken string, each separate and ringing.

"Laurel, it's been almost twenty years since I came riding in to Red Cedars. You're more beautiful now than you were then."

The unwilling eavesdropper's eyes stung. Would anyone be able to say that to her twenty years from now?

Laurel laughed and little bells rang. "And Dr. Adam Birchfield is even handsomer."

Etched against the moss-covered rock, Adam's face shone with a light that caused Rose to cover her mouth. "Thank God you are the one He knew would complete my life. Dearest, all these years, through drought and hard work, two steps forward and one step back, if you could do it all over, would you leave Red Cedars and come to me again?"

Laurel hesitated and the listening Rose held her breath. Then in a choked voice her mother said, "I would come, only far sooner!"

When Dad caught her close with a little cry, Rose escaped undetected. A knowledge she didn't know she possessed whispered inside her wildly beating heart. *This is love as God meant it to be, enduring, sustaining, real.*

Why should the name Carmichael Blake-Jones immediately flash into her mind? Rose dismissed such premonitions in her usual style. Yet now as the sky changed to gold and purple and gray and she reluctantly mounted Mesquite for the ride home, memory of the two who were dearer to Rose than anyone on earth settled into her heart's treasure chest to be stored, taken out now and then, and cherished.

❧

News that ran the range like wildfire temporarily replaced thoughts of love from Rose's mind. When Nate rode in from Antelope with another letter from Michael he also delivered the news that Old Man Turpin had sold his Circle 5 ranch to an easterner.

"Wish I'd known," said Thomas Brown, scratching his head as he looked at his grandson. "We might have swung it and added to the Double B."

Grandma Sadie, bright and perky as ever, said, "Land sakes, old man, don't you think we have enough to do around here without adding another ranch?"

Thomas grinned and Rose saw the fondness in the gaze he turned toward his wife. "The young people are growing up. Maybe one of them will want a ranch."

Nate squirmed under his grandfather's direct gaze. He still hadn't told anyone except Rose about his struggle over the future. His younger brother, Sam, grinned back at Grandpa Thomas. "Not me. I'm gonna be a doctor like Uncle Adam." With a flash of the mischief that characterized Nate, young Sam drawled, "Too bad you didn't buy it for Rose. She could be a female rancher. She'd do a good job, too," he added.

"You just bet I would. If I had the Circle 5 I'd tear down those saggy fences and build a strong corral and then build a house with enough windows to see all five peaks that show up there."

"Does anyone know anything about the new owner?" Columbine put in. Her light brown hair lay in carefully set curls and her usually languid brown eyes sparkled with excitement. "Does he have a family? Will he be living on the Circle 5?"

"Uh, Old Man Turpin says everything was handled through what he calls 'a young upstart of a Rock Springs lawyer.' The name on the papers is a Mr. Prentice." Nate meticulously refrained from mentioning one small detail: he had encouraged the new owner to use a name other than Blake-Jones. Michael had chosen his mother's maiden name and in correspondence had frankly told the lawyer he preferred the countryside didn't know his real identity until a later time when he would disclose it. Neither did Nate report how the lawyer verbally raised his eyebrows but buttoned his lips in respect to his eccentric client's wishes.

"The lawyer is rounding up hands, doing some of those repairs you talked about, Rosy, and in general, sprucing up the Circle 5." Repressed excitement oozed from Nate.

Rose glanced at him sharply. "You act as if you struck the entire deal."

Nate grinned his particularly maddening grin. "Well, I did bring home the news, didn't I?" He tweaked her braid. "Ready for a ride?"

"Five minutes." She raced upstairs to get a jacket and the sombrero she liked best for riding.

Trail companions Mesquite and Piebald stood waiting by the time she arrived. She'd had some trouble convincing Columbine and Sam this wasn't a good time for them to come along.

"Come on, Columbine, I'll take you," she heard Sam say and some of her guilt fled. She had to tell Nate a piece of news of her own. In the letter she'd managed to slip away and read, Michael shared that after a long time of serious thought he had decided to take time off from his teaching position and do some traveling.

*Don't stop writing,* he wrote in the concise hand Rose had come to admire. *Send letters in care of M. Curtis and they will be forwarded.*

"M. Curtis?" Nate wrinkled his forehead. "Who's that?"

"Who cares?" Rose said impatiently and swung to the saddle. Her auburn braid flipped over one shoulder; she felt Mesquite stamp his hoof, ready for the ride. "What if Michael—Mr. Blake-Jones comes out here?"

Nate had never looked more innocent. "What if he does? I told you he's a grand guy." He vaulted onto Piebald and gathered the reins. Not until their usual race ended with him a length ahead did Nate casually add, "Don't you want him to come?"

"I don't know." Panting, her face as pink as her name, Rose slowly dismounted and dropped to the needle-covered knoll they loved. "He hasn't sent a picture, although I did when he asked for one."

Nate choked and she whirled on him. "What's wrong with you?"

He coughed. "Then you wouldn't know him if he came riding up to you." He jerked off his big hat and slapped dust from his jeans with it until Rose indignantly moved away from him. "Any other reason you aren't pitty-patting to see him?"

She ignored his sarcasm and drank in the familiar scene before her. Gazing at the rolling hills and tall mountains, she was filled with the strength and peace of the psalmist David: "I will lift up mine eyes unto the hills, from whence cometh my help."

"Nate—" A childlike tremble brought seriousness to her cousin's face. "It's been wonderful to write and tell him about Wyoming and hear about his life. Sometimes, though, when you meet someone about whom you have certain ideas, you feel disappointed."

"I know, Rose Red."

The hated nickname slipped by without a murmur. "I just don't want anything to spoil the way things are right now." She opened her arms wide to the panorama before them.

Nate stayed quiet so long she looked at him in surprise. He lay on his stomach, chewing a blade of grass. The expression in his eyes touched his faithful friend's heart. "Here I am worrying about what may never happen while you're struggling. Are you any closer to an answer?"

"I think so." New manliness shone in the dark gaze he tore from the mountains and turned on her. "Nothing shattering has happened, but every time I see Dad's tired face filled with a look beyond explaining I see myself." He shifted. "Does that sound stupid?"

Rose shook her head. "Have you talked with him or Aunt Ivy?"

"I won't until I'm sure." Nate moodily returned to his survey of the valley below. "If it were any other job I'd probably be shouting it from the housetops. Like Sam's hung on your dad's pants leg from babyhood talking about being a doctor."

"I understand, Nate." Rose put her sturdy, tanned hand over her cousin's and love flowed between them.

"You're a good kid, Rosy." Nate turned his hand over, gripped hers, and sat up. "Sometimes I think we're almost twins." The next moment he flung off such sentiment and reverted to his usual self. "Why don't we ride over to the Circle 5 tomorrow?" Only the look in his eyes betrayed how important these few moments had been to him.

"Why don't we take Columbine and Sam?" she suggested and sprang lightly to her feet. "Seems we've spent most of our lives running away from them. Lately Columbine has acted lonely."

"Let's fill our saddlebags with grub so we can take all the time we want." Nate leaped at the idea. "Can't go in the morning, though. Grandpa needs help mending fences or they'll start looking like those tumbledown ones on the Circle 5."

"Never!" She laughed. "Besides, this Mr. Prentice is going to fix them, you said."

A curious light came into Nate's eyes. "He's a real good fixer, according to Old Man Turpin's lawyer."

That night the entire household including the four young Birchfields turned in early. Usually the cousins quietly visited for a time after Thomas and Sadie went to bed. Tonight they wanted all the sleep they could get and planned to arise even earlier than normal so work could be done and they'd have time for their ride.

Rose could scarcely believe how excited Columbine was over getting to go. She observed her younger sister pulling on boots and retying her scarf for the third time. "How tall are you now?" she asked.

"Still just five foot three." Columbine's fair skin flushed. "I look taller in boots, though, don't I?"

"You really do." Softened by her own thoughts of romance and growing up, Rose curbed her impatience at Columbine and gave her sister a hug. "You may be short, but you're a lot more grown up than you used to be."

"So are you," Columbine told her. She glanced down and her dark lashes made little half-moons on her pink cheeks. "Ever since you started getting letters from Nate's friend and teacher you've been well, nicer." She looked up and Rose saw sincerity in the brown eyes.

At that, Rose swiftly looked in the mirror. Had she really changed? Her image denied it: same auburn hair in a fat braid with the end curling, same dark brown eyes. Or were they really the same?

Rose shivered but quickly hid it from her observant sister by shrugging her shoulders under her worn riding shirt. Her little pretense did not fool Columbine.

"We all change, Rose. Remember when Paul said he put childish things away when he became a man?" She set her sombrero on her brown curls and finished, "I'll be sixteen in mid-September. You'll be eighteen less than two months later. Many girls our age are married and some have babies." Her face glowed. "Who knows when God will send a special someone like Dad or Uncle Nathaniel, or even like Nate?" Laughter bubbled from her and died. "We have to be ready."

*What if God already had sent someone, a teacher named Michael?* Rose crushed the thought but a rich blush caught her unaware.

# Chapter 5

Alone with his thoughts and unable to sleep, Nate Birchfield had at last fled the Double B into a starry Wyoming night. In the distance faint snatches of song could be heard, most likely night riders checking their herds. Several neighboring ranchers had reported missing cattle recently and rumors that a new and daring rustler band had moved into the area were adrift. Increased efforts to protect the animals were in place because as one wise rancher put it, "The way I see it, if a man steals our cattle he strips the food off our tables."

Tonight, however, Nate's mind could not be troubled with livestock. The smell of sage and wildflowers, the crooning of the night wind and soft neighing from the corral called him. Fifteen minutes later Piebald and his rider quietly walked away from the Double B and broke into a trot, then a canter, and at last a full gallop. Nate knew the dangers of galloping a horse at night—gopher holes and unexpected shadows that made a horse nervous—so he kept to the well-traveled road to Antelope. Long before reaching its outskirts, he slowed Piebald and turned toward a patch where the faithful horse could graze.

Rose's question haunted him. Although Nate had determined to have the summer free, he hadn't been able to outride or outrun God. More and more he felt the challenge of the ministry.

"Never could understand how folks could think a preacher's a weakling," he mumbled to the swaying evergreen branches. "Seems to me if a fellow's going to work for God, it will take everything he's got." He found a fallen limb and dug the end of it into the ground. A great lump came to his throat. How many times had he seen his father down the town's worst men with courage and flashing dark eyes? A view from a crack in a building or a partly drawn shade showed much. Nate had watched Antelope's minister comfort the dying, tell the story of Jesus to a scantily clad woman dying from a careless gunshot in the saloon where she worked, and pray with parents whose only child died of fever.

If he lived to be older than Methuselah, Nate wouldn't forget that last scene. He had sneaked out of the house the way he often did when his father was called in the night, following at a discreet distance. He never knew what compelled him to go, perhaps fear for his father's safety or the desire to be on hand in case he needed him.

That night he shivered in the cold outside the crude log home that held tragedy, and more, and listened.

"Don't talk to me about God," bellowed the young father who always smiled at Nate and Sam. "What does God know about how I feel? Why didn't He make my boy get well? He's my only son, you hear me? God didn't spare my only son!"

Nate stood awed at the grief, forgetting how cold he was, waiting for his father's answer. When it came, it nearly rocked the young boy out of his shoes.

"God knows exactly how you feel." No mumbled apology or stumbling comfort but truth, raw and searing. "God lost His only Son, too. He could have spared Jesus but He didn't. He watched the very people He loved enough to send that only Son hang Him up on a cross and spit on Him. Oh yes, God knows what it is like to lose an only Son, and because He has gone through it, He can and will help you, if you let Him."

A loud cry mingled with the softer weeping of the bereaved mother. "It's all right, Steve," Nathaniel continued. "God understands your pain and anger. He knows it's like the poison my brother, Adam, has to get out of festered wounds before they heal. Don't be ashamed. Right this minute God is probably weeping right along with you."

Nate vanished into the night. He never told his father what he heard but neither did he forget it. Now on a far different kind of night years later, Nate wondered. Had his soul been touched that moment that seemed like days ago? Had God placed it into his heart to trail his beloved father for this purpose?

The peaceful night offered no answers; God would choose the time and place for further revelation. Nate led Piebald back to the road, mounted, and again built up to a full gallop, his hair streaming back and his face aglow. Perhaps he imagined it, but when he silently prayed for answers the wind seemed to respond *sooon, sooon,* and home at last he tumbled back into bed content to wait.

Nate didn't awaken until Sam's eager hand shook him with the reminder that fences waited and so did the girls.

A collective gasp went up from the cousins when they reined in on the crest of a hill that gave them a view of the Circle 5.

"It looks like an anthill I saw after I accidentally stepped on it," Sam told them.

Rose glued her gaze on the multitude of men working below her. "Mercy, how did Mr. Prentice get so many so fast?" she gasped, almost unable to believe her own vision. "Why, they've already torn down the old corral and refenced. Look!" She pointed to the barn. "It's been shored up."

"And it's getting a new roof," Nate said with obvious satisfaction.

"They aren't doing anything to the house," Columbine complained. She patted her horse with pretty, gloved fingers and giggled. "There can't be a Mrs. Prentice or she'd insist that the house be repaired first!"

"I wouldn't," Rose cried indignantly. "If new stock is coming in, especially horses, the corral and barn are more important. Once they're done, there's plenty of time before winter to fix the house."

"I can just see Mr. Prentice," Columbine retorted. "He's probably a paunchy, middle-aged retired banker who reads western stories. He won't take kindly to sleeping in a house with a leaky roof."

"How do you know it leaks?" Rose demanded, her cheeks on fire. "It looks all right to me." She glanced at the shabby cabin. "Besides, your paunchy, middle-aged retired banker will be a whole lot healthier if he will throw down some blankets under one of those big pine trees and roll up in them for a few nights."

Nate had a sudden coughing spell that left him red-faced and panting. He finally croaked, "Let's ride down and see what the workers have to say."

The clatter of hooves announced the visitors' arrival even above pounding hammers and chewing saws. First to notice and greet them was a blond-haired, amber-eyed man who appeared to be in his early forties. At perhaps five feet nine inches he looked taller because of his heeled boots. Rose wondered why his eyes narrowed almost to slits when he looked first at her, then at Columbine.

"Welcome to the Circle 5." He doffed a new-looking sombrero and stooped gracefully into a low bow. "You are—?"

"Nate and Sam Birchfield and our cousins Desert Rose and Columbine." Nate swung out of the saddle and held out his hand. "Are you the new foreman?"

"You might say that." He laughed carelessly. "Won't you step down? I'm Daniel Sharpe. Glad to meet you."

A little bell rang deep in Rose's mind. She looked at Nate, whose puzzled face reflected her own uncertainty. Surely she had heard the name before in a way that made her glad Nate was there.

"You're really fixing the old place up, I see." Sam broke the awkward silence. In the moments that had passed, a look from Nate told Rose Nate had remembered Daniel Sharpe. A spate of explanations by the new Circle 5 foreman ended when Nate interrupted at the first possible moment.

"Sorry to rush off." The words rolled out easily but Nate herded his little band back to their horses. "We have quite a ways to ride."

"Of course you do," Dan Sharpe agreed amiably. Yet Rose felt the sarcastic flick of his look toward her with its hint of boldness.

"Goodbye, Mr. Sharpe." Columbine never let an opportunity pass to practice her innocent wiles. "Do come and visit us. We're staying at the Double B and—" A sharp jab in her ribs brought a look of astonishment toward her sister but effectively ended the farewell. "Why did you do that?" Columbine demanded the moment they were out of earshot.

"Don't tell the story of your life to every stranger you meet," Rose snapped.

"Why not? He seemed nice and he's going to be our neighbor and—"

"Some neighbor!" Nate exploded. "Don't you know who Dan Sharpe is?"

"The new foreman of the Circle 5," Sam put in and laughed. It faded into the mountain air when Nate glared at him.

"Who *is* Daniel or Dan Sharpe?" Rose asked. "The name sounds familiar but I can't remember where I've heard it."

"I didn't either, at first." Nate's lips set in a white line. "Then it hit me. He's the crook who robbed the Rock Springs bank almost twenty years ago."

"That nice man?" Columbine's brown eyes looked disbelieving.

Nate spit out his words. "That nice man also kidnapped Aunt Laurel and held her in a lonely mountain cabin, along with my mother who trailed them! If Dad and Uncle Adam hadn't gotten Running Deer to track them, who knows what might have happened!"

"I remember now that Dad said a man named Dan Sharpe went to prison for robbing a bank, but I never heard the rest of the story," Rose cried. "How could anyone be so wicked?"

"I guess he fell for Aunt Laurel then Mom when they first came out here," Nate continued. "You probably wouldn't have heard the rest of the story, so keep your mouths shut. It's coming back now. You know when I was little kid how I used to hide under the couch and listen to everything?"

"Last year?" Rose inquired sweetly.

He ignored her. "Well, what happened was that Dan got hurt at the cabin and after Aunt Laurel and Mom found the bank loot they got him tied up. They knew if Antelope found out Dan had held them prisoner some of the men would hang him. They couldn't stand that so they made a deal that Dan would admit the robbery but they swore not to tell about the kidnapping. I remember Aunt Laurel saying she was so glad they had because otherwise they would always have been filled with hate and Christians aren't supposed to hate people. Mom and Aunt Laurel never told anyone."

"My stars, how romantic!" Columbine breathed. "Just imagine, getting kidnapped and carried off, then forgiving the perpetrator of the dark deed!"

Rose's new sympathy for her sister died with what had to be a direct quote from one of Columbine's syrupy novels. "Don't be ridiculous."

Columbine's eyes opened wide. "I think the poor man shows

in his eyes how much he's suffered." She gave Sam a dark look when he snorted. "Well, he does. All that time in prison. They must have let him go for good behavior."

"Or because his sentence was up," Nate put in. "If you have any idea of seeing Dan Sharpe, Columbine, forget it right now."

She tossed her head. "I still feel sorry him. Wouldn't it be beautiful if he came back to show everyone he had repented? We're told to love our enemies, aren't we?" She giggled. "Since we don't have any real enemies, does he count?"

"You won't be seeing anything of him," Rose told her. "He wouldn't have the nerve to face Mother and Aunt Ivy." She touched her heels to her horse, eager to put miles between her and the man whose amber eyes had glowed like a mountain lion's.

Rose's evaluation proved to be false. On the next Sunday afternoon Dan Sharpe rode in to the Double B and hitched his shining buckskin horse to the rail as if he worked there.

The usual Sunday afternoon gathering of family and friends lounged on the wide porch. Hardwick, the grizzled owner of the nearby Lazy H, sat tilted back in a chair. When the visitor appeared, the chair crashed to the porch floor and the sturdy man leaped to his feet. "By the powers, is it—it can't be Dan Sharpe?"

In the frozen silence that seemed to chill the warm afternoon, Dan Sharpe slid from his saddle with pantherlike grace. "Howdy, folks." H pushed his spotless Stetson to the back of his shining head and removed it in one easy motion. "Glad to see so many of you congregated here."

Rose quickly glanced at Nate, who shook his head in warning. Sam and Columbine stared open mouthed, but Rose didn't trust the look in her pretty sister's face.

"Sharpe." Thomas Brown offered a noncommittal greeting

then slowly got up, but Rose noticed he didn't offer his hand. Neither did anyone else.

Dan's gaze traveled from Nathaniel and Adam Birchfield to their wives, Ivy Ann and Laurel. A sardonic smile vanished so quickly Rose wondered if it had really been there. "I just wanted to come tell you all that I had a lot of time of think these past years in my, er, accommodations. This is by way of an apology for the wrong trails I rode in the past." Dan's frankness of speech and manner brought surprised gasps from his listeners.

*He's enjoying playing the prodigal son.* Rose could almost hear the words. *I don't think he's sorry at all. For some reason it's necessary to him to put on this humility.*

Columbine's I-told-you-so smirk and the fatuous smile she bestowed on the penitent man left Rose trembling with rage. Couldn't she see through Dan Sharpe, standing there hat in hand?

To Rose's amazement, Uncle Nat crossed the porch and held out his hand in welcome. "This is good news for all of us, Dan."

Rose thought she would explode when the self-invited guest had the audacity to murmur, "The influence of the two Mrs. Birchfields long ago is what made me realize how much I'd left my early teachings."

"So what are you doing back in these parts?" Hardwick squinted, and Rose had the feeling he was no more convinced of Sharpe's sincerity than she.

"When I no longer needed my former accommodations I looked around for a job." Innocence and gratitude didn't quite erase the preying look from Dan's amber eyes. "The word got out about the Circle 5 being sold. I went straight to the Rock Springs lawyer who is handling the sale and threw myself on his mercy."

Rose felt laughter bubble inside her when she compared the

literary tastes of Dan and Columbine. *Threw myself on his mercy* faithfully appeared and reappeared in Columbine's stories, at least the few Rose had been able to wade through.

"So you're getting another chance." Nate's voice sounded hoarse but deceptively bland. One dark eyebrow raised slightly, a sure signal to Rose how her cousin felt.

"I think it's wonderful, Mr. Sharpe," Columbine gushed. Her carefully nurtured complexion blended perfectly with the rosy gown she wore.

"Thank you, Miss Columbine." Dan turned Rose's way. "Well, Miss Birchfield, aren't you going to welcome your new neighbor?" Little devils seemed to dance in his strange eyes.

"Welcome, Mr. Sharpe," Rose obediently repeated then lightly jumped to her feet. "Here, take my chair. Nate and I are going to fix cold lemonade. It's such a warm afternoon." Her plain white dress that she wore under protest on Sundays fluttered about her.

"May I help?"

"Oh no, thank you. Nate is the only one I need." Let him find the hidden meaning in that if he can get the look from his eyes that she detested. Admiration from the range riders always carried respect. The measuring examination of her by Dan Sharpe did not.

Before she and Nate stepped inside, Rose heard Dan begin another verse of how sorry he was and that he planned to make the Circle 5 a paying proposition. "For himself, not for the new owner, I bet." Nate attacked the lemons as though he had Sharpe in his two strong hands. A worried look showed his concern for that new owner. "Mr. Prentice may find himself broke and ruined if my instincts are true."

"I can't understand why Uncle Nat treated him so warmly." Rose took glasses from the cupboard and put them on a tray.

"Dad feels there's a spark of God in every person and we must always try to fan that spark until it grows into a fire that purifies even the blackest heart," Nate told her.

"Columbine certainly seems to agree," Rose said bitterly. "Just listen." She and Nate leaned closer to the screened kitchen window, open to capture what little breeze there was. Dan Sharpe had shifted his chair closer to the girl and his bent head showed rapt attention.

"It's truly an inspiration for someone who has been bad, well, mistaken, to admit it and go on from there." Columbine's high, clear voice made Rose feel sick.

"We'll stop that in a hurry." Nate finished squeezing the lemons as if his life depended on it, dumped in sugar and cold water, and vigorously stirred the pitcherful until Rose warned him it would break from the onslaught. A few minutes later Nate marched back out onto the porch followed by Rose with the glasses. "Come and get it, folks." He glanced at Columbine. "Say, are any of those delicious cookies left you baked yesterday?"

"Of course."

"Would you mind getting them, Columbine? Rose and I will pour and pass."

His strategy worked. Dan Sharpe courteously stood until Rose finished passing the glasses, and although she hated it, Rose settled into Columbine's chair. Nate finished pouring the lemonade and dropped to the chair on Dan's other side.

"Is the new Circle 5 owner planning to take possession soon?" Nate queried innocently.

Dan's careless laugh sent dismay playing up and down Rose's spine. "I doubt it. He's an eastern dude who won't know anything about handling cattle and horse and riders. I'll be in full control, so he won't have anything to worry about."

*Oh, won't he?* Rose wanted to yell. *If you were in full control of the Double B I'd be worried sick.* She bit her lip. Now was *not* the time to show animosity, with Columbine crowded close beside her obviously drinking in every word Dan Sharpe uttered.

Somehow they got through the hideous afternoon. Rose talked and laughed and rejoiced when Sharpe's attention turned more and more to her, with Columbine, Nate, and Sam background figures. Suppose she could win the man's confidence and learn why he had really come back. Or would her playing with fire result in an unknown blaze she wouldn't be able to stop? Undecided, she unconsciously heaved a great sigh of relief when all the company left, Dan Sharpe last of all.

That night Nate Birchfield wrote an urgent, troubled letter to Carmichael Blake-Jones, care of M. Curtis, with an underlined request that the letter be forwarded immediately.

# Chapter 6

Carmichael Blake-Jones had always hated his long name, a name made even longer with "Carey" as a middle name. "Carmichael Carey Blake-Jones," he often scoffed. "It's probably as long as I was when I came into this world." Now, for the first time, it came in handy: he could choose bits and pieces for his nom de plume. At Mercy's urging, Michael intended to arrive in Antelope and, if possible, find work on the Circle 5 under the short and simple alias Mike Carey, Nondescript enough to pass in the West yet simple and familiar to Michael, the name was unlikely to trip him up when someone addressed him that way.

When all the legal papers that gave him ownership of the Circle 5 arrived, he laughed at himself. Who would purchase an unseen ranch in an unknown state on the word of a former student? His doubts were somewhat subdued when he remembered the integrity of Nate Birchfield, evidenced in all their former dealings.

When Carmichael Carey Blake-Jones, alias Mr. Prentice, alias Mike Carey, swung aboard the train muttering Horace Greeley's famous piece of advice, "Go West, young man," he was still filled with a kind of awe at his own daring. If a self-styled prophet had told him a few months ago he'd be cutting ties with everything he knew and setting forth in search of adventure, Michael would have laughed. Now Mike Carey merely smiled. A few turns of the great wheels and he'd be around the first bend.

"Don't forget everything we discussed," Mercy called from her position trackside. Mischief curled her lips upward and

Michael saw the despairing what-on-earth-now look his sister Caroline gave her husband.

"I won't." He waved until Mercy's dainty lace handkerchief became a small white spot then vanished when the train gathered speed.

The same journey that had thrilled the Birchfields and Browns years before severed the young teacher from his past and effectively changed Michael into Mike Carey. At Mercy's instigation, he had selected rough clothing to fit his new station in life and she had insisted on washing it a few times so it no longer looked new. She had also insisted that he deliberately scuff the new boots so their shine wouldn't betray him.

A dozen times Michael laughed at the determined girl but secretly marveled at how knowledgeable she had grown concerning Wyoming. "Clothes may look worn, but how am I going to conceal the fact I am a tenderfoot?" he demanded.

Mercy even had an answer for that. Her round face dimpled. "Easy. You don't go straight to Antelope. You stop off before you get there, stay a few days, find a deserted cabin or someplace where you won't be bothered, then practice roping and shooting all by yourself."

"You think I can learn all that in a few days?" He shook his head in disbelief. "And all this time I thought you were smart for your age."

She refused to be baited. "You already ride, except you'll have to get used to a western saddle. I'll bet you find out the rest isn't as hard as you expect it will be."

Now, with every *clackety-clack* of the wheels carrying him closer to the ranch he couldn't even begin to know how to run, Mike wondered. He found himself turning to God, as he had tentatively begun to do throughout the summer. Long talks with Mercy, who loved the Lord and didn't hesitate to

condemn her uncle for the bitterness he confessed, had rekindled in his heart the desire for the companionship with God
he once treasured. The many hours on the train gave him time
to remember all the things Mercy and he talked about at the
end of the day.

Two weeks later Mike felt ready to plunge into the world
of the Circle 5. He had followed Mercy's advice to the letter, found an out-of-the-way spot and shot up trees, fence
posts, and a multitude of tin cans. Once he had been caught
out overnight when he inexpertly tied his rented horse and
shivered under a tree until a compassionate moon shed its
light and he could see the way back to his shack. Mike Carey
learned that night why cowboys and ranchers hated walking
and cherished even the poorest excuse of a horse. The boot
heels so needed for riding had not been designed for a man
afoot.

Every time Mike hit his target, he whooped. At the end of
such active days he discovered how good even the simple meals
he could manage tasted. Not that he didn't miss Mandy's cooking! A dozen times he told prairie dogs and chipmunks, "I just
have to get her out here." Their interested expressions made him
laugh.

At first, Mike hadn't wanted anyone in Wyoming to know
who he was. After much reflection he changed his mind. The
time might come when he would need the backing of someone
respected and trusted. His Rock Springs lawyer—recommended
by Nate as the "only guy around if you want an honest lawyer"—
fit the description. The afternoon before Mike planned to head
for Antelope, he sought out the attorney, introduced himself,
and disclosed his plan to get work on his own ranch. The lawyer's "you may just get by with it" meant more to Mike than
anything he could have said.

The beauty of the Wind River Range topped anything Mike had ever seen. In the moment he first glimpsed the peaks and valleys, silver streams and forests, grazing land, and piercing blue sky, he turned traitor to the stormy Atlantic he had loved. He had all he could do to keep from racing the strong and spirited quarter horse he had purchased in Rock Springs on the advice of his lawyer. "His name's Peso and it fits him," the attorney said. "He came to me in partial payment of a bad debt. I don't have need of a cutting horse, but you will."

Mike stroked the horse's powerful, reddish-brown neck. "Why is he named Peso?"

"A peso is a Mexican dollar and a good quarter horse can pivot on a spot just about that small." A wintry smile lightened the attorney's eyes. "In case you're wondering, a cutting horse does just that, cuts or sorts out cattle from a herd."

"Thanks." Mike grinned at his own ignorance. "Think I'll ever learn what I need to know to run the Circle 5?"

"I wouldn't be a bit surprised. Besides, your foreman knows ranching and cattle. I hesitated when Dan Sharpe came to me because he spent some years in prison for robbing the bank here in Rock Springs, but—"

Mike felt like Peso had kicked him in the stomach. "You mean my foreman is a bank robber?"

"Former bank robber," his lawyer reminded him. "Out here we tend to give folks second chances if they are worth it."

"And Dan Sharpe is worth it?"

"He appears to be sincere. As the gray beards say, truth will win out." The wintry smile reappeared. "Just keep your eyes wide open and don't be afraid to contact me if you need to."

Mike raised one eyebrow in the way that made his face look more innocent than ever. "Is there anything I need to know about the rest of my employees, uh, ranch hands?"

The attorney's rare laugh rang out and he unexpectedly dropped a heavy hand to Mike's shoulder. "Just that they're a bunch of rowdy, lovable, ornery, soul-trying boys, some still in their teens. They will play tricks, wait to see how you take them, drive you crazy, and once you pass their tests, settle down into a loyal crew who will stand behind you in high water. . .and its companion."

Sobered, dreading those tests yet determined not to fail, Mike gripped the other's hand, then swung into the saddle. He caught the approval in his lawyer's eyes and secretly rejoiced over the hours he had spent riding back home. At least he didn't have to learn that, along with everything else!

"Now, you can't help your accent," his new mentor told him. "I'd recommend listening a whole lot more than you talk. You'll learn more that way, too," he said cryptically. "Good luck; you'll need it. One more thing: never lend that horse to anyone."

Mike turned Peso north, the advice ringing in his ears. "Well, Peso, looks like strange pastures ahead. Wonder why he said never to lend you to anyone? I hated to show any more ignorance than I had to. Maybe it's the custom of the country or something."

Peso's steady *clip-clop* covered miles of road winding upward, bringing them closer to Antelope. Once Mike reached Antelope there would be little time for riding. To be more authentic, he had left most of his money with the Rock Springs lawyer. "Two reasons," he told Peso, whose soft nicker and toss of head encouraged confidences. "First, if I show up with money folks are bound to be suspicious. Second, if I don't have money I'll have to get a job right away." Mike couldn't decide if his intelligent steed's snort showed agreement or disdain for his new owner.

Years before when Adam Birchfield stood on the crest of

a hill and observed Antelope for the first time, he thrilled to the scene. Later, Laurel and her family did the same. History repeated itself when Peso scrambled up a steep place and Mike Carey gazed down into the valley. Early evening shadows and swaying branches softened the rawness of the still-frontierlike town with a purple haze. Only the dim strains of tinkling pianos from the Pronghorn and Silver saloons at either end of town drifted up. A deceptive peace radiated from the town caught between the supper hour and the inevitable promenade later in the evening. Mike slowly rode down the winding road. Every smell, sight, and sound became meaningful.

Armed with Nate's detailed instructions and a letter of introduction from the Rock Springs lawyer, Mike passed through Antelope's business center. The dry goods store, the general store with a surprisingly clean window and attractively arranged display of canned goods and merchandise, and a harness and blacksmith shop all seemed familiar to him because of Nate's crude drawings. Mike finally turned and came to a log church topped with a spire so like the ones in New England that a flash of homesickness touched him. He eagerly looked at the low, log parsonage Nate had described and felt a deep sense of guilt. Could he deceive Nate's wonderful minister father and charming mother? Perhaps he should bypass the welcome he knew Nat and Ivy Ann Birchfield would offer to keep from blundering and giving the whole thing away.

He retraced his way to a large building on a side street with a neat sign outside that read ROOMS. Better not to chance exposing his identity at the Birchfields. Besides, Nate had said he spent most of the summer out at his grandparents' ranch. After a good night's sleep, Mike would decide what to do next.

It didn't take long to arrange for Peso's care at the livery stable and get a room. "Just one night?" the proprietor asked. He didn't seem overly curious, just friendly.

"I hope so." Mike's open manner served him well. "I heard in Rock Springs I might be able to get work up here."

"What can you do?" The man acted more interested.

"Ride, shoot, rope, some of each."

"If you don't mind working for an ex-convict, Dan Sharpe's lookin' for riders." The proprietor eyed Mike keenly.

"What kind of man is he?" Mike parried and tried to hide the exultant leap of his heart.

"We're all waitin' to find that out ourselves." The big man laughed. "Used to be Dan Sharpe was as popular around here as the next one. Antelope's willin' to give him another chance."

"Antelope sounds like a mighty fine little town," Mike said. He signed *Mike Carey* on the register and his landlord peered at the name.

"I used to know some Careys up Montana way. Any kin?"

Mike's spirits plummeted. "No, I'm from parts east of here," he said vaguely. "How much for the night, and is there a place I can get something to eat this late?"

The proprietor named a sum so small Mike almost gave himself away laughing, especially when the big man added, "Reckon Mother can find you some supper if you ain't partic'lar."

"I'm not." Mike breathed easier.

An hour later, filled to the bursting point with the first good meal he'd had since he left Mandy, Mike strolled around the little town. He avoided the Pronghorn and the Silver but instead familiarized himself with the different stores and said howdy to a few loungers. He almost came apart when he overheard one of them whisper in a voice loud enough to be heard in Rock Springs, "Who is that feller? S'pose he's lookin' for somebody?"

Mike beat a hasty retreat and laughed all the way back to his spare but spotlessly clean room on the top floor of the rooming-house. Mercy would squeal when she heard her uncle had been mistaken for a gunfighter!

He slept deeply and dreamlessly and awakened to a rosy dawn. A chill was in the air in spite of the promise of another gorgeous and warm day. *Must be the altitude,* Mike thought. Right after breakfast where he briefly met the few other inhab-itants of the roominghouse, Mike headed for the livery stable. Peso stood munching oats and lifting one foot as if impatient to be gone.

"Thanks," Mike told the hostler. "By the way, how do I get to the Circle 5 from here?"

"Thataway." The leathery faced man pointed but shook his head. "You sure you want to ride out there on this horse?"

"Why not?" Astonished, Mike stopped with his hand on the reins.

The hostler cackled. "That's a mighty fine horse, he is. An' Dan Sharpe just natur'ly takes to fine horses."

"Not Peso." Mike laughed and mounted. "I don't sell my friend here."

"I don't remember sayin' anything' about *sellin'* the horse." The hostler's warning floated after Mike but he just waved and didn't answer. His lawyer's advice came back, *Listen more than you talk. . .you'll learn more.* It had already paid off.

Mike had thought his cup of delight filled when he first saw the Rockies and the Wind River Range. Those moments fled into nothingness when he rode through flower-blessed meadows, up long slopes, and across streams and reined in on the same little knoll above the Circle 5 that the Birchfield cousins had mounted days before.

In involuntary tribute to his Creator, Mike swept his hat off and bowed his head. Could any spot on earth be closer to a little bit of heaven? The five beautiful peaks visible from where he sat dwarfed his very soul. No wonder the original owner, whoever it had been, named the ranch the Circle 5. "Dear God, I could be happy here the rest of my life," Mike whispered from behind the swelling in his breast.

The next moment he jerked as if stung by a bee. The vivacious face of Desert Rose Birchfield that Mike had memorized from her photograph flitted into his mind, completing the picture of years ahead. He saw her kneeling beside him with her tanned hand in his as they dedicated their lives and home to their Master; he saw her thick braid flying above her horse Mesquite, her face laughing yet serious.

Peso raised his head and neighed.

"None too soon," Mike chastised himself. But a dull red glowed in his face and he took a shaky breath to steady himself before making his approach to the Circle 5.

To his amazement, Dan Sharpe little resembled the hardened criminal Mike had imagined. His genuine welcome contrasted with the curious looks from the busy hands. "Say, stranger, are you looking for work?"

"I sure am." Mike dismounted and noticed the admiration in Sharpe's face.

"Good horse there. You didn't steal him, did you?" Underneath the foreman's banter lay something sinister.

"Haw, haw," echoed from the surrounding riders and put Mike on his mettle. He gave his most disarming grin.

"Seems like it was the other way around," he declared. "I never did such horse-trading in my entire life!" He chuckled at the true statement that merely failed to include it was the *only* horse-trading he'd ever done.

"What can you do?" Sharpe demanded, a wary look in his catlike eyes. "Besides ride. I can see that."

"Rope some, shoot some." Mike had the feeling Sharpe's slouch hid a wild beast ready to pounce at the slightest provocation.

"Are you being modest or can you shoot?" one of the hands called.

Before he replied, Mike caught the significance of the question. Obviously the Circle 5 men were more interested in his skills with a gun than with a rope. Could he pass their first test and begin to win the respect he must have to also inspire their loyalty?

"Toss something," he told the riders. His searching gaze discovered a tin can off to one side. "Throw that." While one of the hands reached to get it, Mike silently shot a prayer into the blue Wyoming heavens. *Please, dear God, help me to do my best.*

The can flashed silver in the sunlight. *Spang!* Mike's first shot caught it in the air and sent it flying. The noise drowned Mike's surprised gasp. He hadn't been able to practice on moving objects in his sojourn before reaching Antelope. Thankfulness filled him and left him a bit lightheaded.

"Why didn't you shoot again?" Sharpe's amber gaze bore into Mike. He uncoiled from his relaxed position.

"Why waste bullets when one shot does it?" Mike calmly returned although he wanted to howl along with the hands who evidently liked his humor.

"I guess he can shoot—some," one offered drily.

"Do I get the job?" Mike prodded.

"Yeah. Who are you, anyway? On the dodge?" Sharpe couldn't leave off worrying the bone of contention Mike's shot created.

"Mike Carey." He ignored the second question. "Where do I bunk?" He bit his lip, glad for the few western words Mercy had taught him.

"You sound like an easterner," Sharpe said disparagingly.

Mike's shoulder muscles tensed. If he took that kind of talk even from his new boss he'd lose the ground gained with the shot. "You have something against easterners?" His innocent, round face must have reassured Sharpe, for the foreman immediately shook his head.

"Naw. Some eastern guy named Prentice bought the Circle 5 and he's got the cash to make it a paying ranch." A little smile that didn't reach Sharpe's eyes left Mike edgy and fighting not to change color.

"I don't know any easterner who shoots like that," one hand called.

"That's 'cause you don't know no easterner a-tall," another drawled and the first grinned and admitted it.

Mike turned to Peso and led him to the watering trough. He could feel the gaze of a couple dozen pairs of eyes boring into his back.

"Oh, Carey," Sharpe said.

Mike turned but said nothing.

"Before you sign on there's just one thing." Sharpe's brittle laugh didn't fool Mike one bit. "That's a good quarter horse, and when we start herding and rounding up I'll take him. You can have one of those." He waved to the score of horses in the corral.

A low murmur from the watching hands strengthened Mike. So did his lawyer's warning. Without a word he gathered Peso's reins, turned him from the trough, and mounted.

"Where do you think you're going?" Sharpe's voice cut the still air like a bowie knife.

Mike deliberately rounded his eyes. "I'll get a job somewhere else. No one but me rides Peso." He touched his heels to Peso's flanks but was stopped by Sharpe's voice.

"Just testing, Carey. Climb down. Nobody else touches Peso."

# Chapter 7

The new Mike Carey gloated with every nail driven, every improvement made to the Circle 5 ranch. Enchantment lay in each sunrise and sunset, in lazy evenings at the end of satisfying hard days and in the thunderclouds that gathered above the peaks. It still seemed impossible that he owned the Circle 5.

Yet more important to him than the knowledge that he daily proved himself to his fellow cowboys was a return of the old companionship with his Lord. Mike hadn't realized the depth of his emptiness until one early evening when he rode Peso to the knoll above the ranch and drank in the sweet night air. Now he whispered into the gathering purple shadows. "Thank you, God. . ." and left unsaid those things in his heart too deep for words.

Another day he faced the wild wind, rejoiced in the magnificent thunder and lightning, and then raced for the warmth and safety of the bunkhouse. Snowflake-sized raindrops pounded the earth and filled the air with the pungent fragrance of crushed sagebrush.

At first the Circle 5 cowboys drew an imaginary line with Mike alone on one side. To his amazement, few of the tricks he'd expected came. The second night Mike and the hands slept out when driving strays from the draws. Mike awakened to feel a gentle tug on his blankets. He opened his mouth to yell, remembering the campfire talk of coyotes so bold they sneaked into camp and dragged off blankets. Red-faced, lovable Joe Perkins had warned, "Coyotes out here sometimes get rabid. If ever you feel your blankets a-movin' just holler and we'll come a-runnin'."

Just before Mike hollered loud enough to be heard back in Concord, he remembered something else: the hastily concealed snicker followed by a glare at the boys from Joe. Mike clamped his lips shut and quietly investigated. His searching fingers discovered a taut rope. In a lightning move, he leaped from his blankets and with a mighty heave jerked the rope. Joe Perkins lurched then fell almost at Mike's feet, still holding the rope.

"What the—" A dozen cowboys sat up in their bedrolls. Mike couldn't tell in the starlight whether they had been rudely awakened or merely feigned surprise. He leaned down, helped Joe to his feet, and cried, "Thanks, pard! If you hadn't lassoed that doggoned rabid coyote I'd be foaming at the mouth soon." He whacked the ludicrous figure on the back. "Boys, I never knew how grand you were until now. I'll just bet you've been doing night watch for me all along." He stretched his mouth in a wide yawn. "That ornery old coyote's probably still running so we can all sleep better." Shaking with concealed mirth at the significant silence around him, Mike rolled up in his disarranged blankets and seconds later emitted a series of loud snores, his ears alert to the low rumble among the cowboys.

"I'll be hanged!" Joe's hoarse whisper faithfully carried his chagrin. "Think he really thought that? Or is he smart?"

"Mebbe both," someone else answered.

"Makes a man feel lower than a jackrabbit's belly to pull meanness on a man who *thanks* you for it," a third grunted.

"No more sneakin' around at night for me," Joe promised. "It's a wonder he didn't shoot! You all saw what happened the day he rode in."

Again Mike silently thanked God for steadying his hand on that momentous occasion. Only to Nate, who had carelessly ridden out and passed the time of day with the boys then managed to get Mike aside for a few minutes had the new ranch owner confessed his shock when that bullet went straight.

Outside of a few other obviously half-hearted attempts that Mike's keen senses sniffed out and foiled, the boys abandoned attempts to make his life miserable. Joe did annoy Mike by sometimes attempting to imitate the eastern twang in Mike's speech but threw up his hands in defeat when Mike innocently said, "You sound kind of funny lately, Joe. Are you feeling all right?" He later overheard another just-among-the-hands conversation where the men unanimously agreed "wasn't no fun pesterin' a feller who don't seem to know when he's bein' funned."

All Mike's good nature combined with his innocent expression soon sponged the imaginary line. Yet a single incident welded him solidly into the chain of loyalty among his comrades. Hot, dusty, and wearier than he'd been in his life, Mike and the others rode into the ranch late on Saturday afternoon. According to range custom, they were free over Sunday except for those who had the misfortune to draw night duty. Mike could barely wait for Sunday. So far he hadn't been off the ranch or surrounding area, but now he could attend church in Antelope and meet the Birchfields, and Desert Rose. His pulse pounded and he admitted that every step he and Peso had taken in the time he'd been at the Circle 5 had more or less been directed to that end.

Fate in the person of Dan Sharpe decreed otherwise. Mike knew without being told the foreman had taken a blind, unreasonable dislike to his new hand. Mike gritted his teeth and prayed his way through the dirtiest range jobs assigned to him. He would not whimper. He also realized for the first time how loving your enemies left them speechless. Although Sharpe well hid his feelings, the loud "haw-haws" of his men when Mike blandly raised his innocent blue gaze to his boss and whistled over his work rankled him.

"Why'd you let him put it over on you?" Joe Perkins demanded of Mike once when Sharpe had been particularly overbearing.

"I want to keep my job on the Circle 5." Yet Mike caught the doubt and disappointment in his new friend's eyes and inwardly sighed. Must he sacrifice the hard-won respect of his trailmates because Sharpe spurred him?

Prayer emboldened Mike for the next brush with his boss. When Sharpe arrogantly strolled into the corral where the tired hands were unsaddling and rubbing down their equally tired horses, Mike's lips set in a straight line.

"Oh, Carey, there's a bad break in the south pasture fence. Too late to fix it tonight so you'll have to do it tomorrow." The amber eyes held watchfulness.

Perkins slapped dust from his jeans with his hat. "Aw, boss, have a heart. Mike's put in the last two Sundays doin' chores."

Sharpe quelled him with a lightning glance, and the other hands shifted uneasily or kept busy with their horses.

Mike slowly turned from Peso. "When did you learn about the fence break?"

"Yesterday, but what does that matter? I gave you an order. You'll get out there at daybreak and fix that fence." Sharpe's eyes glowed with anger.

"Why didn't whoever found it fix it?" Mike laughed and rounded his blue eyes. "Seems funny for someone just to ride in and say the fence is broken instead of repairing it."

"Fix the fence or get your time," Sharpe snapped and strode away. His boot heels rang on the hard earth.

"I don't believe the fence is even down," Perkins burst out. He eyed the amount of light left in the sky, calculated, and swung toward Mike. "How about us takin' a little ride?"

"Right now? I thought you were going into Antelope with the boys." Mike thoughtfully glanced at the western sky as Joe had done.

Perkins scuffed his boots. "Do you want to go or don't you? I kind of hanker to see that fence for myself."

"Sure, but I won't take Peso." He slapped the quarter horse on the rump and Peso lazily ambled off to graze.

Joe grunted agreement. They chose fresh mounts from the bunch in the corral and fifteen minutes later headed toward the south range, chewing on biscuits filled with chunks of beef provided by the accommodating cook.

"Well, she's down all right." Joe reined in when they reached the fence. He slid from the saddle and carefully examined the pulled-up stakes. "Hmmm."

Mike joined him. "What is it?"

Joe tilted his big hat farther down over his eyes and drawled, "It either took a buffalo, a mean steer, or a man with a lasso to pull up those stakes."

"Meaning. . ."

"Meaning I don't know many buffaloes or mean steers who up an' jerk out a dozen posts all in a row just to be doin' somethin'." His lips narrowed to a slit. "Well, let's put 'em back where they belong." He pulled on heavy gloves and grimaced. "Nothin' a poor cowpoke likes better on Saturday night than fixin' a derned fence!"

Hours later the two rode home through a silver night so incredibly beautiful Mike wished he could just settle down for the night and watch it change from moment to moment. At Joe's suggestion, they had chosen a shortcut that took them off Circle 5 land and across a chunk of property between the Browns' Double B and Hardwick's Lazy H. Suddenly Perkins's low warning halted Mike.

"Somethin' funny here," Joe whispered. "There ain't supposed to be lights on that parcel. It's never used 'cept by the Lazy H for grazin'. They pay fees to the owner, whoever he is." His arm shot out and gripped Mike's shoulder. "Stay here and don't make noise, no matter what." The next moment Joe slipped off his horse and vanished into the dark shadows cast by trees and kissed by a night wind.

An eternity later a gunshot alerted Mike who still held the bridle of Joe's horse. It took all he could do to keep his own horse and Joe's from pitching. Then, silence. The moon had slid behind a cloud and Mike peered ahead. Joe had told him to wait, but how could he, not knowing what that shot meant? With a quick prayer for guidance and help, Mike sprang from the saddle and tied the horses to a nearby tree. He couldn't take the chance of leaving them with reins standing as nervous as they were. No lights penetrated the darkness when Mike crept forward.

What seemed like a mile was in reality a few hundred feet between the horses and the point where Mike stumbled over something in the path. His heart leaped to his throat. Long, dark, and grotesque, a figure lay motionless at his feet. "Joe?" Mike dropped to his knees, felt for Joe's heartbeat, and his hand came away wet and slippery. He smelled it—blood.

The sympathetic moon crawled from behind its cloud and shone directly on Joe's pallid face. His eyes opened. "Pard, get outa here. Now! Five of 'em; they may come back." He struggled to sit up and fell back senseless.

Every instinct for self-preservation screamed *run* in Mike's ears. He shook his head to clear it, snatched off his scarf, and jerked open Joe's jacket and shirt. "Thank God!" The wound he expected and found was high, away from the heart, near the hollow in Joe's shoulder. Mike stuffed the scarf against the seeping blood and ripped off Joe's scarf and wadded it against the gaping wound where the bullet had gone out of Joe's back. Perkins moaned and the pads shifted. Mike shed his jacket, tore his shirt into strips, and bound the lifesaving pads into place then forced

Joe back into his shirt and jacket.

Every ounce of Mike's newfound strength and a broken, "God, help us, please," sustained him. Once the bandages lay firm, he considered then crept forward. He must ascertain that Joe's attackers had gone before attempting to move the cowboy he had learned to admire and love. Only the faint *thud, thud* of hooves fading in the distance could be heard. *"They must not want anyone to know who they are or what they're doing,"* Mike surmised. The silver night had become the stuff of which nightmares are made. Somehow Mike got Joe into the saddle of his horse. Yet he reeled until Mike knew he'd never stay upright. They'd have to ride double and put the second horse on a lead line. If only good old Peso were here instead of this strong but flighty stallion!

Streaks of dawn caressed the sky by the time Mike and his injured companion reached the Circle 5. With his last spurt of energy he got Joe down and into the bunkhouse. Willing hands who had awakened from what little sleep they had after getting home late from the Antelope saloons fumbled and proved more bother than they were worth. Mike sent the soberest of the bunch to town for Dr. Birchfield and ordered the others to stand back. "We won't remove the bandages until the doctor comes," he told them. Bleary-eyed and unshaven, they bore little resemblance to the singing bunch who had come in from the trail dusty but eager for their night in town.

Disgust filled Mike. When he took over the Circle 5, he wouldn't stand for drinking. If it meant running the ranch with a half crew or doing it all himself, so be it. For an instant he wanted to rail at them all, tell them to look at what they were doing. His shoulders sagged, aching from the long night's strain.

"Pard?" Joe's weak whisper drove all condemnation away.

"Here," Mike triumphantly pressed Joe's hand. "Don't try to

talk. The doctor will be here soon."

Joe's face wrinkled. His pain-glazed eyes locked around the bunkhouse. "Aw, you brought me home! How come you didn't save your own skin?"

Mike felt rather than saw the ripple of shock that froze the others around them. His voice rang. "Joe Perkins, if it had been I who got shot, wouldn't you have done the same?"

A grin more like his usual look sat strangely on the pale face, but Joe's eyes flashed. "Reckon I would." He licked dry lips. "Gimme some water, will you?"

The cook sprang to get it and Mike remembered something. "Did anyone tell Sharpe?"

"Naw, he rode out right after you did," someone volunteered. "Said he wouldn't be back until tomorrow. Didn't say where he was goin'."

Why did a strange feeling brush wings in Mike's mind? Too tired to identify it, he stumbled to a wash basin, cleaned up as best he could, and sat down to wait for the doctor.

His first impression of Dr. Adam Birchfield indelibly etched itself on Mike's brain. Tall, dark, and authoritative, he said little while ministering to Joe except to state he had been given just the right attention and would heal in a short time. Not until he completed his work and washed his blood-stained hands did he turn his piercing black gaze that betrayed his relationship to Nate toward Mike. "New hand? I think Nate mentioned you." His grip proved to be everything and more Mike expected of the legendary man Nate had described. Mike met his gaze squarely.

"Mike Carey."

"Have you studied medicine?"

"No, I just knew the blood had to be stopped. I prayed a lot, too," Mike added frankly.

In the paralyzing stillness that greeted his astounding

announcement, the tick of an old clock sounded loud. Then Dr. Birchfield said, "Well, thanks to *both*, your friend will be fine." He yawned and the black eyes danced. "I'd better get back to Antelope. Our population is due to be increased any minute and I'll be needed." He gripped Mike's hand again, nodded to the rest of the hands, and walked out.

"Can we get some shut-eye now?" someone plaintively asked and it started a rush to the bunks.

Hours later Mike came out of a sound sleep when the bunkhouse door crashed open and heavy-booted footsteps crossed the scrubbed wooden floor. "Where's Carey? Peso's here so Carey must be, too. He's through. Any time I give a man an order and he ignores it—what's wrong with *you*?"

From the shelter of his blankets, Mike grinned and waited for the fun to begin. He could see Joe propped up against a roll of blankets, his bandaged chest visible through a half-opened shirt.

"Well, boss, you'd be short one cowpoke if it weren't for Mike Carey," Joe drawled in his most maddening way. His hands curled around a cup of coffee and the steam spiraled up to hide his expression, but Mike heard the glee in his voice and grinned again.

"Carey!" Dan Sharpe appeared absolutely flabbergasted. "Perkins, get that stupid look off your face and start talking."

With all the insouciance Joe possessed, he began. "Me an' Mike thought we'd go on an' mosey down to the south pasture to the fence last night instead of him waitin' until today. See, he wanted to go to church, an'—"

"Forget what he wanted." Sharpe's eyes looked more like a lion's than ever. "What happened?"

"We found the fence all righty an' fixed it. Funny thing about that." Joe's steady gaze bored right back into Sharpe's.

"Anyway, when we got done the moon had come up, so I said we'd cut through that piece of land between the Double B and the Lazy H."

"You *what?*" Blood poured into Sharpe's face and he made a quick convulsive movement that sent the same feathery tingle into Mike's mind that had been there the night before. Sharpe's hands clenched into fists. "What happened?"

"Don't know for sure." Joe scratched his head. "We saw some lights where they shouldn't have been. I told Mike to hold the horses an' I crept up toward the lights. I could see five figures."

"Recognize any of them?" A curious waiting settled on Dan's features and his knuckles showed white.

"Naw. Someone took a shot at me. Next thing I knew Mike was there stuffin' clothes on me. I told him to get out while he could. Didn't know but what those jaspers were hangin' around. He didn't. He packed me in."

From his viewpoint, Mike saw Sharpe's hands uncurl. The blood receded from his face, leaving it colder and more chiseled than ever.

"He must be dead," the foreman said disparagingly and glanced toward Mike's bunk where he lay prone, his eyes now closed.

"I ain't the lightest feller in the world," Joe said quietly. "An' it's a long way from where I got shot to the Circle 5. Besides, now that the fence's fixed, no reason why he shouldn't sleep, is there?"

With an inarticulate mumble, Sharpe turned on his heel and slammed out the door. Its bang would have roused the dead so Mike opened his eyes, threw back his blankets, and sat up. "Joe? How's the shoulder?" He stretched and yawned.

"Sorer than the time I fell on a cactus." Joe's mouth twitched. "The boss was here. You get the rest of the day off. Too late for church, though. It's gettin' on toward three."

A pang went through Mike. He had really looked forward to attending church. "Maybe next week." He dressed, shaved, and ate a breakfast that even made the cook's eyes pop then decided to ride off some of his stiff muscles.

"Which direction are you headin'?" Joe demanded when Mike stated his plans for the afternoon.

"Thought maybe I'd ride back out the way we came home last night," Mike said casually, but he knew his high color betrayed him. Would he never get over the childish trait of blushing? Must run in the family. Mercy had it, too.

"Not until I'm able to go with you," Joe hissed. Mike turned to see the deadliest look he'd ever noticed in Joe's sharp gaze and Joe repeated softly, "Got that? Not until I go with you. Promise?" He held out his hand.

"Promise." Mike gripped Joe's hand and remembered what the Rock Springs lawyer had said about the Circle 5 cowboys. *Rowdy, lovable, ornery, soul-trying. . .once you pass their tests, they'll settle into a loyal crew who will stand behind you in high water and. . .it's companion.* The look in Joe's eyes showed more plainly than words how that prophecy had come to pass.

# Chapter 8

A flurry of excitement greeted the Browns and Birch-fields when they reached the church yard that Sunday morning. "Wonder what's happened?" Rose craned her neck to see. "Nate, help me down, will you? How I detest dresses!" She pushed down the bothersome skirts and smoothed her hair. Laurel insisted that she either wear it in curls or put it in braids on top of her head for Sunday, and Rose hated that as much as the dresses.

"Did you hear the news?" a friend gushed. "Your father got called out to the Circle 5 early this morning. Joe Perkins got shot by unknown riders and the new young man we've been hearing about—Mike something—bandaged him up and got him to the ranch."

"The way I heard it is that this new hand is making a name for himself. Seems the first day he got there he put on a demonstration of shooting that convinced the hands he might talk like an easterner but he sure could shoot western!"

"What new hand is that?" Rose whirled on Nate. "Why don't you ever tell me anything interesting? Not that I care about any old cowboy," she added, then whispered in Nate's ear. "After all, *my* Michael is above showing off to impress people."

"How do you know?" Nate's black eyes twinkled.

"I just do." She smirked and adjusted her collar. "Drat this dress." She swept into the church with a chuckling Nate right behind her. "Oh dear." She stopped short. Just ahead of them stood Columbine, her hand in Dan Sharpe's. Color came and went in Columbine's face, set off by her simple blue and white gown.

"Mr. Sharpe." Not a trace of emotion colored Rose's greeting. Unperturbed, the dapper man released Columbine's hand and smiled at Rose. "Miss Birchfield, Nate." He inclined his head toward the girls' glowering cousin. "I was just asking Miss Columbine if you young ladies and your cousins would like to ride over to the Circle 5 and—"

Rose started to freeze him with an "Impossible!" but she quickly reconsidered. Once Columbine thought her family was persecuting the foreman her romantic notions would swell into a situation worthy of the Montagues and Capulets.

Nate had no such qualms. "I think Dad's about ready to start. Why don't we discuss it after church?" He adroitly escorted a reluctant Columbine into a nearby pew, then Rose, before placing himself on the end.

If Dan Sharpe saw through the move he didn't let on. "After church, then," he murmured and skillfully placed himself in a pew just ahead and across the aisle where Columbine's admiring gaze couldn't help focusing on him.

It took all of Rose's concentration to overlook the arrogant man and listen to the sermon. On this Sunday Reverend Nathaniel Birchfield had chosen to speak about loving your enemies and praying for those who despitefully use you. Rose frankly admitted in her heart, *Dear God, if I prayed for Dan Sharpe it would be for You to remove him to another range and then soften his heart!* The next second shame filled her. Quick to anger, she struggled for the meekness she knew God required of His children. *I'm sorry, God.* She quickly added a postscript to her unspoken prayer. *It's just that Columbine acts so fascinated and Dan Sharpe's more than twice as old as she is plus a million times older in experience.* Rose turned her head slightly and love mingled with impatience for her sister brought moisture to the long, downcast lashes.

Columbine looked so demure, yet her eyes told other tales when she cast glances across the aisle to the pew ahead. Rose involuntarily shivered. Never, never, never must Dan Sharpe win Columbine! Dared she herself go back to the plan to attract him? She set her lips firmly. If that is what it would take to open Columbine's novel-blinded eyes, so be it. The rest of the sermon, closing hymn, and prayer blurred while Rose gathered courage for the distasteful task ahead. When the congregation spilled out open doors into the sunny world, she had herself under control.

"About that visit, this afternoon would be perfect," declared Dan Sharpe from his position a step behind the girls.

Rose stuck her tongue in her cheek but forced a smile and an upward sweep of lashes worthy of Miss Columbine. "Our parents have strict rules about Sunday riding except to church," she told him. "Perhaps another time."

"How are the rules about Monday riding?" Dan asked. His sardonic look showed he would not be deterred.

Rose hesitated just long enough to feign modesty. "If Nate and Sam are free perhaps we can ride over tomorrow."

"I'll expect you. Don't bother with food. My cook will pre-pare dinner." He smiled, shoved his hat on his tawny hair, and walked to his horse, his posture ramrod straight.

"Isn't he just the most exciting man you ever knew?" Columbine whispered in her sister's ear, so low that only Nate caught the words.

"He's one of the most dangerous men I ever knew, little cousin." Nate's black eyes flashed as he glared after the retreating Dan Sharpe, impressive as always on his beautiful buckskin. "If you have a brain in your head you'll stay away from him."

"How can I when he seems so devoted?" Columbine shot back.

"You ninny, can't you see he only pays attention to you when Rose isn't around?" Nate stood his ground.

A look of doubt crossed Columbine's face and Rose could have hugged Nate. Now that the seed of distrust had been planted, the elaborate scheme Rose had concocted to disillusion her impressionable and foolish sister could proceed.

Opportunity to further her intentions came the next day when the four cousins rode to the Circle 5. Although their foreman-host scrupulously treated the girls the same, Rose saw big-eyed Columbine watching every glance Dan Sharpe sent her way, measuring it against some inner yardstick. A few times Rose noticed Columbine biting her lip in vexation and the glow her younger sister wore like a cloak faded. Rose secretly rejoiced.

All the crosscurrents didn't keep the Birchfields from enjoying their day. The open admiration of the Circle 5 hands who gathered for the midday meal restored some of Columbine's good humor. Near the end of it, a bowlegged cowboy bashfully approached the grassy area a little distance from the cluster of men who had finished eating and gone back to work.

"Beggin' your pardon, boss, but Perkins is feelin' real poorly. Might be some purty visitors would lift his spirits." The messenger stood his ground when Sharpe snapped back at him.

"Get back to work, Haley. The young ladies have better things to do than hold some cowpoke's hand who didn't have better sense than to get himself shot up."

Haley cowered slightly but he would not be silenced. "You might recollect Perkins was on his way back from doin' his job when he got shot up." Haley's bright gaze searched Sharpe and he added softly, "Seems to me a man like that deserves some considerin'." He backed away wrapped in the dignity of the range that falls on hard working men when they are right.

"I should fire that fellow," Sharpe muttered, then laughed

and shrugged. "If I did, I'd lose half the others and with all the work to be done around here. . . ." He hunched his shoulders eloquently, but Rose caught the glowing embers of resentment deep in the foreman's eyes.

"I don't mind at all visiting this man, Perkins, is it? If it will make him feel better, we should see him." Columbine prettily clasped her hands and a gentle blush tinged her face.

Rose saw Sharpe's scowl and quickly jumped up. "I don't either, Columbine. Mr. Sharpe, would you take us to him?" She mischievously added, "Remember what Reverend Birchfield said about visiting the sick? My stars, I didn't know we'd have the chance so soon!"

Defeated, Dan Sharpe silently led them to the bunkhouse. The door stood open and only one man occupied the large room.

"Perkins, Miss Rose and Miss Columbine came to say howdy." Sharpe's look at the injured ranch hand sent chills up and down Rose's spine. She hesitated but Columbine walked close to the bunk where the cowboy lay. "I'm Columbine and this is my sister, Desert Rose," she told the feverish man. "Oh dear, you do look miserable." With the skill that always amazed those who only saw the flirtatious side of Columbine, she located the water pail and dipper with one glance, a basin and cloth with a second. She brought water and gave it to Perkins then bathed his face. "There, isn't that better?"

An ugly laugh from behind Rose warned her of the foreman's growing anger. She stepped to Columbine's side and slid a protective arm around her then said, "Mr. Perkins, we have to be going, but I hope you get well soon."

Some of his usual spirit surfaced. "I sure will, now. An' I'm Joe, not Mr. Perkins." But he didn't waste much time on Rose. He looked back at Columbine with a glance that shouted he had been stricken for a second time when she ministered to him, and this time straight to the heart. Rose intercepted the startled recognition in her sister's face before a burning blush spread over her white skin.

Rose exulted, wanting to do a war dance of joy. Let her get interested in this young cowboy and she's bound to compare him with Dan Sharpe to Sharpe's disadvantage. Even sick and "feelin' real poorly," Joe Perkins was obviously quite a man.

Before they told Joe good-bye, curious Sam could not repress one question. "What happened, anyway?"

Joe suddenly looked older. He compressed his lips and Rose got the distinct impression he wasn't telling all he knew. "My pard Mike an' me were ridin' home. We crossed that section where Hardwick runs his cattle. Someone took a shot at me an' Mike packed me in."

"Mike?" Nate raised an eyebrow. "I don't remember meeting anyone today named Mike."

"Mike Carey. He's just been here a little while but he'd done proved himself." Joe's eyes brightened. "Once you meet him, why, he just ain't easy to forget."

"We really do have to go," Rose reminded Nate. She smiled down at Joe then looked toward Columbine. "When you're feeling better, come see us at the Double B. During the summer we're there more than at home in town." The spirit of mischief prompted her to add, "Mr. Sharpe comes by now and then. Perhaps you can ride over together."

Her remark backfired. When the little party got back outside, Sharpe managed to corner Rose for a minute. "I'll hand it to you, Miss Birchfield. Thanks for getting your little sister all soft and sympathetic toward Perkins." His lips curled in an unpleasant smile. "It will free me to turn my attentions to the girl I really admire."

A surge of disgust and anger opened Rose's lips, but a warning signal in her brain went off just in time. "We'll see about that," she said, mounting Mesquite in record time to get away from the Circle 5 and its domineering, overconfident foreman.

"He seems nice, doesn't he?" Columbine dreamily said and relaxed in the saddle.

"I think he's obnoxious, wicked, and sickening." Rose let off the steam that had been building ever since she first met Dan Sharpe.

Columbine jerked on her reins so hard her horse danced and nickered in protest. "Why, Desert Rose Birchfield, what a mean thing to say. And when you only talked to him for a few minutes. I declare, you get more peculiar every day!" She stared at her sister. "He seems like a perfectly pleasant boy, and if you took such an unreasoning dislike to Joe Perkins, why did you up and invite him to come visit us?"

Rose hid her astonishment and smiled at Columbine. "Sorry, Columbine, I was thinking of someone else. Joe does seem nice, and if I'm a judge of cowboys—and I should be after living around them all my life—he will come calling the minute he can ride again."

Did Columbine whisper, "I hope he does" or did Rose imagine it? She couldn't be sure, for her sister leaned forward, called in her mount's ear, and galloped ahead.

The long, lovely afternoon's golden edges had begun to dim when the little band rode across the needle-covered stretch that led to the bald knob overlook and home. Nate and Rose had taken the lead with Columbine and Sam trailing a little behind. Glorious splashes of rose, red, orange, and pale violet stained the sky and reflected in the handsome faces of the riders.

Rose turned from the burning sky to the overlook point. Surprise straightened her spine. "Someone's there." Her brows knitted. "Why on earth would a lone rider be here at this time of day?"

"Come on, we'll find out." Nate hallooed and the figure turned. Rose gasped. Bathed in the sunset glow, a man stood etched against the far peaks in clean, clear lines.

The distance between the riders and limping figure diminished. Rose's observant eyes showed a man about Nate's height but a little stockier, a rueful grin spread across a good-natured face, lupine-blue eyes, and a shock of curly golden hair escaping from beneath a worn sombrero.

"Hello! I seem to be in your territory."

The unfamiliar accent didn't belong to Wyoming, yet Rose found it pleasant.

"Nate and Sam Birchfield and our cousins Columbine and Desert Rose," Nate quickly identified. "Looks like you took a bad spill."

"It wasn't Peso's fault," the stranger quickly replied. Rose liked the defensive and affectionate way the cowboy glanced at the quarter horse standing a little way back from the promontory. "I got so busy watching that special display of God's handiwork" —he waved toward the ever-changing sky—"I didn't pay attention, and Peso stepped in a gopher hole." The boyish laugh made Rose's lips twitch in sympathy. "Next thing I knew he was standing there and I was lying on the ground looking up at him. By the way, I'm Mike Carey."

"Really?" Rose flushed, disgusted at her involuntary response. We just came from the Circle 5 and Joe Perkins mentioned you. . . ." Her voice trailed off in embarrassment.

"He tends to exaggerate the little service I did for him," Mike said matter-of-factly, rubbing his leg with a dusty hand.

"Are you badly banged up? Can you ride?" Nate asked.

Carey looked surprised. "Sure I can. I just figured as long

243

as we were stopped I'd enjoy the scenic view for a while before heading back to the ranch."

Rose stared at the pinkened glaciers on the high peaks and the purple-shadowed valley. "You called it God's handiwork. You must be a Christian."

The disappearing sun turned Mike's hair to burnished gold. "Yes, except for a time I—"

Nate interrupted. "It's good to meet you, Mike." His face shone in the wavering light. "We have to get home, though. Ride over to the Double B when you can. I'd like to have you meet Grandpa and Grandma Brown."

Mike Carey's steady gaze fixed on Nate. "I had planned on coming to church yesterday but it didn't work out. I will, the first Sunday I have off." He smiled a singularly sweet smile at the girls and grinned at Sam. "It's quite a ride back to the Circle 5 so I'll be on my way." He limped to Peso, mounted, raised a hand in farewell, and rode out of sight.

Quiet Sam, who now and then stunned his elders with rare bits of wisdom, observed, "He sure doesn't act like most of the cowboys around here. How many of our hands would get pitched off a horse and just sit on the ground looking at the mountains and sky?" He shook his head. "Something funny about him."

Nate exploded in much the same way Columbine had when she thought Rose was criticizing Joe Perkins. "Funny! Why say that? Is there any law that says a—a cowboy can't appreciate Wyoming scenery, 'specially when he's a Christian?"

"No law," Sam returned good naturedly. "It's just not usually done in these parts."

The girls laughed and Nate couldn't help joining in. Sam's droll face became shadowed, reminding them of the miles still to traverse before they reached the Double B.

*"Once you meet him, why, he just ain't easy to forget."* Joe Perkin's

evaluation of the new hand floated in the graying twilight air and Rose found herself defending him, even as Nate had done. The look in his deep blue eyes revealed the cowboy's unwillingness to be praised for bringing Joe in amid adverse circumstances *and* the reverent way he had given God credit for the world around them. Yet Sam was right, too. Mike Carey fit no mold that turned out cowboys. Where had he come from? Had he drifted up from Arizona or Colorado, perhaps away from a past that pursued him? There had been something in the way he confessed that for a time his Christianity—what?

Rose took comfort in the thought that whatever it might be, evidently he had worked through it. The next moment she grew disgusted with herself. Why should she care about a chance acquaintance? True, Nate had invited Mike Carey to visit the Double B, but she didn't have to waste time on him or any cowboy.

Her breath quickened. It had been some time since she had received a letter from Carmichael Blake-Jones. Now *there* was a man worth dreaming about if she were a girl like Columbine, always conjuring up romance behind every tumbleweed. A new realization came to her. No wonder she had been interested in Mike Carey. The moment she heard his name it reminded her of Michael.

She laughed aloud and wouldn't explain why when Nate asked her what was so funny. Imagine comparing polished Carmichael Blake-Jones with the dusty, limping, inattentive Mike Carey. She laughed again for pure joy. How wonderful it was that out of all the young men in the world, Michael had answered the advertisement! Would he ever include a visit to her Wyoming home in his travel itinerary?

Rose felt a blush start at the open collar of her soft riding shirt and lazily spread to her temples. How would she feel if he came? Would he love and appreciate the country of her birth, the hardships and glories, tragedies and hard work that sometimes left her feeling caged yet held her in a grip of iron? Would he gaze from the promontory and feel the thrill that swept through her each time she went there, the same awe she had seen mirrored in Mike Carey's blue eyes when he openly recognized God's handiwork? Or would Carmichael Blake-Jones be untouched, unable to look beneath the surface to find beauty in a raw and far from civilized land?

Rose's earlier joy dwindled and a feeling of depression rode side-saddle with her in the last few miles home. Deep in her heart she prayed: *Dear God, it would be better for him never to come than to compare my home—and me—to his eastern ways and friends. I felt You led just the right one to answer my advertisement, but perhaps You only mean for me to have a friend far away.*

She hesitated, longing to add as she had been taught, "Thy will, not mine, be done." Instead she whispered so low even Nate couldn't hear her. "I don't know why, Lord, but I can't say it and be honest." For long, sleepless hours that night Rose sat by her window, stared into the silver world, and wondered why.

## Chapter 9

The photograph had not done her justice.

Mike Carey carefully withdrew from his pocket the well-traveled photograph Nate had sent of Desert Rose and the duplicate she had mailed to him at his request and studied them. The spiritual quality of her face, the glistening auburn braid, the tanned skin, and her taunting dark brown eyes Mike Carey had just seen for the first time.

Neither had the photographs shown the litheness of her body, the charm of her smile, or the strength of hands that held her horse's reins lightly but yet with total control.

Burdened by his guilt, Mike's face contorted. If he had realized the power of her glance to penetrate his soul, would he have agreed to Nate Birchfield's mad scheme? His mobile mouth stretched into a wide smile that seemed to lessen the guilt. "I'm afraid I would have answered even sooner," he confessed to Peso, who obligingly whinnied in agreement. Mike carefully rewrapped the photos in the little square of oiled silk that fit in his breast pocket and kept them free of sweat and dust just above his heart.

August had become a series of memories. The hard work continued, as did Mike's battle of wits against Sharpe, who seemed determined to make him quit. A few encounters with the Birchfield cousins on the range had resulted in an invitation to the Double B with a lovestruck Joe Perkins who stared at Columbine the entire time and announced on the way back to the Circle 5 that he intended to marry her as soon as he could!

By mid-September, fall roundup was underway as well as

plans for Columbine's sixteenth birthday. With the starting of school, she and Sam had gone back to their parents' home in town, but Rose and Nate continued to spend a great deal of time on the Double B. Mike and Joe had been invited to the party in the big white frame house outside Antelope that Dr. Birchfield had built for his family several years earlier, but neither had been able to attend. Black-faced with rage, Joe privately branded Dan Sharpe with several choice names when he sent the two out on night duty the afternoon of the party.

"Can't stand havin' competition," Joe said bitterly and slammed one fist into the palm of his other hand. His shoulder had healed quickly and his splendid strength put him back in the saddle long before Mike expected it.

Mike managed to hide his disappointment. "Which girl is he after? He's more than old enough to be their father."

Joe's jaw set and his blue eyes flashed fire. "Besides, there's stories about him and a woman in Rock Springs—" He broke off and dull color rose in his already-red cheeks. "He can play the gentleman all he wants but it don't make him one. As for which girl he's after, I've been figgerin' it out. 'Pears to me he wants Miss Rose but she acts like she ain't interested even when she's bein' friendly. Now her sister's different."

"How?" Mike couldn't help smiling at his cowboy philosopher friend.

"I know she likes me," Joe said without conceit. "But there's somethin' in her eyes when she looks at Sharpe that plumb scares me. I once saw a little girl look that way when she faced a rattlesnake, kinda fascinated-like in spite of herself."

"What happened?" Mike demanded.

"Why, I just up and shot the snake to save the girl." Pure devilment replaced the shadows in Joe's eyes and Mike threw up his hands but didn't forget the story and its ending. He couldn't blame his partner for being attracted to Columbine. At sixteen, her fragile beauty matched her name. Yet Mike suspected the same hardiness that permitted wild columbine to survive the elements and still raise its beautiful head existed in the budding woman.

"Any more words of wisdom in that noggin of yours?" Mike asked. He wanted to add *especially about Desert Rose* but held back. If Joe Perkins once got onto him, Mike's peace would "vamoose" the way Joe complained the ornery cattle did at roundup time.

Joe cocked one eyebrow and grinned. "I hear this party won't hold a candle to the one Doc and his wife are throwin' for Miss Rose in early November." Satisfaction brightened his face. "Roundup will be over an' everythin' snugged down for winter. We'll be right there with shinin' faces an' our company manners to help ree-joice that Miss Rose is eighteen." He heaved a long, deep sigh. "Before then, though, we've gotta round up some critters. Can't understand why Sharpe's sellin' now. The way I heard it, the new owner wanted to get more cattle, not less. Sharpe'll probably buy in the spring, but it smells funny to me."

A thrill of danger and warning kept Mike from giving away that the owner of the Circle 5 couldn't understand, either. Should he contact his Rock Springs lawyer? Mike shook his head in answer to his own question. He'd watch and wait.

Nothing had prepared Mike for autumn in Wyoming. Although he came from an area of hardwoods that put on a spectacular and colorful show in the fall, it no way overshadowed the spectacle he now rode through daily.

*It's hard to describe,* he wrote to Mercy. *Maybe it's the distant mountains that make the difference or the shining streams I never dreamed I'd see anywhere as wonderful as New England when the*

249

*leaves turn, but Wyoming is just as grand.*

Mercy's reply came in a few weeks. *I'm so glad it's beautiful there, too. How's our house—and my room—coming? I'm already working on Father and Mother. By spring I hope to have worn them down to where they'll wire you and beg you to take me so they can get some rest.*

Mike laughed over her letter but thoughtfully considered her question. He could find no fault with Sharpe's management of the Circle 5 except so far nothing had been done toward replacing Old Man Turpin's cabin with a more substantial house. The cabin had been reroofed and chinked against the coming winter. The bunkhouse offered comfort and warmth. The barn and corrals and fences stood in mute evidence to hard work. Once Mike casually asked Joe, "Isn't the boss going to build a house? Seems to me I heard rumors the eastern owner might visit come spring. I doubt he will want to bunk with Sharpe."

Joe just grunted. "I saw some plans stretched out on the table in the cabin when I had to see Sharpe one day. He musta noticed me lookin' at them 'cause he said someday the Circle 5 would be the finest ranch with the biggest an' best home on it anywhere near Antelope." He tapped his thumbnail against his teeth. "After roundup we'll probably get stuck with cuttin' trees if Sharpe plans to get a house started before the snow flies."

As if on Joe's schedule, the day after the roundup ended, Sharpe called the hands together. "You all know there aren't enough cattle left on the Circle 5 to keep you on over the winter." He paused and Mike glanced at Joe, glad his friend had told him how things were on the range in wintertime.

Sharpe shoved his hands against his hips and continued. "I can use any of you who want to quit for the winter and come back in the spring when I rebuild the herd. Now's the time for a nice, long vacation if you want one." His smile held little real amusement.

"I'll keep on those who are willing to cut and haul logs, lay floors, and play carpenter."

The men looked at each other and one older man said, "Not me, boss. I'm a cowpoke and it about killed me just fancying up the barn and fence and corral."

"Same here," others agreed.

"Fine. Pick up your time and I'll see you back in the spring." Sharpe stood waiting, his amber eyes half closed. "Any takers on my building offer?"

Mike shoved a sharp elbow in Joe's ribs. Joe glared at him, caught the silent signal in Mike's face, and in an offhand voice said, "I don't mind stayin'. I've got kinda used to my bunk."

A few others grudgingly muttered they'd stay, mostly older men who had wives and kids in town and rode in when they could.

"How about you, Carey?" Sharpe's question came just a shade too casual. "I suppose you'll want to look elsewhere for a winter vacation spot."

He might as well have added, *and don't come back,* but Mike chose to ignore the underlying message. His response was typically cheerful in the way he had learned stuck a saddle burr under his boss. "I'm with Joe. Say, Cookie's staying, isn't he?" Mike grinned at the rotund cook who served as the best advertisement of his culinary skills. Cookie grinned right back and nodded.

"I always hankered to see a house built out of logs that had to get cut down," Mike finished and bit the inside of his cheek to keep from roaring at Sharpe's barely concealed fury.

"Decided." Sharpe yanked his gaze away from Mike and jerked his head toward the cabin. "I'll pay off you who are leaving." He led most of the men away and the others dispersed, leaving Joe to grumble.

"How come you done volunteered me to cut trees? You know anythin' about it?"

"Not me." Mike threw back his head and laughed a ringing laugh that brought a scowl to his friend's usually cheerful countenance.

Joe looked toward heaven as if seeking patience and help, then hissed, "Are you up to somethin'?"

Mike stopped laughing. "Look, pard, if we light out we'll have to hole up somewhere for the winter. How much of your wages have you saved?"

"Some." But Joe's scowl disappeared.

"If you're going to impress Dr. and Mrs. Birchfield as a suitable candidate for their youngest daughter's hand you can't do it broke," Mike said. "Chances are if we wintered in town you'd end up hanging around the saloons playing cards, maybe getting shot up, certainly broke by spring. Staying on the Circle 5 means good food, a warm bunkhouse, and wages all winter."

"But I hate choppin' an' cuttin' an' poundin.'" Joe turned a tragic gaze on Mike and spread his hands out helplessly.

Mike fired his strongest shot. "Think what a good impression you'll make on the Birchfields. How can they, especially Columbine, resist a sober, hardworking cowboy who turns his back on idleness and evil and proves himself worthy to call on them when we aren't snowed in?"

"You shore paint a pretty picture," Joe said sourly. He shoved his hat down over eyes gone speculative and added half under his breath, "Might not be so bad at that."

"We'll be riding in to church and—"

"Church! I ain't set foot in a church since I got to the Circle 5."

Joe suddenly shoved his hat back and stared at Mike.

"Then it's time you did." In a single heartbeat Mike knew one of the finest things he could ever do would be to lead this wild, loyal rider to God. "Look, I don't say much because no one wants to get preached to in the bunkhouse, but if you want a pardner who'll be there even when I can't, One who won't let you down no matter what, you'll start getting acquainted with Jesus. I've heard you tell a dozen times about someone you know who fit your description of 'someone to ride the trails with.'" Mike took a deep breath, then released it. "Try asking Jesus to ride the trails with you and I tell you, you can get through anything. I've never told a soul in Wyoming, but last spring both of my parents were killed in a railroad accident."

Mike ignored Joe's little movement and rushed on. "For weeks I took it out on God, blaming Him for not saving them. They were the emptiest weeks of my life. God hadn't turned away from me; I'd left His presence behind me. It took a long time, and I still don't know why He let my folks die, but I know this: He loved me and you and everybody enough to send His only Son to die for our sins. He took our punishment, Joe, and I'm going to keep Jesus as my trailmate as long as I live."

Joe stood there thunderstruck. Mike half turned and said hoarsely, "Think I'll go for a ride."

Joe's quiet voice stopped him. "Think Sharpe will let us off Sunday?"

Mike nodded, too filled for words. He swung back and held out a work-hardened hand and grasped Joe's. Something in the steady blue eyes told him his witness for Jesus Christ had taken hold in the albeit rocky soil. Given time and patience, watered by friendship and prayer, God grant that it would grow and bloom.

Rose restlessly drummed her fingers on the table in the Birchfield living room. When Columbine, Adam, and Laurel all looked up inquiringly she burst out, "It's been ages since we went camping. Dad, can't you take a little time off? If we wait much longer it will be too late in the year."

Her father laid aside the medical journal he had been reading in a rare time of relaxation at home. His dark eyes thoughtfully reflected the maturity of all the years on the frontier. "Let's see, I don't have any mothers due to bring new life into the valley for a week or so. All the broken bones are healing well and, as far as I know, no one has scheduled any emergencies for a few days. Laurel, would it hurt Columbine to miss a few days of school?"

"Of course it won't." Columbine flounced herself closer to Rose. "I'm way ahead on my lessons."

Her mother's eyes sparkled. "I wonder if Nat and Ivy Ann and the children are free. Remember how wonderful it was when our families went into the mountains two years ago?" She glanced out the window into a perfect October day. "Rose is right. If we go it has to be soon. Look how low the snow is on the peaks, even though this is an unusually warm fall."

"This is Wednesday." Adam stood and stretched. "Why don't I walk over and see if the other Birchfields are interested? We can ride into the hills tomorrow and set up camp, stay over Friday, and come back Saturday in time for Nat to finish his sermon."

Laurel still gazed at the mountains. "I rather suspect Nat will be preparing his sermon the whole time we're gone—and what better place to feel close to God than in His beautiful creation!"

Adam couldn't resist teasing, "What if Sam isn't way ahead on his lessons?"

"He will be. He always is," Columbine said confidently. In the past few months she had begun to appreciate her quiet but fun-loving cousin and to develop a kinship with him similar to that shared by Rose and Nate.

Early the next morning the two families set out. In the years since Laurel and Ivy Ann came to Wyoming, their riding skills had become even more accomplished than when they rode the fields and hills near Shawnee, West Virginia. They stopped at the Double B just long enough to tell Thomas and Sadie where they were going and how long they would be gone, a frontier precaution. Wyoming in her gentlest mood still concealed a darker side waiting for those who failed to respect her many faces.

What a day to remember! Rose was in her element. Columbine left behind her airs and reverted to a simple girl who loved her family and the unexpected treat. The boys and their fathers talked of fishing and setting up camp, while Laurel and Ivy Ann shared the simple joy of being together.

By midafternoon the little band reached the spot Adam had selected after consulting with Nat. Few places among the crags offered such natural beauty, good water, and grass for the faithful horses. Soon eight pairs of hands had erected what Rose called HIS and HERS tents, spread bedrolls, started a fire, and begun preparations for a hearty camp supper. The sandwiches they had brought from home and eaten on the trail were only a memory as sizzling steaks, potatoes roasted in the ashes, canned peaches, and the cookies Columbine had found time to make before leaving Antelope were eagerly devoured.

By common consent, campfire talk turned to singing. Civil War songs and ballads gave way to hymns, and circled around the final embers of their fire, their hands joined, the Birchfields bowed their heads and Nat offered a prayer.

Love for her God, her family, and her country swelled within Rose. She could hear Columbine's quick intake of breath and feel Nate squeeze her fingers in a way that told they felt the same. Through the open flap of the tent Rose saw stars that looked close enough to touch, and she fell asleep snuggled against Columbine with a prayer in her heart and her fingers against a letter that had come the day before.

Sometime in the night the drum of heavy rain on the tent awakened her. Columbine slept on, but Rose slipped out of her blankets and let down the tent flap, then mused for a time before falling asleep again. The second time she awoke the rain had stopped and she heard her father calling.

"Get up, everyone! We have to get out of here."

Fear clutched Rose, and she shook Columbine awake.

In record time the campers got dressed and hurried out into a gray dawn. "What's wrong, Dad?" Rose asked, trying to rub sleep from her eyes.

"I don't know and neither does Uncle Nat, but we don't like it."

Rose followed his gaze to the stream nearby that had purled its welcome the day before. Now it looked muddy and sullen.

"With all this rain there should be more water in it," Adam explained. He looked up the stream to where it vanished around a bend. "Something is holding that water back: beaver dams, downed trees, maybe debris. When or if that something gives way, a wall of water will race down the stream bed and our trail is right alongside of it."

"What about going up and over?" Nate asked. Rose saw the concern in his face.

"Not enough food and no guarantee what the weather will be," his father said. "Hurry and get packed and mounted. Laurel, Ivy Ann, don't stop to cook. Do the best you can with whatever we can eat while we ride. Nate, Sam, girls, saddle the horses while Uncle Nat and I pack the ponies. Wait!" He stopped them. "First we must pray."

This time fear ran through the circle even though Nat's calm petition for God's help restored Rose's normal heartbeat. After the *Amen* each person ran to break camp, and in far less time than expected, the line of eight riders and two pack ponies had begun their descent of the mountain.

An hour later, the deluge came. Hastily donned slickers protected the riders to their knees, but hats soaked through allowed streams of water to trickle down their necks. The winding trail became treacherous and slippery with mud. Even the horses so carefully trained to pivot and withstand obstacles found themselves sliding. Only the expert horsemanship of the riders kept them going.

The rain went on and on. "Think we should stop and build an ark?" Nate muttered.

Rose stifled a nervous giggle and Columbine sniffled. But the stream next to the trail continued to flow its even, muddy water. How long could this cloudburst continue and not sweep away even the firmest, most immovable obstruction?

"If we can make it five miles more, we leave the stream and go up," Adam encouraged. "From there we have a series of slopes and don't have to worry about a flash flood."

Down the trail they climbed, one mile then another. The rain didn't let up. Three miles, then four elapsed. Drop by drop the downpour lessened until Rose's heart beat high with triumph. Just one mile more! She patted Mesquite and the roan snorted and stepped over a slippery rock in the trail.

A half mile from the junction where the trail and stream parted company they came to the narrowest place in the canyon. Rock walls on both sides frowned down on the wet riders even though the capricious skies had long since turned a deceptive blue shade.

"Watch the horses, ride as fast as you can without sacrificing safety, and God help us all," Nat ordered. He drove the pack ponies ahead at a fast clip. Laurel and Ivy Ann followed, then Rose, Nate, Sam, and Columbine, with Adam bringing up the rear.

*Boom!* The sound echoed down the canyon, and Rose tasted raw fear.

# Chapter 10

O f all the miserable times to get caught out a thousand miles from nowhere, this beats everythin'!" Joe Perkins turned his coat collar up around his neck and glared at Mike Carey. "You an' your dumb idea to go huntin' while Sharpe's in Rock Springs."

"How did I know it was going to rain?" Mike defended himself and poked at the little fire in front of them that sputtered its protest against the storm. "Cookie said he sure could use some fresh venison, so I told him we'd get some."

"An' dragged me along with you." Joe grunted. "We could have gone courtin' instead of spendin' the night out here." He waved at the blackness around the complaining fire.

"They aren't home." Mike didn't have to identify who *they* were. "One of the boys who rode in for the mail said he met Nate Birchfield at the post office and Nate said his folks and the girls and their folks were going camping in the high country for a couple of days."

"Why'd they want to do that this late in the year?" A little worry line crossed Joe's face and sent a quiver through Mike's veins.

"They probably didn't know it was going to rain, either," he reminded Joe.

"Who does in this country?" The worry line didn't go away. Joe tugged off his boots, turned them upside down over stakes he had driven in next to the fire and stretched his feet toward the little blaze. "Looks like the rain's letting up some. If we can get our socks dry maybe we can also get a little shut-eye. The tarps'll help." He waited until the drizzle stopped for a time and

259

spread his tarp on the ground, waterproof side down. He tossed down the blankets that had been wrapped inside the tarps and finished by covering the hard bed with Mike's tarp, waterproof side up. "I hope you don't snore."

"Only when I'm pretending to be asleep," Mike reminded, stifling a grin at the memory of the day Sharpe stormed into the bunkhouse spitting death and destruction.

Never in his entire life had Carmichael Blake-Jones, alias Mike Carey, spent such an uncomfortable night. He went to bed cold, stayed cold, and woke up a dozen times, still cold. It didn't help that Joe slept like a hibernating bear and only roused himself long enough to yank the tarp over their heads when the rain increased.

Along with his physical torment, Mike couldn't help remembering the worry that creased Joe's forehead. When the gray dawn came, the stiff cowboys struggled into their boots. The fire had dried the inside a bit, but the downpour in the night had soaked them again. "Why didn't you stick them under the tarp?" Joe asked. A trace of his permanent grin lightened the mood. "I'd have done it myself but I guess you noticed once I fall asleep it takes a lot to wake me up."

"I noticed," Mike let it go at that. Then he said, "Joe, uh, you don't think the Birchfields would get into trouble, do you? They've lived here a long time."

"Only a fool or newcomer tries to predict Wyomin' weather this time of year," Joe spit out. "Everythin' looks all bright an' beautiful like yesterday. Then along comes these innocent-lookin' puffy clouds that get their heads together an' the first thing you know, *bang!* You've got a storm." He eyed the sulky sky. "There's more to come. Did Nate say where they were headin'?"

Mike started to shake his head *no* then stopped. "Wait, I

believe he did. Our rider said something about the gulch trail being the prettiest place around, what with all the color."

Joe jerked erect. His apple-red cheeks lost their color. "Saddle Peso." He ran to Splotch, the pinto he liked best of the Circle 5 horses. "I reckon we'd better mosey along an' meet them comin' out."

Something in Joe's voice stilled the million questions knocking in Mike's brain. He forgot the rain, his growling empty stomach, everything except the fact the Birchfields might be in danger.

"Now's the time to pray to that God of yours," Joe said as he climbed into the saddle, wheeled Splotch, and touched him with his boot heels. "Come on, will you?"

Mike mounted Peso and in two jumps came even with Joe. "All right, pard, let's have it. It's worse imagining things than knowing how they really are." He had to raise his voice to be heard over the steady drum of the horses' feet.

"Couldn't be worse if they get caught on the gulch trail an' a wall of water comes racin' down." Joe's fixed gaze on their own trail didn't waver an inch. "It all depends on how far they went, how fast they started out this mornin' an' if they got past the point where the trail leaves the creek." A steely gleam that crept into Joe's eyes when he glanced at him confirmed Mike's fears.

"How far are we from there?"

Joe grunted. "Far enough, but we're a darned sight closer than if we'd had to come from the Circle 5."

"Just maybe God knew we'd be needed and that's why we got caught out last night," Mike reflected.

"Maybe." Joe's lips set in a grim line and Mike lapsed into silence, pouring out his concern in an unspoken prayer.

An eternity later Joe called, "One more hill."

COLLEEN L. REECE

Panting from their run, Peso and Splotch scrambled to the top of the rise and plunged over, sliding on wet needles and grass.

*Boom!* A distant reverberation chilled Mike and Joe swallowed hard. Heedless of possible danger, they urged their horses down the slope.

⌘

Before the echoes died in the narrow canyon, Nat bellowed, "Ride for your lives and don't spare the horses!" He whacked the pack ponies with his leather quirt until they whinnied in terror and bolted down the trail. The others followed, slipping, regaining their balance.

*How much time did they have before churning waters poured toward them?* Rose wondered. She expertly guided Mesquite, conscious of Columbine's half-sobbing breath behind her and Nate's encouraging, "Steady, Piebald, easy." The half mile to safety dwindled to one-fourth of a mile. The trail widened slightly and Rose's death grip on her reins loosened. The pack ponies were out of sight. Nat swerved his stallion to one side, close to the cliff, and motioned Laurel and Ivy Ann past, then Rose.

The vanguard of the flood waters reached them, a roiling, hungry monster seeking vengeance after being restrained miles above. "Go, Mesquite!" Rose screamed. He snorted, stretched out to his full length, and leaped away from the relentless tide. Laurel and Ivy Ann had reached the junction where the stream went one way, the trail the other, up an incline to a flat bench-like formation. Their weary horses forged ahead and stopped on top, trembling and spent.

A wall of muddy water hit the others like an avalanche. Mesquite swayed but kept his footing and nimbly sailed over a rushing log, staggered, then stamped his way to safety.

Rose turned and cried out in despair. Below her the other horses fought valiantly. Piebald made it to the junction and raced toward the bench high above danger. "Oh, dear God, please help them!" Rose couldn't tear her gaze from the awful scene. Logs, some upright, rode down the gulch, smashing this way and that. Nat's stallion stood braced against the rock wall, up to his knees in sucking water. "Head your horse this way," he shouted to Columbine. Her face shone paler than the flower whose name she wore, but she tried to obey.

The next instant a branch grazed her horse's flanks causing him to rear. Columbine stayed in the saddle, but Rose could see that her sister's strength had been tried to the utmost.

Nat's stallion went down. Adam's horse attempted to swim but the current made it impossible. To Rose's horror, her father disappeared in the sweeping torrent around the bend. Nat's magnificent animal regained his precarious position.

"Rose!" Columbine's pleading voice beat in her sister's ears but was replaced by pounding hooves and men shouting. Nat grabbed for Columbine and missed, and his wild cry rose above the tumult. Both Nat and Columbine went under when the big stallion and the girl's mount stumbled and fell, to reappear, but unable to brace the flood.

Something sang over Rose's head, and she whipped around. Joe Perkins had thrown his lasso. It fell far short of Columbine but close enough for Nat to grab it and be hauled in. Regardless of her own safety, Rose stumbled toward the edge of the bench. She couldn't just stand there and do nothing! Nate tackled her and brought her down. "You can't save her, Rosy. Only God can do that. Look, *look*!" he shrieked.

Mike Carey had urged Peso into the river. Strong and powerful muscles rippled in the quarter horse's shoulders. With his knees and left hand clenched to keep in the saddle, Mike's right hand readied his lasso. Then he, too, passed out of sight around the bend, leaving only the thundering flood to taunt the mortals shivering on the little bench of land.

Mike only had time for a quick prayer before entering the now river-sized stream. The moment he and Joe saw the trouble no question arose as to their duty. Mike waited long enough to see Joe's rope fall short of Columbine before he charged into the river, appreciating to the fullest the horse he rode. After that he had no thought for anything except getting to Columbine before a crashing branch knocked her out. When he surged around the bend and saw the girl clinging to the branch of a tree only God could have kept from crushing her, he gave a cry of joy. Yet Columbine remained in danger. How long could she hold on with the treacherous flood waters pulling at her?

Mike cast a quick glance ahead and again cried out. Downstream a stumbling figure at the edge of the water showed Adam Birchfield and his soaked horse making their way to safety. The gulch widened at that point but Mike saw how it narrowed again into what had to be a drop-off. "Dear God, I have to get her out here or not at all." His fingers tightened on his lasso. "Hold on, Columbine!" he yelled as loud as he could.

For the second time in Mike's life, another human being's life depended on him, and he knew as surely as when he had saved Joe that he had to act at once. There would be no time to recoil his rope if he missed.

Peso gained on the frail craft that supported the girl and finally drew even. Mike screamed into the heavens, "Give me Your help, oh God," and threw the rope.

The rope missed the girl but caught on the branch she held. With daring born of desperation, Columbine released one of her hands from the branch, lunged for the rope, and somehow got it over her slender shoulders. Mike saw her lips move while he tightened the lasso around his saddle horn. "Now, old man!"

All the breeding that made Peso the best roundup horse on the range sprang into life. Inch by inch he fought his way until he swam close to Columbine. Mike clasped his knees against Peso's heaving sides and, bending from the waist, scooped Columbine into his arms not a moment too soon. A purple bruise showed where floating debris had struck her. Her light brown eyes looked black with emotion.

"All over but the shouting." Mike tried to smile and saw her tears start. A few minutes later Peso gained the shore in spite of his double burden and Mike slid from the saddle, laid Columbine on his tarp, and hurried to where Adam lay gasping a few hundred yards away.

"Are you all right, sir?" He helped the dazed man sit up.

"Laurel, Rose, the others? Columbine? Oh, dear God, tell me they're not all dead." His prayer brought weakness to Mike's knees, but he shook Adam until his eyes cleared.

"God has saved every one. *Every one,*" he repeated. "The others are back at the junction of the trail. Columbine's just below. Peso and I fished her out."

Adam still looked confused, and Mike shook him again.

"I don't know if Columbine's hurt. She needs you to look at a bruise on her face."

The appeal for his God-given skills reached the doctor as nothing else could. With Mike's help, Adam limped downstream and grabbed Columbine into his arms.

Mike looked away, back at the flood waters that had already begun to abate until only muddy grass showed how they had spilled over their banks.

"I'll build a fire," Mike said. "If I can find dry wood."

"Do you have dry matches?" Adam's expert hands checked over Columbine to make sure no bones were broken.

"Always. A candle stub, too." Mike found a sturdy branch from the flood, whacked open the trunk of a dead tree and scooped out the dry inside. Before long a tiny fire smoldered. A few soggy biscuits from the saddlebags offered sustenance.

"I expect the others in a few minutes," Adam said. "The water is down and they can pick their way. What did I tell you?" He pointed upstream to where horses and riders gingerly came between discarded logs at the edge of the gulch. "Good. The pack ponies didn't get wet at all. We'll have hot food before long."

Rose's eyes looked like drenched brown velvet pansies when she saw Columbine sitting up against a saddle, bedraggled but safe. She gave a little cry. "We prayed so hard. Thank God. How did He save you? Joe Perkins dragged Uncle Nat out after his horse went down."

"He did?" The glory in Columbine's eyes sent a sheepish grin to the cowboy's red face. "Dad stuck on his horse and the flood swept him close enough to shore so he could get out. I thought I wouldn't make it when I lost my stirrups and the current got me." Stark horror returned and Rose hugged her, but Columbine bit her lip and went on. "I grabbed a branch on a log that came toward me. Just when I knew I couldn't hold it any longer I heard a yell to hold on. Someone threw a rope and it caught the branch. I got it around me and then I don't remember what happened." Her dirty fingers explored the bump on her head. "I guess something hit me. Then I was in Mr. Carey's arms and he got me out and—oh dear! I'm going to cry." The tears she had held back so long threatened to drown Rose, who still held her close.

"We couldn't believe that you'd leap into that flood," Nate told Mike. Color returned to his white face.

"I didn't stop to decide," Mike admitted and patted Peso's neck. "I'll tell you, if it hadn't been for God and this old man here—"

"Don't say it," Rose pleaded and tightened her hold on the sister she had never before known she loved so much until she almost vanished in the dirty, rolling waters.

Joe Perkins didn't say a word, but Rose noticed how serious he looked when the others talked about God saving them. Her cold heart warmed. *Maybe someday. . .* She didn't finish her thought. Right now they needed to get home.

"We lost two horses," Adam said. "Columbine's and mine. There's a chance they'll get out somewhere below and come home, but even if they don't, that's a small price compared with—"

"With what could have happened," Laurel finished quietly.

"We'll redistribute the pack ponies' loads onto the other horses and Rosy and I will ride them bareback," Nate offered.

"I'll ride a pack pony and Miss Birchfield can ride Peso," Mike corrected, without looking at Joe Perkins who made a funny sound in his throat. Was he thinking of Mike's boast months ago that no one would ride Peso but his owner?

"After all we've been through, this Mr. Carey and Miss Birchfield business sounds downright unfriendly." Nate's spirits had already bounced back.

"I agree if Miss, er, Rose does," Mike quickly inserted.

A lovely light shone in her eyes. "I do. Thank you for the loan of your horse, Mike." She stepped into the stirrups and stood while he adjusted them to her shorter height. "Now let's go home. Not to Antelope, but to the Double B. We can get dry there and Grandma will feed us." She paused. "That includes you two," she told Mike and Joe.

"Grub sounds good to me," Joe said heartily, and a murmur of assent rippled through the stained but thankful band.

Hours later, in the crisp, clear evening, Mike and Joe rode home to the Circle 5. Bright stars guided their way, yet none glowed more brilliant or beautiful than the girls' eyes when they told the cowboys goodnight and thanked them again. Mike didn't notice how much distance they had covered in silence until Joe heaved a sigh. "I reckon that trailmate of yours came in mighty handy today."

Mike's heart lurched with gladness. "I reckon He did," he repeated. When Joe didn't respond, Mike added, "He's waiting to be your trailmate, too, as soon as you invite Him along."

"I know." Joe sighed for a second time. "A feller'd be an ungrateful cuss for not acceptin' Him, wouldn't he?"

Mike reined in Peso, their forms silhouetted in the starlight. "Joe, I'd give almost anything in the world to have you accept the Lord, but it can't be just because He sent a miracle and saved the Birchfields today."

The pale light didn't hide Joe's astonishment. "Who said anythin' about that bein' the reason?" he demanded. "Didn't you say Jesus came to save everybody an' died to do it?"

"All those who believe and claim the promise." Mike didn't move a muscle. The night wind held its breath and the mountains loomed as if waiting for Joe to answer.

"Well, I guess if He wants a poor, sinful cowpoke who's sorry, I'm willin'." Joe rode away before Mike could recover his wits enough to realize what had just happened. How like Joe Perkins to confess his sins and invite Jesus to be his trailmate in his own unique way! A few long lopes and Peso overtook Splotch. Mike didn't say one word. He just held out his hand and gripped Joe's and sealed the brotherhood between them.

An errant thought that maybe someday they might truly be brothers in the eyes of the world as well crossed Mike's mind, a thought only shared with his loving and merciful Creator.

# Chapter 11

Nate Birchfield never expected God to solve his dilemma by sending a flood down a narrow gulch and scaring the daylights out of him. All summer and into early fall he had sought God's guidance about going into the ministry. When it came time to think about returning East for school, Nate had to confess to his parents the reason he didn't want to go. If he lived a million years he wouldn't forget the look on his father's face.

"I—I feel like I might be called to be a minister, but I need some time," Nate implored. "I have to be sure."

"We understand, Son." Nat placed both hands on Nate's strong shoulders. "Unless God specifically calls you, you must never take on yourself this work."

All the time Nate rode and teased Rose, helped out on the Double B, and lay awake nights, his mind stayed close to his decision. Then on a soggy chunk of benchland above a death-dealing stream his answer came.

He could pinpoint the instant, the one that Columbine was swept around the curve and his mother screamed. Nat was still at the end of Joe's rope getting hauled in. With all his boyish heart, Nate longed to comfort his mother but had no words. If only he were like Dad who seemed to say the exact thing needed for every occasion! All he could do was to put his arms around Ivy Ann and hold her until Nat finally reached the bench and took over.

The next day he sought out his father. "Dad, does being a minister tell you what to say when people need you?"

Wise Nat! He made no effort to explain things to his son in

an easy way. "I believe God gives us the words but only after we have done everything we can to prepare, which means praying, fasting, and studying the scriptures. It's like when your mother cans for winter. If she puts up fifty quarts of peaches, most of them probably won't be needed for a long time, unless you're around with your big appetite!"

Nate grinned but listened intently, and his father went on.

"Learning the Bible verses is like that. It may be a long time before we need all of them." He paused and his face softened.

"But when you do, you know they're right there waiting," Nate said. "Just like the peaches."

"That's right. Yet times come when all our knowledge and wisdom fail. That's when the Holy Spirit steps in and guides our thick and stammering tongues." Nat's eyes glistened. "I believe you are very close to finding answers to your questions, Nathaniel. Be patient and don't try to rush God. He answers the way He chooses in the time He chooses." A kindly thump on his son's shoulder betrayed the father's joy and peace that had come with years of struggle and hard work.

Nate had never felt closer to his father. Gradually his questions ceased. Not that he had all the answers—he probably never would. Yet the growing knowledge of what trail God called him to ride became a certainty. A few days after the flood Nate and Rose rode to their favorite bald knob viewpoint. With Columbine and Sam back in school, extra chores fell on the older brother and sister and left less time for rides.

Desert Rose sat on the dry, needle-covered ground, her jean-clad legs pulled up, arms wrapped around her knees. The drenching rain had muted the once-gorgeous fall colors, creating a somber scene. "It's sad, isn't it, the dying of the year. Soon the snows will come and bury all this—" She waved at the rolling hills and mighty peaks.

"Yet we know that life in the trees isn't dead, just sleeping until spring," Nate reminded. He abruptly added, "How anyone who watches the seasons change and sees the dry, barren trees put on green after the snows and not believe in the resurrection of Jesus is beyond me."

Something in his voice turned Rose's dark gaze from the valley and mountains toward her cousin. Gladness filled her. "You've decided."

"I have." His unflinching face showed the hours of struggle that had changed him from a boy to a man. "I told my folks last night. It's all settled. After Christmas, I'm going away."

"Oh no!" But Rose instantly regretted her selfish cry. She blinked hard. "I'm happy for you, Nate, really I am. It's just that I'll miss you. Where are you going?'

"Back to Concord and Grandpa and Grandma Birchfield's." The quietest smile Rose had ever seen on Nate's face appeared. "I'll study hard until summer, come back here, then go for one more year. After that is up to God."

His reverent trust almost unleashed her tears, but Rose valiantly held them back. She mustn't spoil this precious moment with foolish regrets. A new thought came. "Why, you'll see Michael!" Warm color swept to the roots of her hair.

"He isn't there, remember?" Nate changed to the laughing companion she adored.

"Well, he won't stay away forever, will he?" She flounced a few inches away from him. "My goodness, he will have to work again when his vacation is over."

Nate choked. "Oh, I can't imagine him not working." He grinned. "I'll wager that if he stays in a place long he will find some kind of job while he's there." Nate lay back with his head on his crossed arms and stared at the sky. "Rosey, have you ever been sorry you took my dare and wrote to *Hand and Heart*?"

"No." The word shot out. She nervously plucked at the button on her shirt sleeve. "I made a wonderful new friend."

To her mystification, a look of—was it relief?—crossed Nate's face. "Then everything will be all right." He sprang up and gave her a hand and together they walked to the patient Mesquite and Piebald who stood with reins hanging. "By the way, have you seen anything of Mike Carey lately?"

To her annoyance, Rose found herself blushing again. "Not since they came home with us after the flood. Why?"

"Just wondered." The teasing left Nate's eyes. "You like him, don't you?" he asked irrelevantly.

Rose stared at Nate. "Of course I do. Don't you? He's the nicest cowboy around and he doesn't make sheep's eyes at me the way most of them do. He must have been a gentleman to have such good manners."

A curious stillness settled between Nate and Rose that lasted until after they mounted and headed down the long slope toward the Double B. At last Nate said in a hard voice, "You think a cowboy can't be a gentleman? Isn't that a bit snobbish?"

Angry flares streaked Rose's face. "I didn't say that. It's just that Mike Carey is not like our Wyoming riders." She dug her heels in Mesquites sides and he pranced away before her cousin could reply. Yet his question stayed with her. *Was* she guilty of snobbery, a trait she hated? Rose impulsively wheeled Mesquite back toward Nate. "I'm sorry, Nate. I guess some of the old South is in me, you know, the importance placed on family lineage and all that."

Nate visibly relaxed and his old friendly grin came out like the sun after a shower. "Rose Red, you just need a strong man like me around to keep your feet on the ground."

"Don't call me Rose Red," she automatically protested, but she couldn't hide the little smile his comment brought.

Hours later, not even the whisper of a smile remained. The same brooding atmosphere that had hung over the Double B and other ranches in 1892 when the Johnson County Cattle War raged in north-central Wyoming plagued the ranches again. Rose remembered the newspaper accounts during that time. Cattlemen suspected their herds were being rustled but had no proof. Owners of the large ranches made a list of suspects, imported two dozen Texas outlaws, and formed a force of over fifty-five men called the Invaders. They raided the Kaycee ranch near Buffalo and killed two men.

When word of the killings reached Buffalo, a group of armed men rode out after the Invaders and confronted them on the TA ranch, but federal troops got there in time to prevent any slaughter. Although the Invaders stood trial in Cheyenne, witnesses didn't show. The Invaders were set free and the so-called war ended.

During that time Antelope breathlessly waited, armed and ready in case the violence spilled over into the little mountain hamlet that liked to call itself a town. When nothing extraordinary happened, the townspeople and ranchers got back to the business of daily living, but many remembered sleepless nights when the slightest noise brought husbands and fathers out of bed.

No one knew how or where, but talk of a new band of rustlers now ran rampant. Folks who hadn't oiled up guns except for hunting took down their firearms in case they were needed. Grim-faced riders reported missing cattle and horses. Some told of seeing lights in uninhabited areas. Unease and furtive glances between formerly friendly neighbors increased the tension. Who could be trusted? Rustlers could be living right in the middle of honest people, masquerading as others had done under the guise of upright citizens. Even the approaching celebration of Desert Rose Birchfield's eighteenth birthday couldn't compete with the restless waiting.

On November 2, 1895, a light snow fell then surrendered to the late autumn sun. *Why don't I feel grown-up?* Rose wondered when she awakened and hurried to her window. *Is it because everyone acts so worried?* A flash of perception stilled her fingers on the curtain. *Perhaps I don't want things to change.* She expressed that idea to her mother in a private talk later that morning.

Laurel smiled the contented smile of a happy woman, but her rich brown eyes held understanding and memories. "I felt very much the same way twenty-two years ago," she confessed. Her beautiful hands, slim and graceful yet strong, lay idly in her lap. "Because the years after the war were so hard, Ivy Ann and I didn't have an eighteenth birthday party, but oh, what a glorious celebration we had on our twentieth birthday!" She laughed. "I can't say it was the happiest night of my life, but now I see it as a turning point. I had walked in my twin's shadow far too long, and it wasn't good for either of us."

"Then Dad came." Rose loved the story.

"Yes." Dreams turned to joy but Laurel shook her head. "I'm afraid I had some very un-Christian thoughts toward Ivy Ann over Adam!"

"I wonder if I'd have the courage to do something as outrageous as traveling alone to Wyoming from West Virginia in a time when women wouldn't dream of such a thing," Desert Rose mused.

Laurel cupped her elder daughter's face in her hands. "My darling girl, when you fall in love I shudder to think what outrageous thing you may do." Her gaze probed deeply into Rose's heart. "One thing I know, whatever that thing might be, I know that with your faith in your heavenly Father you will never act in any way except an honorable one." She pressed her lips to Rose's tanned forehead then changed the subject.

"I know you don't like dresses, but isn't your party gown lovely?" She glanced at the cobweb-like white froth swaying gently in the breeze from Rose's open window.

Rose scrutinized the dress from its tiny standup collar to its puffy sleeves and fitted bodice down the sweep of flaring skirt to the wide hem. "It's beautiful." She giggled. "But I'll never forget how outraged the dressmaker acted when I told her I would *not* be laced into an instrument of torture to make my waist smaller and that I would *not* wear any hourglass dress." Rose stretched and admitted, "She did a wonderful job, though. Since it's my first dress from a dressmaker, I'm glad. Besides, after I wear it tonight I'll pack it away and it will do for a wedding dress. I suppose whoever—I mean whomever—I marry will like it." She felt warmth all over when the name Carmichael Blake-Jones came to mind. *How would he react if he could see her in this white confection?*

Rose suddenly felt she was holding on to childhood with one hand and mentally reaching toward womanhood with the other. *Please, God, don't let me. . .don't let me what?* Rose broke off her unspoken prayer and quickly substituted: *Just keep me strong and true to You. Make me worthy of my mother's trust, and Yours.*

The change from boyish, laughing rider to what Columbine labeled "a vision of loveliness" vanquished even the rumors of rustling from the birthday guests' minds. The moment Desert Rose donned the gossamer gown, so modest yet enhancing, and submitted to her sister's expert arrangement of her long, shining auburn hair, a certain wistfulness hovered in her eyes.

Mike Carey, resplendent in the dress suit some whim had included in his packing, couldn't keep his gaze off the slender figure that had taken on some of Columbine's deceptive fragility. Yet a feeling of loss for the thick braid of hair, jeans, and old shirt haunted him. Tonight Rose Birchfield bore little resemblance to the Desert Rose in the picture above his heart. He couldn't know how her pulse raced when she saw the transformation his dark suit made. Even for church Mike had clung to more casual attire so Joe, who now went with him, wouldn't feel outclassed.

Dan Sharpe turned out to be most thunderstruck. His tawny eyes gleamed above his sparkling white shirt front and dark suit. Alarmed by the predatory look in those eyes when he greeted her, Rose braced herself for his dreaded move. Immediately Dan turned to Columbine, whose pale blue and white dress made in much the same style as her sister's set off to perfection her brown hair and light brown eyes. Although Columbine looked kindly on dashing Joe Perkins, some of the old dazzlement remained in her eyes when she faced the immaculately attired foreman.

Thomas Brown had taught the girls, "If you have a job to do, do it. No sense putting off hunting down a skunk if it's under your house and you have to get rid of it." The longtime advice lent courage to his granddaughter even though her lips trembled with unspilled laughter. How would Dan Sharpe feel if he knew she considered the next hour even more disagreeable than hunting down a skunk?

Rose didn't have to do much to encourage Dan. Just after the generous supper and cutting of the tall white-frosted layer cake with its eighteen candles, Dan whispered, "It's so warm in here. Will you walk outside, Miss Rose?"

"It is warm," she agreed and took his arm in spite of the dark look Nate sent her. She barely heard Sharpe's lavish compliments on how he had fallen in love with her until they reached a clump of cottonwoods.

Suddenly bands of steel pinned her arms to her side and Dan kissed her full on the mouth.

"Oh–h!" The soft sound effectively separated them. Unknown to Rose, Columbine and Joe Perkins stood a few feet away in the moonlight.

"You monster!" Rose forgot the role she played in a wave of fury. Her right hand lashed out and struck Sharpe in the face with such force he staggered. "Get off the Double B and don't come back, ever." For the moment, she didn't care about range hospitality that made such an order taboo. "Go! Do you hear me?"

Dan's left hand slowly went to his cheek. His eyelids half closed over his eyes. "When a lady encourages a gentleman, she should expect what she gets."

Joe roared with rage and leaped forward, hampered by Columbine's clutch on his arm. She cried, "No, Joe. Don't ruin Rose's party." She looked appealing at Sharpe, her only interest in him obviously to stop a fight. "You'll go, won't you?"

"Of course." Venom sprayed from Dan, but he turned to Rose. "You'll regret this. I honestly cared for you, just as I did your mother and her twin." He strode to where his buckskin waited, slid into the saddle, and rose away without a backward glance.

Rose's sense of fair play scorched her. Never in her life had she felt so unclean, so cheap. His unwelcome kiss lingered on her lips and she scrubbed it away with a lacy handkerchief. She couldn't scrub away her guilt. It didn't matter that she had tempted him to save her sister. Shame filled her like flood waters in a gulch.

Columbine ran to her and helped smooth her mussed hair and dress. Practical when expected to be helpless, she drew her sister around to the kitchen door, slipped inside, and brought water. Rose drank some of it and patted her burning face with the rest. She dried her hands and face on the big clean handkerchief Joe solemnly offered. "I'm ready to go back in now," she told them. Surely the excitement would cover signs of her heaving emotions.

Nate met them at the door. "Where's Sharpe?"

"He found out he had to leave," Joe drawled into the puddle of silence that greeted Nate's question.

Nate looked suspicious, but Joe blandly stared him down.

"How about some music?" Columbine took charge and Rose longed to hug her. "If everyone will gather around the piano we'll sing. Now if all of you would come to church every Sunday we'd have quite a choir, wouldn't we?"

In the ripple of laughter that followed, Rose glanced around the room, seeking one face, one pair of reassuring blue eyes. "Why, where is Mike Carey?"

"Funny thing. He stepped outside a little while ago, came back in almost before the door closed behind him, and muttered something about having to get back to the Circle 5. He looked kind of sick. I asked him if he wanted me to ride with him or get Joe and he just shook his head and said he'd be all right." Nate's gaze never left Rose's face.

"Why didn't you have father look at him?" Columbine demanded.

"It wasn't that kind of sick. He looked more like something had hit him square between the eyes."

Rose felt ice form in her toes. "He was only outside a few minutes?"

"More like one minute, or even thirty seconds." Nate

shrugged, and Rose bit back hysterical laughter. *What had Mike Carey seen in those thirty seconds?* Probably too much, and not enough. The kiss, certainly, but not the aftermath. In his one quick glance from the doorway to the cottonwoods he could not have seen her reaction.

All pleasure in her party died a quick and final death. Rose wanted to rip off the white gown, climb into her riding clothes, and head Mesquite away from the laughing throng.

Continuous prayers for forgiveness and the strength to survive until the last of the guests left kept a smile on the tortured girl's face. After cleaning up the dishes, her family retired, except for Nate. When he turned to make a laughing remark, she had gone to her room and no amount of calling at the door brought more response than, "Goodnight, Nate. I'll tell you everything tomorrow."

Crouched on her bed in the fluffy gown, Rose waited an eternity until the ranch house lay still. Then her cold fingers struggled with fastenings and she removed her birthday dress. She even carefully hung it up, conscious of the expense her parents had gone to so she would be pleased. Maybe someday she would be able to wear it without feeling those strong arms around her. She shuddered and forced the memory away, pulling on her jeans and shirt. She added a warm jacket and her sombrero and carried her boots.

Step by step she descended the stairs like a wraith. She had no plan in mind, no firm destination. She could never overtake Mike Carey and, even if she did, how much respect would he have for a girl who led a man on until he felt his kiss would be welcomed, even returned?

Armed against the cold night with warm clothing and the sting of hot shame, Rose quickly saddled Mesquite. She admonished him to silence and led him across the carpet of leaves under the cottonwoods before mounting. Even then she kept him to a walk until the range stretched before them in the moonlight. Now she could safely call in his ear and thrill to his smooth swift gait, and perhaps put to rest memories too painful to bear.

# Chapter 12

Mike Carey rode away for the Double B angry, depressed, and disillusioned. How could the girl he had grown to love allow a man such as Dan Sharpe to hold her close? Even in the pale moonlight there had been no mistaking the way the dark and white figures merged. Darkness and light, purity and innocence against evil.

Why had he ever come to Wyoming, anyway? The lure of now-dimmed dreams had captured him and now mocked him. Should he ride back to the Circle 5 and pack his gear, head to Rock Springs, and catch the first train back to Concord?

"Never!" The word rang in the still night. What kind of man was he to give up just because Desert Rose Birchfield had fallen from the pedestal where he had placed her? She wasn't all of Wyoming. He loved the mountains and valleys, the rushing streams and wildflowers, the vivid leaves and cold mornings as if he had been born among them. Besides, a kiss didn't mean Dan Sharpe had put his brand on Rose. Mike's jaw set. He hadn't hung around to see what happened after the kiss. . . .

"Whoa, Peso." He reined in so sharply his horse snorted. What a fool he had been. Perhaps Rose could have used his help if Sharpe had kissed her without her consent. He almost turned back then laughed harshly. Too late now to retrace his steps and charge back to the ranch like a knight in armor. Neither could he be sure his chivalry was needed.

For several minutes Mike and Peso stood statue-like in the trail before moving on toward the Circle 5. Yet in those minutes the distant sound of hooves increased in volume until Mike knew someone galloped toward him from the Double B.

Probably Joe, come to find him. Nate would have told Joe how abruptly he left the party.

Mike impulsively guided Peso off the trail and into the deep black shelter of a clump of nearby trees. He couldn't talk to Joe now. "Quiet, Peso," he whispered when the singing hooves drew near. The next moment Mike straightened in the saddle, his mouth hanging open. The rider wasn't Joe Perkins but Dan Sharpe, grim-faced in the moonlight and riding an already lathered horse as if death and destruction chased him.

What did it mean? Puzzlement gave way to glee. No happy sweetheart rode away like that. Rose must have rejected the foreman's advances. Relief nearly unseated Mike. He waited until Sharpe disappeared over a hill before riding back to the trail. His boss didn't look to be in a mood for company. More like a mood for murder. Mike's hands convulsively tightened the reins. All the distrust he had felt since arriving on the Circle 5 rose in a surge of suspicion and he hurried Peso along, always keeping far enough behind Sharpe to escape detection. Even when the foreman heard hooves he'd assume it was some of the hands going home from the party.

Peso trotted up a hill that gave a view of the trail ahead. Mike couldn't believe his eyes. As far as he could see, that trail lay empty in the moonlight! Of all the strange things. Mike blinked and stared again. No movement ahead. A chill crawled down his spine. Had Sharpe discovered someone following him and taken cover to ambush the rider?

*Don't be an idiot,* Mike told himself. He jerked his gaze from the trail and quickly examined both sides of the valley through which it ran. Mike took in a deep breath.

A buckskin and rider appeared on the edge of the section of land between Hardwick's Lazy H and the Double B, *the same land where Joe Perkins had been shot that night weeks ago.*

"All right, old man, we'd better find out what's going on." Mike tethered Peso instead of letting the reins hang loose. Slipping and sliding in his dress shoes, he longed for the heavy boots he usually wore but hadn't stopped to change into when he hastily left the party. After a dozen steps he took precious time from his pursuit and raced to his saddlebags and changed. In those seconds Sharpe gained distance, although he had slowed his horse's pace considerably. Mike ran from cover to cover and when Sharpe pulled in the buckskin, he found refuge in a prickly bush to the ruin of his dress suit.

The clear air carried sounds perfectly and Mike lay prone, listening with all his might.

"That you, boss?" An unfamiliar voice called.

"Who are you expecting? The governor?" Sharpe's voice showed his vile mood, and Mike raised his head and parted the bushes so he could see. He almost gave himself away when Sharpe started flinging off his dress suit and white shirt then stepped into work clothing and carelessly stuffed his good clothes into his saddlebag. Last of all, Sharpe tied a bandana across his face just under his eyes and pulled his big hat low. "Ready?"

Four similarly clad men, complete with bandana masks, circled Sharpe. One demanded, "What took you so blasted long? We gotta get these cattle outa here before yore hands start home."

"Keep your shirt on," Sharpe barked. "Miss Desert Rose Birchfield's party will last for hours yet."

Mike gritted his teeth and prayed for help. He passionately wanted to leap out of hiding and smash Sharpe's face for the way he said Rose's name.

"Haw, haw, guess it will at that. Well, let's get on with it." The clatter of hooves and creak of leather slowly faded. Mike sat up and rubbed his eyes. Had he really seen five masked men sitting there planning a night raid of Hardwick's cattle? "Ouch!" He rubbed his hand. Both the prickly bush and the incredible scene were real. The question now was, what should he do? Ride back to the Double B for help? The whole Hardwick crew was at the party.

Mike deliberated. Five men against one offered odds only overcome in adventure novels. Trying to hold up the holdup men would be insane. What if he tracked them so he could find out where they took the rustled cattle? Could he do it?

"I have to," he muttered. "If I go get help it will mean shooting and killing. If I can identify the men then find the cattle the law will get them."

His heart thumped, anticipating the long night ahead. He climbed the hill back to Peso, sighed with regret that he still wore the suit, and stepped into the saddle. "Old man, Carmichael Blake-Jones never in his wildest imagination pictured anything like this." He chuckled. "Wonder what Mercy will say when I write to her about it? She'll probably wish she'd been here with me!"

Hours later Mike wearily tailed the five riders and about thirty head of cattle they hazed off toward the mountains. Shock chased away his fatigue when he saw Sharpe's chosen path— across the edge of the Double B not far below the knoll where Mike first saw Desert Rose. The fickle moon darted in and out of gathering clouds, casting eerie shadows on the sinister scene.

Five minutes later raindrops spattered the earth. Mike threw on the slicker he'd learned always to keep rolled behind his saddle. It concealed his dress suit as well, with his pant legs stuffed into his high boot tops. If he were spotted, he could pass as one of the riders. He took further precautions by searching his saddlebags for a neckerchief and knotting it around his neck. He'd observed in following the rustlers that once they left the section of land with their stolen cattle the men pulled down their masks, but left them handy.

"Hey boss, someone's comin'!" a hoarse voice warned. Mike froze and strained to hear. Above the slow-moving shuffle of cattle came the clear, rhythmic sound of hooves. "Get your masks on and keep the cattle moving," Sharpe called. "I'll take care of the jasper. Probably a night herder."

The moon chose that moment to reveal the exciting happenings below. Mike stifled a cry when he saw the gun in Sharpe's hand. He wheeled, still unobserved. He must cut off the unsuspecting rider before Sharpe got to him.

*Too late.* Peso with all his skill couldn't intercept the racing roan. . . .

"Please God, no!" Mike whispered, unable to tear his gaze from Mesquite, carrying Desert Rose into danger at a dead run.

A hiss from Sharpe betrayed his fury. "You!" He snatched the bandana mask from his face.

"What are you doing on our land and with our cattle?" Rose's voice rang like a hammer on an anvil. Mesquite slid to a stop.

Sharpe doffed his hat. "They aren't your cattle. They were Hardwick's, but they're mine now."

"You beast!" She raised her quirt and struck him full in the face.

Sharpe's gun spat and the bullet sped past Rose within inches. "That's the second time tonight you've struck me. It won't happen again." He kept the gun trained on her. "I'll shoot to kill if I have to." His eyes glittered. "That shouldn't be necessary, however. I have other plans for you. Strange how history really does repeat itself, only this time the ending will be different."

Rose fearlessly challenged him. "You know you will be found out and hanged this time, as you would have been before if Mother and Aunt Ivy hadn't kept still."

Mike saw the powerful convulsion of Sharpe's shoulders. "So they broke word and told after all."

"They did not!" Rose's voice went to a high pitch. "Nate accidentally overheard them talking and he told me."

Sharpe shrugged. "Just as well. Now, young lady, you're going with us." The gun pointed steady while he dismounted.

"I am not! I won't tell if you'll let me go." For the first time she betrayed her fear.

"Moffatt, get over here," Sharpe ordered at the top of his lungs and one of the four men with the herd rode back. "Tie her to the saddle and blindfold her."

Moffatt grunted. "I never bargained for nothin' like this." Obviously reluctant he obeyed but only after spirited resistance from Rose.

"I won't gag you if you promise not to holler," Sharpe told the bound girl just before Moffatt wrapped a scarf over her eyes that blazed hate at her captors.

"Why should I holler when there's no one around?" she burst out and squirmed helplessly against the ropes. "I'm not stupid, Dan Sharpe."

He cursed. "Shut up. The first noise out of you and you're gagged. Moffatt, put her horse on a lead line behind mine then halt the cattle." His teeth gleamed. "Miss Birchfield and I will ride ahead so any tracks will be stamped out by our new herd."

Mike felt sweat crawl under his collar. Only the knowledge he could be of better help to the girl by remaining undiscovered held him from taking his chances and holding up Sharpe and Moffatt. *Keep cool,* a little voice inside commanded. *It's your— and her—only chance.*

Bad as things were, they got worse. Sleet that chilled and washed out tracks fell until Mike's hands turned numb. Misery washed over him. Yet the faith of his childhood that had returned since he reached Wyoming routed total despair. Surely God would make a way. Mike clung to this thought and kept his distance from the herd and riders ahead.

Dawn streaked gray and the rain had turned to snow before Sharpe's trek ended. The exhausted men and cattle had been led across rocky patches, down slopes and up trails Sharpe must have learned by heart. Mike had thought he knew the country from combing the draws for wandering cattle, but he'd never come across the sheltered valley hidden deep in the mountains like a pocket in a cloak. To his amazement a snug cabin awaited the riders, old but in good repair. How he longed to warm himself at the crackling fire Moffatt built that sent smoke curling into the snowstorm! Shivering outside an uncurtained back window, Mike noticed the snow had increased until it had already filled the tracks behind them. How could he survive if he remained? Yet could he bear to leave Desert Rose here with this gang of outlaws, especially the ruthless Dan Sharpe?

He crept away from the cabin and stamped life back into his hands and feet. Taking advantage of the heavy snowfall, he even dared to build a tiny fire. If the rustlers smelled smoke they'd associate it with their own fire. Next to the trunk of a large spruce the snow barely sifted through the tightly inter-laced branches, and Mike managed to sleep.

He awakened to take stock of the situation. The best thing he could do was abduct Rose and get her away, soon. Threat of another storm offered possible protection. Everything would depend on how things lay in the cabin. Mike crept back to his post and rejoiced. Rose lay on a bunk just inside the window to the left, concealed from the main part of the cabin by an old blanket someone had strung up.

At least she hadn't been mistreated or she wouldn't sleep

so soundly. He wormed his way around the cabin and pressed his ear to the crack in the door. At the first words he heard he clenched his hands and set his teeth into his lower lip.

"I'm agin it." Moffatt's glare matched the looks on other faces. "Forcin' a girl like her to marry's a pure shame, an' kidnappin's likely to get us hung."

Sharpe's ugly laugh made the hair rise on the back of Mike's neck. "Once I've married her, it won't be kidnapping but elopement. Wives can't testify against their husbands."

"Count me out." Moffatt spat into the open fireplace with its blazing logs. His grizzled countenance turned toward the silent three grouped near the fire. "Me an' the boys'll be ridin' out soon as the snow quits for sure. You can send us our share when you sell the critters." His suggestion carried the weight of an order. "I wouldn't advise any funny business neither."

"Oh, you'll get your money. You always have, haven't you?" Sharpe rolled a cigarette, lit it and puffed out a cloud of smoke that hid his face.

"There never was a skirt mixed up in our dealin's before," Moffatt reminded.

"By all that's holy, I didn't ask her to stick her nose in." Sharpe leaped to his feet so fast his crude chair crashed to the floor. "Now that she has, I'm going to marry her and even old scores."

"And just how do you plan to do that?" a new voice demanded. A tanned hand shoved back the frail curtain partition and Desert Rose Birchfield stepped toward the men. "It takes a minister to marry folks, and somehow I just can't see Uncle Nat taking kindly to performing a ceremony for us."

*Magnificent!* Mike wanted to shout. The sleep had given Rose new courage and strength.

Evidently Sharpe's men thought so, too, for Moffatt laughed

and the others joined in.

"Shut up, all of you!" Dan Sharpe glared at his men then at Rose. "Justices of the peace marry folks, too, and I just happen to know one not more than two miles from here due east."

"You're lying," Rose laughed scornfully. "No decent justice of the peace would be holed up out here in the winter unless—"

"Unless he is a rascal who needed to get away," Sharpe finished smoothly. "I'd rather have married you in the proper way then have a rascally man read the lines, but then circumstances don't always allow for all the nicer things in life."

"And you think such a ceremony will hold? When the moment we get back to civilization I'll tell what really happened?" Rose laughed in Sharpe's face. "You must be mad."

Sharpe's tawny eyebrows rose almost to his hairline. "You turned eighteen yesterday, my dear girl. With both my justice of the peace friend and myself swearing this is an elopement and that you left the Double B and came after me of your own will, we'll be married proper and binding."

Rose whirled toward the other men and cried, "You're going to let him get away with this?"

Moffatt shrugged and the others shifted uneasily. "We didn't ask to get in on this an' we're agin it, but we're ridin' out soon as we can. This other ain't none of our business."

"You—you—" Sheer fury cut off her indictment and Rose ran back behind her curtain and pulled it into place.

Weak from holding himself back, Mike slunk away. Not until he could trust himself to speak rationally did he dare creep back to the little window. Rose sat huddled on the bunk, all the fight she had shown earlier gone. Mike tapped gently, then again. She turned. Hope replaced fear in her glorious eyes. She glanced at the curtain then imperiously waved Mike away from the window and opened it a crack.

"What are you doing in there?" Sharpe bellowed.

"Getting some fresh air," she yelled back. "Who can stand all the smoke?" She defiantly pushed the window up more.

"Don't get any ideas about trying to run away from your bridegroom-to-be," Sharpe taunted. "On foot in the snowstorm that's coming you'd get maybe fifty feet." He laughed delightedly.

Mike reached for the two hands she held out to him. "Quick, don't ask questions. Can you slip out after they're asleep?"

Her cheeks whitened. "I'll try, but if they catch you—"

"They won't. God will help us." He saw color return, but she clung to his hands.

"Mike, you're here, you're involved?"

"I can't explain now. If you start out and anyone challenges you, tell them you're going to the—the—"

"I understand." Her eyes looked enormous. "Where will I find you?"

"I'll be watching." He pressed her hands, smiled, and fled into the safety of the woods.

Endless hours after when the early November dark had come, Mike stood by Peso, ready and waiting. No danger of discovery now. The expected snow had come again, and the large lazy flakes showed every intention of multiplying and continuing for hours. The glow from the fire that had streamed through the window earlier dwindled. Silence replaced the occasional laugh and sporadic conversation. Still Mike waited.

The cabin door opened. A bundled-up figure stepped onto the porch, silhouetted against the dimly lit interior.

"Where are you going?" Sharpe's voice followed.

"Where do you think I'm going in the middle of a snowstorm in the dark?" Rose flung back and slammed the door. She ran down the single step and into Mike's arms. He tossed her onto Peso's back in one easy motion, swung up behind her, and started off. Mesquite, whose saddle lay in the cabin, followed.

She didn't speak until they were out of earshot of the cabin. "Where are we going?"

"I've asked myself that a thousand times this afternoon," he said huskily. "We've got maybe ten minutes' start on them, the way I figure. A few minutes before they miss you, more to saddle up and find our tracks. In this snow and dark it may take some time."

"They'll expect me and whoever has me to aim straight for home." Rose shuddered. "There are so *many* of them. Do you have a gun?"

"Yes."

"Promise you won't use it unless—"

"I promise." His arms around her tightened. "Rose, if they catch us Sharpe will kill me and marry you the way he said. The others won't interfere. I'm not so sure they'll even follow us, but we can't take that chance. I know this is all terrifying and I wish there were another way, but if there is I just can't figure it out."

He took a deep, unsteady breath then let out a croaky little laugh. "Rose, will you go with me to that justice of the peace and marry me—tonight?"

She jerked up and Mike added, "It's for your protection. If you're already married, there's not a thing Sharpe can do about it. I doubt even he would kill me and marry my widow all at the same time."

# Chapter 13

Alifetime ago Laurel Birchfield had told her daughter, *"I know that with your faith in our heavenly Father you will never act in any way except an honorable one."*

Now, trapped by the storm and Dan Sharpe, Rose wondered. Could she live up to that trust?

Faithful Peso continued to breast the storm under a double burden. Suddenly Rose said in a broken voice, "I can't marry you, Mike, even to save my life. Marriage has to be between two persons who love each other or it can't be blessed by God."

"I have loved you ever since I saw you," Mike quietly said. "If you can't learn to care, I'll never ask anything of you except the right to protect you until I can get you back to your family."

*He loved her.* Mike Carey loved her. Why should the fear and gloom that closed in around them suddenly lift? Dazed, torn between an idol created through letters and a strong man who had braved both elements and man to save her, Rose's feelings churned. Carmichael Blake-Jones suddenly seemed so far away, so vague...she had never even seen a picture of him! Mike Carey, cowboy, was here. She thought of his golden hair, his round, appealing face, and most of all the blue eyes anyone on earth could trust. When he vowed to protect her and ask nothing in return she knew she had nothing to fear. Too tired to sort through her fears any longer, Rose shakily said, "I'll marry you."

How different she felt when Mike's arms tightened protectively around her from when Dan had pinioned her against her will! One man gave freely, expecting nothing, while the other selfishly demanded and took.

Mike's hold tightened. "I hope you will never regret it, Rose.

It's the best I can do for you."

She longed to comfort him, to tell him she appreciated and cherished the dearness of him, but mute lips could not form the words. Her newly awakened feelings were still too fragile and perhaps born only from the perilous situation. A little sob came but she disguised it by saying, "You—I'm not really dressed for a wedding."

"I fell in love with a girl with an auburn braid on a roan horse," he told her, and again Rose marveled.

"You saw him kiss me?"

"Yes, and I ran from it. I learned what you did when out on the range Sharpe said you struck him for the *second* time."

Rose felt the heat of gladness fill her veins.

Long before they reached the renegade who still carried the title justice of the peace Rose felt they had come ten miles, not two. Yet she thanked God for the ever-increasing storm. There was little likelihood that Sharpe could trail them quickly. Besides, why would he suspect their destination? A ripple of nervous laughter escaped, and Mike's arms around her tightened.

"Are you regretting your promise, Rose?"

"No." She shivered in spite of the warmth from Mike's strong yet respectful hold. "It just isn't—I didn't think—you have to admit this isn't exactly the kind of wedding a girl imagines."

"I know." Did the husky voice whisper "dear" before Mike said, "Whatever happens, you'll be safe."

She lapsed into silence and Mike concentrated on Peso. The strong horse carrying a double load snorted and hesitated at times but picked his way when Mike wisely let the reins lie loose. A lifetime later Mike wordlessly lifted Rose from the saddle and they stamped their way to the door of a crude hut. Mike pounded and called, "Business for you, sir. We're eloping."

*Eloping!* Some of Rose's confusion fled but when Mike held

out his hand and said, "Come," she obediently followed him into the dim interior of the hut. A quick survey in the lamplight showed it was clean. She sighed in relief and looked at the justice of the peace.

"How'd you know I lived here?" the paunchy, balding man demanded, laying a rifle on the table.

"Sharpe told me. I work on the Circle 5. Can you marry us?" Mike's voice sounded strained.

"I'll hitch you tighter than a peach and its skin," the older man bragged but turned a sharp look toward Rose. "How old are you?"

"Eighteen."

"Names?" The justice of the peace stuck a pair of pince-nez on his nose and procured from a makeshift bureau a stubby pencil and a dirty piece of paper.

"Desert Rose Birchfield." The words had trouble getting out of her parched throat.

"Michael Carey. . ." A loud crash cut Mike off. He backed into a chair and it overturned. "Sorry."

Rose would remember the brief ceremony only in flashes. ". . .take this man. . .love, honor. . .take this woman. . . love, honor. . ." The only words that sounded clearly in her tired brain came when Mike answered the questions with a ringing, "I do." Her own whispered responses evidently satisfied the justice of the peace for he concluded, ". . .pronounce you man and wife." He slowly removed his glasses and added, "You may kiss your bride."

Rose saw the poignant look in Mike's blue eyes before he caught her close, whispered in her ear, "We can't let him be suspicious," then tenderly, almost reverently kissed her lips.

"Sorry I can't offer honeymoon accommodations, but she can use the extra bunk and you'll have to roll up in front of the fire," their unwilling host grudgingly told them. "Night's not fit for critters, let alone humans."

"I'll take care of the horses." Mike's warning glance stilled the protest forming on Rose's lips. "We thank you." The bewildered girl admired his coolness, but when he stepped out into the storm to stable Peso and Mesquite, she nearly panicked. Something in the justice of the peace's knowing look infuriated her.

"Well, Desert Rose Birchfield eloping with a ranch hand!" He slapped his thigh and cackled. "Never thought I'd live to see it."

She summoned up every bit of ancestral southern pride to sustain her as she looked through him. "My *husband* and I appreciate your hospitality. I'm sure you will be well paid."

Greed brightened the small watching eyes, and when Mike came back in and pressed money into his hand he grew positively affable. "Don't forget to sign the wedding certif'cate," he reminded.

"Go ahead, Rose. I'll just dry my coat first," Mike told her. She shakily wrote her name where the justice of the peace pointed, not reading the remarkable documents. She did wonder why it took Mike so long to sign his name. Perhaps he felt as unsure as she. Too tired to care, she roasted in front of the fire until her riding jeans and shirt and socks felt dry then gratefully crept into the rough but clean blankets on the extra bunk, knowing she would never sleep. Fatigue and strain thought otherwise. Long before Mike closed his eyes and shut out the walls of the hut, Rose's soft breathing showed that she slept.

Had he done the right thing? Had his love for her prompted his bold action? Or had there been no other choice? *Dear God,* he prayed, and shifted on the hard floor, *examine my heart and forgive me if I have done wrong.*

Sometime in the night the snow stopped. The Wyoming sun burst over a nearby mountain peak in a glorious flood. It first touched the tall, evergreen tree tops, then the snow-crowned roof of the shack. At last it sent an exploring finger through the single window and into the hut. Still the weary three who had been up until the early morning hours slept. Climbing higher, the sun began to melt the snow. Rose awoke when a *plop-plop* outside the window warned that the storm had passed. At the same time Mike sprang up and the justice of the peace stretched himself and muttered something inaudible.

How could he have slept so long in time of danger? Mike chastised himself and pulled on his boots. "May we trouble you for some breakfast?"

Mellowed by the generous money donation of the night before, their host produced bacon, surprisingly good coffee, and a mountain of flapjacks. An hour later Mike and Rose rode away down a trail they were told was a shortcut back to the Double B, mentally making note of the location so a posse could come as soon as weather permitted. The going proved hard. Rose insisted on riding Mesquite bareback for a time, but the roan's hide grew wet and slippery from kicked-up snow. Again Peso resumed his stalwart pose and carried double.

When they reached the familiar bald knob that meant home lay near, Rose's eyes filled with tears. Everything seemed so unreal. She turned to Mike and again saw the poignant blue light in his eyes that betrayed so much.

"You—you promised—" She swallowed hard. "Mike, could we just keep still?" She hardly believed the look in his face. Relief? A lessening of strain?

"Whatever you say." He laid his hand over her gloved one. "It might be better not to shock your family just yet."

Rose shivered at the *just yet* but managed a wavering smile.

"What shall we tell them then?"

"The truth." He acted surprised, and she straightened. "Let me do the talking," he said quietly.

She numbly nodded, and the horses picked their way down the slope and across the level ground to the ranch house. The warm sun had melted snow in the open and the earth felt soggy from the moisture.

"Thank God, Mike has her!" rang from Nate, who raced toward them on Piebald, his raven hair tossing wildly. "Where have you been?" He stopped his horse in front of them.

"Wait until we reach the ranch," Mike told him. "Rose is worn out, and we don't want to explain but once."

A little later, warmed and fed, Rose quietly listened while Mike told her grandparents and Nate a condensed version of what had happened. "Rose decided on a midnight ride and ran into Sharpe and his band of rustlers stealing Hardwick's cattle. I happened to be trailing Sharpe and saw the whole thing. Sharpe took Rose to a cabin he must have had built for his secret meetings. I managed to get her attention and let her know I was there. She slipped out in the night and the snow covered our tracks. We found a shack for the rest of the night and came home."

"Is that all?" Nate looked at them suspiciously and acted disappointed. "We looked and looked for you, but the snow defeated us."

"What more do you want?" Rose demanded. "Seems to me that cattle rustling, being abducted and carried away and rescued all in the same night should be enough for anyone, even Columbine," she mischievously added.

"I would have been scared to death," Columbine confessed, then blushed. "I–I'm sorry I ever felt sorry for Dan Sharpe!"

Rose escaped to her room in the wave of laughter that

followed, but not before Thomas Brown said, "Mike, are you too tired to take a ride over to Hardwick's with me?"

"Not at all." His voice floated to where Rose stood halfway up the stairs. "Except—I don't think Sharpe knows I saw him. Maybe it would be better for me to head for the Circle 5 and poke around, see if I can find anything incriminating."

"Good idea," Thomas agreed. Rose heard the stamping of his heavy boots. "Come on then, Nate."

Only after the men left did Rose realize that she hadn't even thanked Mike for saving her. Remorseful, she sprang to her window, but Mike and Peso were too far away to hear her call.

All the way back to the Circle 5, Mike sternly suppressed the desire to gloat over the way things had turned out. Suppose Sharpe turned toward the justice of the peace when he could find no trace of Rose? On the other hand, why should he? The deep snow should have obliterated their tracks. Sharpe would probably think Rose had ridden off on Mesquite and headed home. Even if he did go to the justice of peace he would find no evidence of Mike Carey, unless he could get that name out of the Carmichael Blake-Jones signature Mike had used. Back and forth, back and forth his mind seesawed until he reached the corrals at the Circle 5.

"Where in tarnation have you been?" Joe Perkins, ruddier than ever, met him at the corral gate.

"Got caught out. Stayed in a shack." Should he confess to Joe who he really was? With all the intrigue and danger swirling around him, Mike knew he could use some staunch support. He searched Joe's loyal face and made a snap decision. "Come up to the ranch house with me, and I'll tell you a story."

"What kind of story?" Joe followed Mike's brisk steps after Peso had been freed and rubbed down. Clinking spurs and the rolling gait of the cowboy on foot made Mike grin.

"First, we're going to search the house."

"We're *what*?" Joe gasped and his blue eyes popped. "Are you plumb loco? If Sharpe catches us we'll be goners." He drew a brown forefinger across his throat.

Mike figuratively fired both barrels at once. "I saw Sharpe and four men steal about thirty head of Hardwick's cattle last night, but it's my word against theirs. If I can find proof—bills of sale, that kind of thing—we can get him." His face hardened. "Joe, those cattle came right to that piece of land where you got shot."

Joe stuck both hands on his hips. His eyes narrowed to slits. "So-o-o, either Sharpe or one of his rustlers tried to kill me."

"Looks that way to me." They had reached the porch of the ranch house. Mike checked to see no one was around and pushed open the door. "Come on, let's get us some evidence."

"Say, I got a grudge against Sharpe, but how come you're so het up to get him?" Joe demanded when their search turned up nothing.

"Keep your lip buttoned, but I own the Circle 5."

The dumbfounded cowboy stared then shoved back his hat and sadly shook his head. "Aw, now I know you're loco."

"I'm not." Mike laughed at Joe's expression. "My real name is Carmichael Carey Blake-Jones—isn't that a monicker?"

"But the owner's a Mr. Prentice," Joe argued.

"Prentice is my mother's maiden name." Mike hadn't dreamed how much fun he'd get in unmasking himself to Joe.

"One of us is crazy, and it shore ain't me," Joe solemnly announced.

"Neither of us is crazy, and as soon as we get this mess cleared up, how would you like to be the new Circle 5 foreman?" Mike told the dazed cowhand. He couldn't help but wickedly add, "Nice steady job, foreman. A man could think about getting married. Especially when the way I see it is, a foreman needs his privacy. I plan to build a brand-new home in the spring, and there's bound to be logs and window glass enough left for a sung three-or-four-room cabin over there." He waved toward a pretty knoll maybe a quarter mile from the ranch house.

"Have I died an' gone to heaven already?" Joe gasped. His mighty hand shot out and gripped Mike's. "Put her there, pard. Now how're we gonna trip up Sharpe? By the time we can get into that little hidden valley you know he will have moved those cattle on."

"I know and I've been thinking. First thing I'm going to do is pick a fight with our present boss when he gets back." The plan sprang full blown while he talked. "Then I'm riding into Rock Springs. I'll get myself men who are getting pretty fed up with some of his doings—"

"How do you know that?" The pupils of Joe's eyes turned to steel points.

"Overheard them last night while Sharpe was holding Rose Birchfield captive."

"Wh-at?" Rage filled Joe's face and he leaped for the door.

"Hold it, she's home safe. The men wanted no part of it. What I thought I'd do was let word get around I'm for hire and not particular about what I do."

"You'll be walkin' a narrow trail," Joe warned. "Why not let me do it?" His eyes glistened.

Mike hesitated, tempted. Joe had far better skills than he. No, he wouldn't ask another man to kill his snakes.

"You lay low right here on the Circle 5 and protect my— our—interests," he ordered. "Joe, I don't have to tell you what this means to you and me and the Wyoming range."

A second strong grip of hands and they slipped out of the ranch house. Not a moment too soon, either. Joe's keen vision observed a dot in the distance and he softly laughed. " 'Pears to me, our boss is ridin' in a big hurry." He laughed again without mirth. "Reckon your chance to pick an argument's comin' quicker than you thought."

"Good." Mike's blood leaped high. "Back me, no matter what I do, all right?"

Joe only nodded but Mike had the feeling the lithe body beside him was poised to spring should it be necessary. They lounged against the corral fence until Sharpe galloped in, his face dark with anger.

"Why aren't you working?" he yelled. "I don't pay no-good hands to stand around with their hands in their pockets. Either get busy or get your time."

Mike sprang erect. "I'm taking my time, Sharpe. We've worked like slaves, and you know it. Well, no more. Are you coming with me, Joe?" He shot a secret glance of warning toward Joe who glanced down and drew circles in the ground with his boot. "Well, are you?"

"Uh, sorry, but I reckon I'll stick." Apology shone in the blue eyes, and Mike had to look back toward Sharpe to conceal his gleam of triumph.

"Of all the—I thought we were pards." Mike worked himself into a simulated rage. He took off his sombrero and threw it on the ground. "This Circle 5's one fine place!"

"That's enough," Sharpe barked. His face fairly shouted his glee over finally getting rid of the cowboy who had been a burr under his saddle ever since he rode in. "Pack your gear and get out, Carey. You'll have what's coming to you ready by the time you are." He dismounted and tossed his buckskin's reins to Joe. "Rub him down, Perkins."

"I don't know if I can stick it," Joe burst out the moment Sharpe got out of hearing distance. "With you gone, the boss will treat me lower than Wyomin' dirt." He sighed. "Just don't make it too long, pard. I mean, boss."

"Just pard," Mike told him and noticed how Joe smiled in relief. "One other thing. If we meet in town, don't act too friendly and be sure and drop some hints here and there on how funny I've been acting. Wonder out loud if I'm guilty of something nobody knows and that's why I've gone back on you."

"Aw, Mike, I can't do that!" Joe protested. "At least, not to the Birchfields."

"You have to or we'll never get Sharpe." Mike walked toward the bunkhouse and softly reminded, "Everything will work out but a lot rides on how well you play your part." An hour later he rode into Antelope and acted out the disgruntled jobless cowboy to perfection. After staying overnight, he headed for Rock Springs, thankful for the continuing fair weather that had followed the snowstorm.

A week later he returned, properly deputized and eager to put Sharpe back behind bars. From the frosty glares he received Mike knew Joe had done his work well. Word reached Mike that Sharpe had boldly ridden to the Double B and called on Desert Rose, blandly assuring the Browns and Nate he had found the girl injured from a fall and so delirious she thought she was being abducted. Sharpe even offered to bring in his men to verify the story and only shrugged when Rose turned on him and said he lied but refused to allow her parents to take action against him. Mike realized she must be protecting him, and he prayed for self-control to carry out his work.

# Chapter 14

One winter afternoon shortly before Christmas, Rose sought out Nate and led him to a quiet room away from the Browns. "Nate, I've heard rumors about Mike Carey. What do you know?" She watched him with eyes made keen by torment.

Nate started to speak then closed his lips in a straight line. When he finally opened them again he only said, "What have you heard?"

Cold fear settled in Rose's heart. "That time he rescued me, I've never been able to figure out why he happened to be there." She restlessly pleated the fine blue wool of her gown. "Now range gossip has it that Mike's quit the Circle 5, is drifting and —"

"I can't talk about it," Nate cut in, looking like a thunderhead. "Say, what do you hear from your traveling friend?"

Rose looked down at her nervous fingers. "I—we won't be writing again. Things were getting out of hand so I told him it would be best to break off our correspondence."

She didn't add as she could have done that the decision came after tears and prayers. If she relinquished something fine and wonderful, yet the God who had helped her so many times sent the courage to tell the truth. A few days after she came back to the Double B, she wrote to Carmichael Blake-Jones and told him she had married and wouldn't be writing again. She thanked him for his many pleasant letters and said how much she appreciated them. She didn't tell him that if what she suspected were true, her shadowy husband wasn't the Christian cowboy she thought him but in all probability a rustler.

"Is that the letter you gave me to mail?" Nate asked in a choked voice and hid his face in his hands.

"Yes, I know you admire him a lot and I do—did too."

"But I remember bringing you a letter from him after that," Nate protested, his head still down.

Rose almost blurted out the whole story but bit her tongue. She simply couldn't explain without telling about her marriage. Rose fervently hoped Michael wouldn't mention it in a letter to Nate! She replied, "Yes, he wrote once."

"What did he say?" Nate appeared to be holding his breath.

Tired of deceit, Rose went as far as she could. "He said I had broken his heart. That he fell in love with me when he saw my picture." She glared at her cousin. "See what you started? That's not all. Do you know who Mr. Carmichael Blake-Jones is?" She didn't wait for Nate's answer but excitedly went on. "He's also Mr. Prentice, the new owner of the Circle 5, *and he expected to take over and run the ranch.* Probably in the spring. Oh dear, what am I going to do?" A hated tear fell and she angrily brushed it away.

A curious blend of amusement, concern, and pity made Nate's face a closed book, and he patted her arm. "I have a feeling that in time everything will work out just fine, Rosy. Wish I could be here to see it." Disappointment vanished when he squared his shoulders and smiled. "Oh well, the sooner I go and learn what I must the quicker I can come back and serve the Lord."

Rose put away her own troubles. Yet when Nate left her depression came. She had to tell her parents of the hasty marriage and before Carmichael Prentice or whatever his name really was came, but how could she, now that Mike might have turned to rustling? Had he? She couldn't believe it. Range rumors had to be wrong and this aching sense of loss merely a test of her loyalty. The last thing she needed was Michael's arrival to complicate things even more.

᠀

Christmas passed. Nate swung aboard the eastbound train, leaving Rose desolate. Without her cousin or Michael's letters she fell prey to her own thoughts. Columbine and Sam offered companionship when they weren't in school, but long winter hours stretched and lengthened into January and February. Rose alternated between excitement when Nate's scrawled letters came, filled with boyish admiration for a girl named Mercy Curtis, to melancholy. Her infrequent glimpses of Mike Carey helped little.

Mike seldom came to church and Dan Sharpe seldom missed. Sharpe seemed impervious to slanted stares and whispers from other ranchhands. Hardwick, Nate Thomas Brown, and the others who had gone to the little valley found trampled ground when the snows lifted but no evidence. Sharpe continued his way unhampered. Sometimes Rose, who had chosen to spend most of the winter on the Double B, saw a biding-my-time look in Grandpa Brown's eyes when Sharpe's name came up. At least the winter wasn't one of the worst. Rose and Mesquite could get out at times into the snow-hardened paths and clear, cold days.

"Whatever happened to that nice Mike Carey who used to come over?" Grandma innocently asked one morning at breakfast.

Rose steadied her fork with shaking fingers. "He doesn't work for the Circle 5 anymore."

"Land sakes, how young folks do hop around!" Grandma's keen eyes sparkled. "I'm sorry to hear it. He seemed such a nice, steady young man, not at all like some of our good-hearted but rough boys."

306

Grandpa cut in with an irrelevant remark, and Rose wondered how much or what he had heard but didn't dare ask. Yet she couldn't avoid overhearing the growing whispers concerning Mike Carey, now viewed by much of the range as a man of mystery.

Finally spring arrived and bestowed a mixed blessing. April's mercurial outlook reflected Rose's own up-and-down moods. Memory of her marriage ceremony dimmed until at times she felt it had happened to someone else. Now and then she saw Mike at a distance when she went out riding, but he never approached her. "Probably ashamed to," she told Mesquite after one such occurrence. The thought plummeted her spirits even further, and it took a mile of galloping with the wind in her face to regain her composure.

Driven by doubt and a growing love for the absent husband that Rose at last could deny no longer, she decided she must know for sure Mike Carey's true character. He had risked danger, saved Columbine and then herself. Still, he *had* been right there with Sharpe and his rustlers, and if the latest rumors could be believed Mike had actually been seen riding with some of the worst ruffians in Wyoming just a few weeks before.

Rose had consistently resisted riding near the Circle 5, but one bright morning when Columbine and Sam clamored for her to go with them she consented.

"You won't believe the *gorgeous* house going up over there," Columbine told her. "A second house, actually a big log cabin, is being built just a little way off." Red streaked her fair skin. "Last time Sam and I went the workers were just putting in huge windows. You can see the mountains and hills and valley. What a wonderful place to live."

Sam drawled in his own comical way, "Reckon it could be arranged. Someone said Sharpe's getting ready to leave. If you can charm the new owner, Columbine, the house and view go with him."

A rush of emotion made Rose hastily bend down to check her stirrup. *I hope Columbine has better luck with men than I. First, I have too many in my life and now no one. Mike must have changed his mind, and of course I couldn't keep on writing to Michael.* The thought hurt and made her lash out, "I hope you haven't been over here running after Joe Perkins, Columbine."

Her sister's pretty chin tilted up. "I don't have to run after Joe or any man. He isn't even here when we ride over. He's out with the cattle." Tears burned her eyes at the unjust accusation. "Just because you've moped ever since Nate left doesn't mean you have to act so mean to me." She touched her horse's flanks with her heels and shot ahead.

Sam gave her a look of reproach that clearly told how Rose's own hopes for a close relationship between him and Columbine had come to pass. "She's right, you know." He loped ahead as well.

Rose felt sick and disgusted with herself. "Wait," she called and goaded Mesquite into a gallop. "I'm sorry, Columbine." Even though her sister promptly forgave her, Rose couldn't forget the stricken look in her eyes or the way Sam had responded. Things simply couldn't go on this way. Better to set off an explosion than to keep all her misery bottled up inside.

Three days later the terrible feeling of waiting ended. Rose overheard her grandfather, Hardwick, and several other ranchers discussing a cattle raid planned for that night. Someone had leaked the news, perhaps in the Pronghorn or Silver saloon or to a friend who promptly reported it to the sheriff. "This is our chance to get the whole gang," Hardwick snapped and closed his big hand in a significant gesture. "If the report is true, the rustlers are going for every head of cattle they can get away with then move out of Wyoming pronto."

"Call in every decent man you can get," Thomas Brown ordered. "Leave only enough hands with the herds so the rustlers won't get suspicious, and tell them not to resist. We don't want dead cowboys. The cattle aren't worth that. Pass the word that we'll meet here at ten o'clock tonight."

Rose slipped away, her heart frozen. An inner sense told her Mike Carey would be in the midst of the rustler gang tonight. "He must not," she whispered under her breath and at the same moment flung herself outdoors and to the corral. Her fingers made short work of saddling up, and a few minutes later she and Mesquite began their quest to find and stop Mike while time remained.

$\mathscr{L}$

All during the long winter and early spring Mike's conscience warred with duty. He had sworn to uphold the right, but could God approve of the way he had chosen? A dozen times he considered abandoning the entire scheme, heartily sick of deception and ashamed of the final letter he impulsively wrote to Rose. Not that every word wasn't true. He realized his first sight of her in the photograph had intrigued him and the clear eyes innocently beckoned him. Would she ever forgive him! Nate said yes when they had a long talk. Outside of the justice of the peace, only Nate knew of the marriage one snowy December night. Mike had gone back and further insured the man's silence with a large sum of money. Whether he could be trusted remained to be seen. The gathering storm was bound to break soon and sweep away the need for secrecy. After that. . . At this point Mike refused to consider the future.

His role of disgruntled cowboy, sore at Sharpe, brought in rich dividends. Once after griping how Sharpe had ridden him so hard he couldn't stomach working for the Circle 5 foreman, a disreputable, slouching cowboy approached him. Moffatt, the man who had balked over Sharpe's forced elopement, hinted broadly that he knew a way to get even with Sharpe. A few sessions later Mike learned Moffatt and the others had never been paid for the cattle they rustled from Hardwick.

"Can't understand it," Moffatt confessed. "He always paid up before. This time he keeps sayin' it's too dangerous." He barked a short laugh. "Why's one time dangerouser than another?" He leaned close and confidentially whispered, "I think he's hooked on that Birchfield gal and getting' even. He won't even let us move those critters from where's he's hid them. Says we'll make one more grand raid and clear out." His eyes gleamed. "I figure he's goin' to doublecross us, so we're aimin' to get to the cattle first. Hardwick and Brown and some of the other ranchers are on spring roundup right now. We'll let them get the cows all collected for us then mosey out and start movin' them, the night before Sharpe's big raid."

Mike almost choked in an effort to hide his exultation.

"Are you with us?" Moffatt demanded.

"I'll be there." Mike emphatically shook on it. Under the cloak of darkness, Mike dispatched a note to the sheriff warning him of the raid. Being discovered now had not part in his plan.

Only one flaw appeared in the carefully set up trap: Dan Sharpe's absence. Mike thought about it then smiled and wrote a second note.

YORE BEING DOUBLED XED. RAID TOMORROW NIGHT.

He signed it, *A friend*, then rode out and found Joe Perkins and told him to get the message to Sharpe but not let him know who delivered it. Joe's eyes gleamed with the prospect of action. "I reckon there's goin' to be some mighty surprised fellers," he said.

"I just hope we can get away without any shooting," Mike

told him soberly. Joe looked wise and replied, "It all d'pends on how surprised everyone is."

The next day Mike stayed in town at Moffatt's direction. The rustler said, "Keep your eyes open and mouth shut." Mike wanted to laugh; the advice echoed his Rock Springs lawyer's statement exactly. Yet the impending events made Mike restless. He walked up and down the streets for a time then saddled Peso and rode out toward the Double B as he had done a hundred times in the past few months. Every time the truth had trembled on his lips only to be bitten back. No one, not even Desert Rose Birchfield Blake-Jones, must know his plan. One careless word could destroy all he had worked so hard to set up.

Spring with all its shades of green softened the range. Mike and Peso climbed to the bald knob overlook and Mike dismounted. The drumming of hooves warned him, but it was too late. Before he could remount and ride off, Rose and Mesquite topped the rise and slid to a stop.

"Hello, Rose." Mike had no choice but to remain strong at all cost.

Her face pale in spite of her fast ride, she slid from the saddle. "I came to find you." She stepped close and clutched his arms with strong hands. Her fearless dark eyes gazed into his. "Once you said you loved me. Is it still true?"

"It is." He didn't move a muscle.

"Then ride away from Antelope and don't stop until Peso gives out." Her words fell like small icicles into the late afternoon.

"I can't."

Her self-control broke. "You must!" she cried. "Don't you know what happens to rustlers? You'll spend years in jail. Mike, you said you loved God. If you won't leave for my sake, will you go for His?"

A passing cloud dimmed the sun's increasing rays. Birds

hushed their songs. Mike could only shake his head.

Rich color replaced her pallor, but her steady and searching gaze never left his face. "I'll go with you if you'll go now."

He jerked back as if struck. "You'd do that for me? Why?"

"I can't bear to have you turn from God and be dishonorable." Her long eyelashes drooped and so did her shoulders. Her nerveless hands fell from his arms.

"Why should it matter so much to you?" Mike's head spun. "Why, Rose?" he repeated but she didn't answer.

With a magnificent toss of her head, she stepped back and demanded, "What difference does it make? Isn't it enough that I will go with you? I'm your wife." She paled again and her dark eyes grew enormous.

"You would sacrifice yourself to save me," Mike marveled. For one mad moment he almost gave in. To ride away with Rose offered the strongest temptation he had ever known. Only his inner call to a trait passed down from Puritan ancestors, duty, stopped him. He caught her hands in his. "I'd give everything on earth to do what you ask, my darling, but I can't." He felt the shudder that rocked her body.

"Rose, dearest, trust me for a little longer. I swear before God I am not doing anything wrong or wicked. Will you believe me and go back to the Double B?"

She stared at him, and Mike saw the awful struggle within her soul. Seconds crawled into minutes, but at last she whispered, "I trust you."

With a triumphant cry he encircled her with his arms and kissed her as he would have liked the night they married. Then he tore himself free, led Mesquite close, and waited until Rose mounted. "I promise you will never regret your trust," he told her. "Very soon I can explain everything."

She lifted the reins, but he laid one hand on the pommel.

"Rose, are you learning to care?"

Her sweet lips trembled. She patted his hand then removed it from the pommel. Not until Mesquite danced away with her did she reply in a low call that thrilled Mike to his boots. "Perhaps." Her laughing face turned rosy. She waved and rode away, leaving him shaken and thanking God.

Hours later Rose paced her room. She had come back to the Double B as Mike asked but she never promised to stay there. A quick look out the window revealed dark forms gathering in the starlight. Fear clutched the watching girl's throat. She could not bear the long night of waiting. The moment the riders started, she slipped downstairs to where she had tied Mesquite, already saddled, and mingled with the others. Her sombrero and the heavy coat of her grandfather's she had donned effectively hid her identity. Only her wildly beating heart threatened to betray her.

The surprise Joe mentioned worked in the posse's favor. Moffatt and his men had no suspicions and rode practically into the arms of the posse, whose presence paralyzed them.

Hardwick's stentorian, "Hands up or we'll shoot!" and the zing of well-placed lassos rid the range of the outlaws who had plagued ranchers for months.

"Well, just see who's here!" Thomas Brown whirled toward the big buckskin that had dashed into the circle of men around the prisoners.

"I want every one of these men and Mike Carey arrested for rustling," Dan Sharpe's voice boomed out. "I've been watching them for weeks and—"

"You don't leave us holdin' the gunnysack," Moffatt bellowed. "Me and my men'll take our medicine, but we ain't standin' by while you get away with it." A string of profanity followed. "Sheriff, Sharpe's behind us. We'd akept still if he'd paid us like he promised. Now he can go to jail along with the rest of us and Carey."

"Carey?" The sheriff glanced at Mike, rigid in the starlight.

Joe Perkins stepped down from his pinto, Splotch, and faced Sharpe. "My pard ain't no rustler an' never has been. He was sworn in as a special dep'ty months ago, on purpose to stop this here stealin' of yours."

A gasp ran through the crowd of men. Sharpe's jaw sagged then he reached for his revolver. "Liar! You're in this, too, and I'm going to. . ."

"Go, Peso!" Mike spurred on his quarter horse. Peso's flying leap knocked Sharpe flat. He cursed, aimed, and fired. Mike felt a hard blow in his chest and slumped in the saddle.

Released from their stupor by the shot, a dozen men piled onto Sharpe with Joe Perkins going first. Willing hands hauled Mike from the saddle. Barely conscious, his last thought was, *I fought the good fight and kept the faith.* Then, blackness pierced only by a girl's scream. . . .

✑

While stories of his heroism swept the valley, Mike Carey lay fighting for his life. All the skill Adam Birchfield possessed, the power of special prayer meetings on Mike's behalf, and Desert Rose's refusal to let him go combined in a mighty effort. Day and night Rose hovered close by. When alone on watch, she let the love in her heart overflow and clung to her husband's hands, willing him to live.

Five days after the shooting, Adam took his daughter aside. "He's very near the crisis. If he lives through the night he has a slim chance."

"He isn't going to die." Wan but determined, Rose proudly lifted her tired head.

"Would you have his suffering go on and on?" Adam asked

314

and stroked his daughter's auburn braid.

Rose shook her head as she clung to her father. Yet for hours she prayed Mike might be spared. Not until he sighed deep in his coma, his face waxen, could Rose come to the point where she changed her prayer. "Thy will, Lord, not mine." Better for his suffering to end and hers to go on. She rested her head on his pillow, so weary she could not longer hold it up. Adam found her there an hour later.

"Rose." He gently shook her awake.

She lifted heavy, tear-swollen eyelids. "Is he gone?"

"No, praise God. He's sleeping naturally. Now you must rest." He held out his arms and she flew into their comfort after a quick confirming look at their patient. A few minutes later she fell into a deep, untroubled sleep and didn't awaken until early evening. Adam warned her not to stay long now that Mike had begun the long trail back. He must not talk.

So Rose only said when he opened his eyes, "You were shot. Everything is over and you're going to be better."

Satisfied, he slept again while his body healed. When Rose came into the room, his gaze never left her. Something in his look disturbed her, a shadow she couldn't describe. He said little about the fight except to express gladness the rustlers and Sharpe had been sent to prison. He never mentioned their encounter on the bald knob.

Not until the end of May would Adam pronounce Mike fit enough to ride. The shadow in his eyes grew deeper. Even the welcome news that Nate would be coming soon did not erase it. "Will you ride with me?" he asked when Adam agreed to a short outing.

"Of course," Rose couldn't understand why her heart pounded so at the prospect of a mere ride. They didn't go clear to the bald knob but to a secluded spot by a rushing stream where the cottonwoods seemed to whisper their secrets.

"Rose," Mike began after they seated themselves on a big rock, "will you tell me about Carmichael Blake-Jones, please?"

"Nate told you!" Misery made her stammer. "It was a dare and I never meant any harm. I feel so ashamed." She bit her lip and stared at the churning water, feeling tossed like the leaves that fell and whirled downward.

"Nate says he owns the Circle 5 and intends to run it. Are you in love with him?" Mike shifted position.

"No." She turned and met the blue gaze fixed on her. "Once I thought I might be." She couldn't continue.

He gently took her hand and the poignant light she loved filled his eyes. "Then would plain Mike Carey, the man you married, have a chance at capturing your heart?"

False pride faded. Too many hours of uncertainty and fear had driven it away. "Yes, Mike." She courageously continued to look straight into his face.

"Whoopee!" Mike roared. He dropped her hands, threw his hat into the air, and jumped until she wondered if he had gone mad.

"Stop, stop, Mike. Dad would never have let you come if he'd known you wouldn't be careful. What's wrong with you?" She sprang to her feet only to be caught and swung around. "Mike, stop it. What possesses you?"

"I have a confession too. My full name is Carmichael Carey Blake-Jones." Mischief danced in his every movement.

"You!" Desert Rose wondered if she had heard right. "Then, all this time. . ." Her voice stumbled over her rising anger.

"I never lied to you, Rose. I just didn't tell all the truth. I promise never to deceive you again." He held her away from him. "I also want you to know that I would never have agreed to Nate's prank if I hadn't fallen in love with your photograph."

"But you didn't have a photograph when I wrote the advertisement," she protested, too stunned by the revelation to make sense of it.

"Nate sent your letter directly to me with one enclosed."

"How he must have crowed," she said bitterly and jerked free. "I hate being made a fool of, and that's what you've done."

The same poignant blue light returned. "Desert Rose, far from it. The more I got to know the wonderful girl, the more I hated the underhanded way I met her. Won't you forgive me?" Spent from the exertion, he laughed unsteadily. "I think I'd better sit down again." He seated himself crosslegged on the ground, his face suddenly pale.

Rose's anger vanished forever with a rush of memories that brought back those desperate hours when she saw Mike fading in spite of all she could do. Now she threw herself down and confessed, "When I knew Carmichael Blake-Jones would live in the new home on the Circle 5 I felt jealous of the girl he would marry even though by then I knew I loved a cantankerous cowboy named Mike Carey."

His kiss silenced her. Then Mike pointed toward the mountains. "Soon the snows will be gone from the peaks, probably about the time Nate comes. The wildflowers will be gorgeous. We must finish supervising the building on the Circle 5 now, but God willing, would my wife like a camping honeymoon a little later?"

Rose felt her throat tighten at the prospect. "She would." She stayed quiet within his arms for a moment then said. "Michael, do you think God planned this all along? I could forgive Nate better if I thought that."

"God certainly knew it would happen," he soberly told her. "If I had known just a year ago what a harvest I would reap—" His arms tightened. "There's still a harvest of souls waiting, and what better way to gather them than by Christian living and example? We're just links in the strong chain of His followers who have been given a white field. Our children and grandchildren must be taught the only happiness is in serving our Lord and Master."

"They will be," she assured and rested her head on his shoulder. "If God can take the thorns from a desert rose, He will surely guide us." She gently freed herself, stood, and held out her tanned hand. "Come, we must go home." Hand in hand they walked toward Peso and Mesquite and began their life's journey together.

✍

Mercy Curtis never kept house for her uncle, but she did come to Wyoming a year later. As Mrs. Nate Birchfield, she put to good use all the housewifely skills she had cultivated. She and Columbine Perkins joined Rose in the many tasks pioneer and ranch women performed that helped their husbands proclaim the good news of the Gospel of Jesus Christ. Sam followed in Dr. Adam Birchfield's footsteps as a medical doctor while Nate and Reverend Nat Birchfield tended to the souls of the Wind River Range.

**Colleen L. Reece** was born and raised in a small western Washington logging town. She learned to read by kerosene lamplight and dreamed of someday writing a book. God has multiplied Colleen's "someday" book into more than 150 titles that have sold six million copies. Colleen was twice voted Heartsong Presents' Favorite Author and later inducted into Heartsong's Hall of Fame. Several of her books have appeared on the CBA Bestseller list.

# JOIN US ONLINE!

## Christian Fiction for Women

*Christian Fiction for Women is your online home for the latest in Christian fiction.*

Check us out online for:

- Giveaways
- Recipes
- Info about Upcoming Releases
- Book Trailers
- News and More!

---

*Find Christian Fiction for Women at Your Favorite Social Media Site:*

 Search "Christian Fiction for Women"

 @fictionforwomen